"I WILL NOT PLEDGE OBEDIENCE AS YOUR WIFE."

She studied him again, her gaze steady and without the slightest affectation. "And being absolutely proper and correct means everything to you, doesn't it? Even if it's utterly and completely foolish." Then she tilted her head to the side and asked in all innocence, "Or is it that you can't discern the difference between matters of true importance and those that are trifling?"

"I see the distinction quite clearly, Mistress Curran," Devon answered, coming away from the door. "But I also understand all too well the effects of trying to play the game outside the rules. Since we're to be shackled to one another until such time as your uncle cancels the note of credit, it behooves us to have a clear understanding of expectations."

"I'm to conduct myself as a proper lady at all times, but what might I expect of you, Mr. Rivard?"

Devon gave her a half-smile. "That I'll conduct myself as a gentleman."

Her brow arched slightly as she clasped her hands demurely before her. "It would be the better part of wisdom, Mr. Rivard, to request that the cleric remove the wifely vow of obedience from the ceremony. I have absolutely no intention of uttering such a foolish promise, and I would so dislike creating a scene that might embarrass you."

Devon raked her up and down with bold regard and then offered her a condescending bow. "As you request, my lady," he answered sardonically. "Our circumstances do indeed require adaptation."

Leslie LaFoy

COME WHAT MAY

Bantam Books

New York Toronto London Sydney Auckland

Come What May
A Bantam Book / September 2002

ISBN 0-553-58314-X

Published simultaneously in the United States and Canada

Bantam Books are published by Bantam Books, a division
of Random House, Inc. Its trademark, consisting of the
words "Bantam Books" and the portrayal of a rooster, is
Registered in U.S. Patent and Trademark Office and in
other countries. Marca Registrada. Bantam Books, 1540
Broadway, New York, New York 10036.

PRINTED IN THE UNITED STATES OF AMERICA

OPM   10   9   8   7   6   5   4   3   2   1

For my students

A promise made, a promise kept.

COME
WHAT MAY

CHAPTER ONE

MURDER WOULD HAVE been a kinder fate, Claire thought, resisting the urge to chew on her lower lip. All of her plans had been made around an assumption that had proven to be overly optimistic. How could she have underestimated her uncle's spiteful nature? She sighed quietly. There was no point in chastising herself for shortsightedness. There'd be plenty of time for that *after* she found a way out of the ugly Byzantine maze her uncle had crafted.

If only she'd managed to sleep some the night before. She needed a clear head, a mind that could wrest salvation from thin air. But she'd spent the night pacing her rented room, unable to think about anything except what a black-hearted scoundrel her uncle was. And now all she had to show for the effort was a brain that had all the power and clarity of lukewarm oatmeal. Claire clenched her teeth.

"I hope, Mistress Curran, that you found your lodgings suitable?"

Perched on the edge of the chair, Claire forced herself to swallow past the tightness in her throat, took as deep a breath as her stays permitted, and met the gaze of the man standing behind the desk. "They're more than adequate for my needs, Mr. Cantrell. I appreciate your thoughtfulness and effort on my behalf."

The solicitor lifted a sheaf of papers, perused them briefly, and then cast them down with a soft sigh. "It's the least I can do under the circumstances. I'd like you to form at least a favorable first impression of Virginia hospitality. Devon isn't likely to be as concerned with the warmth of your welcome."

Claire stared down at her lap. She didn't have to remove her worn kid gloves to know that her primly laced fingers had turned a ghostly white. Adjusting the drape of her dress and flexing the blood back to her fingertips, she said, "I'm no happier with the circumstances than Mr. Rivard will be. If a way can be found to escape the situation, I assure you that I'll do so."

Edmund Cantrell arched a pale brow and again picked up the sheaf of papers lying on the desk. "He's not going to believe that you're an innocent party in this affair. You're aware of that, aren't you, Mistress Curran?"

She lifted her chin. "I had no knowledge of either the nature or the contents of the letter before yesterday, and I'll swear such before God. You yourself broke the seal."

"Please," the young solicitor hurried to inject. "I meant no dishonor to you. I know your uncle by reputation, and I'm quite sure that such perfidy is common to his business practices. It's Devon who concerns me. He has a streak of suspicion in him that's both wide and notorious. He won't be as . . ." The man sighed and stared down at the papers as he shook his head.

"As what, Edmund?"

Claire pivoted in the chair, turning toward the office

doorway and the direction from which the question had come. A man stood framed within it, the dark curls on his head only a scant distance from the top of the doorway, a mere sliver of space existing between his massive shoulders and the oaken sides of the jamb. The morning light stood at his back and cast his facial features into gray shadows. But she didn't have to see his face to guess the expression he wore. She could tell much about his state of mind by the broad stance he took in the doorway, by the way he commanded the room into which he faced. He was annoyed at having to be there, and he was determined to dispatch the business at hand as quickly as possible.

She fixed her gaze on the desk before the affable Mr. Cantrell and fought back the wave of panic that threatened to propel her out of the chair, out of the office, down the street, and into blissful oblivion. A sense of pending doom settled over her shoulders even as she silently prayed, *Please, dear God, let this be some other man.*

"As what, Edmund?" the stranger repeated, stepping across the threshold and stripping the woolen greatcoat from his shoulders. He turned toward the young man as though they were the only occupants of the room. "Come now, I'm a busy man and I don't have the time for parlor games."

Claire saw Edmund Cantrell rising to his full height and squaring his shoulders. "I was about to say that you're not nearly as understanding as I am."

Her heart sank with certainty.

Devon Rivard made a soft, dismissive sound before replying, "Hardly a great revelation, Edmund. Your message said it was a matter of great importance. Given the weather this morning, it had better be."

"And it is, I assure you," Cantrell responded, sweeping his hand in a wide gesture toward Claire. "May I introduce Mistress Claire Curran, of London."

For a quick moment Claire considered correcting the details of the introduction, to provide her former title and her proper place of residence, but then just as quickly decided against it. To be a lady trapped in a situation of obviously lower, trading-class origins... Besides, she admitted, the truth of what she was and where she came from wouldn't make a bit of difference in the larger, ugly scheme of things about to unfold. Without a word, Claire rose to her feet with a wholly feigned aplomb.

The young attorney continued with the formalities, saying, "Mistress Curran, may I present Mr. Devon Rivard, owner of Rosewind and one of the region's pre-eminent citizens."

"A compliment undeserved, I assure you," the newcomer said smoothly, turning toward her with the most abbreviated of bows.

He was a rakishly handsome man with sooty eyelashes that framed eyes of darkest emerald, a mouth wide and full and somehow mocking, the corners etched with lines that seemed more faded than faint. Yet it was an intangible something about him that knotted a cord deep in the center of her chest. She named it fear and swallowed as best she could around the lump rising in her throat.

His gaze skimmed the length of her, and she wondered if he knew that her secondhand sack dress was three years past fashionable and that she'd deepened the seams of the bodice to fit her meager attributes. With what little resolve she had remaining, Claire said, "It's a pleasure to meet you, Mr. Rivard. I only wish that the circumstances were of a different nature."

He lifted a dark brow while he offered her another brief bow. "I can't consider unfortunate any circumstance which brings such an attractive young woman into my company, Mistress Curran."

She thought the slight curve of one side of his mouth

belied the compliment, and a flicker of ire coursed through her veins. The sudden warmth steadied her knees and strengthened her resolve. Claire dipped her chin ever so slightly in the direction of Edmund Cantrell, saying, "I believe you'll shortly abandon any such thinking, sir."

To her relief, the sandy-haired young man cleared his throat, lifted several pieces of parchment from his desktop, and began, "Mistress Curran arrived in Williamsburg late yesterday afternoon bearing sealed correspondence from Mr. George Seaton-Smythe. You're acquainted with the gentleman, are you not, Devon?"

Claire watched the tall American stride across the office to toss his cloak over the back of an elegantly carved chair. She judged his height to be at least six and two. His boots were of soft black leather, rising to his knees and conforming to his calves. His frock coat was well tailored, the fit fashionably loose and covering the rest of him from her perusal. Not that she needed to see any more than she could. Everything about him spoke of a powerful man quite used to getting his way. Claire quickly moistened her lips and flexed her fingers at her sides.

"'Gentleman' is a term I'd use only loosely to describe Seaton-Smythe," Rivard replied, his back to her and his attorney. Folding his arms across his chest and fixing his gaze on something beyond the window glass, he added, "I know him only by reputation. The productions of my estate are agented through another house."

Her heart racing, Claire took a long, deep breath, stared at the carpet, and hoped that the attorney would make short work of the ugly business at hand.

"It appears that Wyndom doesn't share your assessment of the man," Edmund Cantrell continued. "On the fourth day of January last he entered into a contract with—"

"For what sum?"

Claire heard the steely edge of anger. The strength ebbed from her legs and she locked her knees before she could collapse into the chair behind her.

"Two thousand pounds sterling," answered the attorney, his voice soft in an apparent effort to ease the harshness of the truth. "According to Seaton-Smythe, Wyndom has been either unwilling or unable to repay the debt."

"Tell me, Edmund ... Did Seaton-Smythe have the gall to pretend that he ever expected my besotted brother to conduct himself honorably?"

Cantrell quietly cleared his throat and went on. "Mr. Seaton-Smythe has offered three alternatives for correcting the unfortunate situation. As his first offer, he suggests that you permit him to legally attach your present and future consignments until the debt is paid in full. Should that be unacceptable, then he suggests that you pay the entire amount, in sterling. Mistress Curran is to act as the courier."

Rivard broadened his stance and didn't look away from the window as he asked, "And the third ... *alternative?*"

Again Cantrell cleared his throat before he spoke. Claire closed her eyes as she listened to him reply, "Mr. Seaton-Smythe has offered to cancel the debt upon delivery of legal proof of your marriage to his niece." Cantrell drew a long breath. "The same Mistress Claire Curran."

She heard the slow measure of Rivard's turn, felt the heat of his attention boring through her. Swallowing back the bitter taste of mortal embarrassment, Claire opened her eyes and met his gaze. Never in all her days had she seen such loathing, such unadulterated hatred in a man's eyes. She opened her mouth to speak, but couldn't make a sound.

"Mistress Curran wishes to find some manner of

evading the proposal," the young attorney offered in hasty rescue.

"Oh?" Rivard drawled, both dark brows slanting derisively. "Do you have two thousand pounds sterling on your person, Mistress Curran?"

The cold mockery of his tone stole what precious little air remained in her lungs. She shook her head mutely.

"Have you, mistress, any property you'd be willing to forfeit for payment of my brother's debt?"

The sun-warmed stones of Crossbridge Manor shimmered bright before her mind's eye. *But Uncle George holds the title.* Her eyes aching from the threat of angry tears, Claire again shook her head.

"If I might be permitted to offer a possible solution?" Edmund gently interceded. "Seaton-Smythe has offered to cancel the debt upon the receipt of proof of your marriage. He made no stipulations regarding the nature of that union or the duration. Perhaps..."

"A divorce?" Rivard supplied, quirking one brow and smiling. "An intriguing idea, Edmund."

The young attorney stared blankly at the top of his desk and shook his head in slow disagreement. "Intriguing, yes, but with attendant difficulties, Devon. As you well know, Virginia lacks the power to grant them, and so the case must be made in England itself. Additionally, acceptable grounds are very narrow and would cause the both of you permanent social scars. I was thinking of a slightly less scandalous way out of the marriage contract. One that we can manage in our own house, so to speak."

"An annulment?" Claire heard herself ask in a stunned whisper. "Are you suggesting that the marriage be annulled after my uncle has pardoned the debt?"

"Not too terribly honorable, I know," Edmund replied. "But it would be escape without complete social ruination."

Devon Rivard's gaze swept her from head to hem,

contempt shining in his eyes and twisting his lips into a cruel smile. "And how quickly the lady thought of it."

The sound of his scorn ignited fires she'd thought carefully and safely banked. The words escaped before she could stop them. "How dare you, sir, cast aspersions on my character. You know nothing of me or my circumstances."

She lifted her chin and appraised him in much the same manner as he had her only a moment before. "I'd rather bed the Devil himself than consider marriage to such a self-consumed fool."

He cocked a brow in slow consideration. Deep within his eyes a flame kindled. "You speak of your circumstances," he said, his voice soft and yet somehow sharply cutting.

She wouldn't explain anything to him. She'd go to Crossbridge Manor—somehow—and do what she could to sort out the disaster her life had become. Stepping around the chair, Claire took her cloak from the wall peg, saying as she did, "I owe you no accounting, Mr. Rivard. And I'll give you none. Seek a solution to your dilemma as best you can, but don't expect me to be a party to it." She draped the woolen cloth over her shoulders and, while fastening the frog at the neck, added, "I'll make arrangements to return to London as soon as possible. If you wish for me to bear your payment to my uncle, please see that it's delivered to my lodgings before I depart Williamsburg. Mr. Cantrell knows where to find me."

She turned to find the attorney staring at her, his blue eyes large in his face. "Mr. Cantrell," she said, dropping her chin in polite acknowledgment, "I sincerely appreciate your kindness and—"

"And how is it that you intend to pay for your passage back to London?" Rivard asked, his tone no kinder than before.

She turned to glare at him. His arms were once

again crossed over his chest, but he had shifted his stance so that he rested his weight casually on one leg. The gaze that met hers was cool and distant. "Perhaps you acquired some jewelry from the woman who gave you that god-awful gown?" he ventured before she could reply. "Might you be planning to sell a bit of it for your ship passage?"

His words struck her like a fist. Her throat tightened and she willed back the hot torrent of words. To speak would unleash angry tears and she would never give him that satisfaction.

"It doesn't matter on which side of the Atlantic you stand," he continued, both his tone and the light within his eyes hardening. "George Seaton-Smythe has the reputation of a wharf rat. That you're of some blood relation to him counts against you. On the other hand, that you're obviously a poor and utterly disposable member of his family speaks in your behalf. He didn't send you here and offer you for sacrifice just to rid himself of an undowered, crumb-gobbling relative. What's his true intent?"

God only knew and she didn't want to attempt to guess. She was frightened enough already. Clenching her teeth, Claire struggled to slow her breathing. "My uncle isn't in the habit of discussing his business decisions with me, Mr. Rivard," she ground out. Once more she turned to the lawyer. "Good day, Mr. Cantrell. And again, thank you for all—"

"No matter," Rivard went on. "I'll discover his motives soon enough. And you haven't answered my question as to how you intend to pay for your passage back to dear ol' London."

Of all the insufferable men she'd ever met... Something deep inside her snapped with an almost audible click. Claire spun about and, arms akimbo, retorted, "Are you always so rude, Mr. Rivard?"

"It's one of the many privileges of class, Mistress

Curran," he retorted with a quick and humorless smile. "And how do you plan to secure—"

"Perhaps, Mr. Rivard," she answered with slow force, "my uncle's made provisions for such. Has that possibility not occurred to you?"

He shook his head slowly. "He made no such arrangements. There wouldn't be any point in doing so." A bitter smile lifted the corners of his mouth as he added, "Your uncle understands the circumstances of Tidewater gentlemen."

Claire narrowed her eyes and studied him. Surely he didn't mean to accept the suggestion of marriage? She watched him flick his cloak about his shoulders.

"Have her at Reverend MacDowell's house at three today, Edmund. And bring with you whatever papers are necessary to satisfy Seaton-Smythe. I'll meet you there."

"I won't!" Claire spluttered, feeling her stomach sink to her toes even as a scalding heat flooded her cheeks. "I won't marry you!"

He turned to her slowly, fire burning in his eyes and his chin as hard as granite. "Indeed you will, Mistress Curran. And without protest. You have no honorable means to secure passage back to London. Accept that you've been deliberately stranded and that lifting your skirts is the only sure means you have to feed yourself."

"Devon!" snapped Edmund. "You go too far, man!"

"Nay," he calmly replied, meeting Claire's gaze. "The lady needs to know how truly desperate her situation is. She can sell herself to many or she can sell herself to me." He took a step closer to her and went on, his voice quiet and hard as he said, "If you choose the former, Mistress Curran, your life will be brutal and mean and short. Choose the latter and know that, when the debt's canceled, you may go your way as chaste as you now stand."

"And as penniless and desperate as her current state!" the attorney countered, outrage crackling through his words.

"I'll give her a dowry," Devon replied. "It certainly won't be much of one, but it'll be sufficient to trap herself another husband."

"Devon, your attitude is unconscionable!" Edmund shot back. "I regret that I ever suggested this...this farce!"

Spinning about, the man strode toward the door. "Hell, Edmund," he cast over his shoulder as he went. "Offer to marry her yourself when she's free. I don't give a damn one way or the other."

"You can't wed on such short notice," Edmund offered quickly. "The banns have to be published. A license has to be secured. And decency demands that there be at *least* a day or two between its issuance and the actual performance of the ceremony."

Rivard paused, his hand on the latch, and turned back. His eyes blazed as he icily replied, "The requirement of the banns, a license, and *decency* can be set aside if the circumstances are sufficiently dire, Edmund, and you well know it. Have her at MacDowell's at three."

The door closed behind him with a finality that chilled Claire's soul.

CHAPTER TWO

*D*EVON STEPPED ACROSS the threshold of the pub and pulled the door closed behind him. The raw wind that accompanied him rolled like a storm through the thick haze of tobacco smoke, clearing it sufficiently for him to identify the men gathered around a gaming table in the back. He offered the expectant tavern keeper only a brief nod of acknowledgment before he strode across the planking toward the circle of gamblers.

As he neared the table, a moonfaced man with a bulbous red nose looked up from his cards and smiled. "Devon, ol' man! Do pull up a chair and join us!"

A strained smile of civility was the best Devon could muster as he replied, "Perhaps some other time, Jasper. Misfortune's shadowed me all morning, and I'd be a fool to give her another opportunity to aggravate the day."

"It appears that ill luck clouds the fortunes of both Rivards, then," Jasper offered, smiling at the stiff young man seated with his back toward Devon. Jasper dabbed at his brow with a lace handkerchief as he added, "Wyndom's spent the past few hours alternately cursing us and his cards."

Devon laid his hand on the thin shoulder before him as he addressed the circle of men. "Then perhaps your ears would appreciate a respite. Might I borrow my brother for a short while?"

The other players cast concerned looks at the notes of credit littering the center of the table even as they offered a mumbled chorus of assent. Devon tightened his grip on Wyndom's shoulder and all but pulled his younger brother up from his seat. The chair legs scraped against the wooden floor, setting Devon's teeth on edge. Wyndom offered petulant words of apology to his fellows before following his brother to the far side of the pub.

"My luck was about to turn," the younger man offered as he stopped before Devon. "I don't suppose that this can wait till eventide, can it?"

"I've just come from Edmund Cantrell's," Devon responded, barely containing his anger.

Wyndom glanced over his shoulder at the game that continued without him. He licked his lips and asked, "And what did ol' Edmund need that was of such urgency?"

"A matter of an account past due," Devon answered, struggling with the desire to grab his brother by the lapels of his fashionable frock coat and shake him until either good sense sank in or his head toppled to the floor.

Wyndom shrugged without looking from the game. "You've seen enough duns these past two years to have become accustomed to them. So has Edmund, for that matter. I fail to see what—"

"This debt's particularly large," Devon growled through clenched teeth, "and it seems Mr. Seaton-Smythe has grown impatient."

Wyndom turned toward him with such speed that his blond curls fluttered around his temples. His blue-green eyes large and his gaunt cheeks even more hollow than usual, he lifted his frightened gaze to meet Devon's and stammered, "But I...I..."

Devon cocked a brow and acidly observed, "I'm glad to see that you can at least muster some embarrassment over the situation. Is it possible that an explanation might be forthcoming?"

Taking a breath that did nothing to still the quivering of his chin, Wyndom replied, "I had a run of bad luck in Philadelphia, and the gentlemen threatened grievous harm to my person if I didn't pay off the wagers. I attempted to gather the sum, but couldn't. I went to one of Seaton-Smythe's agents because I had no other choice." He stared at the floor and whispered brokenly, "They were going to crush my knees, Dev. What else could I do?"

The sound of his brother's anguish dissolved Devon's fury into a hollow ache, a familiar ache of weariness and futility. "Nothing," he said with a long sigh. "Why didn't you say something when you returned to Rosewind? I could have made arrangements to—"

"I intended to pay him back when I recieved the payments for last year's crop. I thought you need never know. You have too many burdens already, Dev. I didn't want to add mine to those you inherited from Father."

Devon shook his head and fixed his gaze beyond the windows of the shadowy pub, feeling his world once again teetering on the brink of collapse. A cold hand closed around his heart as he remembered how, on the last day of his father's life, Philip Rivard had ordered from London a new coach, a Wedgwood china service for twenty-four, a half dozen dresses for his wife, and a crystal chandelier for the foyer of Rosewind Manor.

His father had lived life in fine style, with blithe disregard for the cost. Philip's world had been fashionable and elegant and well beyond his means. In death he'd passed to his eldest son the impressive array of his earthly possessions and one of the Tidewater's most neglected estates, including its crumbling manor house and its staggering debt—a debt so enormous that every moment of Devon's life revolved around saving his inheritance from the demands of creditors.

"Devon?"

His brother's plaintive whisper brought Devon's attention back to the present. Pushing aside the dark thoughts, he focused on Wyndom's fearful eyes and darkly offered him the words that had become his credo. "What's done is done and we'll have to make the best of it."

Laying his hands on the younger man's shoulders, Devon went on, saying slowly and clearly so there'd be no mistaking the issuance of a command, "Go to the livery and hire a carriage. While you're waiting for it to be readied, send someone to Rosewind with a message that Mother and Aunt Elsbeth are to prepare a guest room. We should arrive in time for the evening meal."

"God," Wyndom choked out, a line of perspiration suddenly beading his upper lip. "It's not Seaton—"

"No. Thank the Lord for small favors," Devon replied, managing a wry smile. "George Seaton-Smythe remains, as far as I know, in London. His niece will be our guest for an extended time."

"His niece?" Wyndom's eyes again grew large in his thin, waxen face. "Have you met her, Dev? What's she like? I've heard that the Seaton-Smythe women have bovine tendencies and the dispositions of spoiled lapdogs."

An image burst into Devon's mind: a picture of a slim young woman with hair the color of spring honey, flashing violet eyes, creamy skin, cherried cheeks, and a defiant chin. The memory warmed his blood in a way he found particularly irritating. "Yes, I've met her," he replied, shaking the vision from his head. "And Mistress Curran is more akin to a barn cat than a lapdog."

"As you said, thank the Lord for small favors," Wyndom offered with a relieved sigh and a half-smile. "Although the Lord could have been just a bit more generous. Barn cats aren't known to be too terribly friendly. Hardly the sort of creature to curl up with you on a cold night and purr at your touch."

"I have absolutely no interest in sharing my bed with Mistress Curran," Devon snapped, his ire once again rising. "While her presence at Rosewind may be lengthy, it's also decidedly temporary and purely business in nature."

"A situation I can't wait to hear you explain to Darice Lytton."

Devon scowled at his brother and snapped, "I have no obligations to Darice."

His brother lifted both brows in his usual expression of skepticism and smiled. "I'm willing to wager that the good widow thinks quite differently on the matter."

Through clenched teeth Devon growled in quick retort, "It's your willingness to wager that's mired me in this predicament. You'd do well not to remind me of—"

"What predicament?" Wyndom scoffed with a dismissive wave of his hand. "A houseguest? I fail to see how one additional person at Rosewind will undo your grand scheme of austerity and frugality."

Leaning forward, Devon spoke low and hard. "That one additional person is to be my wife."

"Wife?" His brother's voice rose in pitch and broke. "Oh my God! Dev! You can't be serious! For God's sake, why?"

"Seaton-Smythe will cancel the full amount of your debt upon proof of my marriage to his niece. I find myself in a situation similar to yours of a year ago. I have no other choice." He watched Wyndom cast a glance over his shoulder at the men playing cards, noted his brother's quickened breathing. *Sweet Jesus and all the saints*, Devon silently cursed. *Will he ever act like the grown man he is?*

"What are people going to say, Dev?" his brother whined. "How are you going to explain this? You can't possibly tell them the truth!"

"I'm not going to tell them a damn thing," Devon replied. "Let them think what they may."

"You can't!" Wyndom implored, taking a step to close the distance between them. His voice dropped to a mere whisper as he added, "They'll assume the worst. There'll be stories of impropriety and a forced marriage."

"It *is* a forced marriage."

"Is she ... ?" Wyndom asked, slanting a brow and holding his hands before his abdomen.

"I don't know and I don't care," Devon growled through his teeth. But, by God, it was a terrible possibility. Why hadn't it occurred to him already? He was usually quicker of mind.

"If she's not and it becomes apparent ..." Wyndom again looked over his shoulder. His voice dropped another degree. "People will say you married her for money."

"And what Tidewater gentleman marries for any other reason?" Devon countered.

Wyndom shook his head. "Dev, you can't do this. The debt's mine. Let me marry her. It's only right."

"Seaton-Smythe set the conditions and—"

"But everyone would expect me to do something so impulsive and ill-considered. It's my nature." Wyndom laid a pale, slender hand on his brother's forearm. His whisper held a note of panic. "If you marry her under such hasty circumstances, everyone will think our finances are desperate."

Devon stepped away, drawing his arm from his brother's grasp. Raw anger surged through his veins and into his words. "They *are* desperate, Wyndom. How many times must I explain that to you? Should Seaton-Smythe choose to do so, he can bring us to absolute ruin. He made the offer to me. What if you were to be substituted as the groom and he were dissatisfied?"

"Why would he object?" Wyndom countered, drawing himself up to his full height. Still, he had to tilt his head back to meet his brother's gaze as he added, "I'm a man of property."

"You're also a man completely without a sense of responsibility or accountability. What property you hold is at my bequest," Devon retorted. "And it's mortgaged to the hilt."

Wyndom continued, undaunted, "I've my own fields and within a few short years I'll be quite able—"

"I won't stand here and repeat an argument we've already pursued to exhaustion," Devon replied with bare civility. "I have neither the time nor the temperament to deal with your grand illusions today. Now, if you want to preserve your fragile facade of public dignity, you'll get to the livery and fetch a carriage."

"And what are you going to do?"

"I'll do what I must to salvage what I can."

"What am I to tell Mother in the note? And Aunt Elsbeth?"

Devon closed his eyes and took a deep breath. "I'd suggest the truth, Wyndom. And try to avoid your usual embellishments. The situation will be difficult enough without having to untie the knots of your convoluted stories."

Wyndom sighed and brushed imaginary lint from the sleeve of his coat. "Mother won't be pleased when she hears the news."

"And five minutes later, Mother won't be able to recall a single word of the missive."

"Aunt Elsbeth won't be pleased either."

"Elsbeth," Devon countered, "is our mother's sister

and companion. If she wishes to continue to live at Rosewind, she'll have to be accommodating."

Tugging at the linen lace that extended just beyond the cuff of his coat, Wyndom sighed. "I suppose that they'll be placated by the thought of planning a wedding. Women do seem to enjoy that sort of thing."

"The vows are to be exchanged at MacDowell's house at three today."

Wyndom's fingers froze at their task. A full second passed before his head snapped up and his gaze locked with his brother's. "Have you lost your mind?" he demanded in a hoarse whisper. "What about publishing the banns? This is scandalous! People will talk! Don't you remember what Father always said? 'Our reputation is our most valuable possession.'"

The frayed cord of Devon's patience broke. "I'm sick of living in the shackles of public appearance. Damn them all to hell and back."

"You *have* taken leave of your senses, Dev. And I won't be a party to this nonsense."

Devon narrowed his eyes and fixed Wyndom with a piercing look. "Have the carriage at MacDowell's by three or suffer the consequences." Without another word he brushed past his brother and strode out.

The heavy wooden door shook from the force of his exit. He paused on the wooden walk just long enough to settle the hat on his head and to take a deep breath of the cold, damp air. As a frosty cloud rose and wreathed his head, his anger cooled and his thinking cleared.

Wyndom was right, but only to a limited degree. The world of the Virginia upper class did indeed rest on the careful maintenance of public appearances. To a man, they were indebted beyond sanity, beyond any reasonable hope of ever freeing themselves from economic bondage. And yet, to a man, they pretended their personal situations were secret. No one spoke openly of the vast debts owed to him or of his to others. As a group, they gambled their futures on uncertain politics, unstable markets, blind faith, and hopeless, pathetic promises.

Devon clenched his teeth, vaulted down the stairs, and yanked the reins of his horse from the iron ring. As he mounted, the cold leather of his saddle creaked in protest. To his way of thinking, the sound epitomized the straining of his world. Squaring his shoulders, he wheeled the white gelding about and set off across the square, his mind filled with the likely consequences of the day.

Speculative discussions of his hasty marriage to Mistress Claire Curran would spread throughout Williamsburg before dusk had descended on the community. Within a week, the news would have been carried as far north as Philadelphia and as far south as Charleston. The situation would be the chief topic of conversation among those of the propertied class for some time to come.

Devon knew the mental habits of his fellows well. There'd be two avenues of discourse regarding his marriage to the niece of a London trader. Some would contend that his financial situation was tenuous in the extreme—that he'd wed to forestall a legal suit against Rosewind. Others would argue that the sudden marriage exhibited his business acumen—that through the exchange of vows he'd acquired a most enviable line of credit.

A sardonic smile lifted the corners of his mouth as he considered the shortsightedness of his brother's fears. Within a fortnight the two separate lines of public speculation would meld into one. He'd be regarded as a quick and daring businessman, a virtual paragon of colonial ingenuity and spirit who had turned a truly desperate situation to his advantage.

It didn't matter whether the assumptions were true or false. It mattered only that the perception existed.

The continuation of the Tidewater aristocracy rested on just such illusions... and on the unspoken understanding that to challenge one man's facade would bring the world down about every man's ears.

Yes, he knew the intricate rules that governed his existence, and he knew the consequences of failure. An image of auctioning away Rosewind formed in his mind. With a low growl he banished the dark vision. The pitiably dressed, fiery-tempered Mistress Curran was, without doubt, the last woman he'd have chosen to marry if he had free say in the matter, but prudence clearly demanded he accept the situation with as much public grace as possible. He'd vowed to save his estate and secure his future. If Claire Curran was an expedient means to that end, then so be it. And heaven help her if she, or her conniving uncle, tried to stand in his way.

CHAPTER THREE

SOMEWHERE A BELL SOUNDED the eleventh hour of the morning. Claire sat on the chair in Edmund Cantrell's office listening to the long, full notes and feeling the world close around her. How had matters gone so awry? And why now? She'd borne her uncle's correspondence and conducted his business negotiations countless times over the past four years. This time had seemed no different. She'd had no inkling, no warning that he was about to banish her to the deepest, darkest corner of the world. Had she missed some clue that should have served as a warning?

Hoping the young attorney wouldn't notice her trembling hand, she raised the glass of brandy to her lips and took a careful taste of the dark fluid. The memory of Devon Rivard's mocking eyes played on her mind; the soft, cutting timbre of his words still rang in her ears. Her blood raced icy through her veins, driven by the frantic pounding of her heart.

"There. Now isn't that better?" Edmund Cantrell asked, a kind smile dimpling his cheeks.

No. Nothing's better at all, she wanted to sob. Instead, she fixed her gaze on the carpet and managed a weak nod as the liquid seared a path down her throat.

Leaning back against his desk and folding his arms across his chest, the young man continued, "I've always maintained that there's nothing quite like a good brandy to put one's concerns into their right perspective. I know it's hardly proper for a lady to take strong spirits, but I believe that under the present circumstances, propriety might be temporarily set aside."

"You're most kind," Claire heard herself reply.

"It's the least I can do, considering it was my poor judgment which placed you in such unfortunate circumstances. I'm sorry, Mistress Curran. Please believe that. If there's anything I might do..."

"If you'll draft a letter of credit against my uncle's accounts sufficient to pay for my return to London, I'd be most appreciative," she answered, her gaze still fixed on the carpet. "I'd like to leave Williamsburg as soon as possible."

A long silence filled the room. She looked up to find the young man standing with his hands thrust deep in his coat pockets and wearing an expression that appeared to be a mixture of disgust and despondency.

"I truly wish I could honor your request," he finally said. "But your uncle didn't authorize any drafts on his accounts in your behalf. I can't do so without his written consent. Had I the resources, I'd gladly pay for your fare myself."

Claire moistened her lips with the tip of her tongue and swallowed past the growing lump in her throat. Despite her resolution otherwise, her voice was an incredulous whisper as she asked, "Are you saying that my uncle never intended for me to return to London?"

With a long sigh, Edmund Cantrell nodded. "I'm afraid that I must admit that, as usual, Devon was correct in his assessment. Your uncle knew the bargain would be accepted and that there'd be no need to arrange for your transportation back to England. I'm so very sorry."

A shiver ran up the length of her spine as her stomach knotted hard and cold. Memories of Crossbridge Manor assailed her. It took every measure of her dignity to calmly say, "Surely, under such extreme circumstances, allowances could be made."

He shook his head and stared down at his feet. "Were your uncle's reputation other than it is, I'd encourage your hopes, but unfortunately..." He looked up to meet her gaze. "I believe the situation warrants bluntness, Mistress Curran. Among Tidewater gentlemen it's often said that George Seaton-Smythe would sell his mother for the right price. While that statement's an obvious exaggeration, it's woefully apparent that he is willing to sell his niece."

"Only because his mother's dead," Claire muttered, lifting the glass of brandy to her lips. The rich liquor slipped easily down her throat but did nothing to loosen the frigid fingers that gripped her heart and soul. She sat on the edge of the chair, stunned by the gravity of her circumstances, her thoughts careening through the dark memories of the recent past and then vaulting ahead to a future whose shadows loomed as heavy and sad as those behind her.

She considered both for a long moment. Her past had been written by others, and she'd dutifully played the roles they'd assigned her because she'd had no other choice. And the future...A quiet inner voice offered another, reckless course. Claire nodded to herself and instantly felt the coldness of her dread begin to ease. The future belonged to her and to no one else. She'd make of it what she would. She'd defy her uncle's efforts to forever consign her to the end of the world, to shackle her to an insolent and resentful stranger.

Claire rose to her feet and extended the brandy glass toward the attorney. "My father was always quick to remind me that only mortal fools resist the will of the Lord. Perhaps Papa was correct," she observed with a faint smile. "Since there appears to be little hope of altering the tide of events, I'd best be getting about the acceptance of them."

Edmund Cantrell nodded as he took the glass from her hand. Setting it amid the papers littering his desk, he said, "You're a most sensible young woman, Mistress Curran. A trait quite desirable and yet so uncommon these days. Devon is a very fortunate man indeed."

"He won't consider himself so," she countered softly, "if I arrive at the church in my present state." Offering him a gentle smile, she extended her hand, saying, "I do appreciate all the time you've so graciously given to my concerns this morning, Mr. Cantrell. I'll return to my rooms now so that you may get on with more pressing matters."

"Allow me to escort you, Mistress—"

"Nonsense," she interjected, fluttering her hand in a gesture of good-natured dismissal. "I won't hear of it. You have tasks awaiting your attention." She smiled at him sweetly and, in the manner she had seen her cousins use with great effectiveness, tilted her head to gaze at him through the tips of her lashes. "Thank you, but no, Mr. Cantrell. Your offer is most gallant, but if I've managed to travel across the Atlantic Ocean, surely I can find my way down a Williamsburg walkway."

He bowed in acquiescence. "Then I'll call for you at the inn this afternoon. Shall we say at half past two?"

When she nodded her assent, Edmund Cantrell took her hand in his, bent politely over it, and then let her depart.

Moving resolutely down the street, Claire glanced

up at the gray wall of clouds rolling in from the west and wondered if they portended the same weather change in Virginia as they would have in England. After a moment, she shrugged and, lifting the hem of her skirts, lengthened her stride. While she sensed a fair chance of snow in Williamsburg before the afternoon was out, she knew with absolute certainty that Satan would be sleigh riding in hell before she married Devon Rivard of Rosewind.

DEVON EMERGED from the silversmith's shop, tucking the paper-wrapped ring into the pocket of his waistcoat and glowering. Mistress Claire Curran would be his wife in name only. The nature of their relationship didn't require a wedding band, and yet he had just spent a goodly sum to acquire one for her. The price of bowing to social expectations rankled his sense of practicality. It'd be the very last extravagance where Mistress Curran was concerned, he promised himself, reaching for the reins of his mount.

As he swung up into the saddle, his gaze drifted down the street of the small burg. Several women, well bundled and carrying market baskets, scurried along the way, their heads bowed before the onslaught of the westerly wind. A young man with a worn and battered leather valise tipped the brim of his hat to them as he stepped aside to allow them unhindered passage.

Devon narrowed his eyes and studied the slight figure. A name refused to come to mind, but he knew that he'd seen the youth before. Perhaps the lad was one of those employed as a runner for the House of Burgesses. Or perhaps he was simply one of the many students who studied at William and Mary and whose faces were familiar about the town but whose names were generally either not known at all or not worth remembering.

Devon shrugged and turned his mount into the

wind. He had far more important matters to occupy his mind. Lunch at his favorite pub appealed to him at the moment. Food, hot and substantial, might ease the cold heaviness that had been sitting in the pit of his stomach for the last hour. And if eating failed to ease his anger and growing uneasiness, he'd at least be in the right place to attempt to drown them.

THE REMAINS of his noontime fare had long since been carried away. His third brandy had just arrived at the shadowed corner table when a blast of cold air intruded upon Devon's memories of an impossibly tiny waist and wondrously full, tempting lips. Gratefully, he blinked aside his inexplicable fascination with Claire Curran's physical attributes and looked about him, determined to find a more winsome creature to consume his imagination.

Even as he did, the same young man he'd seen earlier in the street stepped across the threshold of the tavern and pulled the door closed behind himself. Devon frowned and took a slow sip of his brandy. Who *was* the boy? And why did he feel so damn compelled to ferret the answer from the recesses of his brain? Better this benign puzzle, he told himself, than the insanity of wondering what the Devil's handmaiden might look like stripped out of her secondhand damasks and linens. He settled his shoulders against the high back of the worn wooden settle, tilting his head so that the deeper of the shadows fell across his face and hid his appraisal.

After a moment, the boy stepped smartly to the bar and began, "Good afternoon, sir." He waited until the man behind the counter paused in wiping a glass and raised a brow in silent question.

"I understand that I may find Mr. John Starnes dining in your establishment," the lad continued. "Would you be so kind as to point him out to me?"

"Over there," the keep replied with a quick thrust of his chin, indicating a man seated two tables to Devon's left. "Wearing the plum-colored coat."

Devon contemplated the young man's rhythm of speech, knowing that he'd heard it before but unable to place it within his memories. His frustrated mind presented him with yet another image of his accursed wife-to-be, with an image of her cheeks flushed with anger, her eyes blazing, her small breasts rising and falling. Devon took another sip of the brandy and stared at the boy. The rudeness of it be damned. No other diversions had presented themselves and he simply couldn't abide another moment of Mistress Curran's haunting.

"Excuse me, sir," the lad began, coming to a halt before Starnes's table. "Your store clerk said that you wouldn't mind having your meal interrupted for just cause. If the truth's otherwise, I'll gladly wait until you've finished."

Devon took another sip of his drink and watched as John Starnes blotted his lips with the linen napkin, set it beside his empty plate, then sat back in his chair before he looked up at the newcomer and asked, "What matter of business do you wish to discuss, lad?"

The boy adjusted his grip on the valise, then squared his shoulders and lifted his chin.

Much like Claire Curran does, Devon's mind instantly noted. His heart lurched at the implication and his blood instantly heated. *Surely not,* he silently assured himself, narrowing his gaze to better study the back of the figure standing before Starnes.

Slight shoulders. The cut of the jacket hid far more of the youth's form than it accented. Long legs. On a young man they'd be considered far too spindly; on a woman, exotically coltish, the kind of legs a man could easily envision wrapped about his hips. He cursed his lack of foresight; it hadn't occurred to him that morning to more closely inspect the goods Seaton-Smythe had offered in trade. If he'd demanded to see beneath Claire Curran's skirts, the matter before him at the moment might have already been resolved. He certainly wouldn't have found himself in the awkward situation of appraising the physical form of what could turn out to be another male.

"... services of a person with excellent penmanship and experience in both keeping account ledgers and dealing with London merchants," he heard the young man explaining in even, educated tones. "I was also told that should you find such a person, they'd be expected to leave for England immediately. I have such skills and experiences and have come to offer my services, sir."

Starnes cocked a brow. "Do you have letters of reference?"

"No, sir."

"May I inquire as to why not?" Starnes asked, leaning forward to place his elbows on either side of his plate. He steepled his fingers.

The young man moved his feet slightly farther apart, lifted his chin up another notch, and answered, "I find myself in Williamsburg at the behest of my most recent employer. Unfortunately, he neglected to provide the funds necessary for my return to London, and therefore I'm forced to seek employment with another."

Something quivered deep within Devon. Whether in anger or excitement, he couldn't be sure. He tossed the remaining brandy down his throat in one quick motion.

"Is your former employer in the habit of neglecting such matters, boy?" Starnes inquired, looking his prospective minion up and down. "Or is there a particular reason for his having left you stranded on our fair shores?"

The lad again shifted the weight of the valise in his hand. "I can only tell you that he didn't anticipate the outcome of the business I was directed to conduct in his behalf."

"And the name of your former employer, lad?"

"George Seaton-Smythe."

Devon contained the enraged snarl that rolled up his throat. But just barely. The temptation to vault from his seat and drag her from the pub threatened to overwhelm everything else. He shoved his empty glass aside and slid forward, intending to act on his outrage. The soft voice of his tattered judgment whispered that he had more to gain from letting her play out the farce than in putting an immediate halt to it.

"And what's your opinion of him?" he heard Starnes ask.

"I won't speak ill of a man who's paid my wages for four years, sir."

"You're loyal to the man despite the difficulty of your present circumstances?" Starnes pressed. "Difficult circumstances, I might add, which are quite attributable to him?"

She looked at a point on the wall beyond his shoulder. "Despite my circumstances, sir."

God, but she's a consummate actress, Devon observed acidly. *The perfect picture of stalwart loyalty in the face of adversity.*

"What assurances will I have that you won't abandon my business once you reach London?" the merchant asked a moment later.

"My word of honor is the only pledge I can offer you, sir," she said solemnly.

Devon clenched his hand into a fist to restrain himself. How many hours had it been since she'd pledged to abide by the terms of her uncle's heinous proposal? His conscience suggested that she'd promised nothing at all, but he ignored its pathetic voice.

Starnes looked skeptical. "How old are you, lad?"

"A few months shy of twenty and one," she supplied and then hastily added, "I've traveled extensively for Mr. Seaton-Smythe during the course of my employment and have dealt with a number of sensitive business situations to his great satisfaction."

"And what was the nature of the business that brought you to Virginia?"

She took a step back, stiffened her spine, and raised her chin. "I'm not at liberty to discuss another man's affairs, Mr. Starnes," she countered, her tone pleasant but firm. "I hope you can understand my position. I would guard your affairs in the same fashion."

Trust that conniving minx, Starnes, Devon silently warned, *and you'll count yourself lucky if all she cuts is your purse strings.*

"What's your name, lad?"

"Crossbridge, sir," she answered. "Clive Crossbridge."

Starnes nodded slowly and pursed his lips. "I'll need some time to think on the matter," he decided, pushing his chair back from the table and rising to his feet. "Can you return to my place of business this evening around six o'clock? I'll have made my decision by that time."

She hesitated. "Six o'clock it will be, sir," she finally replied with a nod. "At your store."

"I believe promptness to be a desirable quality, Mr. Crossbridge."

"As do I, sir," she assured him with a bob of her head. "I'll be there at the appointed hour." She offered him a crisp bow as he walked past her. "Until then, sir."

Devon watched her glance about and then meander toward the bar, noting that she fished about in her coat pocket as she went. When she propped her booted foot on the brass rail, laid a coin on the bar, and with a nod of her head indicated the ale keg, the last thread of his restraint snapped. Casting his napkin on the table, he quickly stood and, swearing beneath his breath, went to put an end to her charade.

Being forced to marry a penniless woman he didn't want was bad enough, but having that woman parading around town dressed in men's clothing, soliciting employment, drinking ale in a pub . . . He clenched his teeth as he casually made his way toward the oaken counter. Mistress Claire Curran had much to learn about being a proper lady and even more about being an acceptable member of the Tidewater aristocracy.

His blood thundered an unholy beat through his veins as he neared the slight figure standing before the barkeep. She glanced up at his approach, and in the merest fraction of a second, he saw realization, fear, and decision ignite in the depths of her violet eyes.

CHAPTER FOUR

WHILE SHE VAGUELY HEARD the ragged measure of her breath, Claire keenly felt the pounding of her heart. Certainty thundered loud and hard through her brain. Devon Rivard had long legs and knowledge of the town to his advantage. She'd lose any footrace with him; running from him was out of the question. With no choice but to stand her ground, she held her breath and waited for the arrival of Satan himself.

He came to stand beside her at the bar, the muscles of his neck taut with barely suppressed rage, his hands balled into fists. Claire smiled tightly and then, with every ounce of her courage and resolve, deliberately turned her back to him and picked up her mug of ale. She threw a goodly portion of the brew down her throat in a manly fashion and heard the low, coarse words he muttered beneath his breath.

He turned slowly and ever so deliberately laid his forearms on the bar beside her. She could feel the heat radiating out of his body and across the scant distance that separated them. There were at least a half dozen taverns in the little town of Williamsburg. How had she managed to choose the one he was in? Could her luck run any worse than it already had? Was God punishing her for some great wrong she'd unknowingly committed?

His words came quietly but edged with cold command. "You will step away from this bar, pick up your valise, and quietly make your way to your lodgings, where you will change into appropriate attire."

She glowered into her ale, furious at his presumption to command. It took several raging heartbeats for her to muster enough calm to ask, "And if I don't?"

Devon stared unseeingly into the stack of glass mugs lining the counter behind the bar. Sweet Jesus, the woman had a steel spine. The last thing he wanted to do was create a public scene. To physically drag what appeared to be a young man out of a public tavern would be bad enough, but when everyone learned that the boy was really a woman and that woman the wife he'd so hastily wed... What would be left of his reputation wouldn't be worth having. Of course, if they learned that he'd done nothing to address her outrageous behavior, he'd be in the same disgusting predicament. He was damned if he did and damned if he didn't. And he resented the hell out of her for putting him in that humiliating position.

"You have to come out of here sometime," he whispered, determined to win one way or the other. "Either before six to keep your appointment with Starnes or in the wee hours of the morning when the keep closes shop. Know that whenever that time is, I'll be waiting for you. And the longer I wait, the madder I'm going to be."

Claire swallowed down her heart. Damn her uncle to hell and back for using her in such a callous way. Damn him for giving her into the hands of such an arrogant bastard. And damn the bastard for his cold willingness to bully and threaten her just as her uncle had. She needed time to think of a way out and sought it in the distraction of her ale mug.

His hand shot forward and clamped around her wrist with a speed and strength that caught her breath.

"Don't," he growled, "compound your sins."

Claire tried to pull away, but his fingers only tightened around her wrist. She felt his pulse race through the whole of her body, felt her own heart surge and then traitorously match the beat. In that instant the axis of her fears shifted. Being forced to marry this man wasn't the worst of the fates that could befall her. Unwittingly inviting him to take physical intimacies posed a far greater danger. The tavern suddenly felt smaller, confining, stifling. She had to get out of there, had to find a way to put some distance between them.

"Bastard," she swore breathlessly. "Let go of me."

"When I do," Devon countered, part of him desperate to do just that, another part wanting just as badly to pull her against the length of his body, "you will leave quietly and wait for me just outside the door. I'll bring your valise as the pretext for following after you. Understood?"

Fire flashed in her eyes as she looked up at him, but she nodded. Her acquiescence surprised him and made him wary, but, being a man of his word, he immediately loosened his grip. The wave of relief was still washing over him when she stepped back and yanked her frock coat into place.

"Do not think for one moment, Mr. Rivard," she said quietly as she turned toward the back door, "that our contest is over and that you've won."

He watched her go, amazed at the depth of her defiance. Did she really have the confidence to go with it? Or was it all just bravado? And why the hell was she so mad at him? It was her uncle who'd set the trap and sprung it. He was just as much an unsuspecting victim of

George Seaton-Smythe as she was. And he hated it, resented being a powerless pawn just as much as she obviously did.

But if she thought he was going to cry friends over their common fate, she could very well think again. She was a social disaster waiting to happen, and unless he got her under firm control, she'd undo what little good would come of the public speculation regarding their marriage. In the end, he told himself as he scooped up her valise, it didn't matter whether her defiance was real or contrived. It had to come to an end.

Her arms hugging her midriff, Claire stood in the cobbled courtyard at the rear of the tavern and glanced toward one end of the long alleyway and then the other. Large red brick buildings stood sentinel on either end, effectively corking her into a bottle. If only she'd spent yesterday evening and that morning exploring the city itself. If only she knew enough of it to find a safe place to hide until she could slip away in the night. She could find a way to make the money necessary to buy her passage back to England.

An honorable way. She could do books. Cook. Keep house. She had once spent her days maintaining a home, running a farm. She'd excelled at it all, had enjoyed every moment of those years. All she needed was for someone to trust her, to give her a chance. She could do it again. She hadn't forgotten how. James City. Yes, she needed to get back to the port. Someone there or nearby would certainly understand her plight and take pity on her.

A blast of warm, smoky air wafted over her, and Claire instinctively jumped and whirled about, regretting that she hadn't already run away and bracing for the next onslaught. Dear Lord, he was such a tall man and so powerfully built. The handle of her valise was invisible in the clutch of his hand, the weight of her meager belongings seemingly nothing for him to lift as he silently held it out to her.

She would have scrambled away then, but even as she took her bag in hand, he seized her upper arm, his hand easily encircling the whole of it, his grip viselike.

"Do you often run about dressed as a man?" he asked quietly, his green eyes blazing as his gaze slowly raked her from the top of her head to the toes of her boots.

Ignoring the heat suddenly fanning across her cheeks, Claire took a steadying breath. She waited for his attention to return up the length of her body before she coolly replied, "As a point of information, Mr. Rivard, yes, I do."

He swallowed hard and then his lips compressed into a hard line as he considered her with narrowed eyes. "Where are you lodged?" he finally asked.

Her heart skittering in renewed panic, Claire answered, "I won't tell you."

The merest shadow of a smile touched one corner of his mouth as he cocked a dark brow and calmly said, "Then you leave me with no choice but to strip you out of these clothes right here."

Claire felt her eyes widen, her insides shrink. Even as the voice of inner reason urged her to run, she heard herself gasp, "You wouldn't dare!"

He laughed, and she heard the distinctive notes of a man who knew he had, at last, gained the upper hand. "I would indeed," he assured her, his eyes sparkling with hard amusement. His full mouth curved upward in a mocking smile. "Our nuptials are within the hour and I have no intention of standing before a cleric with my bride masquerading as a boy. You'll go naked before you go as you're now clothed. The choice is yours, Mistress Curran. You have three seconds to make it."

His smile broadened. "One..."

Every instinct told her that he'd carry out his threat; that she faced the most dangerous man she'd ever met. Yes, he would strip her clothes from her where they stood. And take great pleasure in doing so. Breathing suddenly became a labored, torturous process too difficult to bear...

"Two..."

"The Grissell Hay House," she snapped, as disgusted with her own cowardice as she was with his smirking sense of superiority.

DEVON FOLLOWED her into the small rented room and kicked the door closed behind them while saying, "Change into whatever you possess that might pass for reasonably respectable. The dress you had on in Edmund's office will do."

From the center of the room, she faced him, her shoulders squared as always, that defiant spark lighting her violet eyes. With her hands balled into tiny fists at her sides, she said quietly, "You're loathsome."

"And you're a bit of bad baggage," he countered, moving back so that his body blocked her access to the door. "We appear to deserve each other." The color and expressiveness of her eyes fascinated him. At the moment, they reminded him of the sky during the gathering of storms. What would they look like, he wondered, in the throes of physical passion? And in the quiet lull of the afterward?

Devon frowned and banished the wayward thoughts. He nodded toward the valise she'd tossed on the bed. "We haven't much time. Change your clothing."

"Only when you've turned your back," she demanded with all the haughtiness of an offended duchess.

He laughed outright, shaking his head. "So that you

can bash me over the head and make another attempt at escape?" He leaned his shoulders back against the doorjamb. Crossing his arms over his chest and one ankle casually over the other, he looked her up and down in the way he knew irritated her. "I'm no fool, mistress. Besides, in less than an hour's time you'll be my wife. The bargain's not of my making, but I believe I have every right to see the merchandise I'm acquiring."

He watched clouds of doubt scuttle over the spark of her instant anger. "You promised, before a witness, that I'd leave this farce of a marriage untouched."

"Don't flatter yourself," he countered. "I have absolutely no intentions of bedding you. Not today. Not ever. You don't appeal to my senses in the least." Even as the words left his mouth, a cynical inner voice scoffed, *Liar.*

"But if you don't immediately begin to properly attire yourself," he continued, roughly forcing his mind to the matter at hand, "I'll be forced to accomplish the task for you. And bear in mind that I feel no compulsion to be gentle about it."

She glared at him once before turning her back on him. He watched in amusement as she roughly stripped the coat from her shoulders and flung it on the bed. Her shirt followed within mere seconds and Devon's sense of victory suffered a quick demise. He sucked in his cheeks and shifted his stance, told himself that wisdom lay in observing propriety, in looking away while she unwound the bindings that had flattened her chest.

But he couldn't. God, he couldn't take his gaze from the flawless cream of her skin, couldn't keep it from roaming over the inviting length of her slender neck and down the elegant sweep of her shoulders and arms. It dropped lower to touch the curve of her hips where it disappeared into the waistband of her breeches, and he found himself again wondering about the provocatively long legs hidden by the woolen fabric.

The inner voice came again, this time soft with mockery. *You want her.* Devon swore beneath his breath. If the little half-naked hoyden ripping open the valise appealed to his baser instincts, it was only because he hadn't sought any release since he and Darice Lytton had parted ways. He could change that situation easily enough. He could set aside his suspicions, and Darice would forgive him at the first caress.

His gaze wandered over her again, his already heated blood warming even more at the sight of her bent over the now open valise. Devon forced his attention to the low ceiling of the room, but a flutter of white instantly brought his attention back to her.

"Where's your maid?" he heard himself ask as he watched her pull loosely laced stays over her head and down over her torso. Odd, he mused, he'd never disliked the idea of that particular garment before.

"I don't have a maid," came the distracted reply.

"Am I to assume that you've traveled from London unaccompanied?"

She glanced at him over her smooth, alabaster shoulder. "Since I suspect that anything I might offer in way of explanation would be ignored, I'll leave you to think whatever you like."

Christ, he frankly had no idea what to think of her. She'd been charming in a countrified way at their introduction in Edmund Cantrell's office. Then she'd bristled with all the indignation of a peer insulted in the House of Lords. The masquerade as a young man had been well crafted. She'd calmly stood her ground when confronted at the bar. In the courtyard behind the tavern, she'd been the vulnerable and skittish maiden. Now she played the cool, unflappable lady of quality. Claire Curran apparently changed who and what she was with the unexpected suddenness of spring weather.

Devon smiled to himself. Solving the puzzles of people had always intrigued and entertained him. The secret lay in throwing them off kilter; goading them to anger was the simplest means to that end. "And would the worst I could imagine about you be so very far off the mark?" he asked.

She took a dress from the valise, the same dress she'd been wearing when he'd first met her. "I owe you no accounting of my circumstances, sir."

He cocked his head, his mind reeling back through all the words they'd exchanged that morning. "That's the second time in our brief *courtship* that you've thrown those particular words at me," he observed quietly, watching her. "Apparently your circumstances are of some consequence to you. As your husband, I have a right to know if they're likely to cause me some—"

"Social embarrassment," she finished with just the slightest hint of derision in her voice. Her scorn was fully apparent when she added, just under her breath, "How utterly predictable."

"Are they likely to need an explanation to my friends and family?" he pressed, his pride smarting from her tiny assault and demanding that she pay for it. "There must be a very good reason George Seaton-Smythe thought to concoct this desperate plan to marry you off. An indiscreet affair, perhaps? A petty theft?"

She whirled about, her hands on her hips, her chin set in hard resolve. She studied him for a long moment, a moment in which he watched appraisal and deliberation quench the vibrant spark of anger and darken her eyes to the color of midnight.

"At his death, my father's estate in Herefordshire passed into the hands of Seaton-Smythe," she supplied, her manner as controlled as that of any barrister he'd ever seen. "As my husband, you're within your rights to demand the property as my dowry payment. When this marriage is finally annulled, I want it deeded to me as my settlement."

Devon gave a derisive snort. "Along with a sizable annual sum to maintain it, I presume?"

"I neither need nor want anything from you," she stated blandly, turning her back on him and beginning to rummage through her valise. "Besides," she added in the next heartbeat, "the very fact that you're so easily bowing to my uncle's scheme tells me that you don't have so much as a sovereign to spare."

The first of her words had taken the wind from his sails. The latter deeply wounded his already bruised pride. But he knew better than to stumble, flinging words right and left, into the trap she'd lain. If she honestly thought he had the power to demand anything and that Seaton-Smythe would be disposed to do anything so kindly and unprofitable as to give away valuable property, then she deserved to have her illusions come to a shattering, painful end. "Done," he said even as he wondered if that single utterance might have been one too many.

"I want the agreement in writing," she went on as calmly as before. "Signed, witnessed, and sealed before we exchange our vows."

It was an interesting and unexpected turn. Very businesslike. And sensible. What an intriguing puzzle she was. Solving it probably wouldn't take very long, but it was a diversion in a world that didn't offer too many pleasant ones. Devon smiled. "Has anyone ever mentioned that you're a cold-blooded little mercenary?"

She twisted her mannish, braided queue up into a knot at the nape of her neck, then turned toward him. Holding the arrangement with one hand, she took a hairpin from her lips and nonchalantly pushed it into place while she answered, "Circumstances frequently dictate adaptations."

"You're fond of that statement, aren't you?"

"It's the Curran creed." She smiled and arched a

delicate brow. "What's the credo of the Rivards? Might makes right?"

Didn't she know she was courting his wrath? He knew that she was fully aware of what she was doing and the likely consequences. Apparently she didn't have the good sense to be frightened. No, that wasn't true either. If there was one thing he'd learned about Claire Curran in the single hour of their acquaintance, it was that she possessed both intelligence and common sense.

How many facets were there to this woman? What would she be like pinned between him and soft linen sheets? It didn't matter, he assured himself angrily. Thoughts of throwing her down on the bed were simple aberrations, the product of the day's turmoil and nothing more.

"Finish your dressing," he instructed with a curt nod toward the valise. "We'll be late to our own wedding if you continue to dawdle."

"I am finished dressing."

Her calmness added to his irritation. "You're still wearing breeches and boots beneath your skirts."

"No one will know."

"I'll know."

She studied him again, her gaze steady and without the slightest affectation. "And being absolutely proper and correct means everything to you, doesn't it? Even if it's utterly and completely foolish." Then she tilted her head to the side and asked in all innocence, "Or is it that you can't discern the difference between matters of true importance and those that are trifling?"

"I see the distinction quite clearly, Mistress Curran," Devon answered, coming away from the door. "But I also understand all too well the effects of trying to play the game outside the rules. The ripples of the slightest social censure often produce financial disasters of great proportion. Since we're to be shackled to one another until such time as your uncle cancels the note of credit, it behooves us to have a clear understanding of expectations."

"I'm to conduct myself as a proper lady at all times," she said evenly, her gaze locked with his. "That much has been made abundantly clear. What might I expect of you, Mr. Rivard?"

Devon gave her a half-smile. "That I'll conduct myself as a gentleman."

Her brow arched slightly as she clasped her hands demurely before her. "Am I permitted to observe that your role in this farce grants you a latitude of conduct far greater than mine?"

"You may indeed," he answered, deciding that he could bear being married to Claire Curran if she were to maintain the temperament she now displayed. If such were the case, he could afford to meet her halfway. "I assure you that I'll take reasonable care to be discreet."

She nodded and stared down at the floor at her feet. After a moment she softly said, "How civilized of you."

"Very."

Her gaze came up ever so slowly to meet his. Her eyes were beautiful...sparkling sapphires and diamonds...and he heard himself seize a deep breath at the sight. Only as the smile curved her lips did Devon realize that until that instant he hadn't seen Claire Curran truly angry.

CHAPTER FIVE

FROM THE INSTANT he'd filled the doorway of Edmund Cantrell's office, Claire had known that Devon Rivard possessed an uncommon strength, a force of will wholly unlike that of other men. She was wrapped in it as she stood beside him, feeling tiny and frail and consumed by a sense of mortal dread that seemed to have taken up permanent residence deep in her soul. For the first time in her life she half doubted her ability to overcome an obstacle thrown across her path. The possibility oddly both chilled her to the center of her bones and warmed her blood.

Claire tried to still the trembling of her hands by focusing her attention on the others around her. Edmund Cantrell stood on her left, still holding the documents she and Devon Rivard had authored and signed before the ceremony had begun. On Devon's right stood his brother, Wyndom, shifting restlessly and casting sidelong glances at her. He wasn't anything at all like Devon. Short and slight and blond and exceedingly nervous. He reminded her of some of the tiny, exotic birds she'd seen during the dozen or so trips she'd made to the Caribbean for her uncle.

The vicar was a portly, almost bald older man whose eyes clouded with pity whenever he happened to glance her way. Which thankfully wasn't very often. Pity only made the dread harder and colder and ever so much more paralyzing. She should have run when she'd had the chance in the tavern courtyard. Or bolted out the door of the parsonage in that moment when Devon Rivard had released his hold on her arm so that he could sign Cantrell's papers. But she hadn't. She'd foolishly stood her ground every time, for the sake of dignity. Not that dignity had done anything to help her escape or even delay her fate. Had she had her wits about her, she'd have demanded the moon and stars in exchange for her participation in this farce. Instead she'd settled for the hope of getting Crossbridge back. She was a mouse. A pathetic, timid, quivering little mouse.

"Mistress Curran?"

She started, instantly noting the quick, nervous glance the vicar cast at the man standing beside her.

Rivard didn't so much as turn to look at her as he quietly commanded, "Say 'I do.'"

Oh, how she wanted to say "I don't. I won't ever." How desperately she wanted to pick up her skirts, turn, and haughtily walk way. Only she had nowhere to go and no way to get there. And Hell's Hound would only come after her and drag her back.

"I do," she said, grateful that at least the words hadn't come out in a mousy squeak. The vicar swallowed hard and gave her another pitying look.

"Go on, sir," Devon Rivard said, his tone every bit as imposing as his physical presence.

Closing his book with an audible sigh of relief, the vicar said, "I now pronounce you man and wife. What

God has joined together, let no man put asunder." He smiled weakly and glanced back and forth between them before venturing, "You may now kiss your bride, Mr. Rivard."

Claire knew the instant he turned toward her that he intended to do just that. His knowing smile, the slant of his brows, and the hard glint in his eyes told her he meant to use the opportunity to punish her. Let him do his worst, she challenged inwardly. She wouldn't cringe in maidenly horror and make a fool of herself. If he wanted the clergyman, Edmund Cantrell, and his brother to see him behave like a beast, far be it for her to attempt to salvage his honor. She was busy enough trying to preserve her own. She let him slip his arms about her shoulders and waist without struggling; lifted her face and closed her eyes, determined to endure his assault without so much as a whimper.

He pulled her against the length of his body, not roughly as she had expected, but with a gentle persistence that caught her off guard and instantly sent her heart racing. Pressing his lips to hers, he slowly, thoughtfully caressed her mouth, his tongue reverently tracing the fullness of her lips. In a skittering heartbeat, he shattered her calm and sent a liquid heat singing through her veins. Of their own accord, her hands came up to lie against the broad, hard, muscled planes of his chest. His heartbeat strummed against her palms in welcome and set her own pulse dancing.

Slowly his arms tightened around her and his kiss deepened, devouring her softness. His mouth demanded a response and she instantly, willingly surrendered. She pressed her open lips to his, blood pounding in her brain and her knees trembling.

A tiny cry of regret escaped her lips when he drew away and set her from him. Mortified at her eager acceptance of his kiss, she bit her lower lip and stared at the floor. She would have preferred death to the ache that now battered her body and soul. Lord, what he must think of her.

"We'll have to do that again," he whispered in her ear as he took her elbow and turned her toward the door. "There's no telling where it might lead us."

"You...you..." she sputtered, choking on a curious mixture of elation and fear. She swallowed, focusing on the entry hall and willing her courage to the fore. "You promised I'd leave this marriage untouched," she finally managed to say.

"I did, didn't I?"

Clear notes of amusement rang in his admission, and she inwardly groaned. "Indeed you did," she answered, her voice remarkably even.

"Ah, my dear Madam Rivard," he said, his tone easy and laughing. "I do believe that you're going to have to make some adaptations."

"You have no honor," she retorted, trying to wrench her arm from his grasp.

His eyes darkened and he tightened his grip. "I'm a man in debt up to his chin. What honor I ever possessed, dear wife, I mortgaged long ago."

THE WIND WAS HOWLING out of the north, the skies leaden gray and dropping lower with each passing second. Devon scowled up at them, thinking that they matched his mood perfectly. And then, as though God had decided that he was entirely too optimistic, the first hard spittle of snow blew in from the west.

Swearing under his breath, Devon drew his unwanted wife to a halt on the front steps of the vicarage and surveyed his options. The carriage sat in the road on the other side of the stone fence, the driver hunched into his cape and standing beside the door, waiting. Two horses—his own and Wyndom's—were tethered to the rear of the vehicle, stamping their hooves and sending up great clouds with every breath. Part of him wanted to get away from the woman at his side, to put as much time and distance between them as possible. Another part of him argued that the sooner they reached a full understanding of his expectations, the better.

"Beastly weather, isn't it?" Wyndom asked as he and Edmund Cantrell came to stand on the steps with them. "I loathe these spring snowstorms. The best that can be said for them is that the thaw comes quickly and melts it all away. I sincerely hope the driver thought to heat some bricks for our feet."

"You'll be taking your mount back to Rosewind," Devon declared, his decision made.

"You can't be serious. I'll freeze to death."

"Considering your role in today's disaster, it would be a just fate."

"Maybe I'll stay in town this evening."

"Maybe you won't."

"Maybe," Edmund snapped, "the two of you might continue your petty conflict after the lady has been seen out of the elements."

Before Devon could do any more than glare at the man, Edmund stepped to Claire's other side and presented his arm. She took it, leaving Devon with no other gentlemanly recourse but to let her go. He stood there, hearing the whistle of the wind but only vaguely aware of its bite. He was, however, keenly aware that wild boars had better manners than he'd displayed in the last ten minutes. He hadn't just kissed Claire Curran at the conclusion of their vows, he'd practically consumed her in front of God and everyone else. And then, angry with himself for his lack of control, he'd manhandled her out the door to let her stand in the raw wind while he bickered with his brother.

She might well be only a half step up from a gutter-snipe, but she also seemed to be a hapless victim caught in the web of her uncle's scheming and his own desperation. Until proven otherwise, she deserved to be treated with basic kindness. And it rankled that Edmund had recognized and acted on that fact before he had. The smile she gave the lawyer as he handed her into the carriage rankled even more.

"You'll ride your horse and be home in time for dinner tonight," Devon declared, leaving his brother on the steps and striding forward.

Wyndom was still whining in protest as Edmund blocked Devon's way through the gate. "It's not her fault that her uncle's a blackguard and your brother has cotton for brains."

"Agreed and point taken," Devon admitted. "I intend to apologize for my lack of manners."

"Good," Edmund countered, making no effort to move away. "Although I wouldn't blame her if she refused to accept it. You've behaved like a complete ass today."

"I don't like being blackmailed." He didn't like being scolded, either.

"I'd venture to say that Mistress Curran isn't at all happy about being given away like an old shoe. She is, however, enduring the unpleasant situation with far more grace than you've managed to exhibit."

Edmund would be singing a decidedly different tune if he knew about the woman's masquerade in the tavern. Devon smiled tightly and held his peace. "I said that I'd apologize. Now kindly get out of my way so that I can get on with it."

After a moment's hesitation, Edmund stepped aside, saying as Devon walked past, "I'll be out to Rosewind to check on her welfare as soon as the weather clears."

"Bring your own brandy," Devon called without looking back. As the coachman snapped open the carriage door for him, he said, "The younger Mr. Rivard will be riding the sorrel. Please see that it's left for him."

The man nodded and closed the door, instantly plunging Devon into a dark world without the slightest evidence of heated bricks. He lowered himself into the rear-facing seat and reached over to lift the window curtain. Light, meager and gray, spilled in on a wave of cold air and allowed him to see the woman on the opposite seat. She sat primly, her gloved hands folded in her lap, her gaze meeting his squarely. Even in the dim light, he could see the spark of anger in her dark eyes.

"I wish to apologize for my earlier lack of manners and general hostility," he said tautly, resolved to get the task done so he could move on to more important matters.

"Just out of curiosity," she countered, "would you be inclined to offer your regrets had Mr. Cantrell not berated you?"

He sighed, wishing she hadn't heard the exchange. "I'd determined they were necessary prior to his lecture on the subject." Not by much and only because Edmund had shown him up on the steps, Devon silently admitted. But that was a point of information the woman didn't need to know. It was to his advantage to let her think that he'd come to the conclusion entirely on his own.

She opened her mouth as though to speak, then apparently thought better of whatever words she'd intended to fling at him and pursed her lips. The carriage rocked gently on its springs as the driver climbed into the box. As they began to roll forward, she drew a deep breath and said, "I accept your apology on the understanding that it is offered sincerely, that it covers the entirety of your behavior since our initial meeting, and that it marks the point of a new beginning in the conduct of our relationship."

Devon cocked a brow. Settling back in his seat, he considered the stranger across from him and mentally added yet another role to those he'd already seen her so ably play. "Did you teethe on law books?" he wondered aloud.

"Mathematics," she countered, a small smile flirting at the corners of her mouth. "The law books came soon thereafter, followed by the sciences and philosophy."

Clearly, she'd expected to surprise him, to set him back on his heels. She had, but he wasn't about to give her the satisfaction of showing it. He drawled, "A most atypical education. Did anyone happen to instruct you in the more traditional feminine arts? To provide you with the skills that might be of some practical use to you in life?"

Claire forced her gaze to her hands so that he couldn't see her disappointment. Devon Rivard was without doubt exceedingly handsome, but apparently, like so many others of his sex, he wasn't the least bit concerned with whether she possessed the skills necessary to assure her own survival. All he cared about was whether she had the ability to make *his* life more comfortable. Being the temporary wife of this particular man wasn't reason enough to grant him any greater allowance than she had others.

"Do you require a needlepoint pillow?" she asked, looking up at him and feigning demure interest.

He blinked and tilted his head to the side. Amusement gilded his voice as he replied, "If I did, could you make one?"

"Of course I could. And the florals would be botanically accurate."

His right brow edged slightly upward. "How long would it take you to make it?"

Claire smiled sweetly. "I think you'd be quite fortunate to have it just before you died of old age. I tend to find needlework rather boring and tedious. Given a choice, I'd much rather spend my time with a good book."

He studied her for a long moment and then said,

"You'll find an extensive library at Rosewind. Books happen to be one of the few commodities we have in abundance."

There was also a large library at the Seaton-Smythe house, but women were permitted in the room only to see to its dusting. It had been so long since she'd had the luxury of choosing something she wanted to read. On her travels she'd had to be content with whatever material a fellow passenger had been willing to loan her. If Devon Rivard was actually giving her tacit permission to read the books he owned... It would be a little slice of heaven she'd thought she would never see again. It might even make the waiting to be free of him slightly bearable.

"I look forward to perusing the titles," she ventured blandly, trying not to reveal her hope. It would be foolish to give him a weapon to use against her. "Is it an old collection?"

"Yes and no," he supplied. His gaze went to the carriage window curtain. "My father valued books only for the favorable impression they made on his houseguests. To that end, he had his agent purchase and ship over the entire library of an English estate. Parts of the collection are quite old. But it's been housed at Rosewind for only the last fifteen years or so."

"Your father's view of books isn't at all uncommon," she observed, thinking that his father and her uncle shared a similar attitude in that regard. "How do you see them, Mr. Rivard?"

"I've read every single one of them. Twice," he answered, his attention still on the world beyond the carriage. "And my name is Devon. Mr. Rivard was my father. I prefer to avoid the possibility of any confusion."

Claire nodded and was about to ask that he address her by her Christian name when he said, "At my father's passing, life at Rosewind changed dramatically."

She could tell him much about how the death of a parent changed life, but nothing in his manner suggested that he was interested in commiseration.

"There are some realities you should know prior to our arrival there," he went on, his tone cool and flat. "You'll find Rosewind Manor to be exceptionally well appointed. If, however, you should happen to look beneath the surface appearances, you'll discover that the grand manor stands as a true testament to pretension, empty illusions, and even emptier pockets.

"In short," he added, bringing his gaze to meet hers, "you've been shackled to a man who, two years ago, inherited an estate teetering on the verge of bankruptcy. I've made little progress in reversing our fortunes, and if this autumn's crop falls even slightly below spectacular, this coming winter will find the Rivards living in a tent in the woods. And a borrowed tent at that."

It occurred to her that Edmund Cantrell might have offered her a cursory explanation of Devon Rivard's circumstances prior to his arrival in the office. Had she known something of them beforehand... "And I've become another burden added to those already weighting your shoulders," she offered quietly. "I'm truly sorry."

He blinked and then quickly shrugged, saying, "It's done and we'll have to make the best of it. What do you know of colonial society?"

"Very little in a practical sense," Claire admitted, trying to see the logic in the sudden conversational turn and finding none. "What foreign traveling I've done for my uncle has been largely confined to the Caribbean before this trip."

"There's some small consolation to be found in the knowledge that I'm not the only man in His Majesty's American colonies to be in debt up to his eyeballs." He smiled ruefully. "We excel, however, at pretending otherwise. As a society, we take great pains to avoid any public discussion of our individual finances. Privately, we've woven a net of personal loans that bind us together hip and ankle. If one man goes down, he pulls the rest of us with him."

Claire understood what he was telling her, understood just as clearly all that he'd left unsaid.

"I will *not* be the man who falters," he assured her. "I have no doubt that you'll be quickly informed of my ruthless determination to make life for the inhabitants of Rosewind Manor as miserable as I can. My mother will tell you that, as a result of my miserly ways, the Rivards have become hermits, that my refusal to host lavish social affairs or attend them is a sign of mental unbalance and a fundamental disrespect for my family's needs."

Claire nodded and offered him what she hoped he'd hear as reassurance. "I think that it doesn't much matter where you are in the world. . . . Social affairs require the latest fashions, attending servants in fine livery, lavish gifts, and great quantities of food and drink. All of which are luxuries that come at great expense. Expenses that are difficult to afford even in good times."

His smile was weak and his nod slight. "My mother seems to be incapable of grasping that reality, try though I have to explain it in every way I know how. Her sister, Elsbeth, is a generally shrewish woman who has, over the years, developed criticism to a high art. She feeds my mother's expectations and discontent. If I had somewhere to send her, I would."

"Your mother or your aunt Elsbeth?"

"Both."

"And what of your brother?"

"Wyndom approaches life just as our father did. You'll recall that it's his debt to your uncle that put us in front of the vicar this afternoon. If Wyndom could be sent to a place where he'd be forced to become responsible, he'd have been trussed up and shipped away years ago. Unfortunately, I can't think of where that might be, and I've concluded that it's better to have him where I'm able to keep his damage to a minimum."

Not that he'd been very successful at doing that, she silently observed. "I promise you that, until our contract is dissolved, I'll do whatever I can to earn my keep. I have no desire to be an additional drain on your resources."

"Thank you." He summoned a smile of sorts and added, "I'm sure your uncle will send your belongings once he receives the news of our marriage."

"There's nothing to send," Claire countered. "All the goods I own are in my valise."

"Your uncle's reputed to be a wealthy man. Have I been misinformed?" he asked, his brows knitted as he glanced at the small leather bag at their feet.

"No, you've heard correctly. But George Seaton-Smythe's definition of family is a very narrow one, and I fall well outside of it. I had clothing when the court gave me into his custody, but in the course of four years, I grew and the clothing didn't. He saw no particular reason to replace my wardrobe."

The information seemed to take him aback. He frowned and the crease between his brows deepened. Finally, he nodded and said, "I'm sure my mother has several gowns she wouldn't mind giving you."

Hadn't he just told her that his family didn't socialize? "But I thought—"

"We may not actively participate in the social whirl of Virginia's First Families, but Rosewind Manor is a convenient stopping place for travelers on their way to the capital when the House of Burgesses is in session. I can't have visitors comparing observations and realizing that they've all seen you wearing the same dress."

"Because of the importance you all attach to the pretense of having money?"

"Precisely."

Claire considered him in silence. The Seaton-

Smythes put a high value on social appearances, but they could well afford the necessary trappings. To insist on playing the sport when you didn't have so much as two farthings to rub together was beyond foolish. It was simply insane. No wonder he hadn't been able to reverse the family fortunes.

Devon watched the shadow of disbelief pass across her features. Intrigued by the possible direction of her thoughts, he prompted, "Is there something you wish to say, madam?"

She hesitated, seeming to choose her words carefully. "I can't help but think that your finances wouldn't be quite so desperate if you were a little less concerned with what people thought about you."

At least she was honest. It was more than could be said for most of the people he knew. "I happen to agree with you completely," he conceded. "But that doesn't have the slightest effect on the reality in which we must survive. There are rules governing the conduct of the Tidewater gentry. To ignore them completely is to invite the collapse of the house of cards in which we live. It's a delicate balance of caring and not caring. I expect you to conduct yourself as a lady of the manor should in every regard so that we can maintain the fragile illusion."

She sighed and pursed her lips, then said, "I think it only fair to tell you that I have little patience for social games and no tolerance for the people who play them. My uncle very quickly decided that it was safer to have me conducting his business in the far corners of the British Empire than to have me navigating London social circles."

"You can learn," Devon replied reassuringly. "From time to time the wives of burgesses accompany their husbands to the capital. When they stay the night at Rosewind on their way there, it's customary for the ladies to retire to the salon with their needlework after dinner. You'll have to find a suitable project for yourself and hostess their chatter."

From the opposite seat came a most unladylike snort. "I would rather be shot dead."

They had been doing so well, their conversation easy and smooth. And then she'd had to prove that she was the most deliberately difficult, stubborn female he'd ever met in his life. "You said that you would make every attempt to earn your keep during your stay," he reminded her, hoping to at least shame her into acceptance.

"Have you ever attended such a gathering?"

"No." *Men have more important things to do.*

"Do you have any notion of what it is that women talk about when in their own company?"

"No." *And it's never occurred to me to wonder.*

"Allow me to enlighten you. There are three principal subjects of conversation: their children, their homes, and their wardrobes. If you have none of those, you're at something of a loss when it comes to making a contribution anyone would care to hear."

"You'll have a home to talk about," he countered. "Rose—"

"Rosewind is your home and I am a temporary guest in it," she interjected. "The only true home I have ever known is Crossbridge Manor in Herefordshire, England. I haven't seen it in four years. I don't know if I will ever see it again. I have absolutely nothing to say that these women would want to hear."

She was in a land and community not her own, and he felt sorry for her. "Perhaps," Devon suggested kindly, "you could broaden the conversational range? Take it upon yourself to address a topic or two outside of the traditional expectations?"

She settled back in her seat and after a moment found a small smile. "I've followed Parliament's discussions of the colonial problems," she replied. "I'm aware that there's considerable dissatisfaction here with Crown policies. I could ably converse on that subject. Do you suppose taxation and political representation would be of interest to other women?"

He rather doubted it. She was the first woman he'd ever heard use the words. But using them and actually knowing what they meant were two very different things. "And what's your understanding of the colonial position on those matters?"

She didn't so much as blink before answering crisply, "That the people of the colonies are divided into three groups: those who urge armed rebellion to effect change, those who wish to remain loyal in all instances to the Crown, and those who have no idea what the others are talking about."

True, but it wasn't what he wanted to know. Devon rephrased his question. "Why are some of the colonists opposed to paying taxes?"

She smiled sweetly, her eyes sparkling. "Are you testing me, Devon?"

"Yes," he admitted, his blood warming. "Can you pass?"

Her smile broadened. "In a most basic sense, colonists are opposed to the present taxes because they can't afford them under British mercantile restrictions. If the Crown were to allow the Americans to trade with other nations, profits would be sufficient to make the taxes tolerable and the complaints would end. But the Crown isn't the least bit inclined to let the natural resources of the colonies go to the support of its enemies France, Spain, or Holland, so the restrictions will remain in place and the colonists are left with a choice to smuggle in order to make enough to pay the taxes or to obey the law and politely protest as they go bankrupt.

"On a more philosophical level," she went on crisply, "the colonists chafe at paying taxes to support a government that allows them no say in the creation of the laws that affect them. They argue that being a British subject under common law entitles them to representation in Parliament. To be denied representation is to be denied one of the most basic rights of an Englishman."

Not only did she understand the basic complaints of his fellow colonists, she understood them well. She was a hoyden to the marrow, but she was obviously an exceptionally intelligent one. The combination of traits didn't particularly bode well, though. Especially for a man quite used to being the master of all he surveyed. At that moment he felt a suffering kinship with George Seaton-Smythe. It was an unsettling feeling.

"How did I do?" she asked.

"Quite well," he had to admit. "I'm impressed."

"As I intended for you to be," she allowed, her eyes bright and her grin impish. Sobering only slightly, she added, "Discussing political philosophy is ever so much more interesting than needlepointing pillows."

"You might be surprised to discover that colonial women are more politically aware than their British sisters," he ventured, hoping it was true. By and large, however, he knew they weren't any more formally educated. Custom on that point was one of the few things that hadn't been changed on the journey across the ocean. Which made Claire Curran a decidedly odd duck on both sides of it. If she wasn't willing to pretend to be a normal female, his salon was going to be a cold and silent place. He didn't even want to think of the social ridicule *he'd* have to endure once the House of Burgesses actually convened.

"I certainly hope so," he heard her say. "It would be a welcome change to have an intelligent conversation without having to don a pair of breeches to achieve it."

Hadn't they just had a conversation that qualified as such? Wasn't she wearing a dress? Even as he framed the questions, he saw the answers. Beneath her skirt she was still wearing her boy's clothing. And more importantly, he hadn't contributed one word to the discourse beyond prodding and daring her to expound. How—and at what point—had he lost control of the exchange?

"Speaking of breeches," he began, desperately grasping at the chance to reassert his authority, "you will surrender your boy's costume to me when we reach Rosewind."

She arched a brow. "I will not," she declared, her tone implying that the very idea of doing so was the most ludicrous thing anyone had ever suggested. "If you want my breeches, you'll have to physically remove them from my person. And be forewarned. I won't give them up without a struggle."

She'd fight him? Oh, Jesus. He wasn't the least bit amused by the notion. Stirred, yes, but not at all amused. In fact, the idea of taking her to the floor and removing her clothing was so strongly appealing that it was altogether frightening. But he'd taken the step and was mandated by pride to see the journey through. "Do you think you have any chance of winning the contest?"

"Maybe. Maybe not," she replied with a quick shrug. "But if I should lose, I will at least make you pay a price for your victory."

"And what—other than making me angry—would be the point of that, madam?"

"Remembering the battle," she quipped, "might give you pause the next time it occurs to you to play the imperial lord."

"By law, I *am* your lord," Devon reminded her.

"And why should I feel compelled to respect and obey a law in which I, as a female, had no voice? Colonial men aren't the only ones denied the basic rights granted Englishmen under common law."

It was a most outrageous, preposterous extension of the Natural Rights doctrine that he'd ever heard. To extend the rights of free men to women? *Women?* He was beginning to understand why her uncle had sent her off into the world of men. In addition to being stubborn and willful, she was also a most unnatural woman. Seaton-Smythe had probably considered banishing her the only way to preserve what few positive aspects there were to his public reputation. Even then she'd probably managed to wreak havoc with her flagrant disregard for convention. Marrying her off to a distant, desperate colonial planter had been the only hope the man had of ever sleeping well.

"I can see why your uncle was willing to give up two thousand pounds sterling to be rid of you," he muttered.

"And I, sir," she blithely countered, "can see why you had no wife."

"Bachelorhood was my state by choice."

"Undoubtedly," she laughingly retorted, her brow arched delicately. "No woman in her right mind and of free will would choose to be bound to you."

She'd boxed him into a corner as neatly as she pleased. And he'd all but invited her to do it. When he next saw his brother, Wyndom was a dead man. Even as Devon planned his well-deserved revenge, the carriage slowed and eased into a turn to the north. Glancing out the window, Devon recognized both the stately oaks that lined the drive of Rosewind Manor and the approaching end of the interminable journey.

Turning, he caught and held the gaze of his bride. "Before the night is out, madam," he promised, "you will surrender your breeches."

Claire sighed. If he wanted a battle, she had no choice but to oblige him. And he would learn in the course of it what her uncle had eventually come to accept: Obedience and respect couldn't be attained by swinging a fist. George Seaton-Smythe had sent her away rather than be confronted by that humbling fact each and every day. She could only hope that Devon

Rivard would come to the same conclusion more quickly than her uncle had.

"It should be a most interesting contest, sir. I look forward to it and wish you the best of luck."

The fading daylight was still sufficient for her to see the granite planes of Devon Rivard's smooth-shaven jaw, the light in his eyes that wordlessly spoke of a challenge accepted. A shiver raced up her spine, a shiver that owed nothing to the cold and everything to a sudden shadow passing over her confidence.

Unsettled, she deliberately looked away from him and out the window of the rented carriage. Her first sight of Rosewind Manor came in that moment and took her breath away.

CHAPTER SIX

*T*HERE WAS SO MUCH of it to take in that she could only do so in small parts. The drive on which they were traveling curved gently across the front of the mansion—and *mansion* was the only word she could think of to describe it—passing in front of a set of wide steps leading up to a central door that was protected by a roofed and pilastered extension. The main portion of the red brick structure was two stories high with a hipped roof. No fewer than seven mullioned windows broke the face of the second story on the front side; six windows on the lower story, three on each side of the massive front door. And chimneys... Rosewind Manor had four of them in the central part alone, an internal pair of them on each end.

Flanking the main body of the structure on each side were identical wings. Also constructed of red brick, they were single story and comprised of two distinctly different parts. The outermost portion appeared to be octagonal with a window set in each of the faces she could see. The roof was set in sections, rising and sloping back to abut yet another chimney. Connecting the octagonal portion to the main body of the house was a relatively simple section with a gabled roof and three perfectly spaced windows.

The whole of it was balanced and solid, a monument to a builder who appreciated order and stability. A builder who also possessed great wealth and a determination to display it for all the world to see. Rosewind Manor was positively huge by any standard of measurement. The main part of the house alone was easily half again as large as the Governor's Mansion in Williamsburg. The Seaton-Smythe house in London would have fit into it with plenty of room left over. Their country house would have fit into it twice. As for her own home of Crossbridge Manor ... Somehow *Manor* seemed such a pitiful bit of pretension when comparing her home with that of the Rivards. The main house at Crossbridge was only a third of the size of the central portion of Rosewind alone.

Claire arched a brow, remembering the expenses that had been required to maintain her small home. The costs Devon Rivard bore for running his had to be staggering. It was little wonder that he was so generally ill-tempered. And it was equally clear how he'd come by his lordly demeanor; Rosewind was a castle. Claire smiled ruefully, wondering when the man planned to dig the moat and install the drawbridge.

"Impressed?"

She tore her attention away from the house and gave him both a smile and an honest answer. "I'm relieved that I'm not really the mistress of Rosewind. If I were, I'd be slightly overwhelmed by the responsibilities looming ahead."

"Only slightly?" he asked, clearly surprised.

"And only for a while," she added as the carriage eased to a stop. "Eventually I'd meet even your most outrageous expectations."

"I'd be content, madam," he said as he opened the carriage door, "if someone could meet even the most minimal."

Claire, wondering whether his words were a confession of impossibly high standards or an admission that the household affairs were largely mismanaged, watched him gracefully unfold his huge frame and smoothly exit the carriage. To her surprise, he turned back and offered his hand in assistance. She took it and tried not to rely on it overly much as she climbed out to stand beside him in front of the snow-covered steps. The wind was whipping in hard from the west, stinging her cheeks and cutting through her cloak to arrow into the center of her bones. The snow came in small, icy pellets that crackled and bounced on the stones at her feet, clung to and melted on the warmth of her wool-covered shoulders.

"Mind your step," he said, using his foot to clear a narrow pathway up the steps and drawing her along behind him. "It's slippery. And I can't afford to pay a doctor to set broken limbs."

He simply couldn't be pleasant, Claire silently groused; to be kind and considerate just for the sake of being kind and considerate. For a brief moment he'd been a decent human being, concerned for the welfare of another. And then he'd destroyed the illusion by admitting to his own selfish motives for caring. It would serve him right if she did fall. With just the tiniest bit of luck she could break her neck and be put out of *his* misery.

As he reached the top of the stairs and drew her onto the porch and ahead of him, the massive front door opened as if by itself. Claire started and then recalled the first—and only—time she'd been permitted to use the front door of the Seaton-Smythe house. A servant stood invisibly on the back side, waiting to take their coats. Given all that she'd been told of the family's dire financial straits, it was surprising to realize that they could justify the expense. But then, her beastly husband had made it quite clear that maintaining appearances was vitally important to their survival. Not to mention comfort, Claire added as she was guided into a white marble tiled foyer.

Her hand was abruptly released and, from behind her, she heard the door close and Devon Rivard say, "Good evening, Ephram."

"Good evening, sir."

She turned toward the voice and then froze, stunned by realization. Ephram was a Negro; more accurately, given the lightness of his skin and his features, a mulatto. Even as she blinked in shock, the impeccably dressed Ephram accepted Devon's coat and then bowed in a courtly manner to acknowledge her presence. She dipped her chin in return greeting, her mind reeling. The Rivards didn't have servants; they had slaves. There was a significant difference between the two statuses, and despite all of the traveling she'd done for her uncle and all the places it had taken her, she had never been able to comfortably accept the notion that it was all right for one human being to own another.

Hers was a decidedly uncommon perspective on the institution, she knew. Slavery was known in virtually every corner of the world; the American colonies had no exclusive claim to its practice. And while slaves were owned throughout all thirteen, she knew that the majority of those held in bondage were in the southern ones. She shouldn't have been so stunned to learn that her husband was an owner of slaves. It was logical that he would be, especially being a Virginian. But she was startled nonetheless and she couldn't help but think that it didn't speak at all well of his conscience.

Hearing steps behind her, Claire turned away from

Ephram and the doorway. Coming across the foyer—her wooden heels clicking against the tile—was a living, breathing embodiment of a dressmaker's most stylish moppet. Despite being unable to afford the latest in ladies' fashions for herself, Claire nevertheless knew that no one wore panniers and hoops that wide anymore except to the opera or an evening affair at Windsor Castle. And she could only hope that the impossibly high and intricately arranged hairstyle was a powdered wig that could be removed between public appearances. If it wasn't, the older woman had to suffer from a perpetually stiff neck.

"Devon," the matron declared as she came to a halt so sudden that her hems swayed forward and then back. "I will have a word with you."

"Later perhaps, Mother."

Madam Rivard blindly gestured toward the wide doorway behind her. "Your brother is at this very moment on the verge of collapse from frostbite. He can hardly hold the brandy snifter he's shaking so badly from the chill."

"But he is managing to hold it, isn't he?" the woman's son replied snidely, coming to stand beside Claire. As his mother blinked, he drawled, "Mother, may I present Claire. Claire, my mother, Madam Henrietta Rivard."

Recovering with a start, Madam Rivard advanced, meeting Claire's gaze for the first time and smiling broadly as she gushingly said, "Welcome to Rosewind Manor, my dear girl. Wyndom has only been able to stammer a bit past his chill to tell us that Devon was bringing a guest."

She stopped in front of Claire and took both of her hands in her own to add, "And since my oafish son," she added, casting a quick, censorious glance at Devon, "has neglected to append your surname, I'm placed in the embarrassing position of having to inquire as to which of Virginia's fine families you belong."

Guest? Was the woman just very polite or didn't she know? Uncertain, Claire decided that wisdom lay in giving her the most general of replies. "I am not Virginian, Madam Rivard."

"Ah, British," the woman countered with a smile even larger than before. "I can hear our mother tongue in your voice." She lightly squeezed Claire's hands, then released them and stepped back, saying, "Do let Devon give Ephram your cloak, and come into the parlor so that your bones can warm a bit."

Her son obediently slipped around to stand behind Claire, placing his hands lightly on her shoulders. A warmth flooded into her and rippled all the way to her toes. Disconcerted by the pleasure in the sensation and feeling a desperate need to escape it, Claire held her breath and fumbled to undo the frogs of her cloak. It seemed to take an eternity and she was light-headed and weak-kneed by the time the garment was mercifully lifted away.

Seemingly oblivious to her discomfort, Madam Rivard tucked Claire's arm through her own and led her off in the direction of the wide doorway, asking as they went, "Where in England is your home?"

"I'm of London most recently, but originally from Herefordshire."

"And what is it that brings you to our colony and out to Rosewind, my dear?"

The woman didn't know. The brother hadn't told her. Her stomach knotted with dread, Claire managed a weak smile and replied, "Nefarious scheming."

From behind them, Devon Rivard corrected, "More like exceedingly poor judgment and then miserable luck."

"Oh, I do hear a story begging to be told," Henrietta

Rivard chirped happily as she drew Claire into a lavishly appointed salon. Devon's brother stood directly in front of the hearth, a large brandy snifter in his hand and the tails of his frock coat perilously close to the flames. Another older woman sat perched on the edge of a nearby chair, an embroidery hoop in her hand. Her panniers were every bit as wide as Madam Rivard's, her hair styled in a manner that was only slightly less extravagant. Elsbeth, Claire guessed. Henrietta's supposedly shrewish sister.

"It's been two years since anything even remotely amusing or interesting has happened at Rosewind," Madam Rivard went on, guiding Claire toward the fire. "Devon is positively the most boring man in all of the Americas. Had I not given birth to him myself, I would swear that he wasn't my child at all. Life under his control has become just as stifled as he is. Wyndom, do move over to share the warmth with Mistress..."

Wyndom obeyed, his gaze riveted on his very full glass of brandy, and Claire was deposited beside him at the hearth, her mind reeling and her heart pounding. She saw no choice but answer, "Curran."

Devon, standing in front of the buffet with a decanter in one hand and a crystal tumbler in the other, fixed his brother with a hard look and said, "You didn't send the message, did you?"

"I couldn't think of an appropriate way to frame the words," Wyndom replied without looking up. He took a sip of his brandy before adding, "And, besides, you didn't leave me the time. Arranging for the carriage took all that you allowed."

"You're a sniveling coward."

"Devon!" Madam Rivard gasped, wheeling on him. "We have a guest in our home and you will exercise good manners."

"Mother," he retorted icily, pouring his drink, "You

should know that Claire is more than a mere guest. She's my wife."

Claire couldn't see his mother's face, but it wasn't really necessary. Madam Rivard gasped, pressed her hands to her face, and staggered where she stood. Claire instinctively edged forward, preparing to catch her should she faint dead away.

"Had Wyndom stiffened his spine when instructed to do so," Devon continued, his tone still flinty as he advanced toward the hearth with his drink, "you would have been accorded the opportunity to both receive such startling news and recover from your shock in private. The awkwardness of this moment lies squarely at his feet."

"Nevertheless," the woman with the embroidery hoop said haughtily, "*you* are the son who owes your mother the explanation."

Claire watched fire blaze in his eyes, realizing that despite their sometimes strained and contentious exchanges, she hadn't seen him truly angry until now. With what appeared to be great effort, he deliberately turned his shoulder to the woman and addressed his mother. "Wyndom incurred a gambling debt and arranged a loan from an agent of George Seaton-Smythe in order to pay it."

"I'm not familiar with the name. Is he a Virginian?"

"No, Mother," he replied tightly. "He's British."

"Oh, thank goodness. I would so dislike having our friends know that borrowing was necessary."

Devon scowled at his mother and went on. "Mr. Seaton-Smythe apparently came to realize that my brother's promises aren't worth the paper on which they're written and that I represented the only hope he had of recovering the two thousand pounds sterling Wyndom had borrowed from him."

"I hope that you didn't pay the man that kind of

money," the other woman said, her tone no less imperial for having been pointedly dismissed just a moment before. "Your mother and I have repeatedly submitted our lists to you and have, despite that, done without a great number of necessities for far too long. We haven't had so much as a quarter yard of new cloth come into this house in over eighteen months. The quality of tea we've endured for the last six is positively wretched and we haven't attended—"

"I didn't pay it," Devon snapped, pivoting to glare at her. "If I lack the money for fine tea, Aunt Elsbeth, you can be sure that I don't have it to pay an ill-considered debt that *I* didn't incur."

Ah, yes. She'd been right; it was Elsbeth. And Devon's appraisal of her general manner seemed to be accurate.

"There is no reason to snap, Devon," his mother chided. "I can only hope you stated your regrets to Mr. Seaton-Smythe in a more polite manner."

His regrets? Madam Rivard had absolutely no idea how the larger world worked. Judging by the look in her eldest son's eyes, she was on the verge of getting a hard and brutal lesson on the subject. Claire held her breath and wished herself a thousand miles away.

"Mr. Seaton-Smythe isn't the sort of man to accept regrets," Devon explained, his voice tight. "Politely stated or otherwise, Mother. Anticipating that I wouldn't have the funds, he offered to retire the debt in its entirety if I would agree to wed his niece. Hence, this afternoon, I most reluctantly married Mistress Curran."

He'd been reluctant? Claire's blood heated with outrage even as Elsbeth looked her up and down, her nose wrinkling in obvious disdain. Wyndom absorbed himself in taking a sip of his brandy. Madam Rivard turned to face her, her brow raised.

Refusing to be baited into defending her innocence in the fiasco, Claire straightened her shoulders and met

Madam Rivard's gaze squarely. "We've agreed to have the union annulled as soon as your son receives documents from my uncle canceling the debt. The sham should end by August at the latest."

"An annulment? *An annul—*" Madam Rivard gasped, placed the back of her wrist across her brow, executed a half pirouette while fluttering her eyelids, then daintily crumpled backward.

Claire reacted instinctively, stepping forward and extending her arms to catch the collapsing matron. While Madam Rivard's faint was decidedly graceful, Claire's rescue of her wasn't. The combined weight of the woman's hair, the panniers, the gown, the embroidered petticoats and Henrietta Rivard herself was more than Claire had anticipated and she staggered, desperately struggling for balance. She heard Elsbeth squeak in shock. At the farthest edge of her awareness, she felt the younger brother skitter away, saw the embroidery hoop fall to the floor, and a blur of dark blue.

Then Madam Rivard's weight miraculously left her arms. Claire's hope of recovering her balance was only momentary, though. Even as she tried to get her feet squarely under her, she was abruptly wrenched forward and down. Unable to keep herself upright, she gasped, closed her eyes, and threw her hands out to cushion her certain impact against the floor.

Only it wasn't the floor she hit; it was a heated wall of blue wool and corded muscle. She opened her eyes to find herself on her knees, her arms flung around the neck of Devon Rivard and her breasts pressed hard against the broad expanse of his chest. His emerald gaze met hers and held it as he cocked a brow and a smile played at the corners of his mouth. She froze, her heart pounding furiously, traitorously, at the sight.

"I can manage, thank you," he said softly.

Dear Lord, what he had to be thinking! With all the dignity she could muster, Claire awkwardly leveraged herself against his massive shoulders and gained a respectable space between their upper bodies. But she simply couldn't move her lower limbs and go any farther. Neither could she let go of his shoulders without tumbling back fully against him. Glancing down, she realized the cause of her dilemma. They were both on their knees with Henrietta Rivard trapped between them, cradled in her son's arms with her panniers twisted and her skirts a bunched and crumpled wad held in place by a strong arm encircling her just above her knees.

Claire looked up to meet that unsettling gaze again. "You've caught my skirts in with your mother's. I can't rise until she does."

"Oh, dear God," Wyndom cried breathlessly from behind them. "Mistress Curran, your hem is on fire!"

Claire started and looked over her shoulder to see flames licking a trail along the edge of the only dress she owned. Twisting around, she thought to grab the fabric and haul the flames close enough to smother them with a portion of still-whole cloth.

She'd barely caught a handful when Wyndom stepped close and Devon bellowed, "No! Don't!" just before his brother flung the entire contents of his brandy snifter on her dress.

A ball of bright blue flame exploded upward. Driven by the heat, Claire dropped her skirt to shield her face with her arms as she instinctively turned away. In the same heartbeat, her world careened out of control. Sensation and realization tumbled through her awareness, fractured and elusive, there and gone before she could react. She felt herself roughly jostled and thrown off balance. Steel bands clamped around her upper arms and she heard herself cry out as they lifted her up and then drove her entire body hard against the wooden floor. For a long second there was only the ache that bloomed in her head. As the edge of it slowly faded, normal perception returned.

She was on her back, staring up at the ornately plastered ceiling. Turning and lifting her head, she found Devon in the vicinity of her feet, using her skirt to smother the last of the flames. Wyndom stood beside the hearth, his empty glass in hand and a decidedly regretful furrow between his pale brows. Madam Rivard was sprawled on the floor to Claire's left, her skirts, panniers, and hoops forming something of a tent that the woman was desperately trying to keep from flipping back over her head. The task was made even more difficult by the fact that she had only one hand free. The other was engaged in an equally desperate effort to keep the mountain of hair from falling off her head completely. Elsbeth was trying to help, but her own hoops, panniers, and wig made it impossible for her to bend over and preserve her modesty at the same time.

"Jesus, Wyndom! You're a goddamn idiot."

Claire looked back just in time to see Devon come to his feet in one smooth, flawless, almost feline motion. He wasn't looking at his brother, though. He was looking at her, doing a quick head-to-toe appraisal. Claire found the wherewithal to sit up and quickly smooth down her skirts.

"I was only trying to help," the younger man answered quietly, staring into his empty glass. "My instincts said to throw liquid on it. It never occurred to me—"

"It never does." Devon stepped forward and extended a hand to her. "Are you all right?"

"Yes. Yes, I'm fine," she assured him, gratefully placing her hand in his and accepting his assistance. "And thank you for acting so quickly." She glanced over her shoulder to see what damage had been done to her dress.

"Only your outer skirt is burnt beyond repair," Devon supplied. "Your petticoats are a bit singed, but still quite serviceable. Mother, how are you?"

"Rather rudely handled, I'm afraid."

"Your sensibilities will recover," Devon countered, releasing Claire's hand slowly, clearly watching to make sure she had her balance before he withdrew too far. His gaze lingered on hers for a moment, then he deliberately tore it away to look at his mother. "Are you physically injured in any way?"

"It would appear, at first appraisal, that I am not."

"Wyndom?" he said coolly, "Would it be asking too much of you to help our mother to her feet?"

"Oh!" Wyndom said with a visible start. "Of course not." With his empty snifter still in hand, he dashed to his mother's side and then paused to consider his glass, clearly in a quandary as to what he ought to do with it. His mother flailed her arms as he tried to reach a decision.

Devon groaned quietly and Claire looked up at him just in time to see him roll his eyes. She could honestly understand his frustrations. Wyndom was a generally likable fellow, but he didn't seem to possess even the tiniest sliver of common sense. She was extremely grateful that Devon had been present to put out the fire. Had her life depended on any of the others, she wouldn't be standing there with only a bit of charred fabric to show for the harrowing experience. She'd have been seriously injured. Or dead. The latter, she suddenly realized, would have made Devon's life much simpler. That he'd acted against his own best interests in the situation said something about his sense of decency and honor.

He was certainly a bundle of contradictions, she decided, studying him. Noticing that curls of burnt fabric clung to the sleeves of his frock coat, she reached out to gently brush them away. It seemed the least she could do for him, considering what he'd done for her. She felt his gaze come to her, felt the warmth of his assessment. It was oddly calming, and from the farthest corner of her brain flitted the silly notion that a lifetime of such moments would be rather nice.

She deliberately shoved the thought away and concentrated on brushing a particularly large bit of scorched fabric from the left cuff of his coat. Her hand grazed his in the process and he jerked it away while drawing a hard breath through clenched teeth.

"You've burnt your hand," she declared, reaching for his arm, angry with herself for not thinking of the possibility earlier. He didn't fight her, but stood stiffly as she turned his hand over so that she could see the palm. The skin was a sickly white and she knew that the burn went deep. It needed to be tended immediately.

"A little butter on it and it will be fine," Devon said quietly, seeming to read her mind.

She looked up at him and just as quietly disagreed. "Butter will only seal in the heat and make the pain more intense." At his cocked brow, she glanced over her shoulder to see that Madam Rivard had been righted and that Elsbeth was busily smoothing her sister's skirts. Wyndom was standing there looking as though he was at a complete loss for what to do next.

"Wyndom," she said, drawing his attention to her. "Your brother's hand is injured. Please go out the front door and gather some snow."

Even as Wyndom nodded, Ephram stepped into the doorway, bowed, and said, "Dinner is served."

Wyndom sagged. "Dashedly poor timing."

"Never mind the snow," Devon snapped, easing his hand from Claire's gentle grasp. "I've suffered worse burns and survived. Let's go to the table before we have to add 'cold' to the other shortcomings of the meal." Presenting Claire with his arm, he added, "Wyndom, please try to escort Mother to the dining room without losing her on the way."

CHAPTER SEVEN

*I*T WAS THE ODDEST THING, Devon mused as Claire walked arm in arm with him into the dining room. She'd fallen into step immediately and so they moved as one, their progress even and comfortable. It required no thinking at all and he couldn't help but wonder if she'd be as easy to squire on the dance floor. He'd never in his life considered the possibility of public dancing without offering up a silent groan. But the mental image of partnering with Claire Curran made the prospect not only bearable but inexplicably attractive. Yes, it was most odd. Odd and intriguing.

"Lacking a full household staff," he said as he took her to the buffet against the south wall, "we dine rather informally, serving ourselves. I hope you don't mind."

"Not at all."

Soft and utterly sincere. Considering all the foot stamping and complaining he'd endured since he'd been forced to reduce the staff, her acceptance of the situation was an incredibly welcome change. He gently surrendered her arm and picked up a plate, saying, "Allow me to fill your plate. Do you care for potatoes? I can't vouch for what kind of sauce they're swimming in."

She looked in the chafing dish and caught her lower lip between her teeth. After a moment, she replied, "It would seem to be something cream based. And I'm willing to try anything once. Please fill my plate as you would your own." She glanced up at him to smile and add, "Only smaller portions, of course."

She had the prettiest eyes. When she smiled, they sparkled like sapphires in candlelight. When she was angry, he recalled, they darkened to the color of a midnight sky. She arched a brow in silent question and Devon started with realization. He was staring. And his pulse was tripping through his veins at a ridiculously quick rate. Forcing a smile of his own, he deliberately fixed his attention on the chafing dishes and what passed for food at Rosewind Manor. He carefully picked up a silver serving spoon, mindful both that it needed to be polished and that the movement intensified the throbbing in his hand. He gritted his teeth and focused on the task of serving, determined to fill his mind with something other than the awareness of pain.

He was trying to pry out of the serving dish a slice of what—under the layer of black ash—might be beef when he saw Wyndom escort their mother into the room. Elsbeth trailed behind, looking none too happy about having to walk into the room without chivalrous male assistance.

Claire, standing at his side, was so very different from the other two women. Her figure was trim yet nicely curved. And it existed without the benefit of the outrageous panniers and hoops his mother and Elsbeth strapped around themselves each and every morning of their lives. And her hair . . . It was real, golden and shiny in the lamplight. Thank God she didn't wear it powdered or hide it under a ludicrous wig.

Of course, wigs and hair powder, panniers and hoops were expensive things, and it was obvious that she couldn't afford them. Still, there was something about Claire that suggested that she'd forgo them even if they were within her financial means. Although going without them put her well outside the bounds of social expectations regarding appropriate feminine fashion, he couldn't help but appreciate her unconventionality. It made her seem so much more real; more flesh and blood than an untouchable, fragile china doll. And that was nice. Very nice. Having to always be the courtly gentleman was such a draining way to go through life. He had the unmistakable feeling that, with Claire, a man could actually relax and be himself from time to time without risking the complete collapse of civilization. All things considered...

Devon scowled down at the green mush that had at one point been individual green beans. Just a handful of hours ago, he'd been cursing his luck, Wyndom's stupidity, George Seaton-Smythe's conniving, and Claire Curran's outrageous behavior. And now he was standing at the buffet, scooping and scraping bits of dreck onto a plate for the same Claire Curran and thinking that she was a lovely bit of unexpected fresh air in his life.

Good God Almighty, he'd taken complete leave of his senses. When had it happened? It certainly hadn't been in the carriage. He'd climbed out wanting to strangle her. That same feeling had been with him when he'd drawn her up the icy front steps and into the foyer. But in the moment his mother had advanced on him, berating him for Wyndom's pathetic shivering...

Yes, that's when he'd begun the slide into insanity. He'd been challenged on every front, and in dealing with all the expectations and unpleasantness, he hadn't been able to keep himself from admiring the poise Claire was displaying in the difficult circumstances. He'd forgotten how much he resented her, how deeply she'd angered him in the course of the day.

And then his mother had fainted and he'd found Claire pressed up against him, her arms around his neck. His admiration for her had instantly slipped to an entirely new plane. Then her skirt had caught fire and, when the flames had been put out, she'd taken his hand in hers and asked Wyndom to get some snow so that she could ease his pain. So genuinely caring. So gentle and yet determined. Yes, now that he thought back, he remembered that he'd felt something in his brain snap in that instant.

"I am assuming," Elsbeth said, intruding on his thoughts, "that since your uncle had two thousand pounds to loan Wyndom, you must be accustomed to living in great style, Mistress Curran. Our simple fare must be a considerable disappointment to you."

"Not at all," he heard Claire reply from his side. As he blinked and struggled to bring his awareness back to the reality of the dining room, she added, "Food is food and I'm always grateful to have some put in front of me, Mistress..."

"Whittington," Elsbeth regally supplied.

The tone of her voice sparked Devon's anger and freed him from the tangle of his thoughts. "Everyone addresses her as Elsbeth," he said, gesturing for Claire to precede him to the table. "You may do the same."

"With all due respect, Devon," his aunt shot back, "the choice of how I wish to be addressed by Mistress Curran is mine to make."

He carefully placed the plate before a chair, then stepped behind it to help seat Claire. She shot him a quick look as she smoothed her skirts and settled herself. She was clearly aware of his tension and just as clearly apprehensive about her role in causing it; he could see the regret dulling the light of her eyes. Damn Elsbeth. Her one true talent was a gift for creating difficulties.

He was easing Claire close to the table when he had sufficient control of his anger to calmly reply, "With all due respect, Aunt Elsbeth, I am the master of this household. Claire is my wife. You are my mother's sister." He stepped back to the buffet to pick up a plate for himself as he continued, "You are not Claire's social equal and she will not be expected to address you as such. You, on the other hand, will address her as Madam Rivard until she gives you leave to do otherwise."

"Which brings up a rather pressing concern I've been considering since this afternoon," Wyndom interjected in the breezy way he always used when trying to ease a taut exchange. "Might I inquire as to how we're going to manage conversations having two Madam Rivards under one roof? It could easily become a very sticky web, you know. Having two Mr. Rivards is already complicated enough."

He watched his brother cross to the table and set his plate down in the place beside Claire. "And we certainly wouldn't want to tax your brain any more than necessary," Devon muttered darkly.

"If I might make a suggestion?" Claire asked, turning in her chair to meet his gaze. She offered him a smile to go with the plea shimmering in her eyes. "As Wyndom has pointed out, there's already a Madam Rivard in residence. And since I'm to be here for only a short while, perhaps everyone could address me—and refer to me—simply as Claire."

"Perhaps we could call you Lady Claire," Wyndom offered, his face alight as he plopped unceremoniously onto the chair. "I like that. It has a certain elegance to it, don't you think?"

Claire turned to face the younger man, and while Devon couldn't see her face from his vantage point, he could hear an apologetic smile framing her words as she answered, "Unfortunately, the title isn't appropriate."

"Clearly," Elsbeth muttered under her breath as she helped herself to the green beans. Devon glared at her and considered planting a boot on her hem so that with her next step she ended up on the floor with her face in her food. God, she brought out the worst in him. She always had.

"I was known as Lady Claire as a child, but baronial titles aren't hereditary and it was forfeited at my father's passing."

"Your father was a baron?" his mother asked, crossing to the table with her food. She set her plate down and then stood there, looking pointedly at Wyndom, her brow arched.

Devon scooped up a mass of congealing potatoes and blindly plopped them on his plate as he watched Claire subtly nudge his brother in the ribs while saying, "Yes, madam. The title was granted for meritorious service in His Majesty's Army."

Wyndom vaulted to his feet, nearly upsetting his chair and then careening into the corner of the table in his haste to belatedly exercise good manners. Their mother pretended not to notice his bumbling and turned her full attention to Claire. "He was a hero, then," she said as she sat on the chair Wyndom had pulled out for her. "How exciting. Can you tell us something of his daring feats?"

"I know little of my father's exploits beyond the fact that, in pushing a fellow officer out of harm's way during battle, he suffered the injuries that left him without his right arm and leg and unable to speak."

Oh, Jesus. He'd rather be dead than maimed so badly. Life wouldn't be worth living if it had to be endured with only half a body. Claire's father had been a far stronger man, far braver man than he would ever be.

"So he was a cripple," Elsbeth summarized, pausing

behind her own chair and waiting for Wyndom to seat her.

Devon flung a chunk of meat on his plate, trying to tamp down his anger just long enough to find some words that would express his outrage and yet be somewhere within the bounds of bare civility. Claire spared him the effort.

"Physically," she replied, a hardened edge of steel in her voice, "my father was unable to move about as freely as he wished. Mentally, he remained an indomitable force until he drew his last breath."

Apparently, in the latter respect, Mr. Curran's acorn hadn't fallen far from the tree. And despite his limitations, he'd managed to raise up a daughter who wasn't going to be cowed by Elsbeth's irascibility. Huzzah for Mr. Curran.

"How on earth did your mother manage to endure such trying circumstances?" Devon's mother asked, notes of sincere sympathy ringing in every word.

"My mother—along with both my younger brothers—passed in an influenza epidemic shortly after my father was injured and retired from military service."

As if being half a man wasn't bad enough, Claire's father had suffered through the loss of his wife and sons, too. How and why had he bothered to go on living? Even as Devon wondered, he realized the answer. He'd gone on because he'd had to, because Claire was the only one left and she had needed a father.

"Then who cared for your father over the years?" Wyndom asked, stepping behind Elsbeth's chair.

"I did."

"In a manner of speaking, of course," Elsbeth corrected, allowing Wyndom to settle her at the table. She reached for her linen napkin, adding, "What you meant to say was that, as a lady, you oversaw the servants who actually did the work required."

"Actually, Elsbeth," Claire replied with an even

harder edge to her voice this time, "we had no servants. My father had no inheritance and his military pension went to keeping the fields planted, the food on our table, and the roof over our heads. There was nothing left over with which to pay wages."

"You worked with your hands?" Elsbeth asked, obviously appalled by the possibility.

"It was either do so or starve. Pride and pretension make for a very lean meal."

A fact that Elsbeth would never understand, Devon realized. Neither would his mother or his brother for that matter. All three of them would sit at a table and die waiting for food to be brought to them. Not once would it even occur to them to get up and go about finding and preparing some for themselves. Claire, on the other hand . . .

Settling himself at the table, Devon looked at the mass of unappealing food on his plate and suddenly saw a possibility that had all the glorious promise of a new dawn. "Can you, by any chance, cook?"

"Of course I can."

"And she can undoubtedly scrub the pots when she's done serving, too."

Elsbeth's cutting remark ignited a spark in Claire's eyes. Devon held up his hand quickly. She hesitated for a long moment, then nodded in graceful acceptance and eased back into her chair. Satisfied, he fixed his aunt with a hard look and declared, "There's nothing sinful in an honest day's labor or in rolling up your sleeves to contribute to the smooth functioning of a household. Neither of which, I might add, you have *ever* made so much as an *attempt* to do."

Elsbeth drew herself up with an affronted huff. "I am a gentlewoman."

"You're a parasite," he countered. "You take without giving and invariably complain about what you get. I've tolerated your presence in this house only because my mother seems to find some pleasure in your company and we're bound by the ties of familial blood. But understand me very clearly, Aunt Elsbeth. For as long as Claire resides under this roof, you will treat her with the deference and respect befitting her social station as my wife. If you're unwilling to do that, you may pack your bags and Wyndom will see you safely to Williamsburg."

Elsbeth's jaw sagged. But only for a fraction of a heartbeat. With an almost audible snap, she closed it and snatched up her knife and fork in a way that suggested she was thinking of leaping across the table and plunging them into his chest.

"I do think," his mother said softly, "that you've taken Elsbeth's comment entirely the wrong way, Devon. I believe she meant her remark to reflect her awed appreciation for the breadth of Lady Claire's domestic skills."

"Yes, yes," Wyndom chimed in. "I'm sure she meant no offense."

Not giving him time to offer proof otherwise, his mother chimed in breezily, "Going back to Devon's inquiry, Lady Claire..." She lifted a forkful of potatoes and sighed. "As you can tell, we're in desperate need of someone who can cook something that approximates palatable."

"Lord knows that Mary Margaret tries," Wyndom contributed, adding his own heartfelt sigh. "I was assured, when I bought her papers, that she was an exceptional cook."

"Exceptionally bad," Devon clarified softly and with a wince. He met Claire's gaze and added, "Mary Margaret came to us just over a month ago."

"Well, better poor fare than poisoned fare," Elsbeth piped up. "Before her arrival, we were living under a constant shadow of death."

Claire furrowed her brows, glanced down at her food, and then back at him, clearly puzzled. He saw no recourse except to lay bare the utter stupidity that had gotten them where they were.

"Aunt Elsbeth and Mother heard reports—unsubstantiated, I might add—of a family poisoned by their slave cook," he supplied. "They took it into their heads that Hannah was spending every hour of her waking day plotting our slow and painful demise. And despite her thirty years of faithful and exemplary service to this family, the hysteria reached absurd proportions. Rather than subject Hannah to it, I sold her to Jane Vobe, the owner of the King's Arms."

Claire flinched visibly at the word *sold*. Devon watched her blink and swallow, watched her struggle for words. Did she understand how complicated the web of relationships was? The pain in having them torn apart? Or was she one of those who didn't understand anything at all and opposed the institution based on simplistic principles?

"It must have been difficult for her to be uprooted in that fashion."

Difficult? Oh, yes. It had been difficult. But he wasn't about to admit to anyone that he and Hannah had both cried at their parting, that as he'd ridden away he'd wished with all of his heart that it could have been Aunt Elsbeth who had been sold away. Hannah had been the best part of his childhood, the time spent in the kitchen with her the best part of his every day since he could remember.

"Actually, it was handled in accordance with her request," he answered, attacking the slab of meat on his plate. "In the last few years, Hannah's been keeping Sunday company with Moses, one of Mrs. Vobe's slaves. Mrs. Vobe considered the acquisition of Hannah to be nothing short of a major coup. Everyone was happy: Mother and Aunt Elsbeth, Moses and Hannah, not to mention Mrs. Vobe and her well-fed patrons."

No one but Hannah cared how I felt, he silently

added. Abandoning all hope of cutting the meat, Devon laid down his silverware. Reaching for his wineglass, he affected a brightness he didn't feel and concluded, "The next day Wyndom was dispatched to James City to acquire an indentured servant to take Hannah's place in the kitchen. He came back with Mary Margaret Malone."

"No one has ever heard of an indentured servant poisoning the family food, have they?" Elsbeth inquired, sounding as though the explanation had somehow vindicated her.

"Poisoning is only a matter of degree," he replied dryly. "Slow, god-awful degrees."

"She's a pleasant young woman," Wyndom offered. "And comely, too. She has the most beautiful red hair. It's almost a copper color."

Devon took a sip of his wine and leaned back in his chair, resigned to drowning the gnawing in his belly. "If only those factors contributed something to the edibility of the food she prepares."

"Perhaps," Claire said quietly, also laying aside her silverware in apparent defeat, "it's that she's never been taught how to properly cook." She glanced between his mother and Elsbeth and then hesitantly added, "I'd be happy to do what I can to instruct her."

Lifting his glass in salute, Devon replied with absolute sincerity, "I would be deeply, deeply appreciative of whatever improvement you might achieve."

A smile tickled the corners of her mouth, and a mischievous light suddenly brightened her eyes. He sensed that she saw an opportunity in his need, a chance to parlay his satisfaction to her advantage. What precisely was she thinking? He suspected it had to do with breeches and boots and—for some unfathomable reason—the idea of negotiating for them amused him.

"If you prove successful at the task," Elsbeth said, "perhaps Wyndom can find someone at auction in

James City whom you could train to be a server. Presenting food à la buffet lacks a certain degree of gentility and grace, don't you think, *Lady Claire*?"

The light went out of Claire's eyes as she looked across the table to meet the other woman's gaze.

Ah, my lady Claire, he thought, *if looks could kill I'd be forever in your debt*. Smiling, he studied the color of his wine and drawled, "There isn't any money to buy additional servants, whether they be slave or indentured. Which leaves you with two choices, Aunt Elsbeth. You'll either have to accept and endure the horrific conditions of life here or find someone willing to keep you in a manner more in keeping with your sense of importance."

Elsbeth gave another of her indignant huffs and attempted to rebuff him with silence. His mother frowned at him. And Wyndom shook his head, saying, "I can't help but observe that you're in a particularly foul mood this evening, Devon. Any special reason?"

Devon bit his tongue as an honest answer pounded through his brain. *I've been hungry for a goddamn month. My mother only plays at being the mistress of the household. Her sister is a bottomless pit of expectation and ingratitude. My brother is an idiot. And—lest you've forgotten—this afternoon I was forced to marry a stranger. And—amazingly—aside from myself, the wife I didn't want and don't need appears to be the only other person in this house who possesses an ounce of good sense and is willing to work to earn her keep. What do you think, Wyndom? Are any of those reasons special?*

"It's been a very long day," Devon said tersely, placing his napkin beside his plate. He rose to his feet and turned to Claire. "I'm sure it's been a tiring one for you as well. If you're done with your meal, perhaps you'd like to retire to your room?"

"Yes, I really would," she admitted, putting aside

her napkin as well. "If no one would think it ill-mannered of me to cry exhaustion so early in the evening."

"Of course not, dear," his mother assured her. She looked at him and added, "I'll see to it, Devon. Settling a guest falls within the duties of being the mistress of Rosewind. It's a pleasure too seldom afforded me in recent years."

Which was, of course, his fault. God, he was tired of battling his way through every conversation. "Very well, Mother," he said with an abbreviated bow. "If you will excuse me, please. I have accounts to do."

He walked away, vowing that someday he was going to be a hermit and throw rocks at anyone who came near him.

CHAPTER EIGHT

*C*LAIRE WATCHED HIM LEAVE, with his wineglass in hand, and felt a strange twinge of regret. There was no denying that he'd been contentious throughout dinner, but then his hand hadn't been tended and the pain had to have made him less tolerant of Elsbeth's constant prodding. In a way, she felt sorry for him. Elsbeth would try the patience of a saint. His mother was sweet, but for some reason seemed compelled to make excuses for her sister's nastiness. And Wyndom...Poor Wyndom was everything that his brother wasn't. She felt a little sorry for him, too. Devon never missed an opportunity to criticize or insult him. On the other hand, though, Wyndom constantly said and did things that openly invited his brother's barbed comments.

"Wyndom," Madam Rivard said softly, "Lady Claire, your aunt Elsbeth, and I would like to leave the table."

"Oh!" He vaulted to his feet and then fidgeted in place, his gaze darting between the three of them as he obviously struggled with the decision as to which lady he should assist first.

Claire rose on her own, deliberately removing herself from his mental factoring. Her movement seemed to clarify his thinking. With a huge grin, he darted around the end of the table to attend his mother. Elsbeth waited, her nose in the air and her lips pursed. Yes, Claire could understand why Devon would want to send this woman far, far away.

Madam Rivard, once on her feet, turned to her sister and smiled. "I'll meet you in the salon after I see Lady Claire to her room. Perhaps Wyndom could ask Mary Margaret to prepare us a pot of tea."

Elsbeth nodded and so did Wyndom. Wyndom's nod, however, was noticeably more enthusiastic than that of his aunt. Was Wyndom enamored of the cook? Claire wondered. He'd said she was young and comely. Just how young was Mary Margaret Malone? Claire glanced down at the uneaten food on the plates. Any female older than fifteen would know how to cook. It was basic knowledge that all women were expected to possess and ably practice. Was Mary Margaret a child?

"Shall we go, Lady Claire?"

Claire nodded absently and fell into step beside Madam Rivard, reconsidering a question that had briefly occurred to her earlier. If Mary Margaret had been here a month, why hadn't Madam Rivard or Elsbeth undertaken her instruction? The quick conclusion she'd reached at the table remained the same. There were still only two likely answers: Either they considered the task beneath them or neither of them knew how to cook any better than Mary Margaret did.

If it was the latter, then perhaps the art of cooking wasn't the universal female skill she'd always assumed it to be. And if that was the case, then Mary Margaret's miserable fare might not be a consequence of age at all. It might well be that she was from a social class that hadn't expected her to know how to actually prepare food. Which, of course, begged the question of how she'd come to be an indentured servant.

"Where are your trunks, my dear?"

Pulled from her musing, Claire blinked and looked around her. They had reached the foyer and Madam Rivard had stopped in the center of it, a concerned frown on her face.

Claire, too, stopped. Glancing about, she saw her valise sitting at the base of the stairs leading to the second story. "I have only the one bag," she said, crossing to it.

"That's all? One small valise?"

"Yes, madam," Claire replied, picking it up and waiting for the other woman to join her. "Its contents are quite sufficient for my needs."

Madam Rivard gathered her skirts in hand and started up the stairs, saying, "Your needs must be very small. No wonder Devon's so cross."

Claire considered the two ideas, but couldn't see how one necessarily connected to the other. "I beg your pardon?"

"Devon is a stick, my dear," his mother answered, reaching the top of the stairs and taking a softly glowing candle lamp from a hall table before leading Claire down the carpeted hallway. "He likes his world orderly and patterned and his people predictable. The fact that you have only the one traveling case—and that you see it as entirely adequate—makes you a most unusual woman. It's no wonder that he's spent the evening glowering and snapping."

It made sense in a rather convoluted way. But, while she admittedly didn't know Devon very well at all, she just couldn't imagine that his thinking worked along the rather inconsequential lines his mother claimed. "I'll do what I can to become more predictable," Claire offered in an effort to be diplomatic.

"We would all appreciate it if you would, dear. Devon is really quite difficult to live with even when he's reasonably content with life." She stopped and opened a door on their right, the second one from the end of the hall.

"This, I think," Madam Rivard said, motioning Claire to step across the threshold ahead of her, "shall be your room, Lady Claire. It adjoins Devon's through the other door. It befits a husband and wife and is conducive to whatever agreements they may choose to make for passing through it."

The agreement they had was that the door would remain shut, Claire silently supplied, glancing about the room. Although the candlelight was soft, she could tell that the room was larger than any she'd ever had to call her own. There was a four-poster bed against the far wall, several chests and cabinets, and an armoire large enough to house a family of four. Some items—what looked by general shape to be chairs—were covered with white sheets, and the fireplace was filled with kindling for a fire that hadn't been lit. The walls were painted in what looked like a buttery yellow, and Claire was certain that once a fire burned and the dustcovers were stripped away, it would be a warm and comfortable place to curl up with a good book.

"It's lovely," she said, turning to smile at her hostess.

"If we'd known you were to be staying with us, we would have had the room properly prepared. But as it's turned out..." She offered the barest shrug and set the candle down on a chest. "One never knows how matters will turn out, does one? Oftentimes, it's surprisingly well. One should just accept situations as they are and hope for the best, don't you think?"

She didn't give Claire a chance to respond, but went on breezily, "We'll have Mary Margaret come up tomorrow and remove the dustcovers. She can also arrange the furniture to your liking. Would that be all right with you, Lady Claire?"

"Of course. Thank you for everything, Madam Rivard."

"Oh, please, do call me Henrietta."

Claire hesitated. It wasn't proper to address elders by their Christian name, and the idea of doing so made her uncomfortable. Her parents had been adamant about that particular social lesson. "I'll try," she offered noncommittally.

The older woman smiled. "That's all that I ask. And now I'll wish you a good night and pleasant dreams." Then the woman leaned closer, presenting her cheek for a kiss.

It was such a sweetly maternal thing to do, and it stirred bittersweet memories Claire had long ago put away. "Good night, Mother Rivard," she whispered, pressing a kiss to the woman's powdered cheek.

"Oh, I do like that!" she exclaimed, her eyes bright and her smile broad. "Mother Rivard. Stately and yet approachable. Yes, I like that very much." She stepped out into the hall and, pulling the door closed behind her, added, "Good night again, my dear. Have the sweetest of dreams."

Claire smiled. One had to sleep in order to have dreams. If she didn't get a fire lit and the room warmed, she was going to spend the night wide awake, listening to her teeth chatter. She dropped her valise on the end of the bed and crossed to the fireplace. The tinderbox was on the mantel and she checked it, delighted and relieved to find that it was prepared. She struck the flint and gently blew on the spark. It caught and as the flame grew she bent down and tilted the contents into the waiting kindling. It, too, caught easily, and in seconds the fire was crackling and popping, growing and brightening.

Claire straightened, put the tinderbox back in place, and then looked around the room again. There was a small warmth already coming from the fireplace, but it hadn't yet chased away the chill, and so she set to work, taking a sprig from the fire to light additional candles and then carefully folding up the dustcovers and stacking them neatly on the floor beside the door.

AN HOUR LATER Claire sat in one of the chairs she'd arranged in front of the fire, warming her feet and feeling a deep sense of accomplishment. It had been a lovely room to begin with and, by moving a few cabinets here and a few chairs there, she'd made it even more so. She'd pulled the coverlet and sheets down on the bed so that they'd be warm when and if she ever felt ready to crawl under them.

For some inexplicable reason, though, she wasn't the least bit tired. Lord knew she ought to be. She hadn't slept much last night. And today had been one of the longest of her life. Married against her will to a man who didn't want a wife and considered women brainless ninnies, she'd then been hauled through a snowstorm to be plopped down in the midst of a household that could only be described as . . . well, peculiar.

The cook couldn't cook. The only servant she'd seen had been the one to open the front door for them, and then he'd disappeared. Henrietta Rivard was a nice woman, but didn't seem to have any real concerns beyond the maintenance of good manners. Elsbeth Whittington was a thoroughly unpleasant—and probably unhappy—person. Wyndom Rivard was an affable buffoon whose poor judgment was the reason she and Devon Rivard were shackled to one another. Pouring brandy on a fire . . . Devon might have been a little less blunt about declaring his brother an idiot, but it was largely the truth.

And then, aside from the people, there was the house itself. It might well be grand and stately on the outside, but the inside was in a sorry state. Dust covered the surfaces of all the furnishings, clung to the folds of the draperies, and rose up in little clouds from the small rugs when anyone walked across them. Smudges of soot discolored the windowpanes. The silver, brass, and copper appointments were all tarnished. And it had been so long since the wood floors had been waxed that you could easily see the paths everyone had worn in their coming and going.

Devon Rivard was concerned that she might do something that would crack his facade of wealth and privilege? Claire snorted in a most unladylike way and shook her head. There wasn't any damage she could do that hadn't already been done. The man was the captain of a foundering ship. It was only a matter of time before it went down. With all hands on deck. And, Claire thought darkly, considering the way her luck had been running for the last four years, she was going to be the one blamed for the disaster. Never mind that the ship had been taking on water for years before she'd been forced to join the crew.

Life had been so much simpler at Crossbridge, she mused sadly, staring through the window and into the night. It had been a marginal existence, yes, but an ever so much more simple one. Her days had been her own to do with as she thought best. Her father had respected her decisions and her ability to make them. No one had snapped their fingers and expected her to heel, to sit, to obey, or to beg. She hadn't had to pretend to be something she wasn't, hadn't had to endure being anyone's pawn. The people at Crossbridge were what they were: unpretentious, honest, and hardworking. She had belonged there, was one of them. And she wanted to go home. It was all she'd wanted for four long years.

Tears tightened her throat and welled in her eyes. Claire swallowed and reminded herself that, despite the vast distance between Crossbridge and Rosewind, she was closer to attaining her dream than she ever had been. She'd seen the letter sent to her uncle. She'd read for herself the demand that Crossbridge be titled to her as a dowry. That her uncle would actually capitulate was a slim hope, but it was the only hope she'd ever been given.

If he refused... Claire sighed and pursed her lips. *If?* She knew better than to dream. She knew her uncle. To give her Crossbridge would be an act of compassion and decency. Neither quality was among those George Seaton-Smythe possessed. Greed he had aplenty. And ruthless determination. Cunning, too. But a conscience... What sliver of conscience he might have ever had had withered and died from disuse years ago.

No, there was no *if*. It was a matter of *when* he refused. And what she was going to do after that, after Wyndom's debt had been forgiven and Devon didn't need to pretend he had a wife.

Claire resolutely pushed herself to her feet, crossed to the washstand in the corner, picked up the pitcher, and carried it to the window. Pushing up the lower panel of glass, she filled the porcelain container with some of the snow piled on the sill. The cold blast of air and the icy sting on her hands cleared the darkest shadows from her thoughts. Closing the window, she carried the pitcher to the hearth and set it down. She stood there, watching the snow slowly turn to water and knowing that, come what may, she'd survive. She always had.

HER EVENING ABLUTIONS had been completed, but they hadn't brought her the sense of calm they normally did. Claire leaned her shoulder against the window jamb and surveyed the yard visible below. There was what looked to be a stone smokehouse along with several small wooden buildings whose purpose she couldn't readily identify. A relatively large garden area surrounded what had to be the kitchen. The latter was a rectangular structure made of brick with twin brick chimneys rising from the back side. A pair of windows balanced the plain door in the front wall. No light shone through them and no smoke rose from either of the chimneys.

Claire frowned. Apparently the fires had been allowed to go out, an unwise decision considering the time it would take to rebuild them tomorrow morning. Either Mary Margaret would have to rise early to see to the task or breakfast would be served late. Or cold.

Perhaps, Claire mused, she ought to go out to the kitchen, restart the fires now, then bank them for the morning. She wasn't tired. And the sooner she understood the situation with Mary Margaret, the sooner she'd know how to fix it. Perhaps—for whatever reason—Mary Margaret didn't know that the fires should be banked in the evening. It would be a good first lesson, a relatively simple one. They could progress from there.

Claire was relighting the candle lamp to carry down the stairs with her when she heard footsteps in the hall. She paused and listened to them draw near, pass her door, and then enter the room next door. Devon, she knew, eyeing the connecting door.

Had he done anything to treat the burn on his hand? She rather doubted it. He'd been surprised by her concern for its care, and he hadn't protested when she'd asked Wyndom to go gather some snow. But when his brother had had to choose between the kindness and eating—when insisting on treating his hand would have been an overt admission that it pained him—Devon had pulled his hand back and declared it not worth the bother. Yes, Devon Rivard definitely struck her as the kind of man who would refuse to treat himself purely on the principle that it was unmanly to admit that you were hurting.

She picked up the porcelain washbasin, crossed to the window, and gathered more snow off the windowsill.

Then she stood there for a moment, considering the door between them. She'd prefer not to remind him that it was there. They had an agreement: Their marriage was to be in name only. But she remembered the passion of his kiss in the rectory, how easily she'd succumbed to it, and the thrill that had shot through her when he'd suggested that they might have to explore the avenue further. She'd known that he was only trying to rile her, but... The truth was, she'd masqueraded as a man frequently enough to know that men weren't very good at keeping their pledges of celibacy. Only a fool would open a door and plant the seeds of temptation. At the same time, only a callous heart would let reason prevent the offering of compassion.

She went to the hallway door, opened it, then walked the few steps down to his door. Taking a deep breath to fortify herself, she quietly knocked. After a long moment, it opened and he stood before her, his frock coat removed and his white shirt not only untucked, but mostly undone as well.

Pretending to be male had put her in many an awkward situation through the years, and although she'd always managed to keep from participating in male rituals, she'd seen more than her fair share of masculine chests. Devon's Rivard's was—without doubt or argument—the most spectacular of them all. It was broad and bronzed and darkly furred. And breathtakingly well sculpted. Italian artisans would kill for the privilege to immortalize him in marble.

"Yes? Is there something you need?"

Startled, she glanced up to find one corner of his mouth quirked up and a devilish light in his eyes. Oh, dear God. She'd been staring! Mortified, she dropped her gaze to the snow in the basin. "I thought you could use some snow for your hand," she offered hastily, desperately hoping that he was gentleman enough not to mention her unseemly behavior.

"You shouldn't go out of the house alone. Especially at night."

His words were soft and easy. And for some reason the gentleness of them added to her discomfort. "I didn't," she assured him. Without looking up, she abruptly pushed the edge of the basin into his midriff, making him flinch in surprise and giving him little choice except to take it. As he did, she added, "I gathered it off my windowsill."

"Thank you. I appreciate the thought."

She heard the notes of gentle amusement in his voice. She wanted to look up, to see what he looked like when smiling broadly. She didn't dare. She'd already embarrassed herself once. "You will pack your hand in it, won't you?" she asked, taking a step back.

He shifted his hold on the basin to free his injured hand and then stuffed it into the snow. "It feels better already."

It couldn't. Not that quickly. But she wasn't willing to stand there and disagree with him. Her cheeks were on fire and her heart was beating entirely too fast. "I'm glad. Good night," she said, turning away without looking at him.

"Claire?"

She winced and stopped, then took a deep breath and raised her chin. Before she could actually force herself to turn around and face him, he said kindly, "I'm sorry for the unpleasantness at the table. It will never happen again. I meant what I said: You'll be treated respectfully for as long as you reside in this house."

What had happened to the ill-tempered man she had married earlier in the day? Not that it mattered to her all that much. This Devon Rivard was much more likable. She turned around. His gaze was solemn now, dark and unreadable, as he studied her.

"Elsbeth's behavior isn't at all unusual," she observed. "My aunt and cousins reacted in much the same way when I was thrust so unexpectedly into the Seaton-Smythe household. But I do thank you for the defense. It was far more than my uncle George ever offered in my behalf."

He tilted his head to the side in the way that she'd already come to recognize as his habit when puzzled by something. For a moment he looked as though he was framing a question, then he straightened and said, "I'll see that you're brought several gowns in the morning."

Claire couldn't keep from smiling. "Our earlier disagreement over the necessity of one does appear to be moot at this point, doesn't it?"

He nodded, slowly, contemplatively. "Had you not been wearing leather boots and breeches under your skirt, you might have been seriously injured this evening. Given that, I can see a bit of wisdom in your refusal to give up such practical articles."

He could see a bit of wisdom? Hell had to have frozen. "How far are you willing to extend your spirit of accommodation?" she asked, wary.

"I withdraw my demand that you surrender them."

He'd yielded too easily; there had to be a reason and she was willing to play along to see what it might be. "Thank you."

"But only," he added, "if you'll agree to withdraw your refusal to respect my authority over you."

Ah, there it was. She had to admit that he was very good at maneuvering people, and he hadn't made her wait days for the gambit like her uncle always did. Claire tamped down her impulse to smile and waited, letting him think that she was giving the matter serious consideration. When he cocked his brow, she sighed and said, "I don't suppose it would be fair to expect you to wage the promised battle for my breeches with an injured hand, would it?"

"No, it wouldn't."

So confident. So sure of his victory. Claire smiled.

"Then I'll allow you time for it to heal." He blinked and rocked back on his heels. While he was still off balance, she gave him a brief curtsy and turned away, saying, "Good night again, sir. I'm off to earn my keep."

"What?"

"I'm going down to the kitchen," she answered without looking back. "I can see from my bedroom window that the fires have been allowed to go out. I thought I'd restart and then bank them so they'd be ready tomorrow morning."

"That's Mary Margaret's responsibility."

She could tell by his voice that he'd followed her into the hall. Claire paused in her open doorway and met his gaze over her shoulder. He was puzzled again. For some unfathomable reason his confusion delighted her. "Agreed, but whether out of ignorance or neglect, she apparently hasn't seen to it. I thought I'd make fire-tending her first lesson."

"I distinctly recall you sitting at the dining room table and saying that you wanted to retire. That you were exhausted."

"I was at the time. But once I was alone, I discovered that I had deeper reserves than I'd imagined."

Her heartbeat quickened as he gave her another of his quirked smiles. "A most tactful way, madam, of saying you found your dinner companions taxing."

"To a certain degree," she admitted. "Present company excepted, of course."

"You don't have to lie," he chided, his smile fading. "I know that I'm a beast to get along with. It's my natural tendency." He paused and then shrugged. "If you're determined to go down to the kitchen now, I'll accompany you."

She didn't need an escort. The kitchen was close to the house; she wasn't going to get lost. "I appreciate the offer," Claire said politely, "but, truly, it's not necessary."

"Yes, it is." With two long strides he was beside her and handing back the snow-filled basin. "As I said a few moments ago, you shouldn't go out of the house alone and especially not at night."

"Why ever not?"

"Our slaves are loyal and honest," he answered while pulling tight the laces of his shirt. "The same can't be said for those of other owners. When the sun goes down and work ceases, their slaves have been known to slip off into the night and cause trouble. And you can rest assured that slaves have no exclusive claim to wrongdoing. There are just as many freemen and indentured servants around who are likely to commit mayhem. It's better to be cautious and safe rather than rash and sorry. I'll accompany you to the kitchen or you won't go."

She understood his reasoning, but his presumption to rule her actions rankled. Couldn't he have asked if she would mind if he went along? It would have accomplished the same end and allowed her to accede to common sense rather than surrender to a command. She was about to suggest that he try to be a bit more diplomatic, when he began to stuff his shirttail into the waistband of his breeches.

The movement captured her attention and scattered any thoughts of the kitchen. He'd been wearing his frock coat earlier in the day. His shirt had hung loosely from his shoulders when he'd opened the door at her knock. Now . . . it wasn't just Devon Rivard's chest the sculptors would want to immortalize. The man had a magnificently trim waist and narrow hips. And exceedingly well defined muscles in his thighs. His breeches were tight enough that she could see them ripple and flex at his smallest movement. What would they feel like? she wondered. Higher up, there was a single, large—

Dear God in heaven, she silently swore, resolutely

turning away, heat suffusing her face again. Her heart was going to explode. Right after she fainted from lack of air. What a shameless wanton she'd become. She'd never noticed such things about any man before. And it wasn't as if Devon was the first one she'd ever encountered. In the last four years, she'd met hundreds of men, more than most women were introduced to in the whole of their lifetimes.

"Let me get the candle lamp," she said, walking away before he could notice her blush. "I didn't see any lights burning in the kitchen." To let the mere sight of manly attributes make her so light-headed was absolutely ridiculous, she admonished herself, setting the basin in the stand and then moving around the room to extinguish the extra candles.

"Why do you have the pitcher on the hearth?"

"I melted snow for bathing." Claire picked up the candle lamp and turned to the door. He was watching her, his shoulder propped against the jamb, his arms folded over his chest, and one ankle crossed casually over the other. "My mother didn't see that you had any?"

Lord. Did he have any notion of how rakishly handsome he looked standing like that? Gathering her scattered wits and moving toward the doorway while trying very hard to see him as short, fat, and balding, Claire replied, "It must have slipped her mind. Considering all the strains she endured this evening, I'm not surprised."

He stepped aside to let her pass into the hall, then strode ahead of her to the stairs, saying, "One person in this house making excuses for everyone's shortcomings is quite enough. I don't need a second. My mother's brain is a sieve on her best days, and totally absent on others. There's no need to pretend otherwise. I'd suggest that you simply allow for reality and go on with your own business."

"Don't you think she might be offended by my

presumption?" she asked, following him down the stairs. "I am, after all, a guest in her home. Guests should never presume to take actions or decisions upon themselves."

"It's *my* name on the mortgage. And I expect you to *not* be a burden. I have enough of those already, too." He reached the foyer and headed off to the left, into the dining room. "It's this way."

Claire followed him around the dining room table and to a door at the rear of the room, glad she was wearing her boots. Had she been in feminine shoes, she wouldn't have been able to keep up with him. He had the longest strides. "Don't you need the light to see where you're going?" she asked as he led her into a large butler's pantry.

"I could find my way to the kitchen blindfolded and with my hands tied behind my back," he replied, opening a door.

The crisp scent of snow rushed over her, borne on a gust of cold air. It felt good; renewing and exhilarating. She glanced around her. Not even the dimness of the light could hide the tarnish on the silver serving pieces stored on the open shelves. God only knew what lay inside the lower, closed cabinets—although she was fairly certain that, whatever it was, it needed to be polished. She'd leave the door open for fresh air when she and Mary Margaret tackled the work tomorrow afternoon.

"Give me your hand and I'll help you. The steps are slippery."

She looked to the door to see him standing outside, waiting, his hand extended back to her. Pale moonlight gilded his shoulders and haloed his dark hair. It had stopped snowing, she realized as she stepped forward and put her hand in his. She traversed the short set of steps, waiting for him to remind her that he couldn't afford to pay a physician to set broken bones. He didn't.

"Thank you," she said gratefully when she reached the base.

He didn't release her hand as she expected, either. Instead, he guided her forward, saying, "The walk's icy as well. I won't let you slip."

Claire, clutching the lamp with one hand and allowing the other to be wrapped in the calloused warmth and gentle strength of Devon's, carefully made her way along the walk, wondering yet again what had happened to the man she'd met in Edmund Cantrell's office. How puzzling to have a person change so much and for no apparent reason. It was a change for the better, of course, but it was still absolutely mystifying. They reached the kitchen door and Devon released her hand only so that he could place his own on the small of her back.

"Thank you again," Claire murmured, thinking it wise—considering their beginning—to make sure he knew she appreciated his small courtesies.

"My pleasure, madam," he replied softly, pushing open the door and guiding her into the kitchen ahead of him.

"Sweet Mother of God!"

The voice was definitely Irish and feminine and coming from the far corner of the room. Claire instinctively turned toward it, an apology for surprising the woman on the tip of her tongue. The light from the candle lamp barely reached that far, but it illuminated just enough for her to see a flash of fair hair and a pale expanse of male back. She gasped and froze in her tracks, knowing all too well what she'd interrupted.

"Damn!" Wyndom snapped as he vaulted out of the narrow bed, naked as a jay.

Claire whirled about, unwilling to see any more than she already had, as Devon stormed past her.

"Devon, I can explain. It's not what you—"

Claire cringed as flesh and bone connected with flesh and bone. The impact was immediately followed by another—that of a body crashing hard against a piece of sturdy wood. She could hear Devon swearing under his breath. The sound was low and hard and she caught only the words "goddamn" and "son of."

"Oh, please don't hurt him!" Mary Margaret wailed.

Wyndom sputtered. Devon snarled, "Put some clothes on, woman."

And then, out of the corner of her eye, she saw yet another flash of Wyndom's pale skin. She turned away another degree, but not quickly enough to avoid seeing Devon dragging his brother—arms full of his clothing— toward the door by his hair.

There was a blast of cold air, a thud, and a yelp.

"Claire?" It was a command and she obeyed it, turning to face him. "I'll leave you alone with Mary Margaret," he said, his eyes blazing and his jaw granite. "And if you wouldn't mind, could you make your first lesson one on how meeting the needs of the table come before Wyndom's more personal ones?" She nodded and he went on, "I'll return in a while to escort you back to the house. Do not return on your own. Understand?"

Again, Claire nodded. He left without another word, slamming the door behind him. She stood there, hearing Mary Margaret's movements behind her and wondering whether she'd been confined to the kitchen more out of Devon's concerns about wandering marauders or because he simply didn't want her to see him beating Wyndom senseless.

Lord. Why hadn't she just stayed in her room and waited until morning to deal with Mary Margaret and the kitchen? Why hadn't she anticipated the possibility that she'd find Wyndom and the cook together?

Behind her, Mary Margaret grew quiet. Claire sighed. She hadn't had the good sense to mind her own business and stay in her room, and now there was no choice but to deal with an awkward situation. Just how would the mistress of a castle go about doing that? she wondered.

Staring at the door, an idea came to her. And since it was the only one that did, she acted on it. Setting the lamp down on the worktable, she gathered her skirts in hand and marched outside.

CHAPTER NINE

*C*LAIRE CLOSED THE DOOR behind herself, carefully turned on the icy flagstones, took a deep breath, pasted a smile on her face, and then knocked. It took several long moments, but the door eventually swung open. A tall, large-boned, copper-haired woman stood warily on the other side.

"Hello. I'm Claire ... Rivard," she began. "I assume that you're Mary Margaret Malone?"

The woman hesitated, her brows furrowed. "Aye, madam."

"May I come in?"

Mary Margaret nodded and stepped aside. Claire went past her, moving to the table where she'd placed the candle lamp, before stopping and turning to face the Irish woman. Her smile and determination to begin anew still in place, Claire said pleasantly, "It's my understanding that you've been the cook at Rosewind for only the last month."

"Aye, madam."

Good, the woman hadn't hesitated to answer that time. Claire plunged ahead. "I've always believed in facing things squarely, so I'll just come right out and ask . . . Do you know how to cook, Mary Margaret?"

"Just a bit and not well," she admitted with a weak smile. "And Mr. Rivard be the only one who calls me Mary Margaret. To everyone else, I be called Meg."

They'd successfully crossed the hurdle; they were on to names and easy conversation. Claire relaxed. "Meg's certainly easier to say than Mary Margaret," she replied. "I'm assuming the Mr. Rivard of whom you speak is Wyndom?"

"Aye, madam. The owner of Rosewind."

"Did he tell you that?"

"Aye. When he bought me papers at auction."

That explained a great deal. "Well, I think you should know that he isn't the owner of this estate. His older brother—the man who threw him out into the snow—is the true master of Rosewind."

"Mr. Devil?"

"Devon," Claire corrected, chuckling. "Yes."

Meg considered the door, her eyes blazing. "The lying little . . . If I'd a but known . . ." She turned and met Claire's gaze to add, "I thought I was a savin' meself a warm place to sleep. He said he'd sell me papers if'n I didn't . . . ye know . . ." She glanced toward the bed in the corner.

"A decidedly low thing for him to do. I think you can rest assured that Wyndom won't be blackmailing you for your favors anymore."

"I don't want his bones broken. He really isn't a bad man. A girl could do worse, ye know."

"Yes, I do," Claire admitted, remembering a host of cads from her own past. They had been everywhere in London and especially numerous behind ballroom potted plants and garden hedges. But sharing stories with Meg wasn't why she was here. "If I might change the subject and return to my purpose for coming to the kitchen this evening?"

"Of course, madam."

"I don't mean to be unkind, Meg," she began softly and with a smile, "but the food at dinner tonight was inedible. I've been given to understand that it hasn't been any better at previous meals. Mr. Devon asked me if I'd be willing to undertake your cooking instruction. If you're agreeable, I'm certainly willing to give it a try."

"If'n I'm not, Mr. Devon would be a-thinkin' about sellin' me papers, wouldn't he?"

"It would be the reasonable course. And one made purely in the interest of self-preservation."

"Then I suppose that I've got no choice but to learn, do I?"

It wasn't the enthusiastic response Claire had hoped to hear, but it was better than outright refusal. "Why is it that you don't know how to cook, Meg? A woman your age usually does."

"I've never had to," the woman replied, the tone of her voice implying that it should have been obvious. "Meals was always cooked by the kitchen staff an' served to the maids."

"So you've been a domestic servant," Claire observed, remembering how the Seaton-Smythe household had functioned.

"Aye. Upstairs maid, I was." Her hands went to her hips. "An' I suppose you'd be a wonderin' how it was that I'd be findin' meself papered an' sold off for a scullery maid, wouldn't ye? Well, I'll be tellin' ye the tale so ye don't be hearin' it from others who'd be stitchin' the story with their lies. My employer was a London gent, fine an' fancy an' randy as any goat. Had him a string of mistresses, he did, his wife a knowin' 'bout 'em all. What she didn't know was that he was keepin' 'em by sellin' off her jewels on the sly."

"And there came a day when she discovered something missing," Claire supplied, having heard the story too many times to count.

"Aye, an' the goat didn't have the bullocks to stand up an' confess his crimes. Blamed the maids, he did. Mary Anne O'Malley an' me. We was hauled into the dock, we were, an' declared common thieves. 'Twas prison or be papered an' so we was shipped to the colonies. " 'Twas James City, they said, where we be docked. An' where me papers was bought by Mr. Wyndom."

It was such a common story. But for the grace of God, Claire might have very well have ended up bound into servitude just like Meg. "I'm sorry."

" 'Tisn't yer fault, Madam Rivard. I just want ye to know the true tale in case ye hear the other."

"Duly noted, Meg. And please . . . Madam Rivard is the mother of Devon and Wyndom. Everyone's taken it into their heads to call me Lady Claire to distinguish between us. It seems easier to accept it than to resist."

"Are ye a lady?"

"I was at one point in my life," Claire answered. "Not that it mattered much then or in the years since."

"But ye know how to cook."

"Yes, I do. And well. What are you planning to prepare for meals tomorrow?"

Meg glanced around the kitchen. "Porridge for breakfast. 'Tis easy enough. After that . . ." She studied a ham hanging from a hook in the ceiling, shrugged, and looked back to Claire. "Maybe a ham for the midday meal an' what's left of it for the evenin'?"

"To be prepared how?"

"In the oven?"

"The oven would be fine," Claire conceded. "Have you soaked the ham?"

"Soaked?"

"To remove the curing salts so that it's palatable."

"An' what should it be a soakin' in, an' for how long?"

"Water," Claire answered, knowing that they were going to have to start with the most basic of lessons. "Why don't you go fetch some while I get the fires going again."

Meg dutifully went to the door, picked up the bucket, and then paused to ask, "Ye'll be a cookin' it tonight?"

"Partially," Claire answered, moving toward the hearth. "For the most part, I'll be relighting and then banking the fires so they're ready to go in the morning when you're ready to cook the porridge and bake the daily bread."

"I don't know 'bout bread bakin'."

"I'll teach you. For now, please go get the water for the ham."

Meg went, bucket in hand, while Claire stirred the ashes, searching for a few live coals. They were small, but there and sufficient. She was feeding bits of tinder to them when Meg returned from the well. Claire had her pour the water into a cauldron and then sent her back for more. By the time Meg returned the second time, flames were crackling up from the ashes and the ham had been placed in the cast iron cooking pot. Together, they lifted the massive weight and secured the handle on the fire hook.

Stepping back, Claire considered the brick oven to her right. "Why don't you restart the other fire, Meg, while I see what's in the stores."

With a nod, Meg set to the task. Claire went about lifting lids from the various crates and barrels that lined one long wall of the stone room, from the crocks that, along with stacks of pottery bowls, filled the two open-faced shelves on the other long wall. Flour and salt.

Lard and vinegar. Sugar, both brown and white. Molasses and cornmeal.

"Are ye Mr. Devon's sister?"

"His wife," Claire answered absently, opening the lower cupboard doors. Metal cooking pans were stacked neatly on shelves inside. "We were very recently married."

"Ahhh. 'Tis the explanation then."

"The explanation of what?" she asked, straightening, a flat baking sheet in her hand.

"Why ye hesitated to use his name when ye introduced yerself to me. 'Tis foreign to yer tongue yet."

"Yes, it is," Claire confessed, handing the pan to Meg and pointing to the central worktable. Getting a large bowl from the shelf above, she added, "In fact, I don't know that I'll ever become accustomed to using it."

"Aye, ye will," Meg assured her as Claire crossed to the other side of the room. "Sooner than ye think, prob'ly. 'Tis, to me thinkin', the easiest part of being married."

Using her hand to scoop flour from the barrel, Claire asked, "Do you have a husband, Meg?"

"Oh, I did for a wee while. But he took up with Mary Agnes O'Roarke, an' I'd been married to him long enough to know that she was a doin' me a favor in takin' him off me hands. I let him go an' said a novena for poor Mary Agnes. 'Twas no prize she was gettin'.

"Now, Mr. Devon...I be a thinkin' he's a prize worth a fight to hang on to. Not that I've seen more o' him than his comin' an' goin' from the main house, mind ye. But even from a fair distance, a girl can see he's a handsome, strappin' man."

"More handsome than Wyndom?" Claire teased, pausing as she put the flour bowl on the table.

Meg Malone laughed softly, amusement sparkling in her eyes. "Mr. Wyndom's fair enough o' face, to be sure. He's a bit of a lummox, but it makes me heart light to watch him bumble about. An' truth be told, he's the finest gent what's ever slid 'tween me sheets. Not that others ain't tried, mind ye. Like ye, I be a picker an' a chooser."

"Well, in all honesty," Claire replied on her way to the shelves for the crocks containing lard, salt, and baking powder, "I have to admit that I didn't pick or choose Devon."

Meg came along to help, accepting the larger lard crock and asking, "Yer da picked him for ye?"

"My uncle, actually."

"Ah," Meg sighed dreamily, "but it's got to warm yer heart to know the man was down on his knees beggin' yer uncle fer yer hand. An' the rest of ye that goes with it. Not that a gentleman like him would be mentionin' that."

The image of Devon Rivard down on his knees, begging anyone for anything, was preposterous. She didn't know him well, but she certainly knew that Devon would never humble himself in any fashion. And God help the poor fool who had the audacity to suggest that he consider it.

"Mr. Devon did ask fer ye, didn't he?"

Hadn't he declared her to be the last person on earth he would have chosen to marry had he a free choice in the matter? Or had that been something she'd said of him? It had been a very long day and she couldn't remember things quite clearly. But regardless of who had said what to whom, it was the way they both felt. "It's a very complicated situation," Claire said, putting the crocks down on the table and hoping Meg wouldn't press for a fuller answer.

"Complicated or no, boils down to ye an' the mister makin' the best o' it an' sharin' a bed as husband an' wife, right?"

She thought about lying, but quickly realized that if

getting an annulment depended on witnesses testifying that the marriage hadn't been consummated... "We were married only this afternoon and—"

"This afternoon! An' ye be a spendin' yer weddin' night in the kitchen with me?"

"Hunger rearranges one's priorities," Claire quipped, deciding that she'd come back later to the issue of her and Devon being strangers. And their determination to keep it that way.

"To the end of appeasing that hunger," she went on, "and while we have the oven fire going, I'm going to teach you how to make biscuits. If you'd be so kind as to show me where the larder is. We'll need milk."

DEVON CHANCED A GLARE in his brother's direction and found him sitting on one of the dining room chairs, struggling to push the tops of his stockings up under the lower edge of his breeches. Good God Almighty, the idiot couldn't even get his clothes on in the proper order. The ache in the back of his head deepening, Devon closed his eyes, still not trusting himself to speak and thankful that Wyndom had displayed the uncommon good sense to keep his mouth shut and not push the issue.

"I don't see that who I choose to sleep with is any of your business, Dev. And Lord knows I'm not the first man who's ever dallied with the family cook."

So much for good sense. Deliberately crossing his arms over his chest to lessen the chance of swinging a fist at his brother, Devon answered tightly, "Just because others have committed stupidities doesn't give you leave to follow in their footsteps. Mary Margaret Malone is a servant, and while she may be an indentured one, she's just as much legal property as any of the slaves. The rules that apply to your congress with them apply to her as well. Is that clear?"

"The rules aren't laws," his brother shot back, pulling on a boot. "They're rules you made up because you think that's the way the world should work."

"My roof, my rules," Devon countered simply. "As long as you live here, you'll abide by them."

"They're stupid rules. If Mary Margaret's willing, then—"

"And who do you think is going to be the one who will have to feed and clothe the babe she might well hand you this winter?"

Wyndom pushed his foot into his other boot and shrugged. "If it's my child, then I will."

God, how many times had they had this conversation? Hadn't they had it once already today? When was it going to sink into his brother's pea-sized brain? "You don't own a damn thing in your own right. You have no money aside from the allowance I give you and show absolutely no inclination to earn any on your own. And before you can say it, sitting at a card table hoping for luck to smile on you just once in your life isn't considered gainful employment."

"Not by you, anyway."

"Not by anyone."

"You know," Wyndom snapped, gaining his feet, "you've been a royal bastard to live with for the last two months. I figured it had to do with Darice Lytton kicking you out of her bed and that if there was one bright spot in having Lady Claire forced upon you it was that she might be able to twist you up in the sheets and knock the harder edges off of you. What the hell were you doing in the kitchen tonight? Why weren't you pinning your new wife to the bed like any self-respecting man would be?"

He so wanted to give his brother a flat nose to go with his fat lip. Devon fisted his hands and used every ounce of self-restraint he possessed to keep his arms folded. "We will have this conversation once and only once, Wyndom," he declared with deadly calm. "First, I am not a mindless rutter like you or our father. Second, the decision to leave Darice Lytton's bed was mine, not hers.

"Third—and most importantly—Claire's an intelligent woman who clearly understands that there's nothing to be gained in being shackled to a man on the verge of bankruptcy and whose house could pass for an insane asylum. I don't need another mouth to feed around here or another body to clothe. We're both aware that the long-term existence of this union is in neither of our best interests and that we'd both be better off to legally end it as soon as her uncle forgives the debt—*your debt*—that has us mired together."

"Don't you ever get tired of being so damn honorable and self-sacrificing, Devon? Christ, you've positively refined it to an art. Bed the woman and then swear that you didn't so you can get your goddamn precious annulment when the time comes. No one cares whether or not your testimony is true. Either seduce Lady Claire or go throw yourself on Darice's mercy. I don't give a damn which you do, but I'm sick and tired of you riding my ass from dawn to midnight. Do me—do us *all*—a favor and pick a woman to ride for a change, will you?"

There wasn't nearly enough pleasure in knocking Wyndom on his well-ridden ass, but there was some. His knuckles smarted, but Devon took satisfaction in knowing that his brother's nose had to hurt even worse. He watched as Wyndom struggled to sit up with one hand clamped over the center of his face. "If I ever find you with Mary Margaret again, I'll geld you. That's a promise."

Wyndom glared up at him and snarled from behind his hand, "Don't you think having one foul-tempered eunuch in the family is enough?"

"I'm going out to the kitchen to escort Claire back to the house," he declared, ignoring the taunt. "By the time I return, I expect you to have taken your loathsome carcass somewhere well out of my sight."

"Is Williamsburg far enough?"

"Not by half," Devon replied, turning on his heel and striding through the door to the butler's pantry and out into the cold night air.

Halfway between the house and the kitchen he stopped and expelled a hard breath. It rose in a silvery cloud around him as the cold cut through the linen of his shirt to chill his skin, his blood, and his temper. The pounding in his head eased, leaving him aware of aching muscles and a battered spirit.

God, for two shillings he'd sign it all over to Wyndom, climb on his horse, and ride away without ever looking back. No one would blame him. Even if they did, he'd be far enough away that he'd never have to listen to them. Of course, a war with England was looking more likely every day; he could just be patient, enlist in whatever army his fellow colonists could muster, and claim patriotism was a more noble calling than that of being a warden to ingrates and fools. With any luck he could get himself killed. As fates went, it was preferable to spending the rest of his life here listening to the whining and waiting for the debt to slowly crush him.

Maybe, if revolution came soon enough, Claire Curran could be a widow. She could sniffle into a lace-edged handkerchief and regret the good man she'd had and lost. With a wry smile, Devon continued on to the kitchen. Truth be known, he had no idea how Claire would receive any news of his death. Had he considered the question earlier in the day, he'd have bet Rosewind that she'd have been the first in line to dance on his grave.

But then she'd brought him a basin of snow for his hand. It was an act of kindness he hadn't expected and—considering the way he'd treated her—didn't deserve. His smile broadened as he remembered that moment. The way she'd openly surveyed his chest, her violet eyes bright with appreciation... Until she'd realized what she was doing, of course. And then she'd blushed and stammered and tried to get away. He'd been surprised by that glimpse of an innocent. And he'd felt more than a little guilty for some of the things he'd said to her earlier in the day. They'd been based on assumptions that weren't true.

He pushed open the kitchen door and felt the wave of warm air roll over him. On it was the delectable scent of freshly baked biscuits. He looked toward the central table, half expecting to see Hannah there. But it wasn't Hannah, it was Mary Margaret Malone. Standing beside her was Claire. She looked up and smiled at him. Tendrils of golden hair had escaped their pins to softly frame her face, and flour lightly dusted the end of her nose and both her cheeks. And while she'd donned an apron to protect what remained of her gown, she'd removed the buffon that had added extra inches to the bodice of it. He'd considered her attributes meager that afternoon. Like other assumptions he'd made, that one was wrong, too. A delightful bit of reality had been hidden by that strip of modest fabric.

Devon vaguely heard his stomach growl, but the sound was lost in a larger realization. Claire Curran was a beautiful woman—an intriguingly intelligent, kind, and strikingly beautiful woman. He'd married her, giving her a solemn vow that he'd never touch her. He was going to be sorry he'd spoken so impetuously. He knew it in his bones. Other parts of his person were just as certain and already making him pay the price.

"A good evenin' to ye, Mr. Rivard," the Irish cook called out, holding up a basket and smiling broadly. "An' just in time ye are to sample one of me first biscuits still warm from the oven. A bit of butter an' some strawberry jam to go on it?"

He nodded, regretting that his breeches fit so closely and knowing that wisdom lay in focusing his attention on anything except his wife. "They smell wonderful," he declared, advancing to the table while trying to nonchalantly blouse his shirttail.

"An' wonderful they taste, too, sir. We'll confess to havin' sampled one or two 'fore ye came through the door. The scent was more than we could resist. Be that right, Lady Claire?"

Claire's smile widened. Her eyes twinkled. "Temptation being the powerful force it is..."

God, he could testify to the truth of that. He sat down in one of the chairs, then half rose to pull his shirttail out a bit more.

Mary Margaret nodded. "Powerless we were in the face of it, sir. Powerless."

He could tell them a thing or two about being unable to control temptation. He accepted the thick, light biscuit the cook offered him and took a huge bite. Butter and jam oozed out the back side of it, and he quickly shifted his hold to lick his fingers clean. At the edge of his vision, he saw Claire start, then snatch up the baking pan and attack its surface with a damp rag.

"They're very good," he offered his cook while he watched Claire's intense effort at cleaning. The dusting of flour did nothing to disguise the color flooding her cheeks. "May I have another?" he asked absently.

"To be sure, sir."

He managed to mumble his thanks, but the larger part of his awareness was fascinated by how easily Claire Curran's senses seemed to be stirred. Almost as easily as his own. Or at least so it appeared. Was it only wishful thinking on his part? While Mary Margaret slathered another biscuit with butter and jam for him, he took a chance. "So tell me, Claire...Did all the lessons go as well as the one on biscuits?"

She looked up to meet his gaze. With a tentative

smile she answered, "I do believe so. Meg had been misinformed on a crucial point. We got it sorted out," and then quickly went back to scrubbing the pan.

Devon smiled, wondering just what thoughts were running through her pretty little head. Given how flushed her cheeks were, they had to border on being truly lascivious. Not as lascivious as his own were at the moment, but still...

"An' the fires are banked for the night, sir," he heard the other woman assure him. "Don't know why it never occurred to me brain that they'd be tended the same as those in the upstairs. Here ye go, sir."

Tearing his attention away from Claire, he took the second biscuit offered by the cook. Meg, was it? It was certainly quicker to say than Mary Margaret.

"Meg was a housemaid in London before becoming indentured and..." She stifled a yawn before she could finish, "...being brought to the colonies."

Devon rose to his feet, the biscuit still in his hand. "Are you finally tired enough to truly retire?"

"Yes," she admitted with a sigh, setting aside the pan and the rag. Untying her apron, she came around the end of the table, saying, "I'll be back out in the morning, Meg, to help you prepare the ham."

"Thank ye, Lady Claire. But don't be hurryin' from yer bed too quick, though. There'll be nothin' here needin' tendin' more than yer handsome husband."

The startled look on Claire's face...Devon was tempted to laugh until he saw the color flooding over the swells of her breasts and sweeping up the slender column of her throat. In a fraction of a heartbeat, his amusement was pounded into oblivion by another kind of temptation altogether. Sweet Jesus. No amount of bloused shirt would ever be sufficient to hide the fact that his breeches were becoming intolerably—and embarrassingly—tight. He glanced about, wondering what pretext he could use for yanking the tail out completely.

His gaze fell on the carving block and he instantly opted for a timely distraction.

"Hold this for me a moment, will you?" he said, thrusting his biscuit at a surprisingly compliant Claire. "Meg?" he went on, striding to the block and grabbing the handle of a hefty cleaver.

"Aye, sir?"

He carried it back to the central table and buried the tip of it in the wood. "If Wyndom should make an appearance in your kitchen again, you have my permission to use this on whatever part of his anatomy you think appropriate."

Meg grinned and nodded slowly. "I'll be givin' it some thought, sir. Though seems to me that I'm likely to be takin' a swing at whatever comes up first."

"My thoughts exactly," he agreed, giving her a smile and a wink. "Good night, Meg." He turned away and, being careful to keep himself out of Claire's line of sight, placed his hand on the small of her back and guided her toward the door.

They were outside before he realized that they'd left the candle lamp behind. He thought about going back to get it, but quickly saw the advantage in the relative darkness. What Claire couldn't clearly see wouldn't concern her. Unfortunately, the lack of light didn't give him any respite from temptation. Being considerably taller than she was, all he had to do was look down to feast his eyes on the full swells of her breasts. The biscuit she was carrying for him didn't look nearly as delicious as she did. The biscuit . . .

Devon smiled as a lecherous possibility occurred to him. Did he dare act on it? As he escorted her up the back steps and into the butler's pantry, he realized that it all depended on how Claire would respond. If he frightened her, she'd scurry away and he'd be hard pressed to get within a mile of her for the next fortnight. If she met him halfway, though...sweet Jesus. If she didn't run away, he was going to either be in acute pain or scrambling for a way to renegotiate their conjugal agreement. Or, he reminded himself sternly as they climbed the stairs, he could exercise some self-discipline and behave himself. It would be the intelligent, rational thing to do. His life was complicated enough already.

"You didn't hurt Wyndom too badly, did you?" she asked softly when they reached the upstairs hallway.

"Not as badly as I wanted to."

"It would appear that he doesn't think matters through very carefully."

Devon snorted. "Whether he thinks at all is open to debate."

"Of course he thinks," she countered as they came to stop at her bedroom door. Turning to face him, she added, "Just in a manner very different from you. It has to be difficult for him to exist in your shadow and never measure up to the standards you set. Perhaps you—"

"Perhaps you shouldn't meddle," he suggested. "How I deal with Wyndom is none of your concern. I'll leave Meg to you, you leave everyone else to me, and we'll do fine."

"There are times," she said with quiet defiance, her face tilted up so that she could meet his gaze, "when I honestly think that you see yourself as sitting at the right hand of God."

"Actually," he countered, grinning, "I stand in for him on Tuesdays, Thursdays, and every other Sunday." She didn't want to smile; he could see the corners of her mouth twitching as she fought the impulse. And watching her struggle, he lost his own battle and his mind arrowed back to his carnal fantasy.

"I'll have my biscuit back, if you don't mind."

She blinked, looked disconcerted for a second, and then glanced down at her hand as though she'd forgotten that she was holding it. Shaking her head, she sighed in amused aggravation and handed it to him with a smile.

He took the biscuit with one hand and with his other gently caught hers before she could draw it back. "Wait," he murmured, watching her eyes as he lifted her fingertips to his lips. "You've gotten sticky."

"Devon," she whispered, her voice edged with wariness. "I'd rather that you—"

Whatever it was that she'd intended to say was lost as he kissed the end of her first finger. He saw fear flicker for a second in the dark depths of her eyes and then it was gone, replaced by the bright light of exhilaration. Emboldened, his heart racing, he slowly trailed the tip of his tongue down the length of her slender finger, drew the whole of it into his mouth, and gently suckled it.

Knowing well the skills of seduction, he also recognized the certain signs of surrender. Her lips were parted, her breathing shallow and so very slow. Her eyes drifted closed and she leaned gently toward him, wordlessly inviting him to deeper intimacies. It would be so easy; she wouldn't resist. There was no denying that he wanted to take her to his bed.

And if he did, he'd spend the rest of his life bound to her. And she to him and his fate. Honor demanded that he find the strength to walk away from all that she offered. He had nothing of equal value to give her in return.

Slowly, he released his claim to her finger. "You are dangerously delicious, madam," he said softly while regretfully surrendering possession of her hand.

She swallowed hard and took a deep breath before she forced a smile on her face and managed to whisper, "And you, sir, are positively wicked."

"I won't argue." It wasn't too late. If he reached for her now, she'd come to him. The spell wasn't yet broken. And God help him, he wanted her. "I think we'd do well to keep our distance from one another," he said, desperately hoping she'd either disagree or simply step into his arms.

"A most wise idea." She exhaled with a slight shudder, then turned and opened her door, hurriedly adding, "I'll wish you a good night now, sir."

"Good night, madam," he answered, watching her leave him. "Sleep well."

He stood there for a long while, staring at the door, his pulse thrumming wildly through his veins, his loins aching. And to think that he'd accused Wyndom of being a mindless rutter. If not for Claire Curran's common sense and self-control, he'd be—at this very moment—proving beyond all doubt that he wasn't one bit more disciplined and intelligent than all the Rivard males that had gone before him. He'd been a damn fool to dance with temptation. But, he consoled himself as he headed toward his own room and his solitary bed, he'd learned a valuable, necessary lesson in his rashness: Claire was more intoxicating than the finest brandy, and he had to stay the hell away from her. If he didn't, he'd be the ruin of them both.

CLAIRE LAY IN HER BED, staring up at the canopy over her head, unable to silence the chatter of her thoughts. How was it possible to resent a man's arrogance at the same time that you were irresistibly, physically drawn to him? Heaven help her. If she didn't keep a good distance from him, she'd make a complete fool of herself. One mistake, one witness to it, would be all that it would take to bind them together forever. And bound to Devon Rivard, she would never see Crossbridge Manor again. She would never again have the hope of being free.

CHAPTER TEN

CLAIRE QUICKLY LOOKED over her shoulder at the rear face of Rosewind. Somewhere inside, another door slammed. And then another. She pursed her lips. Had Wyndom finally returned from wherever it was that he'd gone? Was Devon making a rare daylight appearance in the house? Was he looking for her?

Of course not, she assured herself, going back to raking the winter's deadfall out of the herb garden. He'd said they needed to keep their distance from each other, and he'd certainly held to his side of it. If only she could stop thinking about him, stop remembering the rakish way he'd leaned against her doorjamb that first night and given her that roguish half-smile of his. And it would be especially nice if she could stop her heart from ridiculously fluttering every time she thought he might be near. She'd never acted like this in her life. It was embarrassing.

Meg looked up from her work on the other side of

the planting bed and cautiously asked, "Would there be anythin' you'd like to be askin' me, Lady Claire?"

"About what?" she asked absently, bending down to break off a dried sprig of lavender and inhaling the earthy, sweet scent.

"Whatever 'tis that's had ye mopin' and lookin' over yer shoulder at the least noise fer the last week."

She'd admit to looking over her shoulder. She knew that she did it frequently. But sighing and moping? Had she really been such poor company? Resolving to be more aware of her behavior, Claire tucked the lavender sprig behind her ear. "I'm fine. Honestly."

"Well, 'tis with a great an' profound respect that I disagree with ye," Meg countered, her hands fisted on her hips. "Ye're not fine an' 'twould be me guess that it has somethin' to do with Mr. Devon."

Her pulse skittered and, irritated with herself, Claire yanked a dead parsley plant out of the ground with far more vigor than necessary. Dirt rained down and she stepped back, shaking it from her skirt as she summoned her most blithe manner and asked, "Now, why would you think something like that, Meg?"

"'Cause I haven't seen the two of ye together since the first night ye both was here in me kitchen."

Yes, servants noticed everything. Most of them understood, though, that they weren't supposed to share their observations. But then Meg wasn't the typical servant. "He's been very busy with the estate since the snow melted," Claire said, tossing the dead plant onto the heap and studiously refusing to meet Meg's brown-eyed gaze. "And I've been busy with matters concerning the house."

"Ye've been hidin' in the kitchen, pure an' simple, Lady Claire. 'Tis many a time I've wondered if'n we ought to be findin' a bed fer ye to put on the oth'r corner. An' since I'm havin' no luck with gettin' ye to share the burden by beatin' 'round the bush, I'll just be a-comin' at it square on...is there anythin' ye'd like to know 'bout sharin' a man's bed?"

Meg thought...Heat flooded Claire's cheeks. "No. But thank you for offering," she hastily replied. "If I ever find myself in the situation, I'll—"

"If'n ye ever?"

Claire sighed, realizing that she couldn't let Meg make assumptions and that she should have addressed the matter long before this point. If she and Devon were going to successfully annul the marriage, then everyone needed to know that they weren't sharing a bed. Either happily or unhappily. She'd avoided discussing the matter with Meg simply because the time had never been any more right than the words she could find. But the time had now come and whether the words were the right ones or not, she had to say something.

"Ours is an unusual situation," Claire began, finally meeting the other woman's gaze. Meg's eyes were huge, their depths filled with puzzlement. "Devon and I were forced to marry. The circumstances are rather complicated. Suffice it to say that since neither of us wants to be married—and especially not to each other—we've agreed that the marriage will be in name only so that it can be annulled in a few months."

"Blessed Mary, preserve me. Are ye tellin' me that when the two o' ye left here that first night, ye shook hands at yer doors an' went to yer beds alone?"

"I suppose that's something of how it went."

"Well," Meg said with a snort, " 'twasn't what he wanted to do, I can tell ye fer sure. The man was squirmin' the whole time he was in the kitchen. Couldn't keep his eyes off ye. 'Tis surprised I am to hear that he didn't ravage ye out on the flagstones the second the door was closed behind ye."

"He did kiss my finger," Claire offered with a weak

smile, wondering why it was such a relief to share what had happened to her.

Meg blinked rapidly, shook her head slightly, and then said, "He what?"

"I was carrying his biscuit, remember? When we got to the door of my room, he asked for it back. I'd forgotten that I even had it. And when I gave it to him, he caught my hand and kissed my finger. He said it was sticky from the jam. But it really wasn't. It was just an excuse."

"He just kissed yer finger?" Meg pressed, incredulous.

"Well, actually, no," Claire admitted, for some unfathomable reason pleased by her ability to so easily flabbergast the Irishwoman. "He kissed it. And then he licked it."

Meg's eyes lit up and she pressed her hand over her heart as she turned her face skyward and whispered, "Oh, Lord."

"And then he suckled it."

Meg's gaze came back to hers with an almost audible click. "An' ye weren't just a wee bit tempted to throw the man on his back an' have yer way with him?"

Claire grinned and offered Meg a shrug and the truth. "I wouldn't know how to have my way with a man. The only real experience I have with them is in fending them off."

With a soft laugh, Meg asked, "But I'll bet ye were regrettin' that, weren't ye?"

"Actually, I thought for a minute or two that he might take matters into his own hands. So to speak."

"But he didn't," Meg finished sadly.

"Thank goodness," Claire quickly countered. "If he had, my fate would have been sealed. It took all the strength I had just to stand there. There wouldn't have been any left with which to fight off his advance. But, mercifully, he released me and suggested that wisdom lay in trying to avoid each other as much as possible. I agreed that he was right. We've seen each other only from a distance for the past week. It's working out rather nicely."

Meg considered Claire through narrowed eyes. "No doubt," she said slowly, " 'tis the thing to do if 'n yer hearts is set on goin' their different ways."

"I don't see that we have any other course. We're not at all suited for one another."

Meg opened her mouth to speak, but it was Mother Rivard's voice that filled the silence.

"Oh, Lady Claire, I've found you," the older woman declared breathlessly as she fumbled with the latch on the garden gate. Unable to operate it, she ceased her efforts and, clutching the top of a picket in each hand, said with a heavy sigh, "Thank heavens."

Alarmed by the woman's agitation, Claire dropped her rake and pulled off her gloves even as she asked, "Has something happened? Is someone hurt?"

"A note has arrived from Wyndom," his mother answered excitedly. "He's returning home in two days' time. And he's bringing the Lee brothers with him!"

"Guests," Claire repeated, feeling a little foolish for having been so easily frightened.

"Not just any guests!" Henrietta countered. "The Lee brothers! Dear heavens, I hope Devon can understand the importance of this. You need to find him in the fields and tell him the news straight away. He must prepare."

Prepare. Claire's pulse tripped as full realization struck. Guests meant getting the house cleaned from top to bottom, the guest rooms opened up, the sheets changed. And then there was the food and the—

"Oh dear," Mother Rivard gasped, intruding on Claire's quiet panic. "What to wear for their arrival? The pink silk? Or perhaps the green brocade?"

With all that had to be done, Henrietta was worried about dresses? And she'd asked absolutely the wrong person for help with the decision. "I think you should consult Elsbeth on the proper wardrobe for the occasion."

"Yes, yes," the other woman agreed, her smile bright. "That's the thing to do. You will find Devon and give him the wonderful news, won't you?"

"Immediately."

The promise seemed sufficient. Henrietta Rivard, still smiling, gathered her skirts in hand, turned, and all but ran back to the house. Claire watched her go, wondering what it would be like to go through life so blissfully unconcerned about anything more pressing than what dress to wear the day after tomorrow. It had to be nice, she decided. As long as there was someone around who would happily—and competently—bear the responsibilities you didn't see. Henrietta was very fortunate to have a son like Devon.

Turning to Meg, she pulled the sprig of lavender from behind her ear and tossed it away, saying, "I'm off to the fields to share the joyous tidings." With a weak smile, she added, "Of course, I have absolutely no idea why they're so joyous. And would you happen to have any idea of where the fields are?"

Meg absently pointed off to the east, her gaze fixed on the back door of the house. "We're in trouble deep an' wide, Lady Claire. There's too much to be done an' not 'nough time to do it."

"We'll manage," Claire promised, letting herself out of the garden gate. "If you'd prepare a cold luncheon while I'm gone, I'd be most appreciative. And put something on to simmer for supper as well. It's going to be a long afternoon and we're not going to have time to fix anything too terribly complicated."

"That Elsbeth—"

"Don't worry about her, Meg." Gathering her skirt

into her hands, she tossed a quick look at the main house. "She'll be too busy complaining about other things to even notice the food."

Meg called out an assurance and then abandoned the garden for the kitchen. Claire set out on the wide path that led from the back of the house toward the gently rolling, wooded hills to the east, mentally sweeping through each and every room of Rosewind and noting all the tasks that needed to be done in each. The list was long and daunting. If she found any time to sleep between now and the arrival of the Lee brothers, it would be a miracle. There was so much to do, so much that shouldn't have been allowed to reach the state of decline it had.

Suddenly she understood the comment Devon had made that first day: that he'd be happy if anyone could meet the least of his expectations regarding the care and maintenance of Rosewind Manor. She slowed and then stopped, staring blindly down at the dirt road, and wondered why it was that she felt such a keen and personal need to meet his expectations.

The reasons, as Devon had explained them to her, for having a splendid home and offering lavish hospitality were silly at best and, at worst, financially indefensible. And she wasn't the true mistress of Rosewind; Henrietta was. Seeing that Rosewind met the standards of outsiders was properly the obligation of Devon's mother. However, Henrietta's inability to see to the task meant that someone else was going to have to shoulder the responsibility or Devon was going to be severely embarrassed in front of his peers.

Claire frowned. So why was she so quickly willing to accept that obligation to Devon? Why did she care what the Lee brothers thought of his home or of him? She wasn't bound to him or this place forever. In a few months she'd be far away, and what anyone—Devon or the Lee brothers—thought of her wouldn't matter in the least.

And yet, despite all the rational arguments to support her stepping back from the incredible amount of work that needed to be done, she wasn't willing to do that. The Herefordshire gentry had publicly said she was too young to be a proper mistress for Crossbridge Manor. They'd said that her father should hire a manager for the farm and a housekeeper. She'd proven them wrong. And eventually they'd had to not only publicly admit their mistake, but also that no one could have done it better. She'd earned their admiration and, far more important, their respect.

With a smile, Claire looked up from the road. The trees arching overhead were leafed, the colors of green wildly varied and refreshing. She drew a deep breath, enjoying the scent of spring air, of the promise of the world coming new again.

DEVON GLANCED UP from trickling seeds to site his plowing line over the mule's back. Up ahead, at the far end of the field and perfectly framed between the animal's ears, was the unmistakable flutter of rose-colored skirts. Claire. It had to be. His mother and Aunt Elsbeth had no idea where the fields were, and there was no reason for them to have developed a sudden curiosity about such matters at this point in their lives. And the woman watching him, her hand shading her eyes, didn't have red hair. Yes, it was definitely Claire.

He tore his attention away from her and resolutely set it back on the seeds dropping one by one from the spinning barrel and into the freshly dug furrow. Behind him he heard the scraping of metal against dirt as his few remaining slaves covered the seeds he was leaving in his wake.

Why was she here? Had something happened up at the house? Had there been an accident? He glanced up again and decided that her manner was far too patient for there to have been some great calamity. So what *had* brought her out here? he wondered. They'd agreed to avoid each other as best they could. They'd been able to do that quite well for the last week.

Not that she'd been all that distant from his thoughts, Devon silently admitted. But that didn't pose a problem beyond restless sleep and being a bit distractible when awake. No, thinking about her, remembering and turning her words over and over in his mind, didn't count against him in the agreement they'd made.

But her coming to the fields was a clear violation of it. Which, given her compliance to this point, meant that there had to be a very good reason for her having made the effort to find him. And, he conceded with a sigh, the only civil thing to do was turn the mule at the end of the field, stop, and take the time to talk to her. Not that he really wanted to. His mind—hell, his fantasies—didn't need any additional fodder where Claire Curran was concerned.

He managed to give her a cursory nod as he drew near enough to meet her gaze, then deliberately looked away as he turned the mule and reined it to a halt. It took him a moment to disengage himself from the harness and turn back toward her. It was only then that he realized that he should have been thinking of what he intended to say. *What are you doing here?* might well be what he wanted to know, but it was also entirely too abrupt and blunt.

He cleared his throat and frantically searched his brain as he ambled toward her across the newly planted furrows. When close enough to speak without shouting, he stopped, bowed briefly, and asked, "Did you come down here alone?"

"It's broad daylight and the road is clear and wide

enough that no assailant could attack me by surprise even if he were of a mind to." She didn't give him a chance to rebut her claim. Neither, to his relief, did she point out how boorish the question was. Instead, she leaned around him to gaze in the direction of the mule and observe, "If I were in England, I'd think that you were planting wheat. Isn't that one of Mr. Jethro Tull's early seed-drilling machines?"

"It is," he said, wondering how the devil she recognized the implement. "My grandfather bought it on a whim. As it turns out, his whim may be my salvation."

She shifted her attention to the furrow he'd just planted. "Are you using it to sow tobacco seeds?"

Devon smiled. She might know a seed driller, but she didn't know the first thing about the growing of Virginia's sacred plant. He shook his head in answer to her question, then explained, "Tobacco is a rich man's crop. Cultivating and processing it requires incredible amounts of labor, which—thanks to my father's spending habits—I don't have at my disposal. Besides that, the plants themselves consume the fertility of the soil and give nothing back. A man growing tobacco has to expand his holdings so that there's always virgin ground on which to plant it. Since I can't afford to do that, I've been forced to find another crop to sustain Rosewind. Wheat, oats, corn, and rye are my experiments for this year."

"Very wise ones," she replied, smiling up at him. "I've been given to understand that very few Virginians grow the staple crops—favoring tobacco as they do. I'd think that you could get premium prices for your grain in the local markets."

"Oh?" She knew philosophy, planting machines, *and* commodity trading?

"Everyone needs flours," she said, nodding, her expression solemn and most businesslike as she surveyed his half-planted field. "And a locally produced supply can be had more reliably than one imported from another colony. People are usually inclined to pay a bit more for what they can have in hand at the moment than they are to save a few shillings by waiting to buy what may not ever arrive."

Her reasoning paralleled his own. His curiosity stirred, he asked, "And how is it that you know something of commodity trading?"

"I grew wheat and oats at Crossbridge. The difference between selling a crop well and selling it poorly was the difference between eating and not." She bent down and scooped up a handful of soil. Straightening to assess its quality, she added, "My skill at grain trading was one of the first my uncle sought to use to his advantage. His Majesty's Army consumes great quantities of grain, and a trader who can buy low and sell high stands to make obscene profits in the transaction. And understand," she added with a frown, "that dear Uncle George has no compunctions whatsoever about lining his pockets with coins stripped from the King's."

"You don't approve of profit?"

"Not the way he often goes about it," she answered, letting the last of the soil fall through her fingers and then brushing her hands clean. "He's not above having his hirelings burn his competitors' fields and warehouses to create scarcity and drive up prices. And he's been known to substitute poor-quality grains for what he's contracted to deliver and then pay quartermasters to turn a blind eye to that fact."

"Those are serious accusations," Devon pointed out. "How do you know them to be fact?"

She met his gaze squarely. "It wasn't uncommon for me to negotiate the original contract and then be dispatched to attend to the bribery of the quartermasters. I deeply resented being a party to such perfidy."

He could understand her feelings on the matter.

He'd have hated it, too. Not that he'd have gone so far as to be involved once he'd understood the nature of the transactions. But then he wasn't a female and dependent on anyone for his daily bread and the shirt on his back. "May I assume that your protests to being involved in such affairs are what led to being offered up for Wyndom's debts?"

She laughed softly, sadly. "People who oppose George Seaton-Smythe are people who are usually found floating face down in the Thames. No, I didn't protest. I knew better." She mustered a weak smile and added, "But I did make concerted efforts to leave various documents my uncle authored in the care of those I trusted, so that if I were ever hauled into the dock for fraud, I could at least offer a defense."

Honest, intelligent, and forward thinking. Which were probably characteristics her uncle didn't perceive as being entirely to his advantage. If he knew about them. There was a distinct possibility that he didn't, of course. If Claire had saved her uncle's correspondence as a defense, she'd likely gone to some lengths to keep him from discovering it. "A healthy sense of self-preservation is a good thing," Devon admitted. "So tell me . . . Precisely why did your uncle want to dispose of you?"

She considered him for a long moment, her violet eyes darkening, before quietly answering, "To punish me for having the audacity to refuse his advances. And for being strident enough in my refusal to put him in the awkward position of having to explain the six-inch gash across his forehead to his wife and friends."

She was so serious, so decidedly proper about the whole thing. And for some reason he found it all delightfully amusing. It took monumental effort to contain his smile and feign a decorum equal to her own as he asked, "What did you hit him with?"

"A fireplace poker."

Oh, God, he wanted to laugh. "It's a wonder that you didn't kill him."

The corners of her mouth twitched and her eyes sparkled with devilment. "More a pity, actually, because that's what I was trying to do." Her restraint fell away and she smiled broadly as she added, "Should I ever have chance for a second go at it, I'll remember to swing harder."

He grinned, and Claire gave up the struggle to be dignified. Lord, he was a handsome man at any time, but never more so than when he laughed. The sound of his happiness reverberated through her, thrilling and powerful in its effect. It made her want to do or say something that would keep his eyes twinkling and his burdens so obviously lightened. He looked young when he laughed. And so approachable, so touchable. Wouldn't it be grand to be wrapped in his arms, laughing with him?

The mental image stole what little air there was in her lungs. She took a half step back, her knees weak and her mind reeling at the unexpected and dangerous path her thoughts had taken. Dear God, what was wrong with her? Why couldn't she keep her head squarely on her shoulders when she was near him? Why was she so drawn to him? Drawn to him despite knowing that there could never be anything more between them than a temporary marriage of convenience?

Would it be so awful? asked a soft inner voice. *Would being his wife, his lover, really be so awful?*

She started even as, deep inside her, something warmed and swelled, filling her and making her pulse skitter with anticipation. She struggled to breathe, to keep her feet firmly under her. She closed her eyes and desperately tried to summon the memory of Crossbridge Manor's golden, sun-drenched stones. All she could see was Rosewind's rosy bricks. Tears rose in her throat and she struggled to swallow them back, to keep her composure.

He cleared his throat.

She opened her eyes and glanced up to see that the young, carefree man was gone without a trace. Relief slowly rippled through her and although it eased the frantic beating of her heart, it did nothing to soothe the regret she felt for the loss of his laughter. That Devon had regained his normal composure was for the best, she assured herself. She didn't want to make a fool of herself, didn't want to embarrass them both. She didn't want him or his crumbling mansion. She wanted to go home.

He softly cleared his throat again and then, taking a step back himself, tightly asked, "Is there some particular reason you've come down to the fields?"

"Yes, there is, actually," she hurried to answer, resolutely focusing her thoughts on innocuous matters. She took a wonderfully steadying breath and continued, explaining, "Your mother asked me to. Rather excitedly, I might add. A message has arrived from Wyndom. He's returning home in two days and bringing the Lee brothers with him. I gathered from your mother's reaction to the news that these Lee brothers are of great importance."

He snorted and gave her a rueful half-smile. "You can't swing a dead cat in Virginia without hitting a Lee. And all of them are of great importance. Especially the Brothers Lee—Francis Lightfoot and Richard Henry."

Her pulse had quickened again and she slid her gaze back out to the field so that she couldn't see him at all. How could a small, cynical smile have such a powerful effect? "Your mother gave me the impression that the Lee brothers coming to Rosewind was very important to you in a personal sense."

"Richard Henry is a senior member of the House of Burgesses. If a younger man has ambitions of political advancement, he has to have his approval and support."

"Ah, and you have ambitions," she guessed.

"No, I don't," he corrected with a softly wry chuckle. "But Mother has illusions enough for the both of us. I'm willing to fulfill the basic obligations of leadership that come with being a landowner, but I'm not willing to surrender the whole of my life to public service. If I were to do that, I wouldn't have a chance of saving Rosewind from the auction block."

"Perhaps someday your finances won't be so precarious," she offered, chancing a quick look at him.

He shrugged and motioned to one of the field hands as he said, "Then I'll have to find another excuse. The truth is that I don't much care for politics as they presently are. It involves a great deal of talking—talking that seldom results in any sort of definitive action. Every now and then they'll decide to take a stand on an issue, but it's largely symbolic, ineffectual, and either ignored or rescinded the next day. It's pathetic and maddening and makes the whole tedious process a waste of my time and effort. I prefer to take action."

"And the Lee brothers are aware of your feelings on these matters?"

"They'd have to be deaf, dumb, and blind not to have noticed my lack of spirited participation at past meetings." He cocked a dark brow and began to unroll his shirtsleeves. "And I assure you that they're not deaf, dumb or blind."

She wasn't either, and the sight of his nimble fingers and the corded muscles of his forearms was oddly, deeply stirring. "But you'll host the Lees amiably," she said, trying to ground her thoughts again.

"Hospitality in Virginia is a high expectation. One can't scrimp on it without inviting speculation about one's imminent financial collapse."

"And doing anything to invite speculation would be pulling the cornerstone from the foundation of social illusion," she added, taking another deep breath to fortify herself before facing him squarely.

"You do understand," he said, his smile sad and beleaguered. "Saving Rosewind is a point of pride, I suppose. Six generations of Rivards have lived under its roof. I don't want to be known as the Rivard who managed to lose it."

"But you can't be held responsible for the consequences of the decisions made by those who held it before you."

He shook his head. "Six generations from now, no one would know the details of how it was lost, just that it was and by me. I'd rather be forgotten completely than remembered that way. To keep Rosewind from the auction block, I'll do what I have to do."

She could understand his feelings on the matter. Crossbridge had been given to her father when she'd been but a little girl. No long tradition of ownership had come with it. And yet through the years that she'd been its mistress, she'd moved heaven and earth to keep it going. It had been pride beneath her fierce determination to succeed, her refusal to fail. Yes, she could well understand how Devon Rivard felt about Rosewind.

"If there's to be a reasonable hope of impressing the Lee brothers and saving Rosewind, I'm going to need help," she said, narrowing her eyes to see into the days to come. "Is there any chance that you might borrow Hannah from Mrs. Vobe for a few days? In preparing for such auspicious guests, Meg's skills would be best utilized in the house."

He nodded. "I can ask. The worst that could happen is that Mrs. Vobe would say no."

"I'd be most appreciative. I'm going to need every set of hands I can press into duty. The next two days are going to be long ones for everyone."

Both brows slowly arced upward. "You're not thinking of asking Mother and Aunt Elsbeth to lend a hand, are you?"

"Yes," Claire replied, lifting her chin, "actually, I am."

"Doing what?"

Refusing to be put off by his incredulity, she answered, "Polishing, dusting, waxing, washing, cooking. The list of tasks is positively endless."

"Thank you, Zeke," he said, accepting the reins of his horse from the waiting slave. "Have a go at the driller while I'm gone, will you? I'll be back as soon as I can."

Zeke looked at the seeding machine as though it were the Holy Grail. And the way he said "Yes, sir" left no doubt in Claire's mind that, for whatever reason, Zeke felt incredibly honored to have been given the task of planting the wheat.

"I'll do what I can to force their enlistment," Devon said, calling her attention back to him, "but you should know that neither Mother nor Aunt Elsbeth will work willingly. Keeping them to their tasks will involve more time and effort than if you were to simply do them yourself. It's one of the key drawbacks of forced labor."

"I don't have any other choice," she admitted, watching as he smoothly swung up into the saddle. "Not if the house is to be ready in time."

He pulled his foot from the stirrup and leaned down, his hand outstretched. "Your hand, madam."

She understood his intention. She also could see all too clearly the consequences. "Thank you, but I'll walk back to the house."

He eased back a bit, his brows furrowed as he considered her. "Are you afraid of horses?"

"Not at all," she admitted before she could think better of the honesty.

He reached out again. "Then give me your hand so I can pull you up."

"I'd prefer to walk, thank you." She took a step away from him so that she was well beyond his immediate reach. "It would do me good. I need time to think and order my housekeeping plans."

"Think while you ride," he countered tightly. "A Tidewater lady is never seen walking about her estate."

Him and his silly Tidewater rules and expectations. Claire gathered her skirts in hand and turned toward the road leading back to the house, retorting, "I would imagine that a Tidewater gentleman is never seen running his own seed-drilling machine, either. If the rules can be bent for you, they can be bent for me as well. I'll walk if it pleases me to do so."

"You're a most stubborn woman, Claire Curran," he called after her. "Has anyone ever mentioned that flaw?"

She didn't bother to look back. "More than once."

Devon slipped his foot back into the stirrup and eased his horse forward, smiling as he watched her march up the road. So purposeful. So determined to do things her own way. Even when there wasn't any point to it beyond defying him for the sake of defiance alone. He had to give her full credit for pluck and a stiff backbone, though. Unfortunately for her, he had just as much as she did. And no patience with foolishness. Nudging his horse into a brisk trot, he leaned out and down, rode up beside her and, before she could react, neatly slipped his arm around her waist. She squeaked in surprise and clutched his arm tightly as he lifted her up and deposited her firmly on his lap.

"You've met your match for stubbornness," he said quietly in her pretty little ear.

She started and then pried at his encircling arm. "Put me down!" She squirmed and twisted in his embrace.

It was a magnificent and inspiring friction. Devon sucked in a deep breath, trying to decide whether or not he wanted her to realize what she was doing to him. "Oh, sit still and enjoy being a lady," he growled, subtly trying to shift to a more comfortable position under her. "It won't kill you." *And if you don't,* he silently added, *it's going to kill me.*

She didn't stop, of course, and he tightened his arm around her. "Stop struggling, Claire," he growled in her ear. "You're going to fall off and break your neck."

"And then your precious house wouldn't be clean for the Lee brothers."

It rankled that she thought that was what he cared about. "Exactly," he snapped, pulling her hard against his lap and kicking his horse into a canter. With every stride of the animal beneath them, he rose up against her, pressing hard into the folds of her skirt. She went still and everywhere their bodies touched he could feel the tremors that coursed through her. Color flooded the swells of her breasts and swept upward, darkening her cheeks. The scent of heated lavender washed over him, inviting him to lean close, to press his lips to the nape of her neck and fill his soul with the sweet, heady taste of her.

Devon clenched his teeth and deliberately leaned back, knowing that if he succumbed to just the tiniest temptation, he'd be powerless to resist the larger ones. And, at the moment, the most strident one of them all was suggesting that he find a secluded bit of dappled grass, lay Claire Curran down, and admit that having a wife wasn't the worst fate a man could endure.

Maybe it wasn't, but making a woman his wife just because he didn't have the strength of character to hold his needs in check would definitely be the greatest folly he'd ever commit. It was much wiser to suffer a few minutes of acute discomfort than spend all eternity paying for the pleasure to be found in release.

CHAPTER ELEVEN

*I*T WAS DIFFICULT to outwardly pretend that she was unaffected. She'd have had to have been dead not to notice the proof of Devon's physical stimulation. With every rolling step the horse took, it pressed hard against her thigh, stroking upward and then briefly falling away before returning to taunt and brand her anew. No skirt or petticoat on earth was sufficiently thick to pad her to the point of not knowing what it was. And, dear God in heaven, she knew precisely what it meant. Men, when in their own company, often became satyrs who felt compelled to share with every other man—or woman masquerading as a man—their graphic repertoires of tasteless sexual pantomime.

She'd seen much more than she'd ever wanted to; been declared an unnaturally priggish man more times than she could count. But despite all that she'd seen and heard, it had never occurred to her that sharing a cantering horse with a man could come so perilously close to the act of lovemaking. It was frightening to know just how close.

And it was exhilarating, too. Wildly, breathlessly, deliciously exhilarating. There was no denying it. Every fiber of her being was alive in a delightfully new way. It was as though her senses had suddenly awakened from a lifelong slumber, emerging from hibernation starving and demanding that their hunger be sated. They reveled in the waves and layers of sensation there were in being held in Devon's embrace. The scents of sun and soil, of man and leather, wrapped around her, holding her captive more effectively than the steely strength of his arm. The easy sureness of his hand as it held the reins, the bronze of his skin in such dazzling contrast to the white of his linen shirt, the caress of his voice when he spoke against her ear, the solid warmth of his body, the vigor of his arousal . . . if only she could taste him, her senses would be full; she'd be complete.

And she'd be risking the loss of herself. For the second time that day, tears threatened to close her throat. Why was she drawn to this man? Why did he have the power to stir her senses so deeply, so profoundly? How could he so effortlessly scatter her resolve and make beguiling what had always been an unthinkable surrender? Out of all the men in the world, why had her uncle chosen Devon Rivard? Why an impoverished, autocratic colonial man who had sworn to be rid of her as soon as he could?

She was clearly a fool. Worse yet, apparently she was also, deep down inside, a shameless wanton without regard for pride or consequence. A week had passed by the calendar, and yet time and distance from Devon had changed absolutely nothing. She was just as brazenly enraptured now as in the moment when he'd so seductively suckled her finger. If he pressed, she'd likely surrender. What resistance she offered—if she could muster any at all—would be brief at best and half-hearted. Yes, she was shameless. And shortsighted, too.

There was nothing at Rosewind for her but servitude and poverty. While life at Crossbridge had never been anything beyond a marginal existence, at least she had been her own master, free to do as she thought best, to act in her own self-interest. She'd been forced to surrender that freedom to George Seaton-Smythe, and the yoke of submission had chafed every day for four long years. To spend eternity wearing it was a frightening prospect. And to deliberately choose to accept it was impossible. She couldn't allow herself to be weak, to be tempted by Devon Rivard's handsome face and seductive ways. She simply couldn't. She'd have to be strong—stronger than she'd ever been. The course of her life from this point forward depended on it.

They rounded a bend in the road, and suddenly the rear face of Rosewind came into sight. Claire breathed a small sigh of relief. Once they reached it, her present ordeal would be over. They would dismount and stand apart and the temptation would come to an end. She'd pretend that it had never happened. She'd thank him politely for bringing her back to the house and then throw herself into the work needing to be done. She wouldn't have to be anywhere near him for the next two days. And then the house would have guests within its walls, and the requirements of genteel hospitality would keep a dignified distance between them.

After that . . . Claire pursed her lips. After that, she'd have to find some other task that required her concerted attention and offered little chance of encountering Devon. It was the only rational strategy to pursue. She might well be a fool where he was concerned, but only a complete fool would refuse to back away from the edge of the abyss when she had the chance to do so. She wasn't so fascinated with him that she'd lost her

common sense. With self-discipline, she could avoid
making a horrible mistake.

"Do *not* attempt to jump off this horse, madam."

She felt every softly spoken word resonate through
the whole of her body, from her earlobe to where his
chest brushed against her shoulders, to her thighs and
then to the very tips of her toes. It was a decidedly pleasant, warming sensation. Claire clenched her teeth and
summoned some indignation over his presumption to
issue a command. Did he think that she didn't have
enough common sense to know the risks in throwing
herself off the animal?

He reined the horse to a gradual halt at the rear of
the house, then worked his body back, drawing her fully
into the curve of the saddle as he moved himself out of it
and onto the rump.

"Hold your balance," he said, easing his arm from
around her. "I'm going to release you."

There was utter relief wrapped around his each and
every word. She could certainly understand how he felt;
now that he'd put a bit of distance between them, she
could actually take a full breath. He dropped to the
ground behind his mount and then quickly stepped to
the side, lifted his arms, and slipped his hands about her
waist. She looked down at him, noting his tension in the
granite hardness of his jaw and the tightness of his lips.
She could understand that as well; she felt as though
someone had found a spring inside her and tightened it
to the point of breaking.

Placing her hands lightly on his shoulders, she allowed him to lift her from the saddle. The instant her
feet were firmly planted under her, she stepped to the
side, pulling her arms quickly to her sides. He took a
step back, withdrawing his own hands as well.

Before the silence could become awkward, she managed a smile and said, "Thank you for seeing me back
to the house. As I'm sure you want to be off to

Williamsburg as soon as you can, I won't delay you."
With the requirements of politeness met, she turned,
gathered her skirts in hand, and started toward the
steps. The tension inside her eased as she moved away
from him, and she couldn't suppress the feeling of having gained a reprieve as she passed into the cool shadows of the butler's pantry.

Devon considered her and weighed the merits of his
choices. On the one hand, he wanted to put as much distance between himself and skirted temptation as possible. On the other hand, he knew what she intended to
do once she went inside, and he couldn't help but cringe
at the certain outcome. With a sigh, he quickly pulled
the reins over his horse's head and, leaving the animal,
went after Claire.

Catching up with her in the foyer, he fell in beside
her, his hands clasped behind his back. "If you're off to
enlist the assistance of Mother and Aunt Elsbeth, I'd
better go with you," he said when she darted a look at
him. "Not," he hurried to add as they climbed the stairs
together, "that I think you're incapable of stating your
needs and requests. It's more a matter of me being willing to bully them into compliance. You're a nicer person
than I am."

She didn't say anything, but cast him another quick
look as they moved down the hall in the direction of his
mother's and Elsbeth's rooms. He heard their excited
chatter long before they reached the door, and was able
to pick out a sufficient number of words to realize they
were plotting his political rise to the governorship of
Virginia. Steeling himself, he dropped back to allow
Claire to procede him through the open doorway. She
paused, however, to knock and—presumably—politely
announce their presence. He could have told her that
was a mistake. Elsbeth looked up and instantly seized
the initiative.

"Good, you're back," the woman declared, scoop-

ing up an armload of gowns draped over the back of a
chair and advancing toward Claire with them. "We've
been waiting for you." She pushed them at her, saying,
"These need to be washed and pressed," and leaving
Claire with a choice between taking them or letting
them fall to the floor. "And tell Mary Margaret that
we'll be served luncheon here in our rooms," Elsbeth
added as she walked away. "We're entirely too busy to
come down today."

Claire stood there, holding the dresses and considering his mother and her companion for several long moments. Devon watched her, judging by the set of her jaw
that a confrontation was brewing. He waited, inexplicably excited by the prospect. Finally, her voice cool and
firm, she said, "Luncheon, today and tomorrow, will be
cold and served in the dining room as always. If you're
hungry and wish to partake, you may help yourself. Meg
is going to be far too busy to wait on you hand and foot.

"As for your washing..." She dumped the clothing
on the floor and gave the two shocked women a small
smile. "It will get done when it gets done. And since
there exists a distinct possibility that it won't, you might
want to choose something to wear for the Lee brothers
that's already clean."

"I don't like the tone of your voice," Elsbeth
snapped, her arms akimbo and her gaze raking Claire
from hair to hem. "And I care even less for your attitude. Clearly you have no understanding of the requirements of hospitality."

Claire remained unruffled. "I would presume that
guests would expect clean sheets, comfortable rooms,
and decent food, that they'd appreciate being able to see
out of the windowpanes and to take a deep breath without choking to death on the dust raised in their passing
from one room to another."

Elsbeth shrugged. "Those are the concerns of the
house staff."

"In the event that it's escaped your notice," Claire countered, the tiniest bit of sarcasm gilding her words, "we don't have a house staff."

His mother looked perplexed and then suddenly brightened. "Have Mary Margaret attend to the cleaning."

To her everlasting credit, Claire answered kindly, "I'm afraid that far too much has been neglected for far too long for any one person to prepare this house for entertaining. We'll all have to roll up our sleeves and apply ourselves if the Lee brothers are to be properly hosted."

Elsbeth sputtered, "Surely you don't mean to suggest—"

"She's not suggesting, Aunt Elsbeth," Devon interrupted, seeing the end of civility looming large. "She's telling you that you and Mother are both going to help get this house ready for guests."

"Well, I never!"

"Yes, I know," he replied with a sardonic smile. "But that's going to change. Claire is going to assign you a task, and you're going to do it well and without complaining. Is that clear?"

His mother stood there blinking at him as though she were trying to translate his words from Greek. Her sister stiffened her back and glowered at him.

"You'll either help in getting the work done," he said tightly, forestalling his aunt, "or your contribution can be to pack your bags and leave. I'm on my way into town to see if Mrs. Vobe will lend us Hannah for the next couple of days. If your decision is to leave, I'll be quite happy to escort you into Williamsburg."

"Hannah?" his mother gasped, pressing her hand to the base of her throat. "You'd risk poisoning the Lee brothers? Have you lost your mind?"

"Mother," he began with all the patience he could summon, "Hannah is a good and honorable woman. Thoughts of poisoning us have never once crossed her mind. If Mrs. Vobe is agreeable, Hannah will return here and serve us just as ably as she always did. And you will eat what she prepares without complaint. Is that understood?"

His mother blinked some more. Elsbeth huffed and looked down her nose at him to snap, "You're making a mistake that could well cost us not only our reputations but our lives."

"Leave it be, Aunt Elsbeth," he warned, "or I'll poison you myself. No jury would convict me."

Elsbeth gasped and took a half step back. His mother looked stricken and pale. A tension swelled in the room and he wasn't the least inclined to do anything to dissipate it. Claire apparently felt otherwise.

"The issue of who's going to prepare the food aside, Mother Rivard," she said gently, breaking the taut silence, "there are other tasks that must be done. If Hannah can be brought back to take care of the kitchen, I'll assign Meg the task of preparing the guest rooms. She has experience at this. Which leaves the main floor. Ephram can take down the draperies and haul the rugs out for beating. I'll take care of the washing, general dusting, and waxing the floors. That leaves the windows to be cleaned and the brass and silver to be polished. Which would you prefer to do?"

Devon had to admire the way she phrased it all, how she seemed to give his mother and Elsbeth a choice but, in actuality, didn't.

His mother, having been given no room to escape the situation, hesitantly replied, "I suppose that I could wipe a bit of glass. Elsbeth can polish the brass and copper."

It was Elsbeth's turn to blink. She slowly turned her head to stare at his mother in stunned disbelief.

"Thank you, Mother Rivard," Claire went on, smiling and ignoring Elsbeth's reaction. "I'll see you both downstairs shortly. I'll see that you have aprons to protect your gowns." With that, she dropped them a brief curtsy, turned and walked past him.

He shot his mother and Aunt Elsbeth a quick glance meant to assure them that if they didn't come down, he'd see that they regretted it, and then left them. Joining Claire as she marched down the hall, he felt compelled to observe, "They're not going to be of much help, you know."

"I suspect you're right. But thank you for wading in on my behalf. And for foreseeing the necessity of it."

Devon shrugged as they made their way down to the main level of the house. "I know how beleaguered they can make a person feel. Other than Hannah, is there anything you'd like for me to bring back from Williamsburg?"

A letter from her uncle, a letter saying that Wyndom's debt had been forgiven and that he'd gladly sign over the title to Crossbridge Manor. But it was an unreasonable request and she knew it. George Seaton-Smythe hadn't yet received their papers. It would be at least a month before he did and another month after that before she could realistically hope to hear anything in reply. Until then, she was trapped here, trapped in a world where newly discovered passions were at constant war with her common sense and pride.

"No," she replied. "I can't think of anything. But it was kind of you to offer."

He gestured toward the hallway leading off the other side of the foyer and into the eastern wing of the house, saying, "My study is this way."

She went, dropping back to allow Devon to precede her. It was, after all, his domain and one in which she had never been. He stopped in front of an open doorway and, while saying, "Ephram, I hope you're bored senseless with accounting and correspondence," blindly reached back to draw her to his side.

"I've been anticipating a call to other duties,"

Ephram replied, smiling and rising from his seat while he nodded in acknowledgment of her presence. He came around the large mahogany desk and toward them, adding, "I've taken care of the most important matters. What remains to be done here can wait."

"I seem to have acquired a wife with the ability to seize command," Devon explained. "I'm being dispatched to Williamsburg to see if I can retrieve your mother for a few days. While I'm gone, I'd appreciate it if you'd see to the more arduous tasks Claire needs done." Ephram had barely nodded his assent when Devon added with a sly smile, "I'll make it up to you. We'll go fishing tomorrow morning. You know your mother will want fish."

"An acceptable bargain, sir," the slave replied, his smile an uncanny mirror of his owner's. He turned to face her and added, "I'm at your disposal, Lady Claire. What task would you have me attend first?"

She started. His eyes were the same deep emerald green as Devon's. Claire gathered her distracted wits and summoned a smile. "Thank you, Ephram. All the rugs need to be taken out and beaten. Choose any room in which you'd like to start."

He bowed and as Devon moved aside, stepped past her. The two men fell in together and walked down the hall, conversing amiably. She followed slowly after them, watching them in stunned silence, noting the striking similarities in their heights and builds, in the way they moved and carried themselves. From the back, Ephram more resembled Devon than Wyndom did. Claire's steps faltered as other startling realizations swept over her. Henrietta was Devon's mother, Hannah Ephram's. But their father was undoubtedly the same man. Which meant that Ephram was not only a slave, he was also Devon's half brother.

What a very strange world this was. And to think that she'd always considered her relationship with the

Seaton-Smythes to be horribly sticky and convoluted. The difficulties in those relationships paled in comparison to the complicated and tangled web that bound together the lives of those at Rosewind. She could see why Henrietta so rarely focused her attention on the realities of her life. To know that your husband was fathering children with other women, with his female slaves . . .

Yes, she could understand how painful it must have been for Henrietta to see what was going on around her, to acknowledge the betrayal of fidelity and trust. So she'd turned away from it and studiously refused to see anything beyond the smooth facade of gentility and perfection. It was the only way she could avoid being consumed by indignity and despair.

Claire paused in the foyer to look upstairs. She felt deeply sorry for Devon's mother. She was just as deeply grateful that she wasn't going to have to confront the same choices in her own life. Henrietta had had no way to escape; she did.

CHAPTER TWELVE

CLAIRE STOPPED JUST INSIDE and looked around the rather poorly appointed guest room. It was stifling, but they didn't dare open the windows to let in the cool breeze. Not until they'd wiped the dust from the few wooden surfaces there were, hauled out the bedding and the curtains, and shoveled the heap of ash from the hearth. Meg wordlessly left her side, put the basket of cleaning supplies on the bureau, moved to the bed, and then competently set about stripping it.

There was a single wooden chair in the room, and Claire picked it up and carried it to one of the windows. Considering the bracket on which the curtain pole was suspended, she absently lifted her skirts and stepped up onto the seat. Attempting to stand upright and reach, she pitched forward, realizing too late that she'd caught her hem between her foot and the chair seat. Desperately catching the windowsill, she managed to prevent a wholly ungraceful fall to the floor, but not before the front edge of the maple chair had scraped along the entire length of her shin. Pain shimmered through her, bringing tears to her eyes.

"Are you all right, Lady Claire?"

"Yes," she muttered, carefully putting her weight back on both feet. "Damn skirts. Always in the way, always requiring one hand to manage them when you need two to properly complete a task. I positively loathe them."

"Well, bein' as the only other choice ye got is go buck naked," Meg lightly admonished, "I'm thinkin' that ye'd best be about acceptin' the trouble of 'em."

Claire considered the chair, her anger and frustration rising. Meg was wrong; skirts and nudity weren't the only choices. And it was ridiculous to handicap yourself when it wasn't necessary. "While I would be the first to admit that some situations necessitate acceptance," she said tightly, heading toward the door, "I'm of the opinion that others are best handled with a well-considered adaptation. I'll be back in a few minutes. Leave the curtains for me."

"Ye aren't a goin' to cut yer skirts off short, are ye?"

"And ruin a perfectly good dress and petticoat?" Claire answered without looking back. "Hardly."

" 'Tis hardly a good skirt," Meg countered, laughing. "What with the big burn ye have in the back of it."

True, Claire silently conceded as she entered her own room and began to work at her laces. But it still remained the only dress she really had. At Devon's request, his mother and Elsbeth had surrendered some of their gowns for her use—Henrietta quite happily and Elsbeth most grudgingly—but even the simplest of them was of exceptionally fine fabric, had exceedingly low necklines, and required huge panniers to keep the hems from pooling around her feet. Working in them would have been absolutely impossible, and so she'd hung them in the wardrobe until she could find the necessary time and patience to alter them to a more modest and serviceable style. Which certainly wasn't going to be today, she knew. Tomorrow didn't hold much promise, either.

Stripping out of her dress, Claire smiled ruefully. Given the circumstances, she was probably going to have to meet the Lee brothers wearing one of the borrowed dresses as it was—panniers, neckline, and all. The only consolation in the prospect was the fact that neither Henrietta nor Elsbeth had offered her one of their wigs to complete the outrageous ensemble.

She tossed her dress on the end of her bed, crossed to the armoire, and removed her breeches, simple linen shirt, and jackboots from the lower drawer. She considered her bindings, but quickly decided against them. There wasn't any reason to flatten her breasts. She wasn't trying to pass for a man today; she was just attempting to move around as safely and efficiently as males did.

And it felt good, she admitted as she finished dressing and pulled on her boots. Men's clothing was so much lighter than women's. And not at all constricting. You could breathe fully and move so freely. And with boots you didn't have to worry about twisting your ankle or falling off your heels. It was easy to understand why women tottered and men strode. Why women stayed home and men went out to conquer the world.

Claire smiled as she went down the hall toward the rooms set aside for guests. She wasn't all that interested in conquering the world, but the possibility of setting Rosewind to rights had some appeal. And now that she was comfortably dressed, the battle somehow didn't seem nearly as daunting as it had just minutes ago. It was amazing, she thought not for the first time, what a good pair of breeches could do for a person's confidence and optimism.

"Oh, sweet Joseph an' Mary."

Claire paused just inside the room and turned in a

slow circle to allow the wide-eyed Meg to fully appreciate her attire. "Simple and practical," she offered. "And watch this," she added excitedly as she strode over to the chair. She bounded up onto the seat, hopped down to the floor, and then bounded back up. She grinned at the still-stunned Irishwoman. "Impressive, isn't it?"

"An' what if someone sees ye dressed like that?" Meg whispered, glancing toward the door. " 'Tisn't natural, Lady Claire."

"And being unable to move without fear of tripping, falling, and injuring yourself is?" Claire asked, her hands fisted on her hips. "Why should we be denied the freedom men are allowed in moving about?"

"Where did ye come by 'em? Be they Mr. Devon's?"

"They're mine, actually," she replied, turning on the chair and setting about taking down the curtains. "I traveled in the conduct of my uncle's business. And he didn't see fit to provide me with a companion or a chaperone to do so. On the first sojourn in his behalf, I learned the perils of a woman traversing the world alone. Before I left London the next time, I'd been to see an understanding seamstress."

"An' does Mr. Devon know about yer breeches?"

She tossed the curtains atop the linens Meg had piled on the floor and then jumped down from the chair, saying, "As a point of fact, yes, he does."

"An' doesn't he mind ye wearin' 'em?"

"He minds very much, actually," she admitted while carrying the chair to the other window. Climbing up on it, she went on, "But I refuse to surrender common sense and mobility simply for the sake of his sense of propriety."

"Won't he be angry if'n he comes back an' finds ye runnin' 'bout the house dressed like ye are?"

"More than likely," she conceded, pulling the curtains off the wooden rods. "But it seems to me that his most pressing concern should be whether or not his home is ready for guests. Not what his wife wears while she does the necessary work. I intend to point that out to him should he even dare to bluster."

Meg gave her a doubtful look. Claire jumped off the chair with a grin on her face and the curtains in her arms.

"Lady Cl—"

Knowing the voice, Claire cringed and turned toward the door. It was indeed Mother Rivard who stood there, her gaze fixed on Claire's legs, her eyes wide and her mouth agape.

"Merciful saints preserve us," Meg whispered.

"Oh," Henrietta gasped. She feebly fanned her hands in the vicinity of her face and neck. "Oh, oh."

Claire ignored the I-warned-ye look Meg shot at her and said, "Close your eyes, Mother Rivard. Take a slow breath."

"Oh, dear." She swayed on her feet as the color drained from her face. Then, in a warning Claire had already come to recognize, she pressed the back of her hand against her brow and swayed.

"Take these," Claire instructed, shoving the draperies into Meg's hands. She strode across the room and, unencumbered by a skirt, managed to catch the fainting woman much more adroitly than she had her first night in the house. Shifting her hold on Mother Rivard's limp form so that she held her firmly under the arms, Claire sighed and gave the wide-eyed Meg a weak smile. "This is becoming something of a habit, you know. If we loosen her laces, she'll be all right."

Meg nodded, but didn't move to help. Thinking that an attempt to accomplish the task on the wood floor of the room would be too hard on the poor woman, Claire backed out of the doorway and into the carpeted hall, dragging Mother Rivard along with only the heels of her shoes touching the floor. They slipped onto the carpet, instantly raising clouds of dust and plowing a set of narrow, wavy tracks in the pile.

The elaborate wig began to slip to the side, and Claire twisted her hip in an effort to hold it in place, to preserve what she could of the poor woman's dignity. The top-heavy arrangement tumbled off despite the effort, hitting the carpet amidst a cloud of hair powder and household dust. Mother Rivard stirred at its loss, bringing both hands up to cover the flattened silver strands of her natural hair. The movement instantly compromised Claire's grip on her.

Afraid of dropping the elderly woman, Claire desperately tried to shift her hold. "Please don't—" was all she managed to get out before a bellow reverberated through the confines of the hall. Claire started and Mother Rivard slipped another degree in her hands as Elsbeth stormed up the last of the stairs like a dark avenging angel.

"Breeches? Are you wearing men's breeches?"

"Put compassion before outrage," she retorted, feeling Henrietta slipping further from her grasp. "And help me before I drop her."

Elsbeth stopped in her tracks and glowered. Henrietta stirred again, making a feeble effort to get her feet under herself. Her leverage on the woman precarious, Claire couldn't help her beyond hanging on and offering soft words of encouragement.

"Hold there, Lady Claire. I'm comin'."

"Bless you, Meg," she whispered as the woman reached her side and slipped both arms under Henrietta's back. Together, they tilted the older woman upright and onto her feet. She swayed a bit and then found her own balance. Still concerned for her, Claire lightly wrapped her arm around the woman's waist as Meg eased away and went to retrieve the wig.

"I have never in my life seen anything so outrageous!"

Elsbeth declared with an offended huff. "A woman all but baring her legs for anyone to see! Scandalous. Absolutely scandalous!"

"Let's get you to your room, Mother Rivard," Claire said gently, easing the woman around and facing her in that direction. "We'll loosen your laces and then you can lie down and rest for a bit."

" 'Tis apologizing I am for takin' so long to help ye, Lady Claire," Meg said softly as she took up a position on the other side of Devon's mother. "Me brains were not workin' right for a sad minute or two."

"It's all right, Meg. You recovered yourself just in time. Thank you."

Elsbeth advanced another step, her hands fisted on her cinched and panniered waist. "And what would the world be like if everyone wore the clothes of the other sex, I ask you? What if men went out and about in gowns?"

" 'Tis certain they'd not be marchin' off to wars as often an' as boldly as they do," Meg muttered under her breath. " 'Twould be near impossible to be swingin' a sword while holdin' yer hems up."

Claire grinned at the image Meg had painted as together they guided Henrietta through the open doorway of her room and toward her bed. They'd barely gotten her seated on the edge when Elsbeth stomped into the room, her face flushed and her ebony eyes glittering.

"You...you..."

Trusting Meg to keep a steadying hand on Henrietta's shoulder, Claire turned to face the other woman, arching a brow and waiting for her to finish her diatribe. Elsbeth closed her mouth with an audible snap.

"Would you be," Claire asked coolly, breaking the taut silence, "by any chance, however remote, about to make a positive contribution to the situation? Or would you prefer to stand there and glare at me while I loosen your sister's laces and make her comfortable?"

"You're an abomination," Elsbeth declared, her gaze raking Claire from head to toe. "An embarrassment to all womankind. An affront to the very ideas of femininity, gentility, and grace."

"Undoubtedly," Claire admitted wryly. "But I don't faint when I take a deep breath. And I can work at a pace that doesn't require the driving of stakes to determine forward progress."

Elsbeth's chin came up so fast her wig wobbled. She righted it with both hands and a hard yank, then marched toward the bed, waving Meg aside and snapping, "I'm going to tell Devon about this the instant he returns."

"I had assumed you would," Claire retorted dryly, moving toward the door. "Now if you'll excuse Meg and me, we have work to do."

Meg came out into the hall practically on her heels. "Maybe ye should go an' put yer skirts back on," she suggested in a fearful whisper. "Ye don't want to be makin' Mr. Devon angry. Or killin' his mother."

"Meg, look around you," Claire said, throwing her arms out in a gesture that encompassed the whole house. "Look at all that has to be done before Wyndom and the Lee brothers get here. I can either bow to propriety, put on my skirts, and hamper myself as I dash about trying to prepare this house for guests. Or I can be practical and sensible, wear my breeches, and give myself a slight advantage in the contest we're waging against time and expectation."

" 'Tis a brave woman ye are, Lady Claire. Far braver than me."

"And isn't it a sad comment on the state of the world," Claire countered, moving back toward the guest room, "that a woman is considered brave in choosing practicality over convention. I'll carry the things down for washing if you'll see to cleaning the windowpanes."

• • •

HE'D BEEN A damn fool to sell Hannah, he thought as he watched her come out the back door of the King's Arms, a small traveling bundle in hand. He should have let his mother and Aunt Elsbeth starve to death rather than sell her.

Hannah never changed, he realized as she approached him with a bright smile. She'd been gray haired since he could remember. Her eyes had always been quick and bright, her back so ramrod straight and her shoulders so square that no one ever seemed aware that she was a tiny little woman. A tiny little woman with a temper and a willingness to speak her mind in plain, blunt words. What decency and honor he possessed he owed to Hannah's determination to give him the guidance his parents hadn't. What would it cost him, he wondered, to buy her back from Mrs. Vobe?

More than he had, he knew. And more than he was going to have for some time to come. The money he'd raised in selling her was long since gone—for taxes, for seed, for payment of only the most pressing of his father's debts. And there were more of those bills yet to be paid, the creditors growing less patient with each passing day. The only consolation to be had in the situation was that the remaining creditors were in England and that he didn't owe any one of them enough to make the trip across the Atlantic worth the amount they'd collect at this end of it. If war came soon enough . . .

"Mrs. Vobe tells me you're in desperate straits out at Rosewind, Mr. Devon."

There were many levels to his desperation, but Hannah only knew of one, and he didn't want to trouble her with all the rest of them. He smiled and lent his hand to help her up into the front seat of the phaeton as he replied, "Wyndom's returning from God only knows where and bringing the Lee brothers with him. I truly appreciate your willingness to come back for a few days, Hannah. I've missed you. How are you doing? Are you happy with Mrs. Vobe? With Moses?"

She waited until he'd come around the front of the carriage and was climbing into the driver's seat before she answered, "I'm fine and so is Moses. He's a good, Christian man. Mrs. Vobe's an easy woman to work for, very sensible and generous." She paused to study him, her mouth growing smaller with each passing second. Devon braced himself; he knew the signs of a pending inquisition. He'd endured so many of Hannah's over the years that he'd lost count. There was something oddly comforting about the prospect of yet another. He smiled and waited, knowing that she'd get to where she was going in her own time. Hannah always did things her way.

"You're looking thinner than I remember, Mr. Devon," she said as he picked up the reins. "Haven't you bought a new cook yet?"

"Wyndom did," he answered, setting the horse in motion. "An indentured woman. A month ago."

"Oh, Lord. That boy can't be trusted to choose his own clothes and do it right."

"Her name's Meg," he supplied, grinning. "And she's learning. Rather quickly now that Claire's there to teach her."

"That would be the new missus I've heard about."

And knowing Hannah, *he* was going to hear something about it, too. "What exactly have you heard about my wife, Hannah?"

"That she arrived alone in Williamsburg one afternoon and by the very next she was married to you," she replied crisply. "One story has it that she's with Mr. Wyndom's child and you took pity on her. Another has it that the babe is yours. Yet another is that her family wanted to be rid of her and was willing to cancel a debt Mr. Wyndom owed them if you would take her."

"It's the latter." He shrugged. "With the addition of a few details that don't really matter in the larger scheme of things."

Hannah nodded and fastened her gaze on the road ahead. Devon waited, happy with the comfortable and familiar rhythm of conversation with her.

"Everyone says she's very pretty."

"She is. A bit peculiar at times and decidedly head-strong, but definitely pretty."

"Will she be a good mistress for Rosewind?"

"The food's been edible since she arrived," he conceded. "And the silver serving pieces have been polished. The garden's being planted. Aunt Elsbeth loathes her and Mother blinks a lot."

"Then she's doing fine," Hannah pronounced, clearly pleased with Claire's list of accomplishments. "Will she make you a good wife?"

Devon shrugged again. "As soon as we have documents canceling Wyndom's debt, we're going to have the marriage annulled."

"Hmmm."

"Hmmm, what?" he pressed, knowing that he wasn't going to like whatever Hannah was thinking, but also knowing from experience that wisdom lay in getting the issue out in the clear sooner rather than later. Giving Hannah time to stew only made her words sting that much harder.

"I thought," she said after an exceptionally long pause, "that you were done with that Lytton woman."

That Lytton woman. Devon smiled. He'd never known Hannah to so dislike anyone as much as she did Robert Lytton's young widow. But what did Darice have to do with whether or not he wanted Claire for a wife? He shook his head. "I told you at the time that Darice was a passing flirtation and nothing more. I meant it. Darice and I are done."

Hannah snorted. "You had more than a flirtation with her, Mr. Devon, and all of Virginia knows it. There's no point in you trying to put another face on it."

"All right," he admitted, knowing there was no point in trying to claim good virtue. Hannah knew the truth. What she hadn't seen for herself, he'd told her. "There was more with Darice. But that doesn't alter the present reality. We no longer have a relationship beyond that of being neighbors. I haven't so much as laid eyes on her since the week before you went to Mrs. Vobe's."

She gave him that look of hers—the one that, as a child, had always made him glance down to see if he had telltale cake or cookie crumbs on his shirtfront. "Honestly, Hannah. I haven't seen her."

"So then why are you planning to have your marriage annulled?" she asked, looking straight ahead. "Is there someone other than that Widow Lytton woman?"

"There's no one else, Hannah," he assured her.

"Then why are you willing to throw away a perfectly good wife? She can't be shrewish or she and Elsbeth would be the best of friends. Is she ancient?"

"No, she's only a few years younger than I am."

"Is she a wanton?"

He remembered the look in Claire's eyes as he'd suckled her finger in the dark hall that night. She'd been surprised and, for a moment, frightened. But then . . . She would have been a wanton if he'd asked it of her. And there wasn't a doubt in his mind that, the next morning, she'd have been mortified by the willingness of her surrender.

"I've seen nothing in her behavior to suggest moral laxity," Devon answered tightly.

Hannah cast him a quick glance and then went back to watching their progress through the countryside. After another long lull in the conversation she mused aloud, "You said she was pretty, and she can't be empty-headed if she's ably managing the household and teaching this Meg woman how to cook. What's wrong with her?"

Claire was plainspoken, highly opinionated, and didn't give a damn about conventions and social expectations. She was, he realized with a start, just like Hannah.

"There's nothing wrong with Claire," he admitted quietly.

Hannah nodded and continued to study the road ahead. Devon waited in the conversational silence, his chest oddly tight and his stomach churning. It was akin to the feeling he had when he considered the account ledgers: a sense of being overwhelmed and dreading the gray unknowns of the future. But it was different, too. Beneath this feeling there was a vague sense of hope, of there being a tiny ray of sunshine he might see if he could just claw his way through the dismal clouds surrounding him.

"Then the problem has to be with you," Hannah said, intruding on his thoughts. "What's wrong? Did that Widow Lytton give you a disease?"

"No!" He looked over at her, appalled that she'd even think of the possibility. "For God's sake, Hannah. I know enough to protect myself from the likes of Darice Lytton. I'm not stupid."

She met his gaze unflinchingly and snorted again. "You are if you're not willing to take a good woman to wife when one comes along."

"Hannah," he countered, putting his attention back on his driving, "what do I have to offer any woman other than the likelihood of bankruptcy and public disgrace? Besides," he added, shrugging a shoulder, "a wife is nothing more than another mouth to feed, another body to clothe, and another set of expectations that I can fail to meet."

A nod. Another quick glance at him. "She's been spoiled like your mother and Elsbeth then."

"No," he allowed, shaking his head, remembering what she'd told his family of her childhood, what he knew of her life since being given into her uncle's custody. "Claire's practical and sensible. She knows how to work and is quite willing to do so. And she's yet to ask me for a single thing in the way of material comforts. In some respects, she's a very simple, uncomplicated woman."

"Are you listening to yourself?" Hannah asked, turning on the seat to skewer him with a gaze bright with vexation. He was still drawing a bracing breath when she let loose. "I've known you since you were a little bitty baby, Mr. Devon. I gave you your first bath and I know you and how you think. Marrying this woman wasn't your own idea and it ruffled your feathers something powerful, didn't it? And before you could think things through, you balled up your fist and swore before God and everyone else that you wouldn't tolerate being tethered one more day than you had to be, didn't you?"

"More or less," he muttered, wondering if Hannah had been watching the whole damn thing through Edmund Cantrell's window.

"It was more," Hannah countered with fiery certainty. "And having done that, you can't act on your common good sense without having to make a meal out of a great big crow. You and your pride, Mr. Devon."

"Pride maketh a man blind," he grumbled, not at all happy with the turn the conversation had taken. And he'd been a blind fool to think Hannah would understand about sending Claire on her way when the time came. Hannah had been badgering him to marry for years. As long as the wife wasn't Darice Lytton, Hannah would approve of any woman, sight unseen.

"Just because you can quote me back to myself,"

Hannah countered regally, "doesn't mean that you've learned the lesson in it."

A way out glimmered in his awareness and, desperate, he seized it. "It's not a matter of my pride at all. Claire has a home in England. She wants to go back there."

There was the usual pause as Hannah mulled his words, and in the comfortable familiarity of it, Devon began to relax.

"Does she have a man waiting for her at home?"

The idea was startling. And somehow a little bit troubling, too. "I have no idea. She hasn't mentioned one and I haven't thought to ask."

"If she hasn't told you that her heart belongs to another, then it's free to claim," Hannah declared. She turned to look at him as she added, "And in case no one's ever told you so, no bit of dirt is more important to a woman than the man who stands on it. If you were to swallow your pride, she'd be willing to stay at Rosewind."

It was his turn to snort. "You don't know Claire."

"Answer me this question, Mr. Devon," Hannah replied. "Did she tell you that she wanted to go to this home in England before or after you swore to be rid of her as soon as you could?"

He thought back, remembering the conversations they'd had that first day. Had it only been a week ago? It seemed like a lifetime. "After."

"Then your wife has a bit of pride of her own. And no small amount of backbone and gumption, too." Hannah smiled at the road. "Good for her."

He turned the carriage off the main road and up the drive of Rosewind. "I don't see what pride has to do with her returning to England."

Hannah tilted her face toward the sky in the way she always did when she was asking God to let her borrow the patience of a saint. After a moment, she sighed and asked, "What choice did she have when you were railing on as only you can, Mr. Devon? Was she supposed to fall at your feet and beg you not to be unkind to her?"

Beg? At his feet? He chuckled. "Not Claire."

"No woman worth her salt would. No, her only choice was to hold her head up and say that she'd make her own way and do just fine without you. Whether or not she believes it's possible doesn't matter. It's better to starve to death than throw yourself on the mercy of a man who doesn't want you."

"How do you know all this?"

"These eyes have seen a lot in their sixty years," she answered softly. "These ears have heard many a tale, and these hands have dried a river of tears. I may be old, Mr. Devon, but I'm a woman. It's like I've always said: It doesn't matter what color your skin is—"

"We're all the same underneath," he finished for her.

She smiled and nodded. "And that's how I know what I know. If you backed down a bit, so would she, and the two of you could be happy together."

Rosewind loomed closer and closer and with its nearness came a flood of memories. "My mother and father were strangers when they wed," he said softly, driving the phaeton around to the back of the house. "They didn't choose each other; others chose for them. The circumstances are much the same for Claire and me. I don't want a marriage like the one my parents had." He reined in the horse, stopping in front of the kitchen.

"Well, since you're nothing like your daddy and this Claire sounds nothing like your mama," Hannah observed cheerfully as she waited for him to round the carriage, "I don't think that's anything you need to be all too concerned about. Have you thought about taking up again with that Widow Lytton woman since you've been married?"

He froze, looking up at her, absolutely mystified by

the direction her questioning had suddenly taken. "What does Darice have to do with—"

"Just answer the question, Mr. Devon. Have you thought about riding over there?"

He reined in his frustration and extended his hand to help her down. "Not seriously."

"But it has crossed your mind."

He sighed. "Yes."

"That's good," she declared, grinning up at him, her eyes bright and laughing. "Very good."

"Hannah!" he grumbled, no less confused by her response than he had been by her question.

Poking a fingertip into the center of his chest, she replied, "When it's the smells of your own kitchen that makes your stomach growl, going somewhere else for a meal won't satisfy your hunger. Just you remember that."

Turning and heading toward the kitchen, she added, "I'm looking forward to meeting your Claire. I'll set about the regular cooking, but wait until she and I can talk before I plan anything special for the company meals."

He didn't fully understand what it was she was saying about being hungry, but then he seldom grasped the whole lesson at its presentation. It had always been that way. Hannah would plant the seed; he'd mull over it and eventually realize what she meant and how wise she was.

"Hannah?" he called after her, smiling. He waited until she stopped and looked back at him. "It's good to have you home."

Her eyes were soft and warm and full of love. Just like always. "You haven't had anyone to pin your ears back since I've been gone, have you?"

He thought of Claire. "Well," he began, chuckling. The hard look that came to Hannah's face instantly snuffed his amusement. He followed the line of her sight, turning to see Elsbeth coming down the back stairs, her skirts fisted in her hands and held high above her ankles, her jaw set and her eyes blazing.

"Devon!" she snapped, storming toward him. "I will have a word with you right this instant! This is an outrageous affront to decency, and your mother and I *demand* that you do something about it!"

Devon looked over his shoulder and gave Hannah a weak smile. "Usually by someone without a dram of brains and always about the trivial. I'll bring Claire to meet you as soon as I can."

CHAPTER THIRTEEN

*C*LAIRE STOOD AT THE top of the servants' stairs and surveyed the dimly lit attic. Even in the poor light she could see that it was filled to the rafters with a haphazard maze of discarded furniture, paintings, rolled-up rugs, and stacks and stacks of crates and barrels containing God only knew what. Judging just by the sheer volume of it all, it looked as though enough had been discarded through the years to fully furnish another house the size of Rosewind.

To put things out of use simply because you'd gotten something newer and more fashionable . . . it was a testament to a degree of wealth she couldn't even begin to comprehend. There were only four small trunks in the attic of Crossbridge Manor: one that had been her mother's, one for each of her brothers, one that had been her father's. Each containing the physical proof that they had once existed, each item in them an anchor that kept her memories from drifting away with time.

She smiled wryly as she made her way into the

labyrinth. Did the Rivards even know what was up here? Did any of it hold memories for them? Could anyone lay their hands on the top of the stout maple bureau as she was doing and tell her where it had come from, why it was purchased, where it had been put in the house, who had used it? Could they remember how the little white ring had come to mar its top? Could they recall the things that had once decorated the top of it? The articles that had filled its drawers? It had been four years since she'd been forced to leave Crossbridge, and yet, on dark nights, she could close her eyes and in her mind wander through each of its rooms and see everything, remember everything. The settle in front of the fire in the main room, her father's books piled on the seat, his pipe and tobacco jar on the candle table that always sat at its end. The wheeled chair that was kept in the farthest corner of the room, draped with a pretty cloth, as invisible as she could make it.

Claire shook her head to dispel her somber mood. Despite the tiny white ring in its top, the bureau would match the other pieces in the second guest room and help fill its echoing emptiness. Thinking to make the piece lighter and easier to move, she bent to remove the drawers. The lowest one of the three was filled with neatly folded coverlets and bed linens. She removed each article carefully, breathing deep the scent of lavender and marveling at the richness of the fabrics as she set them aside. Velvets and damasks and satins, the softest wools and the smoothest linens—proof of not only great wealth, but also of exquisite taste and an appreciation for comfort. Opening the other drawers, she found more of the same and added them to the soft mound she was building to the side.

The drawers came out of the chest only with squeaking protests, and as she stacked them to the other side, she couldn't help but marvel at the craftsmanship that had gone into the construction of the whole piece. Time hadn't weakened the joints one bit, hadn't loosened the perfect fit of its components. She glanced over at the stored bedding she'd removed, realizing that, unlike everything in the lower levels of the house, they were clean. No dust had risen as she'd handled them. Just the light and lovely scent of lavender.

It would be so much simpler, not to mention faster, to make up the guest rooms with these items rather than to launder, dry, and iron what she and Meg had removed. There was so much other work that had to be done, and time was short. She knelt in front of the pile and carefully considered what was there, then began arranging items together in a way that pleased her eye. Bedskirts and canopies were all that she was missing. Claire glanced around, knowing they had to be there somewhere and trying to guess in which chest, bureau, crate, or barrel she'd be most likely to find them. Looking would be time well spent, she decided, gaining her feet. She smiled. It would be a treasure hunt in the name of practicality. It was odd how life gave you pleasure in the most unexpected ways and at the most unexpected times.

DEVON QUIETLY POKED his head inside the bedroom door and saw only Meg. He left her to her window cleaning and moved on, checking each room as he made his way down the hall. Lord Almighty, it had been a busy morning in the upstairs of Rosewind Manor. He couldn't remember the last time he'd seen it all turned so upside down and shoveled out. All the beds had been stripped down to the ropes. The windows and floors were just as bare. And precisely where the bedding, curtains, and rugs had gone was as much a mystery to him as where Claire had hidden herself.

No, he corrected as he paused at the end of the hall and looked back the length of it; he knew where the rugs were. Poor Ephram had them hung over a metal bar at the side of the carriage house and was beating both them and himself into exhaustion. The dust cloud had been so thick that Ephram had been made not only almost white by it, but decidedly surly. A rest had helped his attitude a bit, but not nearly as much as the swigs of bourbon they'd shared for "medicinal and fortitudinal purposes."

He had promised to come help Ephram with the rugs as soon as he got Claire back into a skirt and his mother and Aunt Elsbeth placated, but he was answered only with rolling eyes and a disparaging snort. Devon wasn't sure which part Ephram considered an impossibility, and he hadn't asked. He'd had a sinking feeling even then that both were going to end up being severe tests of his patience.

A noise from somewhere overhead interrupted his gloomy thoughts, and he stepped back to look up the stairs leading to the attic. The noise came again: wood scraping against wood. With the whereabouts of everyone else in the house accounted for, it could only be Claire. He muttered a curse, took a deep breath, and climbed the steps.

He stopped at the top, instantly noting the disassembled bureau and the piles of bedding that had been spread out around it. Claire wasn't anywhere in sight, but he knew that she had to be somewhere amidst the relics of his family history. He looked over it all with some dismay—he hadn't been up to the attic in years. Somewhere in the heap was the oaken cradle that had held the last four generations of Rivard babies. But just the legitimate Rivards, he corrected himself ruefully. Given his grandfather's, father's, and Wyndom's proclivities, there were undoubtedly rafts of aunts, uncles, cousins, nieces, and nephews he knew nothing about. And there were probably brothers other than Ephram and Wyndom, too. Maybe even a sister or two.

He smiled wanly. Or three or four or more. The Rivard men had never been known for either self-restraint or accepting responsibility for the consequences of their actions.

He'd always thought it had to be something inherited, some trait that, like the color of eyes and hair, was passed down from father to son and led the Rivard men to throw good judgment to the wind at the mere sight of curving hips, long legs, and a comely face. He'd spent twenty-six years smugly convinced that he'd escaped that one bit of ugly inheritance.

But he hadn't, he silently admitted as Claire stepped from between two large pieces of furniture, her arms laden. Sweet God Almighty, he hadn't escaped it at all. What was it about her curves, her legs, her face that had an impact on him no other woman had ever been able to achieve? What was it about her that stirred the Rivard in him so damn deeply?

God, he had to get this confrontation over and done so he could get a safe distance away from her. Just looking at her heated his blood, made his heart pound, and turned his brain to pudding. "Claire."

She looked up to meet his gaze, her eyes widening and her step faltering for a second. "Oh, hello," she said, recovering enough to turn away and put the armload of what looked to be netting atop the bureau. "Were you able to bring Hannah back with you?"

"Yes, Mrs. Vobe was very understanding," he supplied, ambling toward her so that they could speak quietly enough to keep their exchange private. "Hannah's bustling in the kitchen already. I'll take you down to meet her when you have a moment. She wants to discuss her ideas for the menus with you."

"Someone who doesn't need me to think for them," she said with a dry chuckle. "I could weep with gratitude. Not that Meg's a trial," she hastily added, glancing over her shoulder at him. "It's just that she doesn't know where things are any more than I do. Or, for that matter, your mother and Aunt Elsbeth."

"Speaking of whom," he began, remembering why he'd come up here in the first place.

"Have they recovered from their vapors yet?" she asked, turning to face him squarely.

"I don't think they ever will."

"I'm sorry to have so offended their sensibilities," she offered, leaning back against the bureau and crossing her arms over her midriff. "But there's so much work to be done, and knowing how much more practical my breeches are for moving about quickly . . ." She shrugged one small shoulder. "Well, I decided that sensibility was the most important virtue today."

The linen of her shirt was light and through it he could see that she hadn't bound her breasts. Round and full and firm . . . As virtues went, his better ones were taking a beating. Devon forced himself to swallow, to think of something other than the temptation so casually, so innocently standing in front of him. "I can appreciate being able to move freely," he conceded. "But what if the Lee brothers come through the door earlier than anticipated?"

"They'd be exhibiting very poor manners indeed," she instantly countered. "Guests never arrive before the time the hostess expects them. Never. It's just not done."

"Claire, you cannot run around in breeches," he declared, as exasperated with himself as he was with her. "Yes, I'll agree that they're probably a great deal more practical than skirts, but women simply do not wear men's clothes. To do so is absolutely scandalous. I can't and won't permit it."

She studied the floor at his feet, her lips pursed and her brow furrowed. Devon watched her, waiting. The last time they'd dealt with the subject of her mannish clothes, she'd been vehement about her right to wear them. Such calm now didn't bode well.

"How is your hand feeling?" she asked quietly and without looking up.

He flexed it, feeling only the slightest tightness in the healing skin. "Much better, thank you."

Her gaze slowly rose to meet his. Calmly, easily, she asked, "Is it well enough to do battle?"

God help them both if he had to wrestle her to the floor. "You'd lose, Claire," he warned, his pulse racing.

"So you would like to think," she retorted with a confident smile. Unfolding her arms, she pushed away from the bureau to stand squarely on her feet and add, "One of the most interesting aspects of being male is the notion that all of you should be able to defend yourselves. Traveling can be a most boring enterprise at times, and trading pugilistic techniques seems to be a fairly standard way for men to pass the time."

Devon watched in amazement as she carefully widened her stance, brought her arms up, and fisted her hands in front of her face. He didn't know who had taught her that this was an effective means of fighting, but it was clearly someone who had never had to do it. Her balance was all right, but she was too stiff, her pose too committed to the protection of her face; it left the rest of her body vulnerable to a well-aimed blow. And to a man not as bound to formal, fair play as she was.

"I am ready when you are, sir."

"You can't be serious," he cajoled, easing around to her right.

"I am," she replied sternly as she predictably adjusted her position to remain square to him.

She was so small, so naively fierce, so delectably curved. He lifted his hands, palms outward. "I don't want to hurt you, Claire."

"Then surrender the point."

"I can't do that."

Her chin came up a notch and resolve brightened

her beautiful eyes. "Then you have no other course but to defend it, sir."

"Claire..." He saw the blow coming from a mile away. He grinned, silently giving her credit for pluck even as he easily caught her fist in his hand. As he expected, she instantly shifted her stance and tried to free herself from his grasp. He went with her effort, stepping forward to wrap his arm around her waist while he neatly swept her feet out from under her and drove her back and down.

Squeaking in surprise, she landed just where and how he'd intended—atop the piles of bedding and beneath him. Bearing his weight on his forearms, he looked down into widened eyes, felt the wild thrumming of her heartbeat all along the length of his body.

"This is *not* how men fight each other," she announced, too breathless to be fully indignant.

"No, it's how men best women," he drawled softly, smiling. "Admit defeat and I'll let you up."

Anger flashed in the depths of her eyes. "So that I can go to my room, remove my breeches, and hand them—and my common sense—over to you?"

"Would you prefer to have me take them from you here and now?" he taunted as his own pulse raced to match the cadence of hers.

"It wouldn't be as easily accomplished as you'd like to think, sir," she retorted, roughly pulling her hands from between them, clapping them on his shoulders, and then trying to arch up and throw him off. It was a magnificently seductive friction and his loins instantly hardened in appreciation of her effort. He eased his weight down on her just enough to still her movement, just enough to warn her of the trouble she was courting.

Her breathing ragged and quick, she touched the tip of her tongue to her lower lip and met his gaze to whisper, "You aren't the first man to think that he can—"

"I'm tired of thinking," he whispered back, leaning down to lightly brush his lips over hers. "I can't when I'm around you."

His admission strummed over her senses, bathing her in wondrous relief. She wasn't alone in battling temptation, wasn't the only one whose control was staggering before the powerful onslaught. There was soul-deep solace in knowing that, an eternal snare in surrendering to it. She struggled to grasp the crumbling bits of her reason, to save them both from folly.

"Devon..." Her plea was lost in the slow demand of his kiss, in the gently tightening circle of his arms, the tenderness of his possession. Layer upon layer of heady sensation wrapped around her; the muscled hardness and warmth of the body pressed against hers, the quiet hunger for breath, the gentle murmur of discovery, the sun-warm scent of life, the intoxicating taste of things wild and forbidden and dangerous.

Something inside her bloomed and grew. It had no shape, no color, no taste. And although it made no sound, she felt it beckon in a low whisper across her soul. It drew her forward and inward and out, into a billowing darkness, to a place where the only reality was this man's touch and the gnawing hunger it both created and fed. Powerless to resist its siren call, she abandoned herself to it, to the provocative delight of exploring, of touching, of tasting.

Devon knew he was in trouble. But the part of him that cared wasn't in control. Sweet Christ. He ached to know the full measure of this woman, his temptress wife. She yielded to him, met his demands, and came to him, touched him, drew him to her with a gentle intensity that was more than his flesh and blood could resist.

He eased away to kiss a fiery trail down the slim column of her throat, his hand sliding beneath the linen to savor the ardent heat of her skin, to cup the fullness of her breast. She moaned softly, arching into his embrace, his caress, twining her fingers in his hair, guiding his lips across her satin swell and toward the hardened peak.

"Lady Claire? Are you up there?"

He started, instinctively drawing back to fix the location of the voice. Halfway up the stairs, he realized with another start that jolted his already racing heart.

"Yes, Meg," Claire called out, her voice quavering and breathless. "I'll be down in just a moment. Wait for me there, please."

He looked down into deep blue, anxious eyes. God, he couldn't breathe. Hunger, raw and insistent, ached in every fiber of his being. *Tell Meg to go away. Make love to me, Claire. Make love to me.*

She drew a breath, her entire body shuddering at the effort. With a ragged swallow, she extracted her fingers from his hair and let her hands fall limply into the bedding. "I have work to do, Devon," she whispered, the sound so soft that it barely reached his ears.

It arrowed, however, into his reason, piercing the fog of heedless desire. His heart skittered and ice surged into the heat of his veins. Jesus. Sweet Jesus. How close they'd been to committing madness, how mindlessly and happily he would have tumbled over the edge with her in his arms.

"Of course," he said, rolling off her and onto his feet. He thought to offer his hand to help her rise, but before he could even extend it, she vaulted to her feet and snatched up the armload of netting. For a long moment she stood there, searching his eyes, her breasts rising and falling as she fought to breathe. He could feel the tension in her, could sense that she wanted to explain, to apologize, to promise that it would never happen again. But in the depths of her eyes he saw the same confusion that bound his own words to soul-tearing silence.

"Lady Claire? Are ye all right?"

"Fine, Meg," she answered, taking a step back. She

shook her head, her eyes shimmering with regret, and then turned toward the stairs, adding, "I'm on my way down."

Don't go, the fool inside him called. *Stay with me.*

Devon clenched his teeth and watched her walk away. She was at the top of the stairs before he could make his voice work. "Claire?" She stopped, but didn't look back. "I'm not a saint. In breeches, your curves are entirely too inviting," he said with all the control he could muster. "If you don't want my hands on them again, hide them under a dress. Preferably a very loose one with a bodice that goes all the way to your chin."

She caught her lower lip between her teeth and kept her gaze firmly fixed ahead of her. It was a long moment before she replied, "If you and Ephram would be so kind as to bring the bureau down sometime today, I would appreciate it. If it's not convenient, Meg and I will manage it ourselves."

And then she was gone, bounding down the stairs as if the hounds of hell were nipping at her heels. Devon sank down on the bureau, his legs suddenly too weak to hold him. What was he going to do about Claire? About the searing, witless desire she so effortlessly stirred in him? He couldn't send her away. He didn't have the money to ensconce her at an inn in Williamsburg or anywhere else. And even if he did, he suspected that the distance wouldn't be great enough to keep him from stupidity. England might be far enough, but he certainly didn't have the money to send her there. And he couldn't go away himself. There were crops yet to sow, fields that had to be tended.

Folding his arms across his chest, Devon absently stared at the far wall of the attic. Neither of them could leave; they were trapped together, plain and simple. And just as obvious was the fact that Claire wasn't any more able to resist temptation than he was. The odds weren't good for them being able to stand before a judge and truthfully claim nonconsummation as grounds for annulment of their marriage.

Would having Claire as his wife, in every sense and forever, be such a bad thing? Was there a possibility that they could find common ground after the flames of passion died away? Or would they spend eternity loathing each other as his parents had and regretting that they hadn't resisted a fleeting curiosity?

With a snort, Devon rose to his feet. Maybe what he needed to do before he made any lifelong decisions was to ride over to Lytton Hall. Physical need was definitely clouding his judgment, and although Darice was a lot of things, she had always been fairly good at grounding him in that respect. Yes, that was what he needed to do. There wouldn't be time before the Lee brothers arrived, but after they left . . .

Devon frowned at the cringing of his conscience. Claire was his wife in name only. He hadn't promised her fidelity. He'd promised her an eventual escape. By crawling into Darice's bed, he'd be sparing Claire the possibility of being forever shackled to him. Viewed that way, throwing himself at Darice would be a noble act of self-sacrifice.

It didn't feel that way, he admitted, picking up the empty bureau drawers, but with time he'd eventually accept the rightness of it. And Claire, on the day she was able to leave Rosewind and go home, would be most appreciative of what he'd done for them.

Yes, in a couple of days he'd go see Darice and everything would be all right. His conscience twisted again and as he headed down the stairs he decided that perhaps it would be for the best if Claire never knew about Darice Lytton. He didn't want to hurt Claire any more than he wanted her forever bound to poverty and ruin. She was a good person who deserved better, who deserved to be happy.

• • •

HER SENSES STILL REELING, Claire marshaled her composure as she joined Meg in the blue guest room. "I found some filet canopies and bed linens up in the attic," she announced breezily as she dumped them on the dresser top. "If we use them, we won't have to worry about getting the others washed and ironed in time."

Meg, a dust cloth in hand, tilted her head to the side and quickly looked her up and down. "I thought ye were goin' up to look for a piece or two to fill this cave."

"And I found a beautiful bureau," Claire replied, determined that Meg never guess what had happened on the attic floor. "Three-drawered maple. It'll match the other pieces perfectly."

"Are ye all right, Lady Claire? Are ye not feelin' well? Yer face is flushed."

"I'm fine," she asserted, her pulse racing, her fragile facade crumbling under the strain of pretending. She had to escape, to be by herself, even if just for a little while so that she could settle her jangled nerves. "But I need to leave you to the beds while I go down to the kitchen to speak with Hannah about the meals."

Meg's gaze darted in the general direction of the attic stairs and then came back to meet Claire's. "Mr. Devon's back?"

Somehow Meg suspected; Claire could feel the unspoken questions vibrating in the air between them. And Meg would know for certain if Devon came down those stairs while she was still standing there. Facing Devon again so soon would be impossible. She'd barely escaped the attic without dissolving into tears.

"Yes, he is," Claire admitted, quickly turning and walking away. "If you should see him before I do, would you please show him where we want the bureau placed?" She didn't wait for Meg to answer. "I'll be back shortly."

She added cowardice to the list of her other short-comings as she raced down the stairs, through the foyer, the dining room, and the butler's pantry. It was only when she reached the back steps that she stopped to breathe and face the fullness of what had happened. Sinking down on the top step, she buried her face in her hands and quietly moaned. She knew the rules that governed women's behavior: that they were supposed to resist male advances, even those of their husbands. She also knew what men thought of women who didn't. And she hadn't. She'd seen the likely consequences of being pinned between the bedding and Devon's body, and the only protest she'd been able to muster was to whisper his name in what had amounted to an invitation. After that...

She lifted her face, tilting it up into the afternoon sunlight and trying to draw strength and resolve from its warmth. There was no denying that she was drawn to Devon, that she shamelessly enjoyed his touch. And if Devon's words could be counted as true, he was suffering the same temptations where she was concerned.

Claire closed her eyes. In two months she could be free to do with her life as she willed, free of her uncle's demands, free of anyone's control. For four years it had been the dream that had sustained her, that had made all the heartaches and fears endurable. But the hope of someday owning herself would be lost forever if she yielded to desire. She'd be Devon's wife and the mistress of Rosewind for the rest of her days. He would own her, would confine her—mind, body, and soul—to the narrow bounds of what he considered proper and right.

And she would grow to hate him for it. And herself for having traded freedom for the fleeting hope of love.

"Love," Claire whispered caustically, shaking her head. " 'Fool, not to know that love endures no ties.' " She smiled weakly. "John Dryden."

"There is no fear in love."

Startled by the unfamiliar, unexpected voice, Claire instantly opened her eyes and sat up straight. A small African woman stood on the walk just a few feet away, a hint of gray hair visible under the edge of her snowy white mobcap. How long had she been there?

"But perfect love casteth out fear," the woman went on. "The First Epistle of John. Chapter four, verse eighteen." A smile touched the corners of her mouth, and her dark eyes sparkled. "You must be Mistress Claire."

"I am," Claire replied, rising and returning the woman's smile. "And you must be Hannah."

The older woman nodded and then paused for a moment before saying, "Mr. Devon told me you were a bit peculiar at times. He didn't mention that you wore breeches."

Peculiar? He'd been feeling charitable. "Only on occasion. You're not going to faint like Mother Rivard did, are you?"

Hannah chuckled. "I've never fainted in my life."

"Neither have I." Claire smiled, liking the woman already. "Are you going to lecture me on propriety?"

"Like Elsbeth?" She shook her head. "There are a lot of folks in this world who think being proper is enough to make up for their sins and cold hearts. I prefer good, honest people."

"I'll try not to disappoint you."

"Just don't disappoint Mr. Devon and I'll be content."

The matter of Devon's expectations was one she found acutely uncomfortable. Claire deliberately changed the course of their conversation. "Devon said you wanted to discuss menus with me."

For a long moment Hannah studied her face and said nothing. "I think," she finally, slowly ventured, "that your greatest trouble isn't what the Lee brothers are going to eat. And I'm inclined to think that Mr.

Devon is the cause of the shadows I saw passing across your mind when you didn't know I was here."

There was no denying it. Hannah had seen what she'd seen. "It's not so much Devon as . . ." She faltered, surprised by her inability to find the right words.

"As what, child?"

The words were there; so were the feelings. But they were all jumbled and tangled together, no one clearly distinguishable from the others. It was so confusing, the task of sorting through it all so daunting. "As not being sure of my way, I suppose," she finished with a sigh.

"Life will show you the right road to travel," the other woman assured her, gently patting her arm. "It always does. You'll know it when you see it."

Claire wasn't as certain. "I hope so," she offered noncommittally, summoning a smile. "So tell me, Hannah . . . What would you suggest as appropriate fare for the distinguished guests about to descend upon us?"

Hannah's arched brow said she recognized an effort at evasion when she saw one. "It's been a good while since the Lee brothers were here," she said, graciously acceding. "But I seem to recall that Mr. Richard Henry likes his salsify fried."

Claire didn't have the foggiest notion what salsify was, much less the various means of preparing it. But Hannah clearly did and there was immeasurable comfort in being able to trust someone else's wisdom and experience. It had been such a very long time since she'd had a shoulder to lean on.

CHAPTER FOURTEEN

$\mathcal{D}$EVON LOOKED UP from the column he'd just to-
taled and sighed. "Well, I suppose there's something to
be said for the fact that the balances have been worse."

Not pausing in his entry-making, Ephram muttered
to his ledger, "That's not saying very much, sir."

No, it wasn't, but for some reason the reality of
poverty, unpaid taxes, and impending bankruptcy didn't
depress him this morning the way it usually did. "I'm
trying to find a silver lining in the cloud of despair,
Ephram. We've been through this a thousand times before. I say it's been worse. You agree with me and then
assure me that Rosewind will be debt free by summer's
end."

"Yes, I know," his half brother admitted, laying his
quill aside and looking up to meet Devon's gaze. Cocking
a dark brow, he asked, "But by *which* summer? It certainly
wasn't either of the last two. And looking at the figures, we
can both see that it's not going to be this one. Or the next."
After a brief pause, he added perfunctorily, "Sir."

Devon smiled. "I'm open to any suggestions you might have as to how to make more money."

It was Ephram's turn to sigh. "I don't see any. If all else fails, you could do what Thompkins did. Sell everything and make a grand show of returning to the civilized bosom of our dear Mother England. If you'll recall, your father talked often about leaving Virginia and returning home."

Devon's smile faded. *Your father*. Not *our*. It was never *our* father. Because their father had blindly adhered to cowardly Tidewater tradition and refused to formally acknowledge that Ephram was his son. But he hadn't gotten away with it forever. Devon had created a social scandal when, at the age of twelve, he'd decided right was right and that the only honorable thing to do was publicly admit what everyone already knew—that Ephram was his brother. His mother hadn't risen from her bed for over a month. His father had gone to Charleston for that month and the two that followed it. And in the absence of his parents, he'd faced down his very proper English tutor and firmly installed Ephram in the schoolroom. It had been the wisest thing he'd ever done.

"Our father was an Englishman," Devon pointed out. "I'm not. I'm a Virginian, an American. England isn't my home. Rosewind is and I'm not selling her unless I'm forced to by our father's creditors. We can only hope for good weather, good crops, and outstanding prices."

"That," Ephram agreed, "and that the Lee brothers don't eat us out of house and home while they're here and make all the effort irrelevant."

Yes, and that, too. Devon looked out the study doorway and into the hall, instantly feeling again the sense of wonder that had enveloped him that morning as he'd made his way down to breakfast. The scent of food had been glorious, made even more powerful by the uncommon freshness of the house itself. His feet had actually left tracks in the carpets, and the sunlight streaming through the windowpanes had almost blinded him. The silver sparkled, the copper glowed, and the brass positively gleamed. Furniture had been polished until the surfaces could be used as mirrors, and all of it had been moved about and repositioned in ways that somehow made the rooms seem bigger and more inviting. There was a sense of rightness, a completeness about it all that he had never felt before. Rosewind was a new house, the house she should have always been.

He turned in his chair to see that Ephram had returned to carefully entering numbers into the various columns of the estate ledger.

"When," Devon drawled, "was the last time this house looked as fine as it does today?"

Ephram abandoned his entries yet again and narrowed his eyes in an obvious effort to see into the past. After a moment he shook his head and went back to work, saying, "You'll have to ask my mother. Her memory goes back farther than mine does."

At least it wasn't just him who couldn't recall Rosewind ever having been tended as lovingly as she had been for the last two days. He thought back, remembering bits and pieces of his childhood, trying to find a scrap of memory in which his mother had commanded a brigade of bustling slaves and servants. All he could find, though, were snippets of his father coming triumphantly through the door with carters in his wake, their backs straining under the weight of new furnishings. The old had been hauled up to the attic and supplanted with the new.

Nothing had ever been cleaned or refurbished, he realized. It had always been replaced at the first sign of wear or soiling. Nothing held sentimental value; nothing was important enough to keep or put effort into maintaining. No one, not his grandfather or his grandmother, his father or his mother, had ever put anything of themselves into the nurturing of Rosewind's true possibilities. They had spent money by the handfuls and counted it sufficient to impress those with whom they shared the rarefied air of the Tidewater gentry.

But Claire had come at it differently. She'd rolled up her sleeves and put all of her heart into it. She'd made Rosewind more than mere bricks and mortar, plaster walls, furniture and carpets. She'd made it feel like a home.

"Claire's amazing, isn't she?" he mused aloud.

"Yes, she is," Ephram agreed. "Her breeches notwithstanding."

Her breeches. God, he hadn't thought about them today. Or yesterday, either. He'd actually gotten used to seeing her dashing through rooms and up and down stairs in her fawn-colored breeches. But today the Lee brothers were to arrive, and he couldn't afford to be tolerant of his wife's eccentricity any longer.

"Have you seen her this morning, Ephram?" he asked, rising to his feet.

"I caught a glimpse of her as she raced past me in the dining room earlier this morning. I assumed she had been out to the kitchen to discuss something of great import with Mother. I believe she was headed upstairs at the time to speak with Meg."

"Was she wearing breeches?" he asked, hoping for a reprieve.

"Meg is appreciative of the freedom they afford," Ephram replied absently as he considered an account statement, "but she says that she's too traditional to be so daring. She says she'll allow Lady Claire to blaze the trails for all womankind."

"I meant Claire," Devon explained, frustrated and sensing that the Fates weren't going to be kind to him. "Was Claire still wearing her breeches when you saw her?"

Ephram laid the paper aside and met his gaze with a cocked brow and a half-smile. "Do you honestly think you're going to win that battle?"

He had his doubts, but he wasn't about to admit them. Heading toward the door, he muttered, "I'd better go find her and make sure she's in a gown before the Lees get here."

"Good luck to you, sir."

He heard the suppressed amusement in Ephram's voice and turned back at the threshold. "You could at least *pretend* that you're on my side."

The other laughed quietly and then confessed, "It's rather nice to see someone so openly defy you."

"Everyone in this house defies me. Haven't you noticed?"

"Yes." Ephram grinned. "But Lady Claire is the only one who can truly ruffle you with it. It's been most entertaining to watch you rail and sputter and then stomp off vowing to do something the *next* time you see her."

"She'll be in a suitable gown when the Lee brothers get here," Devon promised, wagging a finger at him. "You can mark my words, Ephram."

"Duly noted, sir."

Duly noted, Devon silently groused as he strode down the hall and toward the stairs. God only knew what he was going to do if she refused to change her breeches for a gown. He suspected that he was going to have a choice between out-and-out begging her to have mercy on his social reputation and wrestling her to the floor of her room and forcibly stripping them from her body. If he had to do the latter, they were both going to regret her obstinacy for the rest of their lives and well into eternity. Of course, he had to find her before he could decide just how badly he wanted to impose his will and social conventions. Deciding that he'd start with her room on the off chance that she might be doing the right thing all on her own, he strode down the hall and stopped in front of her closed door.

With a deep breath to sustain him, he rapped his knuckles against the panel and called, "Claire? Are you in there?" There was a faint sound from the other side. His heart racing, he turned the knob on the door and slowly pushed it open, saying softly as he did, "Claire?"

The sound came again and this time he plainly heard it. Claire stood at the foot of her bed, wearing only a transparent rail and a loose set of stays. Tears were streaming down her cheeks. "What's wrong?" he demanded, pushing the door wide and moving toward her. "Are you hurt?"

"I can't get my laces tied," she sobbed, trying to reach around her back and grasp the ribbons. "Meg's busy. I've tried and tried and ..." She choked on another sob and his heart melted.

"Turn around," he instructed, gently taking her by the shoulders and helping her comply. She was too exhausted to resist, too tired to do anything more than stand in front of him, cry, and let him draw her laces.

"The house looks beautiful, Claire," he said softly. "Neither Ephram nor I can remember when we've ever seen it so clean, so perfectly appointed. You've done a magnificent job."

She scrubbed away her tears with the palms of her hands. Her control was still uneven when she replied, "The thanks go to Hannah and Ephram and Meg. And to you, too. I've worked all of you to death."

"You haven't asked anything of anyone that you haven't been willing to do yourself," he countered, tying off the laces. Gently, he turned her around to face him. Looking down into tear-rimmed eyes, he fought the urge to gather her into his arms. "Why are you doing all this for me, Claire?"

She sniffled, but her smile was soft and gentle and certain. "Because I can."

And because no one else in his world would. His heart swelled. "When was the last time you slept?" he asked, his voice a whisper.

"Last night."

If she had, it had been in some corner of the house where she'd been working. "I meant in your bed, Claire. When was the last time you laid down on your bed and properly slept?"

She took a deep, shuddering breath and looked away. "I don't remember."

"Why don't you lie down and nap until the Lees get here."

"I'm too tired to sleep lightly," she admitted, stepping around him and picking up her dress. "If I close my eyes, I'll be lost to the world for a week."

If she didn't lie down for even a short while, she was going to fall asleep on her feet. He reached out and gently caught her wrist. She stilled and looked at his hand for a long moment before bringing her gaze slowly up to meet his.

Taking the dress from her, he dropped it back on the foot of the bed, saying, "I'm deeply appreciative of all that you've done to make Rosewind—and me—look our best. Thank you, Claire."

She blinked and swayed slightly on her feet. "You're welcome," she whispered, looking away and reaching for her dress again.

He stepped closer and, in one smooth, effortless motion, lifted her into the cradle of his arms. She was light and fit against him as though she'd been molded for that single purpose.

Her own arms slipped up to loosely encircle his neck as she weakly asked, "What are you doing, Devon?"

"I'm putting you to bed," he declared, carrying her

around to the side and tenderly depositing her atop the down coverlet. "Close your eyes and rest. I won't let you sleep overlong. I promise."

She stifled a yawn with the back of her hand. "There's work—"

"There's always work, sweetheart. But what remains to be done can wait for another day." He pulled the far side of the cover over and carefully tucked her under it, loosening her stays as he did so. "Close your eyes."

Her eyelids drifted downward even as she murmured, "I have to do my hair yet."

"Your hair is perfect just the way it is," he assured her, smoothing an errant curl off her cheek. "I'd be pleased if you'd leave it to fall free."

"Unseemly."

"Perhaps. But I like it. The world will just have to adapt for us."

A tiny smile touched the corners of her mouth as she drifted off into the realm of sleep. He stood there, watching her, unable to make his feet carry him away. She was beautiful, both innocence and temptation incarnate. There wasn't a man on earth who wouldn't be drawn to her. But how many of them would see beyond her fair skin and luscious curves, beyond the full lips the color of dark, sweet cherries? How many would see the woman she really was?

His throat tightened as, deep inside, the well of his emotions rose, as a need deeper than he'd ever known took quiet, certain possession of his heart and soul. He wanted to lie with her, to take her in his arms and hold her while she slept. He wanted to cradle her head against his shoulder and burrow his cheek into the silken strands of her golden hair. Yes, hold her and pour his strength into her and make her whole, make her happy.

And God help him, he wanted her to stir in his arms, to smile up at him dreamily and draw him closer, to invite him to love her. Not just her body, but all of her.

Devon closed his eyes, swaying on his feet, his breathing ragged and his heart racing with sudden, unrelenting fear. He was on the edge of an abyss. He could feel it, a beckoning darkness from which he knew he could never return. If he stepped toward Claire, if he took her in his arms, the strangling swell of his feelings would be with him forever. He'd be a prisoner to them, his mind and his reason always subject to the tides of emotion.

No, he couldn't do it. He couldn't face the world as less than a whole man. He'd rather die. There had to be a way back from the precipice, he told himself. There had to be a way to escape, to make the fullness threatening to drown him go away; a way to make him forget that it had ever threatened him.

Darice. He'd pour his attention onto Darice. Yes, that's what he'd do. He'd forgotten all about her in recent days. There had been so much to do. But, yes, Darice was his salvation. To hell with all of his suspicions. He'd immerse himself in the safe realm of mindless, unfeeling lust, and it would sate him. It would crush the weakness that Claire stirred in him. Then she'd go away—back to England—and he'd never have to stand at the edge again. He'd be safe and whole. And the only fears he'd have to face would be those of poverty and social ruin. They had always been with him; he knew them like old friends. They were survivable, endurable. Loving Claire wasn't. It went too deep.

Devon turned and walked away. Yes, Darice. He'd let her ride him until he forgot that he'd ever known a woman named Claire Curran.

MEG SLIPPED QUIETLY out the door, leaving Claire standing alone before the cheval mirror, studying her reflection and frowning. Meg's assurances aside, the bodice of the dark periwinkle damask gown was so dangerously scant and tight that the requirements of modesty precluded bending over, reaching up, or taking a deep breath. And her hips . . . Claire closed her eyes for a few seconds and then opened them again, hoping to see a miraculous change. She didn't; the drastically altered hoops strapped around her waist were still too full to be stylish, and the fact that the skirt fabrics had been drawn up on the sides and fixed with bows would be seen for what it was—an obvious attempt to quickly shorten the length.

She knew that she might reasonably expect the Lee brothers to pretend they didn't notice her decidedly unfashionable appearance. But they would notice; they'd have to be blind not to. Henrietta and Elsbeth would also notice. Their gracious lack of comment couldn't be counted on as surely as that of the Lees, however. Henrietta was likely to innocently blunder into an embarrassing remark. Elsbeth, on the other hand, would probably offer an observation out of pure malice. Which would bring Devon swinging into the fray.

If only there was some way to avoid going downstairs. But there wasn't and she knew it. Wyndom and the Lees would be here any minute, and the master's wife refusing to greet guests would be a social sin far more grievous than that of wearing a peculiar dress. Claire sighed and, resolving to endure the ordeal with all the dignity she could muster, turned and left the safe haven of her room.

She'd barely started down the main stairs when Mother Rivard—dressed for a ball at Buckingham Palace—sailed into the foyer, exclaiming, "They're here! They're here!" Elsbeth scurried in her wake, one hand holding her voluminous skirts high above her ankles, the other holding her towering wig in place.

Claire slowly continued down, her stomach heavy

and tight. She reached the foyer itself just as the two other women came to a skittering, skirt-swaying stop at the front door and deliberately slipped into a masquerade of unruffled, genteel calm. Then they stood there, still as statues, while Ephram came smoothly and sedately from the direction of the study, shooting his cuffs and brushing his coat sleeves with white-gloved hands. Devon followed in his wake, looking dashingly handsome and as though he were being led to his own execution.

With as deep a breath as her stays and bodice allowed, Claire moved forward to join the procession making its way to the door. Devon's attention instantly snapped to her, and his step faltered. She stopped, watching his dismal demeanor slip away as his gaze glided up and down the length of her, caressed the swells of her breasts, and then slowly lifted to meet her own. A smile lifted the corners of his mouth as he crossed the foyer to her.

"You look lovely, Claire," he said quietly as he offered her his arm. "There is no fairer flower in all of Virginia."

A blush spreading over her cheeks, she looked down at the floor and fumbled for words.

"Wyndom! What's happened to you?"

Henrietta's concern instantly called Claire's attention toward the door. Ephram stood to the side, the shiny brass handle in hand, his gaze fixed unseeingly on the opposite wall. Wyndom stood in the doorway, his left arm in a huge sling and his weight largely borne by a cane held in his right hand. His face, swollen and misshapen, was an alarming swirl of purplish red and greenish yellow.

"He's been beaten to a bloody pulp, madam," said a tall, spare man who stepped from behind Wyndom to lay a hand on his shoulder.

Another man, slightly taller than the other and with

more flesh on his bones, stepped to Wyndom's other side to add, "We found him lying in a James City street and felt compelled to patch up the poor blighter as best we could. He was kind enough to invite us to visit in recompense for our being such good and noble Samaritans."

Wyndom tried to smile, but the effort seemed to upset his precarious balance and he began to sway on his feet.

"You poor dear," Henrietta crooned, quickly stepping forward to wrap her arm around her youngest son's waist. Drawing him gingerly across the threshold, she added, "You must retire to your room and do nothing but allow yourself to heal. I'll have Meg bring you something to eat and drink. You must regain your strength."

Claire, remembering that the last time she'd seen Wyndom had been the night Devon had forcibly ejected him from the kitchen, looked up at the man standing at her side.

"I hit him twice and that was all," Devon said quietly, seeming to read her mind without so much as glancing at her. "He didn't look like that when he left here. You can stop glaring at me like I'm a heartless felon. Someone other than me lost their patience with him this time."

"If you will please excuse me, gentlemen," Henrietta offered, glancing back over her shoulder at the two men left standing on the other side of the threshold. "I need to look after my son. I will be forever in your debt for having brought him back into the bosom of his family for care."

Both men bowed and Henrietta eased Wyndom across the foyer toward the stairs, saying, "Elsbeth, please come along and assist me."

Elsbeth clearly didn't want to leave the company of the newly arrived guests, but she managed to curtsy and turn her back to them before her smile turned into an angry pout. Yanking her skirts up, she marched to Wyndom's left side. He winced and gasped as she roughly took his injured arm in hand. Claire cringed in empathy and then looked up at Devon, thinking to suggest that he offer to carry his brother up the stairs and spare the poor wounded man the pain of Elsbeth's resentment and his mother's kindness.

"He'll manage," he said softly, drawing her forward. "It's not the first time he's come home battered and bruised."

And then he lifted his chin a bit and raised his voice to a public volume to say, "Richard Henry, it's been ages. Welcome to Rosewind." He stopped, shook the first man's hand, then turned to the other as he added, "Francis Lightfoot, it's good to see you, too. Welcome and thank you for escorting the prodigal son."

He stepped back, turned slightly, and extended his hand to Claire, saying, "Gentlemen, may I present my wife, Lady Claire Curran Rivard." As he genteelly gestured to the shorter and leaner of the two men, he said, "Claire, Mr. Richard Henry Lee."

She extended her hand in feminine fashion and he took it, bowing crisply and saying, "I am charmed, madam."

"As am I, Mr. Lee."

"Please," he countered, releasing her and straightening to smile. "I would be honored if you would call me Richard Henry."

She nodded and Devon drew her slightly to her left, positioning her for an introduction to the other man

"And his brother, Mr. Francis Lightfoot Lee."

"I'm called Francis," he said, bending over her extended hand. He straightened, but maintained his courtly clasp as he smiled and added, "I'm delighted to make the acquaintance of such a beautiful creature. I shall always consider it my greatest misfortune that Devon met you before I did."

She chuckled softly. "You are a shameless flatterer, sir."

He grinned, winked, released her hand, and gave her an abbreviated bow. "So my wife frequently tells me, madam."

She laughed outright and the dread in her melted away. "Please come in and take your ease, gentlemen," she offered, stepping from Devon's grasp to stand on her own. "There are refreshments set out in the library. I'll leave Devon to entertain you, if you don't mind. I need to speak with Meg about seeing to Wyndom's immediate needs."

"Of course, Lady Claire," Francis replied, deliberately putting a doleful expression on his face. "But please don't deprive us of your lovely company for overly long. We shall pine every second you are away. Our hearts will be empty and—"

"It's his brain that's empty," his brother interjected, rolling his eyes.

Devon laughed. "Shall we fill it with brandy and hope for an improvement?"

"Capital idea!" Francis declared, instantly brightening. "I'm utterly parched."

"I'll bid you a good afternoon, gentlemen," Claire said with a polite curtsy. "If you have need of anything before dinner, please have Ephram relay your request." All three men bowed as convention demanded, and she turned away, moving across the foyer toward the rear of the house and feeling their eyes following her every step.

"They've said she's pretty, Devon," she heard Richard Henry say quietly. "They've clearly done her an injustice. She's as beautiful and elegant as you are fortunate and wise to have made her your wife."

She paused just inside the dining room, out of sight and shamelessly straining to hear Devon's response. It came as a low rumble, the words indistinguishable amidst the thundering rush of her heartbeat. Claire sagged, fighting back a wave of surprisingly deep disappointment.

It was exhaustion, she assured herself as she absently resumed her course. She'd simply worked her brain into such a state of numbness that it couldn't efficiently control her strangely careening emotions. It didn't matter what Devon said to strangers about her, about their relationship. Whatever he said to others would be something polite and well within the bounds of social expectations. It was absolutely foolish to think that he might confess how the combination of physical attraction and a well-functioning household was changing his mind about his wife, that he was considering the merits of making their marriage a very real and permanent one.

It was even more foolish to hope that he would, she warned herself as she slipped out the back door.

CHAPTER FIFTEEN

*H*E WAS HAVING the damnedest time keeping his awareness focused on the conversation. Images of deep violet eyes, dreamy smiles, and silken swells kept drawing his mind down paths other than that of being an attentive host. Devon blinked and forced his mind back to his guests. Francis, an empty brandy snifter in hand, was seated in the chair by the window that overlooked the drive. He was watching his older brother, hands clasped firmly behind his back, pace back and forth across the width of the room.

"... establish committees of correspondence for the sharing of information and the coordination of colonial resistance to Crown policies."

Ah, yes, Devon thought, taking a sip of his own nearly full glass of brandy. Richard Henry never strayed far from his passionate interest in the preservation of colonial rights. This particular diatribe was the likely result of his having recently heard from Sam Adams up in Boston. From what Devon had been able to see so far,

Richard Henry and the Bostonian thought a great deal alike on the only issue that mattered to either one of them. Setting up a colonial system of communication was something that both men felt vital to the effective defense of colonial liberty. It had been Richard Henry's primary topic of conversation since the news of the Boston Tea Party had reached Virginia.

"There is a rumor that Parliament is debating a bill that would severely punish Boston, indeed all of Massachusetts, for her failure to pay for the tea destroyed December last."

Devon stared down into his glass, trying to look as though he was surprised and distressed by Boston's predicament. The truth was, however, that he wasn't. And he wasn't going to be any more stunned when they capitulated at the first threat of force. As for distressed... His countrymen's lack of backbone had long dismayed and disgusted him. He'd ceased letting it bother him. It was wasted concern.

"If I might intrude on your conversation, gentlemen..."

He looked up to find Claire framed by the doorway. Smiling at him softly, she added, "With sincere apologies for my inadvertent eavesdropping." She turned toward Richard Henry. "The bill of which you speak has no doubt already passed through Parliament."

The man froze in his tracks. "Are you sure? How do you know this?"

"My uncle is a member of the House of Commons," Claire explained as she eased into the room. "His fellow members frequently come to his home to discuss pending legislation and their strategies. I left England in early March. The night before the day I sailed, my uncle and his friends had a celebratory dinner where they toasted the wisdom and backbone of Lord North and lauded what they expected to be swift passage of the Boston Port Bill."

Since neither Richard Henry nor Francis Lightfoot seemed capable of doing anything more than staring dumbly at her, Devon asked, "Do you know anything of the specific provisions of that act?"

With a nod, she explained, "Boston Harbor is to be closed to all trade until the citizens pay for the tea they destroyed. To that end, the Royal Navy will establish a blockade and General Gage is to be moved from Philadelphia to occupy the city."

"Armed soldiers in the streets again," Francis muttered. He made a *tsk*ing sound. "Boston has ugly memories of the last time the Crown imposed occupation. General Gage's return won't go well."

Claire glanced at the other two men, but addressed her reply to him. "The feeling is that if the merchants' purses can be sufficiently starved, they'll quickly withdraw their support of the radical elements and cross to the side of the King."

"Under most circumstances," Richard Henry said, "and in most places, that would be a logical assumption. But Boston is a world apart from other places, and her circumstances are unique. She will not buckle."

Claire glanced at Richard Henry and then back to Francis. Devon saw not only hesitation in her eyes but the spark of intellectual spirit. His heart oddly light, he raised his snifter to her in salute, saying, "Please speak freely, Claire. Tell us what you think."

She gave him a smile of appreciation and then turned to face Richard Henry Lee. "There are other bills pending in Parliament, and given the conversations I've heard over them, I think it likely that they'll be passed within the next few weeks and months. All of them are designed to break not only the spirit of Boston but of colonial unrest as a whole. Massachusetts is to be the example from which all of you are expected to learn an important lesson."

Richard Henry appraised her in silence. Francis

wasn't as provident. "Do continue, Lady Claire. You have our full attention."

Indeed she did, Devon silently mused, wondering why he suddenly found the conversation more interesting.

"There is a bill," she went on, still addressing the silent Richard Henry, "to my knowledge yet untitled, concerning the administration of colonial justice. Under it, high royal officials accused of capital offenses would be tried in England, not in the colonies, as is the current allowance."

"In England," Devon observed, "they're far more likely to be acquitted than they would be if tried among those whom they've abused."

"Precisely the intent," she replied, giving him another smile. "There's another bill pending that would allow the governor to appoint colonial officials that are presently elected by the people themselves. It would also give the governor the authority to limit the meetings of the colonial legislature to once annually and give him the sole power to set that body's agenda."

Francis said softly, "That would abrogate the original charter on which the colony was established."

Richard Henry finally joined the conversation by slamming his fist into the palm of his hand and bellowing, "It would be the end of colonial self-rule!"

Claire winced and with obvious regret added, "There's also—"

"Good God," Devon groaned. "There's more?"

"Yes," she admitted. "An amendment has been proposed for the present Quartering Act. Under the new provisions, the citizens of a colony would be required to house His Majesty's armies in privately owned and occupied buildings."

"In other words, our homes," Francis muttered. "Our businesses."

"We would be required by law to host the spies among

us!" the other Lee roared in outrage. "To feed them at our own tables and at our own expense!"

Devon sighed and with a wave of his hand called his wife's attention away from the irate man who was once again pacing the width of the room. "Is Lord North deliberately trying to drive us to armed rebellion?"

She considered him for a long moment, her lips pursed. "Pitt and Burke have repeatedly argued that there's more to be gained in allowing the American colonists to govern themselves as they always have," she began. "They hold that the resources of the various colonies benefit the mother country to such a degree that it's in England's best economic interests to tolerate the independent-mindedness of the colonists. Pitt and Burke are both of the opinion that Lord North doesn't understand either the colonial perspective or the likely consequences of trying to manage the American colonies in the same manner as all others."

"In reading the London papers," Francis said, leaving his seat to stand beside Devon at the cold hearth, "we see that the English people agree with Pitt and Burke and that Lord North's punitive legislation is decidedly unpopular."

"Yes, to a certain extent you're correct," she allowed. "The Boston Port Bill is—or was, depending on its current status—debated in secret so that the members of Parliament wouldn't have to fear for their persons should it become public knowledge. Support for the Boston Tea Party is strong among the common people."

"But," Devon rejoined dryly, "it isn't the common people who hold the reins of power and enact the laws."

"No, it isn't," she said sadly. "The members of Lord North's cabinet and of Parliament are all men of business or property. Their chief concern is that in not tightening the reins on the Americans, the colonists will take it into their heads to enact legislation that would cancel the debts they owe to British merchants and investors.

Should that happen, they'd be impoverished. Better that the Americans should suffer than themselves."

"Are you sure that these measures are being seriously considered in Parliament?" Richard Henry asked, his gaze riveted on the carpet passing under his feet. "Do you know that they have a reasonable chance of passage?"

Once again she hesitated, her gaze searching Devon's for some sign of just how far the social conventions of his world allowed her to go. He lifted his brandy glass again in silent assurance. Her smile was soft; the light of gratitude in her eyes, blinding.

"Prior to coming to the colonies," she said to Richard Henry, "I was frequently engaged in the conduct of my uncle's business affairs. Given the nature of transportation and communications, I would often find that circumstances had shifted between my departure from England and my arrival in whatever place I was to transact his affairs. In order to make adjustments for those changes to my uncle's advantage, it was necessary for me to be aware of the general direction of both imperial policy and its economic impacts. To that end, I was always ensconced in a dark corner of his study to listen and learn from his discourse with his parliamentary colleagues."

Devon snorted and muttered, "Never to be heard from on the various topics, of course."

She nodded. "In the Seaton-Smythe household, women are seldom seen and never heard."

It occurred to Devon that her uncle was extremely myopic. Seaton-Smythe had had an excellent mind at his disposal and either didn't recognize the fact or refused to utilize it because it was inside a female head. His gain was Seaton-Smythe's loss, he thought as Claire continued.

"Yes, Richard Henry, I'm certain of the provisions of the pending legislation, the sentiments behind their proposal and consideration, and the likelihood of their eventual passage. Boston will be made to suffer for her impudence. And the intent is for all of the colonies to become—sooner rather than later—subject to the same limitations and control being imposed in Massachusetts."

"We won't tolerate being stripped of our liberties, of the rights of Englishmen," Francis said forcefully. "We can't."

"If England doesn't correct her course," the older Lee mused as he paced, "we'll have no choice but to pick up arms in defense of our freedoms."

Or so Richard Henry Lee and Sam Adams hoped. But if it did eventually come down to armed rebellion, then there were important factors meriting serious consideration. "In your estimation, Claire," Devon drawled, squinting into his brandy, "how stalwart are Pitt, Burke, and the English people in their support of the colonial cause?"

"Pitt and Burke are, at their core, members of the aristocracy. They'll support you only so far. They can't and won't argue for your right to armed rebellion. You would, after all, be committing treason, and anyone who stands with you is likely to be hanged with you as well. Given that, the vast majority of the propertied class will also step back and come into line with Lord North's expectations. Only the very poor will rally to your flags. And, to my thinking, the poor have little they can contribute that could affect the outcome to your benefit."

Her ability to analyze situations exceeded the capabilities of most of the men he knew. If only the discourse in the House of Burgesses were as interesting and informed as the one she'd brought into his study.

"Do the British understand that we have no real desire to be fully independent of the King's rule?" he asked, knowing that only Claire could give him an accurate answer. "Do they know that all we want is the preservation of the liberties we've enjoyed since the first Englishman set foot on this shore?"

"In all honesty, Devon," she replied gently, "they see the colonists as lacking sufficient courage to truly break the bonds that tie you to the mother country. They believe that when pushed to the edge of the precipice, you'll choose to submit rather than jump to your certain deaths."

"I wish I could say that I knew them to be wrong. But for every stalwart heart, there are ten faint ones."

Francis softly cleared his throat. "Where do you stand on the issue of colonial resistance, Lady Claire?"

"Freedom is a very precious thing. To my mind, it's more valuable than gold and jewels and all the money in the world. But is it more precious than life itself? That's a difficult choice."

"You haven't answered the question, Claire," Devon pressed, for some inexplicable reason desperately wanting to hear her say that she'd don her breeches and pick up arms for the cause of liberty. "Where do you stand?"

"I haven't yet decided."

The admission hurt in a way he couldn't quite fathom. His spirits sank, wrapped in an overwhelming feeling of being adrift and utterly alone.

Richard Henry ceased his frantic pacing and from across the room asked, "What concerns are you still pondering, Lady Claire?"

Her chin came up a notch and she took a breath and moistened her lips before replying, "I have many of them, sir. On the one hand, I agree that the colonists are being denied the basic rights of Englishmen and have cause for protest on all fronts—economic and political and philosophical. Your repeated protests and reasoned, earnest pleas for equality and fairness have fallen on deaf ears. I understand how you've become frustrated and desperate enough to resort to more violent acts of protest."

"Understanding doesn't necessarily mean that you approve."

"Cause and consequence go hand in hand, sir. As you escalate your resistance to the rule of the Crown, the Crown becomes more determined to bring you to heel. The plight of Boston serves as a prime example of that. If Boston doesn't capitulate—"

"And she won't," Richard Henry assured her.

Claire shrugged slightly. "If Boston won't compromise, the Crown won't either and there'll be no chance of avoiding bloodshed. Men will die. Fathers, husbands, sons, brothers. And women will grieve for them. An entire generation—American and English alike—will always bear the scars of loss on their hearts. And for what?"

"Liberty," Richard Henry answered, his dark eyes afire.

"The right of free men to govern themselves," Francis offered calmly.

Devon snorted. "Pride."

"Yes, Devon," she countered, meeting his gaze somberly. "When it comes down to it, it's pride. And I have to ask myself why it is that women and slaves and indentured servants are expected to meekly surrender their pride and accept a status that free white men of wealth consider so intolerable as to be worth resisting to the cost of their very lives. That, Richard Henry," she added, turning back to him, "is the central issue which prevents me from declaring support for your cause. You profess a passionate devotion to liberty, but you intend for that liberty to be enjoyed only by men like yourself— wealthy and white."

Devon held his breath, watching Richard Henry fairly vibrate with anger. Dear God, what had he been thinking in encouraging Claire to freely speak her mind?

How could he have forgotten her unconventional views on the doctrine of natural rights? Richard Henry was renowned as a passionate, capable, no-quarter debater. Claire had stirred a hornet's nest.

"I will remind you, Lady Claire," Richard Henry said icily, "that we cannot give to others what we don't possess."

"With all due respect, sir," she shot back, her tone coolly belying the spark of anger in her eyes, "liberty is not yours to grant. It is the birthright of every man and every woman. To place yourself in the position of allowing or denying freedom to any human being, you're claiming for yourself the very right you refuse to let the King have over you. How can I, as a woman, support your resistance of despotism? In the end, would I not simply be trading one despot for another?"

"I will remind you," Richard Henry retorted, squaring his shoulders and stiffening his back, "that not all men are tyrants, Lady Claire."

"By the same token," Devon observed quietly, "not all men are benevolent. I can see the soundness of your logic, Claire. It pains me, but I can see it."

"Thank you," she replied, her smile small but conveying her appreciation for his alliance. "I'll continue to examine the colonial cause with an open mind and some sympathy. But I must be honest and say to you that I'm unlikely to stand with you unless I have good reason to believe that the liberty for which we would all fight is liberty which we will all enjoy."

Before Devon or the others could muster a reply of any sort, she graciously swept the three of them with her gaze, smiled prettily, and bobbed a curtsy as she said, "And I will now leave you gentlemen to your brandy and conversation. Dinner will be served in a few minutes, sirs."

Devon watched her go, a smile slowly spreading

across his face. Damned if she hadn't stood up to Richard Henry Lee and held her own. She hadn't needed him to step into the fray in support of her beliefs and ideas. But she'd appreciated him for doing it, which was warming in the strangest, most intoxicating way. Or, he reminded himself, looking down, it could be nothing more than an effect of the brandy.

"Rivard," Francis said, "that is a most unusual woman."

"She does know her own mind."

"And she obviously has no qualms about voicing it," Francis observed, chuckling softly. "She sounds very much like Tom Jefferson. Although her voice is better for public speaking than his will ever be. You do have your hands full, don't you?"

Devon's smile broadened. "I'll admit that life has been considerably more interesting since she arrived at Rosewind."

"She's right, you know," Richard Henry declared, moving to the desk to retrieve his brandy snifter. "There will be war. It won't come tomorrow. Perhaps not even this year or the next. But there will come a day when the Crown will demand that we choose between our principles and peace. You both know the hearts of our countrymen as well as I do. You know that we'll choose to pick up our weapons and fight for principle."

"No, I don't, Richard," Devon admitted, his good mood evaporating. "For the last twenty years we've endured policies and laws that have been directly contrary to our best interests in every respect. We've paid the taxes to support an army among us, an army that's supposed to protect us from native attacks but doesn't venture outside the safe and secure comforts of our cities. We've surrendered the taxes to pay the wages of colonial administrators who care nothing for the quality of our lives and everything for that of the King and his ministers. For the sake of the privilege of being an oft-abused part of the British Empire, we've allowed the erosion of our freedoms and rights in every facet of our lives.

"And what have we done about it?" Devon went on. Not allowing the other man time to respond, he answered his own question. "We've stomped our feet, shaken our fists, railed at the injustice of it all, then written polite letters to the King and his ministers asking them to please give some consideration to being a bit nicer to us. Tell me why we'd suddenly find our backbones and stand up like men."

"It won't be sudden, Devon," Richard Henry assured him. "It will happen in increments. Slow, decidedly painful increments. But with the passage of the Boston Port Bill, the die has been cast. Boston will not back down. We won't let her. The Crown will press harder and we'll press back. We've endured these last twenty years to learn our lesson well. What we willingly give, the King demands tenfold. We have reached the point of having nothing more to give, the point of having nothing to lose and everything to gain. War will come, Devon."

From beside him, Francis asked, "What will you do, Devon, if your wife can't bring herself to stand at your side when war comes?"

"I don't know," he answered, his mind wrestling with the decision of just how much to tell the Lees about his relationship with Claire. Part of him knew that the testimony of any Lee in annulment proceedings would tip the scales in his favor. To that end, he ought to tell them the entire truth of how he and Claire had come to be married and their determination to go their separate ways at their first opportunity. And yet he didn't want to. Every fiber of his being said the matter was a private one, no one's business but Claire's and his own.

"Do you think that she would return to England

and petition the Crown for a divorce?" he vaguely heard Francis ask.

"Which she would likely get," Richard Henry pronounced. "Being the wife of an avowed rebel would gain her great sympathy from the bench. I imagine that it would be difficult to see her leave, though. She's a most beautiful and intelligent lady."

"She is. And it would," Devon admitted absently, his mind reeling through a myriad of stunning possibilities he'd never even imagined before that moment.

SHE'D NEVER HOSTESSED a dinner party before, but Claire thought it was going fairly well. If the Lee brothers had noticed that the butler and the doorman were the same person, they were polite enough to refrain from mentioning it. They were equally decorous—or blind—about the upstairs maid who was serving them their dinner. Meg was doing a beautiful job of it, and every forkful of Hannah's food had been exclaimed over by their guests.

Devon sat at the opposite end of the table, his mother on his right, Elsbeth on his left. The Lee bothers had been seated at Claire's end, with Francis Lightfoot sitting across from Elsbeth and Richard Henry opposite Mother Rivard. All in all, the seating seemed to allow for easy conversation. Or it would have if anyone but Elsbeth could have gotten a word in edgewise.

"Everyone was there, of course," Elsbeth was saying. "Mr. Custis, God rest his soul, was such a wonderful dancer. We made a marvelous pairing in the quadrille. Despite what everyone says, I do believe he was every bit the equal of Mr. Washington in any Virginia ballroom. Which of course explains why Mrs. Custis, after the death of her dear, dear husband, was so quickly attracted to Mr. Washington. A man who both enjoys and excels at dancing is such a rare creature, don't you agree, Francis Lightfoot?"

Francis Lightfoot Lee, every inch the Tidewater gentleman, smiled, nodded, and murmured something indistinguishable but undoubtedly polite.

Elsbeth smiled and fluttered her lashes, and in the precious lull of silence, Richard Henry Lee turned to Devon and abruptly changed the course of the dinner conversation. "I understand that you're not planting tobacco this year, Devon. That you're experimenting with farming instead."

"I'm planting a variety of crops," he replied, "trying to see which might be best suited to our climate and our market opportunities."

"Devon?" Elsbeth gasped, her hand pressed to the base of her throat. "You're a *farmer*?"

"There's no shame in farming, Mistress Whittington," Francis quickly assured her. "The last time I was at Mount Vernon, Colonel Washington and I spent a great deal of time discussing the coming necessity of crop diversification. Devon is simply ahead of the rest of us in venturing along the new trail."

"And I, for one," Richard Henry added, "am most anxious to hear the results of your experiments. As I'm sure others are. You'd best be prepared to give a full accounting when the House next comes into session. Everyone will expect it."

Devon shrugged and reached for his wineglass. "I doubt that I'll have much to say. I'm still planting the fields. It'll be late this fall before I know the true worth of the endeavor. Claire believes that it'll be quite profitable, though." He lifted his glass toward her, adding, "I hope that I don't disappoint her."

She heard sincerity in his voice, saw the soft light of admiration and respect shining in his eyes. To know that her opinion mattered to him was somehow settling. "I have complete faith in you, Devon. Disappointing me isn't possible."

At the edge of her vision she saw Elsbeth frown. "I thought Lady Claire was planning to return to England in August."

"The possibility has been discussed," Devon admitted with a reassuring smile at the startled Lee brothers. "But circumstances frequently require adaptations. Do they not, Claire?"

"Yes, they do," she answered, wondering what had caused the drastic change in his manner. If she hadn't known better, she would have thought he was genuinely trying to court her affections. "The challenge is to see the advantages in the new situation and accept the change with grace and dignity."

"I would imagine," Elsbeth offered caustically, "that you usually find that exceedingly difficult, if not impossible, to do."

Francis and Richard visibly squirmed, then quickly tried to cover their reaction by focusing their attention on their plates. Devon, his dark eyes flashing, slammed down his wineglass. As he did, his mother looked at Claire and silently begged her to do something to avert the impending scene.

Without time to think, Claire hastily quipped, "Not everyone is gifted with an imagination, Elsbeth." She offered what she hoped passed as a sympathetic smile. "Please don't let your lack bother you. It's nothing to be ashamed of."

Elsbeth drew herself up regally and glared at her, her face mottling with suppressed anger.

Devon smiled and lifted his wineglass yet again, saying, "A toast, gentlemen." He waited until the Lees had raised their glasses before continuing, "To Claire and the beauty and spirit she's brought to our life here at Rosewind."

"To Lady Claire," they said in chorus as they lifted their glasses in her direction. Francis's smile was broad and impish. Richard Henry cocked a brow and winked in wordless congratulations.

"Thank you, one and all," she offered, heat suffusing her cheeks. "But I've done nothing beyond what any wife would do."

"Any *good* wife, Lady Claire," Francis corrected. "Good wives are few and far between. Devon is most fortunate to have found you. I do hope that you're planning to accompany him to Williamsburg when the House goes into session. It's quite the social occasion and I'd welcome the opportunity to introduce you to my own lovely wife."

"And I, mine," his brother added.

She didn't have the wardrobe required for socializing with the wealthiest women in the American colonies. "I look forward to making their acquaintance," she offered diplomatically. "I hope our respective duties will permit our meeting."

"Oh dear," Mother Rivard exclaimed. "Three weeks. That doesn't allow us much time to acquire a suitable wardrobe for you, Lady Claire. I suppose all we can do is travel to James City and throw ourselves on the mercy of a kindly dressmaker."

It would be cruel to let the woman plan and look forward to something that would not, could not happen. "There's far too many tasks needing my attention at Rosewind for me to be traipsing off to James City for new gowns, Mother Rivard. What I already have will do."

Henrietta blinked and knitted her brows. "But..."

"Lady Claire, you are a rare gem." Francis laughingly declared, reaching out to take her hand in both of his. "I beg you to impart your philosophy to my wife when you meet her. I'd be forever grateful if you could spare me the expense of her twice-annual purchasing forays."

"I'll do my best, Francis. It's all that I can promise."

"Should Devon ever prove himself the utter fool and cast you aside..." His smile broadened and he leaned closer. "I have an unmarried son who's every bit the handsome devil your husband is."

Claire chuckled. There wasn't another man on earth the equal of Devon Rivard in any respect. "I'll be mindful of the option, sir."

From the other end of the table, Devon laughed. "You might also be mindful of the fact that his son is all of ten years old."

"Eleven this July," Francis amended. "And at the age, I might add, where he's still somewhat malleable."

Claire looked across the table at Devon and smiled. "Malleable would be nice."

Devilment sparkling in his eyes, he grinned and replied, "Wouldn't it, though."

An unexpected warmth spread through her, deepening the sense of peace that had settled over her earlier. Whatever the reason for Devon's courtly manner, she enjoyed the effect. Having him openly appreciate and admire her...She would remember it forever as the most singularly wonderful evening of her life.

CHAPTER SIXTEEN

*D*EVON BID HIS GUESTS good night at their chamber doors and made his way down the dark hall. Three brandies, a couple of cheroots, and—through the course of the fourth and fifth brandies—a heated debate with Richard Henry over the philosophical merits of extending the concept of natural rights to include women... Yes, it definitely had been an evening of excess. And he'd enjoyed it immensely. In fact, he couldn't remember when he'd finished a day with such an utter sense of satisfaction.

He couldn't keep from smiling. His house sparkled, radiating elegance and heartfelt care from top to bottom. Each course of dinner had been a culinary masterpiece. His guests were not only comfortable, but openly appreciative of the genuine warmth of his hospitality. And he owed the wonderful state of his mind—indeed, his world—all to Claire. Beautiful, sweet, competent, charming, intelligent, articulate Claire. The perfect hostess, the perfect wife.

His step faltered as realization struck him. It was the brandy, he told himself. Brandy combined with the heady rush of a spirited debate and too much tobacco smoke. His brain was foggy and he'd be a damn fool to make any long-term decisions while in his present state. Besides, a man ought to be stone-cold sober when asking a woman to be his wife in every sense of the word. If for no other reason than to assure her that she wasn't agreeing to spend a lifetime tethered to a drunkard. And Claire certainly deserved better than that. She was the best thing that had ever happened to him or to Rosewind.

The smile returned to his face. Thanks to George Seaton-Smythe's conniving and ingratitude—not to mention his own desperation—he'd received the brightest bit of luck of his life. Who would have thought so that terrible morning in Edmund Cantrell's office? He certainly hadn't. And neither had Claire. Had she, too, changed the way she felt about their marriage? Considering the tender regard in her eyes that evening at dinner, how easily she'd laughed . . .

Devon looked along the hall, deciding that if there was light spilling from beneath the lower edge of her door, he'd hang good sense and sobriety. The worst she could do was refuse to discuss anything with a man obviously a sheet or two to the wind.

There were two bands of light weakly spilling out into the darkness, Claire's near the end of the hall on his own side and Wyndom's on the opposite wall and some distance closer. Devon considered them both and his optimism ebbed away. Talking to Claire would have to wait until later. He needed to speak with his brother, to find out what had precipitated the beating in James City and what the likely repercussions would be for Rosewind. Maybe, if God was feeling unusually kind, this time there wouldn't be any.

Stepping up to his brother's door, he knocked, deciding that if there was anything that would sober him quickly, it would be a conversation with Wyndom. He winced at the call for him to enter, wishing that it hadn't come, but resolutely turned the knob and pushed open the door, saying, "I saw the light coming from under the door and thought we might talk if you're up to it."

Propped up against the headboard, his back cushioned by a sea of feather pillows, his brother quipped, "Please, Devon. You saw the light under the door and decided that as long as I was awake, there was no point in putting off till tomorrow the bludgeoning you could do today."

"It would appear that I'm not the first in line for the privilege," Devon countered, leaning his shoulder against the jamb and crossing his arms over his chest.

"But you're far better at it than anyone else."

Wyndom's battered, swollen face and the sling on his arm testified otherwise. Pointing that out, however, wouldn't accomplish or resolve anything. Devon sighed and stared unseeingly at the wood floor between himself and Wyndom's bed. "Might I ask who pummeled you in James City and why?"

"No one you know and it was over a debt."

"A gambling debt," Devon supplied, knowing all too well the pattern of his brother's folly. He brought his gaze up to meet Wyndom's and gently asked, "Has it ever occurred to you that you're not a very good card-player?"

"I suppose you're better than I am at that, too."

How could a grown man stand to hear himself whine like a boy in short pants? "Hell, Wyndom," he answered, suddenly too weary to be exasperated or angry. "Everyone's better than you. Why do you persist at gambling when you never win? When huge debts and a battered body are all it ever gains you?"

"I enjoy it."

"You enjoy losing? You enjoy drowning in debt? You enjoy being physically beaten?"

"You don't understand."

"Well, you're right about that. I don't understand. And I never will," Devon admitted, accepting, deep down inside, that he was never going to be able to change Wyndom; the die had been cast long ago. He could reason, bellow, plead, and rescue until he took his last breath and it wasn't ever going to make a difference in his brother's attitude and behavior. All he could do was limit the damage. "What's the sum total of your current debts? Do you have any idea?"

"No."

Of course not. Thinking about it would require facing reality for a moment or two. "How much do you owe the man who battered you in James City?"

"Nothing," Wyndom snapped. "The matter's been resolved to his satisfaction."

The hair on the back of his neck prickling, Devon observed, "Somehow I don't think the satisfaction of bloodying you was sufficient for payment, either in part or in full. You can't spend satisfaction at the local tavern."

Wyndom haughtily countered, "You might be surprised by what some people will gratefully take in trade."

Jesus. He was tired of traveling this same old path. Resolving that this was going to be the last time he did, Devon asked, "And just what do you have of value to trade, Wyndom? You don't own a damn thing."

"As you are ever so fond of constantly reminding me."

"That's because you keep forgetting it."

"I have my wits and my resourcefulness," Wyndom snapped, sitting up straight in bed, his pale blue eyes sparking with resentment. "It will no doubt surprise you to learn that some people consider my abilities to be of considerable merit. Of more merit than mere material goods and possessions."

"And just how," Devon drawled, "have you used your vast wits and resourcefulness to this James City person's advantage?"

Wyndom settled back into the pillows with a sardonic smile. "That, dear brother, is none of your business."

Dread, cold and leaden, settled in the pit of Devon's stomach. It *was* his business; he could sense it gathering like a storm on the horizon. Dear God, he didn't have the resources or the strength to weather another one. There was only one way out. Resolved to do what he must, Devon said sadly, "I'm afraid that you've backed me into a corner, Wyndom."

"There's a first," his brother replied flippantly. "We should note it in the family Bible."

"That can be done if you'd like," Devon conceded, pinching the bridge of his nose to ease the dull ache blooming in his head. "I'll have Mother slip the notice between the pages for pressing."

Wyndom blinked and looked concerned for the first time since Devon had entered the room. "What notice?"

Devon met his brother's gaze and gently but firmly answered, "You've left me with no choice but to publicly announce that I'm not responsible for your debts—past, present, or future. I'm going to have a legal notice to that effect published in every major newspaper in the colonies."

Wyndom studied him for a long moment as if trying to decide if the threat was an empty one.

Devon shook his head. "I'm done, Wyndom. My tolerance is at its end. I'll send the notices tomorrow."

"You goddamn bastard."

"Undoubtedly," Devon agreed with a resigned shrug. "But I don't have the wits and resourcefulness that you do. I'm tired of cleaning up the disasters that come in your wake. I'm tired of trying to make you see reason. We've reached the point where you're going to stand up like a man—whether you like it or not—and be solely accountable for your actions."

Wyndom glared at him, his jaw set. "As soon as my tobacco crop comes in," he announced regally, "I'll be taking up residence elsewhere."

Devon managed a half-smile. "What tobacco crop?"

"The one that's in the ground."

"I wasn't aware that you've been putting one in. It's an awful lot of hard work for one man to do. How have you managed it without the necessary slaves? We only have a handful of field workers left, and I've been using them to plant my crops."

His brother stared at him, his mouth sagging open and his pale eyes widening with panicked realization. "But," Wyndom sputtered. "Surely..."

"No," he assured him. "No one's planted the tobacco for you as they have in the past. I told you last winter that I wasn't going to, that if you wanted to call yourself a planter, you were actually going to have to *be* a planter. Do you remember that conversation?"

Wyndom dropped his head back into the pillows and stared up at the ceiling. "This is your idea of revenge, isn't it?" he asked flatly. "For being forced to marry Claire. You're punishing me for it, aren't you?"

"This has nothing to do with Claire," Devon corrected, anger suddenly sparking. "It has everything to do with your immaturity and irresponsibility. It goes well back—to long before Claire stepped foot on Virginia soil. She's just as much one of your victims as I am."

Wyndom, still staring up at the ceiling, sighed. "As soon as I receive my payments for last year's crop, I'll be leaving Rosewind."

He could have agreed, could have encouraged his brother to imagine that such an escape was possible, but Wyndom's problems stemmed from having those around him too long support the ease of his fantasies.

"You won't be able to afford to run away," Devon said bluntly. "If you'll recall, you agreed to let me attach your crops for the monies I lent you for planting and for paying your gambling debts to Jasper. You're not going to clear enough to buy yourself a meal at the Raleigh, much less a single night's lodging. You'd best plan to stay right here, Wyndom."

Tears edged Wyndom's voice as he asked, "And do what?"

"Grow up?" he suggested, wishing he didn't feel sorry for his brother. "Be responsible? Make a positive contribution to the productivity of the estate?"

"In other words, be your bootlicking toady." He tried to laugh, but the sound strangled amidst tears deep in his throat. Clearing it with considerable effort, he finally managed to tightly say, "Thank you, but no."

His heart aching for his brother's misery, Devon decided that honor and compassion required him to try reason one more time. "Wyndom, our father's world is gone forever. We can't—"

"Oh, spare me, Devon," his brother snarled, his gaze snapping down from the ceiling. Cold fire flashed in his eyes. "I've heard it all before." Motioning in Devon's general direction, he added, "I brought a mail packet from James City. It's on the bureau by your elbow. Don't neglect to take it with you as you leave."

Devon looked down to see the bundle wrapped in twine. As he picked it up, Wyndom blew out the light. With the packet in hand, Devon backed out of the room, quietly saying into the darkness, "Good night, Wyndom. Tomorrow will be a better day."

"Go to hell."

Struggling against a sense of futility and overwhelming sadness, Devon closed the door softly, turned, and made his way down the darkened hall. The light was still on in Claire's room, and he paused in front of her door, wanting to knock, wanting... He wanted her to hold him, to let him cry on her shoulder. He wanted to pour out his pain and regret and hear her promise to make it all come right for him. He wanted Claire to help him carry the burdens he was bearing for Wyndom, for Rosewind.

Slowly, he walked on to his own door. It was too much to ask of her.

CLAIRE ANGLED THE BOOK to better catch the candlelight, hoping the improvement would keep her mind from wandering. A few minutes later, having read the same paragraph no fewer than three times and not being able to recall a single word within it, she gave up and tossed the volume onto the foot of her bed. Why wasn't she tired? she wondered. The last few days had been physically grueling. By all rights and logic, she should have fallen sound asleep the minute her head had touched the pillow. Instead, she was wide awake and restless, feeling as though there was something important she should be doing.

Climbing out of bed, she crossed to the window and looked down on the kitchen and its gardens. A tiny wisp of smoke rose from the chimney, and the windows were dark. She sighed, knowing that Hannah and Meg had finished their work and retired for the night. Telling herself that she should do the same and simply will herself into sleep, she resolutely marched back to her bed and climbed between the sheets.

She was cupping her hand around the candle flame before blowing it out when there came a soft knock on the door that separated her room from Devon's. Her heart started and she stared at the wooden panel, her pulse and mind racing.

"Claire?" he called quietly, tentatively.

"One moment, please," she answered, throwing off the covers and snatching up her dressing gown. Shoving her arms into the sleeves, she hurried to the door, then paused just long enough to cinch the belt around her waist and take a single calming breath.

Despite the effort, her heart was still pounding and her hand was trembling when she opened the door. Devon stood on the other side, his dinner jacket removed and his shirttail pulled from his breeches. He'd opened the front, affording her a glimpse of dark curls and sun-burnished skin. Her breath caught as her pulse warmed and danced. He cut a dashing, rakish figure in his formal dress, but there was something about him in a casual state of disattire that stirred her senses in the most delicious way.

"I'm sorry to disturb you at the late hour," he said, extending his hand. "But a letter for you was in the packet Wyndom brought from James City. Since it bears the King's seal, I think you might not want to put off reading it."

The King's seal? Certitude instantly struck her. The day of reckoning had come as she'd always feared. And she didn't want to think about it, didn't want to face it.

Taking the folded and wax-sealed piece of parchment from Devon and deliberately turning her thoughts in another direction, she wondered aloud, "How would anyone other than my uncle know to send it to me here? Do you suppose he told the King—or someone representing him—where I am?"

"Very good questions," he allowed, smiling. "Maybe the writer will provide the answers."

Her fear melted in the warmth and ease of that smile. Bless Devon and the way he could so effortlessly relieve her apprehensions. It was magical and she adored him for it.

"Please," she said, resisting the impulse to hug him and resolutely stepping back, "come in and have a seat."

He hesitated, his brows knitted as he considered her.

"Please, Devon," she insisted, motioning to the bench seat before the cold hearth. "Do come in and be comfortable. It's silly to stand in the doorway and deny yourself entrance into a room in your very own house. I promise not to ravage you."

He laughed softly and she retreated again, disguising her flight by focusing her attention on carefully opening the letter. Dropping down onto the edge of her bed, she angled the paper into the light, acutely aware that Devon had stopped at the foot and was leaning his shoulder against the poster, watching her.

"It's from the Court of Chancery," she said aloud as she read. "A grand jury is to be impaneled to hear evidence against my uncle to the end of indicting him for fraud. I'm to appear before the bench as a material witness in the case being constructed against him."

"Are you being investigated for any wrongdoing?"

She heard the note of genuine concern in his voice, and she was grateful for it. "No. It says that an informant has sworn to my innocence in the matter and that I have nothing to fear in rendering a full and truthful account."

"Ah, an informant," he repeated quietly, turning so that his back propped him against the ornately carved poster. "If they know enough of your uncle's business dealings to swear to your innocence in them, then they'd be close enough to him to know his plans for our marriage. That explains how the court knew that you could be found at Rosewind."

"It would have to be someone he trusted as a friend."

"Not necessarily," he countered, turning to smile at

her. "It could just as well be someone invisible. A clerk. A secretary. Someone who, like yourself, was given responsibilities for important tasks and expected to accomplish them without being seen or heard."

Claire mentally ran her eyes over her uncle's home, his offices. "There are several scores of such people in my uncle's life. It could be any one of them. He's not a likable man and doesn't inspire loyalty to anything but the paltry wages he pays."

He nodded, pushed himself off the post at the end of her bed, and crossed to the bench seat she'd indicated earlier. Sitting on the edge with his elbows resting on his knees, he stared down at his clasped hands and asked, "Can you offer your testimony in writing or do you have to physically appear before the bench?"

Claire went back to reading the letter. "I'm to surrender myself into the protective custody of General Gage in Boston, Massachusetts, during the first week of June. I'm to be taken back to England under military escort and transferred into the protection of the court so that I'm available to testify beginning sometime in late July or early August."

Having reached the end of the correspondence, she laid it in her lap and looked up at Devon. He was still hunched forward, staring at his hands. His lips were a hard line, his jaw granite.

"Well," she ventured, trying to alleviate his suddenly dark mood, "it does resolve the issue of deciding where I'll go and what I'll do after our marriage is annulled, doesn't it?" She winced at the sadness even she could hear in her voice.

"And after you've satisfied the court?" he asked without looking up. "What will you do then? Where will you go?"

His kindness and concern only deepened the strange melancholy settling over her. Reminding herself that her problems weren't Devon's, she forced herself to smile, to think of the best possible outcomes. "If my uncle's indicted and then convicted, the Crown's likely to seize the Seaton-Smythe properties to recoup the monies he misappropriated. Perhaps I can persuade the court to give me Crossbridge Manor as a reward for my assistance."

"And if they aren't willing to be so generous?"

"In traveling for my uncle," she countered, scrambling to see other avenues, "I've met a considerable number of good and decent men. Many of them have families. I think several of them might be willing to offer me employment as a nurse or tutor."

"If they aren't? Then what?"

"Do you always expect the worst, Devon?"

"Expecting the worst is a requirement of survival at Rosewind," he replied, pushing himself to his feet. Hooking his thumbs over the waistband of his breeches, he stared into the cold hearth. "And it's amazing how often the worst I can imagine pales beside what actually happens. So answer my question, Claire. What are you going to do if you can't find employment as a nurse or a tutor?"

She was certain that she would; she was educated and reasonably genteel. But Devon was too committed to bleak prospects to accept her assurance that matters would work out well in the end. Thinking that perhaps the ludicrous would pierce his gloom, she laughed and said, "I don't know, Devon. Throw myself in the Thames?"

Slowly, he turned to her and, with the solemnity of a man climbing the gallow steps, said, "You could come back to Rosewind."

God, what she wouldn't have given for his words to have been wrapped in one of his smiles. It would have made all the difference in the world. "Thank you," she replied, hiding her bruised heart behind a smile. "That's most kind of you. Would I be returning as your wife, your mistress, or your housekeeper?"

His brows shot together. "You're my wife."

"In name only. And only for a short while," she pointed out. "In fact," she mused aloud, glancing down at the letter, "with my uncle soon to be embroiled in defending himself from the King's justice, he'll be much too busy to spare us so much as a thought. There's no reason for us to maintain our sham marriage a day longer. He isn't likely to be in any position to bring consequences to bear on either one of us."

He didn't say anything. Instead, he just stood there pensively, his gaze fastened unseeingly on her, his thoughts obviously elsewhere. A troubling elsewhere, Claire decided.

"Devon?"

He blinked at the sound of her voice. "Maybe we should postpone the annulment until after you've rendered your duty to the court. If you're granted Crossbridge or if you find employment that suits you, then we could proceed from there. But if those avenues don't prove fruitful, you could return to Rosewind." He took a long, slow breath before adding, "You know that I don't have much to offer you, but..."

"But it's far more than what *I* have?" she finished for him.

He narrowed his eyes, seeming to have suddenly realized that she wasn't tumbling head over heels to accept his magnanimous offer. "Well, yes," he answered warily.

"It occurs to me, Devon, that I'd rather make my way alone than accept a marriage offered out of pity."

"Pity isn't the right word," he quickly protested. "You've done wonders for Rosewind and—"

"You feel an obligation towards me?"

Again he considered her, hesitating before saying, "Something like that."

Claire smiled thinly. "You have debts enough, Devon. I won't be another piled atop those already burdening you."

"You're not a burden. And you have to know that I find you attractive."

God yes, she did know that. And she was just as drawn to him. But what would bind them when the novelty of physical discovery became tarnished by the common reality of day-to-day life?

"Pity, obligation, and lust," she summarized. "Do you consider those motivations an adequate foundation for a lifelong relationship?"

He was silent, but the truth shone in his eyes. Under it lay the same sorrow that was battering her own heart.

"Neither do I, Devon," she said softly, rising from the bed, the letter in her hand. "And I think it best if we don't let your chivalry or my uncertainty cloud our judgment. The problem is mine and I'll find a solution. You needn't feel any duty to rescue me from the situation. I've been taking care of myself for a very long time. I'm quite capable, you know."

"You shouldn't have to take care of yourself."

In a perfect world, she would be loved and cherished and protected. In a perfect world, all the people that had ever mattered to her would still be alive. She swallowed back the threat of tears and raised her chin. "Circumstances frequently require adaptations, Devon. Remember?"

"And the secret is to accept the changes with grace," he added, nodding somberly as he came to stand in front of her. Gently resting his hands on her shoulders, he said softly, firmly, "Our circumstances have changed, Claire. And yes, you're probably correct in assuming that your uncle's much too preoccupied to worry about how long our marriage lasts. But I won't sign my name to a petition for annulment until I'm certain that you have another course on which you can be safe, secure, and happy. Until then, I'm your husband. There will be no immediate annulment. There won't be an annulment until after your duty to the King's court is done."

Stunned, she retorted, "You can't summarily make pronouncements like that."

"Yes, I can. The law allows it as my right. Accept it with grace, Claire."

She stared up at him, her mind reeling. "You promised," she whispered. "You said that we'd—"

"Circumstances, Claire," he interrupted, giving her the tiniest of impatient shakes. "The circumstances have changed. I didn't want to marry you any more than you wanted to marry me. But I'm not stupid and I'm not blind. Rosewind has never had a better mistress. It seems to me that if I can swallow enough of my pride to confess my appreciation and need, you could do the same so that we could come to an amicable compromise."

"Amicable?" she sputtered, her mind reeling anew. "You want us to be friends?"

"No, that's not what I want at all," he countered, giving her a rueful smile. Lifting his right hand, he trailed his fingertips over her cheek and whispered, "Right this moment, my sweet Claire, I want nothing more in the world than to lay you down on this bed and lose myself in you. Over and over and over again. I want it so badly I ache."

She couldn't breathe and her blood was wildly, thrillingly afire. Her heart begged her to surrender. Reason screamed of the price. "But if . . ."

"Yes," he said, releasing her and taking a single, very deliberate step back. He squared his shoulders and there was an edge of hard-won control in his voice when he continued, "It's the path of no return for both of us. If we travel it, there can be no annulment. That bit of reality is the tether holding me in check. I'll keep you here and safe until you can choose your own way, yes. But I won't hold you here against your will forever. And just as importantly, I won't let desire put me in the position of being a rebel with a loyalist wife in his bed."

Feeling alone, empty, and storm battered, her knees too weak to hold her, Claire sank down on the bed. "You didn't mention earlier that my adoption of your political beliefs was a condition of returning to Rosewind."

He sighed and shrugged. "I thought I'd see which way the wind was blowing first."

"I don't think it's blowing at all, Devon," she confessed, staring at the far wall and trying to swallow down the thickening lump in her throat. "I can't live a lie for you. And I won't live waiting for the day they hang you for treason." *I couldn't bear to lose any more of my heart.*

"Then it would appear that we have nothing further to talk about. I bid you a good night, Claire."

She nodded, unable to speak, consumed by the effort to collect her scattered thoughts and emotions. Vaguely, she heard the door close and she couldn't keep from sagging in relief. How had life become so complicated without her noticing? When had her desires and feelings become so entwined with Devon's?

There were no ready, easy answers to be found, and so Claire shook her head to dispel the troubling thoughts. As she did, her gaze fell into her lap and onto the letter clutched absently in her hand. She perused it again, noting the date on which it had been penned. The fourth of March, just two days after she'd left England. If only she'd known then the set of circumstances unfolding behind her. By the time she'd reached Williamsburg . . . She needn't have married Devon at all.

Except, Claire silently admitted, she didn't feel trapped, as she had that day. That feeling had passed, and now she felt . . . Claire frowned, trying once again to define the various elements of her tangled emotions.

Devon was a good and decent man trying his best to salvage what he could of the wreckage his father had left behind. He worked hard and genuinely appreciated the effort others made to do the same. He dared to explore new directions, and while he wasn't quite accepting of her determination to blaze new trails in feminine fashion, he at least had the grace to silently endure. For the most part.

Claire smiled softly. And patience; Devon might not have an inexhaustible well of it, but he had far more than other men in his circumstances would be able to summon. Which testified to the fact that, beneath his baronial manner, Devon Rivard was really a very kind man with a generous heart. How many men blackmailed into marriage would surrender their chance for freedom to offer the unwanted wife a haven when she had no other?

Of course, Claire ruefully admitted, Devon didn't want anything more than a mistress and a capable housekeeper. The former he could find easily; he was handsome enough that he could have any woman he desired. As for his wanting *her* . . . she was here and not altogether unwilling—a convenient and easy conquest for Devon and nothing more. A housekeeper, though . . . a housekeeper would cost him money and so was beyond his immediate attainment. That was where her true value to him lay.

She might be a dreamer, but she wasn't fool enough to trade her future for a handful of breathless interludes that, in the end, would lead to nothing more than a lifetime of domestic servitude. No, she'd been right earlier. His pity, obligation, and lust and her desperation weren't enough on which to build a life together as husband and wife. And while she and Devon might have reached a point where they could concede a certain degree of admiration and respect for each other, there wasn't much more than that between them. There certainly wasn't any love.

Claire blinked back a sudden, unexpected spring of tears. Love, she silently chided as she blindly folded the letter, didn't matter. Men of Devon's social class didn't marry for love; they married for money—which Devon desperately needed and could never hope to acquire if he remained married to her.

Laying the court summons on the bedside table, she blew out the light and slipped under the covers. In the darkness a truth stole over her. If she had wealth, she'd willingly offer every farthing to Devon in exchange for the hope that maybe, someday, he might grow to love her as much as she was foolishly growing to love him.

CHAPTER SEVENTEEN

$\mathcal{D}$EVON LEANED FORWARD in the chair and handed the legal notice across the desk to his attorney, saying, "It looks sufficient. Thank you."

Edmund nodded, laid it aside, and picked up his teacup. "Is Wyndom aware that he's being cut off?"

"If he was listening, he is," Devon replied, settling back with a weak smile. "One's never quite sure with Wyndom."

"You do know that there's a distinct possibility that he'll end up in debtor's prison, don't you?"

Devon nodded. "But, given a choice between either going in his stead or letting him suffer the consequences of his own actions, I don't see that I really have much of a choice at all. If I go to prison for debts, Rosewind and Mother will be left in his care. He'd gamble them both away within a week."

"If it would take him that long," Edmund observed with a sad shake of his head. "I'll make copies of the notice and send them out on the first available dispatch. They should be published well inside thirty days."

"Thank you." Pushing himself up out of the chair, Devon clasped his hands behind his back and began to slowly pace the solicitor's office. "There's another matter I'd like for you to take care of as well. Claire has been summoned by the Chancery Court to testify against her uncle."

"In person?" Edmund quickly asked. "Before the bench?"

Devon nodded. "A grand jury. She's to surrender herself to General Gage in Boston the first week in June, then be transported under military escort."

"June?" Edmund pursed his lips and stared off into the distance. After a moment, he relaxed with a shrug. "You're not likely to have the paperwork necessary to have the marriage annulled by then."

"That's all right. I've decided to postpone the proceeding for a while."

The lawyer started visibly, then cocked a brow and smiled. "Whenever you're ready to expand on that rather startling pronouncement, I'm more than willing to hear it."

Devon went on pacing, his mind carefully tracing through the maze of his plan. "She intends to petition the court for her family's estate in Herefordshire. It seems to me that she'd have a far better chance of having it granted if she were to have the request phrased by an officer of the court. I'd like for you to draft the petition for her so that she has it in hand when she sets out for Boston."

"But, if I'm understanding correctly," Edmund countered, "she'll be in England and still your wife. Do you intend to have the marriage annulled in absentia?"

His throat tightened. "If that's what Claire chooses."

"You'd prefer to have her come back, wouldn't you?"

The clear notes of amusement in the other man's voice rankled. "Rosewind has never had a more capable mistress," Devon replied crisply. "Of course I want her to return. Only a fool would willingly give up decent food and a clean house."

Stroking his chin, Edmund softly said, "Just out of curiosity, Devon, do you have any personal feelings toward her at all?"

The question, though lightly posed, struck hard, inexplicably taking the air from his lungs and sending his heart into his throat. Unable to unravel or define the jumble of thoughts and emotions suddenly overwhelming him, Devon retrieved his hat from the wall peg, saying, "It's only been a short while. Gratitude is the only sentiment that can possibly grow in such a brief span of time."

Settling the hat on his head, Devon smiled at his lawyer and set about extracting himself from the gentle inquisition. "Thank you for seeing to the legal notice, Edmund. And there's no hurry on the petition as long as it's done by the time she has to sail for Boston."

Edmund rose and extended his hand. Devon politely shook it while thinking that he'd like nothing more at the moment than to wipe the smirk off his friend's face. Forcing a congenial smile, Devon left the office, his anger swelling with every step he took.

Feelings for Claire? How dare Edmund presume to even ask the question. It was entirely too personal. And answering it honestly would have cast him in a very poor light. Yanking the reins of his mount from the ring, Devon swung up into the saddle and set out for Rosewind, his teeth clenched and the likely conversation playing out in his mind.

Why yes, Edmund. I do care for Claire in some respects. She has a narrow waist, beautifully curved hips and delightfully full breasts. Simply looking at her makes me hard. Oh, and have I mentioned that she's cleaned Rosewind from top to bottom and that the Lee brothers think she's a charming and delightful hostess?

Oh, you were thinking that I might have fallen in love with her? How ridiculous. She's as poor as a church mouse, outspoken, opinionated, entirely too independent, and a borderline loyalist. I'm certainly grateful for the change she's brought to Rosewind. It's nice to be able to breathe without inhaling a lungful of dust. But I'm no fool. I'm fully aware of the difference between lust and love. And Claire inspires nothing more for me than the former. As Tidewater wives go, she's utterly unsuitable and I know it.

What? Can you have her when I'm done with her? You most certainly may not!

Why? Because... Well, because...

Devon swallowed past the lump in his throat and focused his awareness on the countryside through which he was riding. Imaginary conversations were beyond inane and accomplished nothing. Except, he silently conceded, to reveal what a pathetically shallow and weak-minded man he was.

CLAIRE STEPPED BACK to consider the arrangement of red and yellow tulips she'd placed in the center of the dining room table and smiled, silently thanking whichever of Devon's ancestors had been inclined to plant thousands of Dutch bulbs. Outside, they were a well-planned, richly colored blanket wrapping around Rosewind. Cut and brought inside, they were bright and cheerful and somehow made the world seem new and bursting with promise.

Pleased with the effect the blooms had achieved in the dining room, Claire picked up the second vase. The parlor, she thought, heading in that direction. The peach and pink flowers would be perfect for the most feminine room in the house. Mother Rivard would especially like them.

And, if time permitted before luncheon, she'd cut a bouquet for the library as well, she decided. Surely Devon and the Lee brothers—once they returned from wherever they'd gone—would appreciate the splash of color and a light, sweet scent while they argued politics and economics, smoked cigars and drank their brandy. It should be a striking, somewhat masculine combination, though. Maroon with creamy white, she decided as she entered the parlor.

The silence was sudden and strained, bringing Claire out of her thoughts and sharpening what had only been the vaguest awareness of conversation. She froze, holding the vase in front of her, and quickly surveyed the room. Mother Rivard and Elsbeth, overdressed and powdered as usual, occupied opposite ends of the settee in front of the window. Across the Persian rug from them, in the center of the matching settee, was another woman, her dark hair piled in an intricate arrangement atop her head, her shoulders bared by the daring décolletage of her gown.

Mother Rivard started, looking nervously between Claire and the stranger. Elsbeth smiled slowly, making the hair prickle on the back of Claire's neck.

"I'm sorry to intrude. I wasn't aware that you had a caller," Claire offered, quickly taking the bouquet to the sideboard. "I'll leave these here and allow you to return to your conversation." Out of the corner of her eye, she saw Mother Rivard rise and smile at the guest. As the stranger also gained her feet, Claire glanced toward the door and tamped down the urge to run.

"Lady Claire," Henrietta said smoothly, "allow me to introduce our neighbor, Lady Darice Lytton." Claire obediently turned as Mother Rivard went on, saying, "She's just returned from Philadelphia and has come over this morning to share all the latest news with us. Darice, this is Claire, Devon's wife."

"Wife?" the tall, voluptuous woman repeated, the coolness of her voice belied by the sudden, hard spark in her dark eyes. She raked Claire from hair to hem, her brow arching ever so slightly as she did.

Despite the pounding of her heart, Claire forced herself to relax, to smile; she knew what kind of woman Darice Lytton was. It had been her encounters with the Darices of London that had driven her uncle to send her far away on business.

"The marriage was most unexpected," Elsbeth put in sardonically. "Apparently, Wyndom owed money to her uncle, and she was foisted off on Devon in lieu of payment. They assure us that the marriage will be annulled as soon as they receive word that the debt has been canceled."

"My," Darice said with a dry chuckle. "Knowing Devon as I do, I can only imagine that he's being positively beastly about the whole thing."

"I do think he's coming around, though," Mother Rivard nervously hastened to assure her. "Lady Claire has been nothing short of a dervish in getting Rosewind prepared to receive guests. Have we mentioned that the Lee brothers are here? They brought poor Wyndom home from James City. He'd had an unfortunate encounter and they were kind enough to rescue him. He's been abed, recovering, since yesterday."

The woman's brow had inched further upward at the mention of Devon's possible acceptance of the situation, and Claire knew that everything Mother Rivard had said after that had fallen on deaf ears. Predators were at least predictable. Claire waited for the thinly veiled insult.

"I suppose that if one is to have only limited talents," Darice observed with an insincere smile, "housekeeping would at least be a useful and employable skill.

Would you happen to be available to clean my house? After being away for two months... well, it certainly could use a little dervish whirling through it."

"I'm afraid you'll have to rely on your own resources, Lady Darice," she replied with every bit of sweetness she could muster. She broadened her smile before she delivered a slap of her own. "Making a comfortable home for Devon fully and happily occupies all my time."

The glint in her ebony eyes hardening, Darice practically purred as she replied, "Aren't you simply precious."

"Precious? Ha!" Elsbeth snorted. "She wears breeches and boots about the house. For all we know, she's probably worn them out in public, too."

"As a matter of fact, Elsbeth, I have. Frequently." All three women gasped and stared at her, their mouths agape. Pleased with having succeeded at undermining the aplomb that Darice used to make people feel inferior, Claire grinned and quipped, "Precious and outrageous, too."

Before they could offer any sort of comment, she added, "If you'll excuse me, ladies. I'm off to check with Hannah on this evening's meal. Will you be staying for luncheon, Lady Darice? Or are you hurrying home to try your own hand at being useful?"

"Of course she'll be staying," Elsbeth snapped, her eyes glittering as hard and dark as Darice's. "We wouldn't hear otherwise, would we, Henrietta?"

Mother Rivard cast a quick look between Claire and Darice, opened her mouth to speak, and then apparently thought better of whatever it was she had been about to say. She pursed her lips, swallowed hard, and managed a weak smile. "It would be unconscionably rude not to invite her to stay."

Elsbeth stared at Henrietta, and Darice blinked furiously. Claire reined in her smile, and then dropped a quick curtsy before she turned and left the room. She ought to be ashamed of herself, Claire silently admonished as she made her way down the hall toward the foyer. She'd not only deliberately baited the woman, she'd matched her insult for insult. It was petty and childish behavior. Her mother had taught her better. Of course, Claire amended, her mother had never been backed into a corner by one of the Darice Lyttons of the world. She'd have sung a different song had her ladylike courtesy been repaid with an unprovoked mauling or two.

"A word with you privately, Claire."

Claire stopped on the threshold of the butler's pantry and turned back, mentally bracing as she watched Darice advance and chiding herself for not having anticipated the woman's unwillingness to allow someone to walk away with the upper hand.

"If it won't take long, Darice," she countered. "I need to let Hannah know we'll be having a guest for the midday meal."

"Then for the sake of brevity, I'll be blunt. You're a very sweet little girl and far too innocent to play the game against someone like me. There's no sport for me in winning under such circumstances. So please, spare us both an unpleasant experience and quietly quit the field without the pretense of making it a contest."

This was the woman's idea of blunt? At the rate she was going, it would take them a month to get to the meat of the matter at hand. "Are we talking about Devon?"

"Devon's the only reason I'd ever visit this pile of rubble," Darice said contemptuously. "Are you aware that he and I are lovers?"

The declaration struck Claire hard, clenching her stomach and driving the air from her lungs. Part of her brain refused to believe it. Another part did, but warned that she couldn't allow Darice to know how deeply she'd been wounded. "I can't recall his ever having mentioned your name, Darice," she answered with a breeziness she didn't feel. "So no, I wasn't aware of any relationship between you. Telling me about it must have slipped his mind."

Darice laughed softly. "Cattiness doesn't become you. You're not particularly good at it. And please allow me to disabuse you of any notion you might have about being good enough to draw Devon into your bed. Oh, you might be able to lure him there once. But while innocence is certainly appealing in its novelty, it lacks any depth. I can assure you that Devon is a man who very much requires and appreciates depth of experience."

Struggling to contain her rising anger, Claire observed dryly, "Experience which you happen to have in abundance, no doubt."

"Not only have I bedded more men than you'll meet in the course of your life, but I've also buried three husbands, each of whom was exceedingly grateful for my skills and rewarded me grandly for brightening the last days of his life."

"Experience and wealth, too."

"Can you offer Devon either of those things? Of course you can't. And you've been here long enough to know how important money is to Devon. You'll have to accept my word on how much he enjoys a talented woman in his bed."

Standing there listening to another woman expound on Devon's sexual expectations... Reminding herself that Devon was her husband in name only didn't cool her temper one bit. "I can certainly see why he'd be motivated to take you to the altar, Darice. Which naturally begs the question... Why hasn't he?"

"My last husband has been dead for less than a

year," Darice explained coolly. "I'm in mourning and can't wed for another two months. Devon's inordinately concerned about public appearances, which is why I went off to Philadelphia. People were beginning to suspect that we were involved, and it bothered him. Since he's powerless to resist temptation, the only kind and considerate thing to do was go away."

"But now you're back and fully intending to take up with Devon where you left off."

With a smile, Darice added, "And I will not tolerate any attempt on your part to stand in our way."

"I wouldn't dream of it," Claire managed to say lightly. Resolving to escape before she did the woman bodily harm, she forced herself to shrug and say, "Well, in case we don't have another opportunity to visit with each other before I leave Rosewind, allow me to extend my congratulations on your inevitable nuptials and wish you and Devon the greatest happiness you can hope to achieve."

"I'm so glad we had this chance to set matters straight," Darice said as she turned and walked away. "I'm sure that you'll someday find a man more in keeping with your ability to hold his interest. Henrietta mentioned that Hannah is back. Tell her I want pheasant breasts in Madeira sauce for lunch."

Claire watched her go, wishing she had something in hand to throw at her. The woman was positively viperous. Not to mention presumptuous and malicious and avaricious. Just out and out onerous. *Devon and I are lovers ... A man more in keeping ...* Fuming, her heartbeat pounding in her temples, Claire spun about and stomped off toward the kitchen.

Hannah, chopping vegetables at the central table, looked up at her stormy arrival. The knife went still and a gray brow arched up. "What's happened, child?"

"We have a guest for lunch," Claire gritted out, her

hands fisted on her hips. "She told me to tell you that she wants pheasant breasts in a Madeira sauce."

Hannah grimaced. "Lady Darice Lytton."

"None other."

Meg shoveled a loaf of bread into the oven and asked, "Who's Lady Darice Lytton?"

"Devon's lover," she shot back angrily.

"Oh, sweet merciful saints preserve us."

Meg's obvious shock and dismay at the revelation was somehow both a balm and a dose of salt on her wounded pride. Claire looked back and forth between the two women, her breathing ragged and her heart still hammering.

"Calm yourself down, Lady Claire," Hannah said softly. "There's another side of the story that Widow Lytton woman hasn't told you."

"Would that be Devon's side?"

"Yes. And when you're ready to hear it, I'll tell it to you." Hannah picked up a cloth-lined basket and handed it to her, saying, "Eat a biscuit."

"I've never in my life loathed another human being as much as I do her," Claire admitted, obediently but absently taking a piece of the offered bread. "What could Devon possibly see in her? Why—aside from her baskets and baskets of money—would he ever consider marrying her?"

"Is that what she told you?" Hannah asked, her hands going to her hips. "That he was going to marry her?"

"Yes. And that I don't have a prayer of being *experienced* enough to . . . to . . ."

"Seduce him?" Meg supplied as she set aside the bread paddle and moved toward the open hearth.

"Thank you. Or keep his interest should I—ever so accidentally—lure him into my bed."

With a deep sigh, Hannah reached out to lay her

hand on Claire's arm. "Put that whole biscuit in your mouth and chew slowly."

Her mind still reeling, Claire stood there mutely unmoving. Biscuit? She wasn't the least bit hungry. She'd probably never be hungry again for as long as she lived.

"Now, Lady Claire. The whole thing."

God. Why not? What else did she have to do? There was no earthly reason to pour any more of herself into pretending to be the mistress of Rosewind. Not when Darice Lytton was waiting in the wings to dance in and claim the title for herself. Claire took a huge, angry bite of the cold bread.

"Listen to me carefully," Hannah began, her tone stern, her words obviously well considered. "It was a long, *long* winter. And Mr. Devon is a man, not a saint. And, being a man, he doesn't always think things through with his brain. And mind you that he's not the only man in this part of Virginia to have accepted that woman's invitation.

"But he swears to me that he's done with her and has been for some time. I believe him. And you should know right here and now, Lady Claire, that even when his thinking was impaired, it never once crossed his mind to marry that woman. Not once. If she's telling you that Mr. Devon's set to walk her up the aisle of the Bruton Parish Church, she's lying to you through her teeth."

She so desperately wanted to believe Hannah. Claire swallowed the lump of bread and said, "She's an absolutely hideous person."

"Yes, she is," the cook agreed. "And God will judge her harshly for her many, many sins."

"But gettin' to God takes too long," Meg complained, bringing the teapot from the hearth. "An' then we don't get the satisfaction of bein' there to watch an' cheer."

"How true," Claire agreed, putting the biscuit down

on the table. Moving to the shelves for cups and saucers, she added, "And it just galls me to know that Darice Lytton even thinks that she's . . . she's won."

Hannah waited until she'd returned to the table with the china before asking, "Won what, Lady Claire?"

"Devon," she replied while none too gently pairing the cups with their saucers. "She thinks she's beaten me in a contest for Devon."

As Meg poured, Hannah tilted her head to the side and considered Claire with slightly narrowed eyes. "Let me ask you a question," she said slowly. "And you think hard before you answer. Do you want Mr. Devon because that Darice Lytton woman wants him? Or do you want Mr. Devon because *you* want him?"

The anger and indignation that had consumed her was instantly gone, leaving her weak in the knees. Clutching the edge of the table to steady herself, Claire suddenly understood why Darice Lytton had been able to rile her so easily. The woman's manner was only a very small part of it. The more fundamental truth was that Darice posed a threat to a deeply buried hope, a fragile, impossible hope that Claire hadn't known she was harboring. Fear crept in to fill the void left by her outrage. "Because I want him," she whispered.

"Ye love him, don't ye?"

Her heart swelled and twisted. "God help me, I think I do."

Hannah passed her a cup of tea, saying crisply, "The good Lord helps those who help themselves."

"So I should help myself to Devon?" she asked, feeling shaky and acutely desperate. "Do I use a spoon or a fork?"

"A knife, I'm thinkin'," Meg briskly answered, taking up her own cup. "Ye hold it to his throat till he sees the wisdom of lettin' ye have yer way with him."

Claire didn't know whether to laugh or to cry. "This is impossible."

"Nah, ye just hold yer ground an' he'll surrender. Shouldn't take more than a second. Two at the most. Smitten to the core with ye already, he is."

Smitten? Claire shook her head.

Hannah took a sip of her tea and then gently pressed, "What's impossible, Lady Claire?"

"Everything," she answered, suddenly so frustrated that she wanted to scream. "Devon desperately needs money and I don't have any. If we annul the marriage as we've planned, he'd be free to find a woman who could save Rosewind for him."

"Money isn't—never has been and never will be—the salvation of anyone or anything." Hannah countered. "Mr. Devon needs much more than what can be bought or sold for shillings and pounds. And there's nothing at Rosewind that can't be mended with care and time."

"He's willing to go to war for colonial rights," Claire went on, her pulse racing wildly. "He could be killed or hanged as a traitor."

" 'Tis true enough," Meg granted, nodding. "But trip o'er his own feet this afternoon, he could. An' fall down the stairs an' be dead of a broken neck 'fore he hits the foyer floor. Life is full o' risks, Lady Claire. Ye can't throw away the good to avoid the bad an' have a life that's worth livin'."

"We have significant philosophical differences. On slavery. On the rights of women. On the necessity of armed rebellion."

"Oh dear," Meg said softly, casting a glance at Hannah.

The older woman met Claire's gaze. After a long silence, she said with granite resolution, "For men and women of good character and kind hearts, there is no difference that can't be bridged by honesty and a genuine willingness to hear. Life is about compromise, Lady Claire. It's about knowing what's important and what isn't. If you and Mr. Devon haven't set yourselves down and had a good talk about what you both, in your heart of hearts, want from your lives, then it's high time that you did."

Meg nodded enthusiastically and Hannah went on, adding, "I'd suggest you start that conversation by asking Mr. Devon about a law he tried to get passed two years ago."

"What law?"

"Ask Mr. Devon. And listen to his answer with both your heart and your mind."

"He's a good man," Meg offered. "Kind an' fair. An' if'n ye were to reach out, sure I am that he'd be willin' to do the same."

Meg was right; Devon had not only been willing to hear her opinions, but had encouraged her to express them. As for Hannah's belief that their differences could be bridged . . . only time and effort would tell. But assuming that they could find a common ground . . .

"That issue aside," Claire said, gathering her courage, "as much as I am absolutely loathe to admit it, Darice Lytton is right. I'm an innocent. I know how to fend men off. I've had vast experience doing that. But I don't have the foggiest notion how to go about seducing a man. Much less how to actually please him."

With a snort, Meg assured her, "Men don't have to be seduced. They're perfectly willin' to do it fer ye. All ye have to do is step up an' say yer wonderin' what beddin' 'em would be like. Once ye've done that, all that's left to do is hang on an' enjoy the ride."

"And men," Claire asked skeptically, "derive pleasure out of simply providing . . . the ride?"

Meg nodded emphatically. Hannah took a sip of her tea.

"Darice led me to believe that it required a female

with considerable artistic talent. Let's not forget experience, either."

"For that Widow Lytton woman, it most likely does," Hannah said quietly, settling her cup gently back in the saucer. "She doesn't have a heart to put into the loving. Giving your body doesn't mean anything if you hold back your heart and soul, Lady Claire. That's the difference between lovers and whores. Lovers give everything they have. Freely and without thought. That's where the pleasure comes from. For the both of you."

Giving voice to her greatest fears, Claire wondered aloud, "What if Devon can't bring himself to love me heart and soul? What if we can't find a common philosophical ground?"

"Then ye give him up an' count yerself blessed to be rid of a man too stupid to be worth havin'."

"Meg's right," Hannah said. "If he can't love you or bend for you, then you let that Lytton woman have him. And gladly. They'd deserve each other."

But did she deserve Devon more? Was she what he needed? Did she have the strength to weather the rebuilding of Rosewind and then to gracefully endure the loss of both the estate and Devon if rebellion came? Was she willing to give up the chance of ever returning to England, to Crossbridge and a life of her own making? Was she willing to give up being an Englishwoman? There were no answers lurking in the wake of the hard questions, only an overwhelming sense of being adrift in a vast ocean of uncertainty.

"I have a great deal to think about and to decide, don't I?" she ventured, suddenly wanting only to be alone. "Perhaps I can start while I pick some tulips for the library. Thank you both for listening to my ranting and for sharing your wisdom with me. I appreciate it more than I can ever express."

"Just don't be wastin' it, Lady Claire. Good advice does ye no good if'n ye don't use it."

"I'll remember that," she promised, already moving toward the kitchen door and the solitary haven of the gardens beyond. She stopped outside and allowed her shoulders to sag. Yes, she and Devon should probably have a serious conversation regarding their dreams and life goals. And before she could ask him to do that, she needed to decide just what hers were.

If anyone had asked her to define them a month ago, she would have had a ready and certain answer: She wanted the quiet, familiar simplicity of life at Crossbridge. But today . . . so much had happened. And all of it seemed to have melded her into someone she didn't know, someone with entirely new hopes and dreams. The change had been wholly unexpected and she couldn't help but wonder if life might bring yet another completely different set of them. Would the mere sight of Devon always make her heart race? Would his rakish smile always make her blood warm and excite her carnal imagination?

Claire smiled. God, she hoped so.

DEVON EASED HIS mount into a trot as he eyed from a distance the black carriage sitting in the drive at the front of the house. More damn guests, he silently groused. Guests who would expect—in the grandest of Virginia traditions—to eat, drink, and be entertained until merry. Claire had undoubtedly welcomed them graciously and invited them to consider Rosewind their home. She was a far better hostess than he was host. Truth be told, she was a far better person in general than he was. Claire didn't have a selfish bone in her body. No one would ever say the same about him.

Wondering who had invaded his home this time, he considered the carriage again. There was a coat of arms on the door, and he narrowed his eyes to bring it into sharper focus. And his heart rolled over in his chest.

CHAPTER EIGHTEEN

*I*F THERE WAS A GOD, Devon feverishly thought as he tied off his horse, Ephram and the Lee brothers had returned before Darice's arrival and were keeping her occupied. And if that God was feeling just the tiniest bit kind, he hadn't allowed Darice a chance to corner Claire alone. A truly benevolent God would have seen that the two women hadn't even had a chance to meet.

Wracking his brain to recall anything he'd recently done that might be considered of sufficient merit to be worth divine intervention, Devon bounded up the front steps and flung open the door. The foyer was empty and he listened hard, praying that he'd catch the low rumble of male voices. He didn't, and with dread filling his bones, he made his way down the hall toward the parlor.

Halfway there, the soft sounds of feminine chatter came to his ears, and he slowed, straining to identify the occupants of the room. He heard his aunt Elsbeth clearly; the woman never paused to so much as take a breath. But where Elsbeth went, so did his mother. It was a given she was in there as well. And Darice had to be, too. Good manners required that she be entertained by the ladies of Rosewind. Which would include Claire. Unless—*please dear God*—she'd managed to find an excuse and beg out of it.

Fortifying himself with a deep breath, he stepped into the parlor. His mother and Aunt Elsbeth sat on the far settee. Darice stood at the mantel, a glass of sherry in her hand, and a smile on her face that said she'd seen him ride up and had been waiting for him. Claire was nowhere in sight and he barely kept himself from sagging in relief. It was only then that he realized he'd trapped himself, that he'd stepped into the den of lionesses for no reason and without a plan for saving himself.

"Good afternoon, Mother, ladies," he said tersely, speaking over Elsbeth's continued prattling.

His mother started, casting a nervous glance from him to Darice. Elsbeth went instantly silent, a satisfied smile lifting the corners of her mouth.

"Devon, darling," Darice all but purred, gliding toward him, her arms extended. "How I've missed you."

His stomach went cold and he deliberately stepped back, pointedly keeping his arms pinned at his sides. "Darice," he said tightly, sparing her only the briefest of glances before asking, "Mother, where's Claire?"

"You could at least attempt to offer a civil welcome to Lady Lytton," Elsbeth admonished sharply.

"Do *not* presume to lecture me on manners, Aunt Elsbeth," he snapped, never having wanted to strangle the woman as much as he did in that moment.

"You needn't look so dark and stormy," Darice said as she came to stand in front of him. Her smile was the pure seduction of old as she whispered, "A temporary wife needn't stand in our way," and reached up to touch his cheek.

He took another step back, deliberately turning his head so that he was beyond her reach. "There's your way and my way, Darice," he said coolly. "They're distinctly separate roads. I thought I'd made that abundantly clear several months ago."

"But I know that you didn't truly mean it," she corrected sweetly. "Any more than you meant the promises you gave Claire at the altar," she added, reaching for him again.

His pulse racing with fearful certainty, he caught her wrist and stayed her, saying only, "Don't."

Tears welled in her eyes and her lower lip quivered as she whispered his name. He'd seen the performance before. Several times. It moved him no more this time than it had the last.

"Darice says we're having pheasant breasts in Madeira sauce for luncheon," his mother blurted. "Doesn't that sound delicious?"

"Where is Claire, Mother?"

"Out in the kitchen?" she guessed.

"Thank you." He released Darice abruptly, bowed crisply to his mother, then turned on his heel and walked away. His only thought as he strode toward the rear of the house was that of finding Claire and putting things as right as he could. God, he was such an idiot. He should have foreseen that Darice and Claire would someday meet. He should have prepared Claire for it. He should have armed her with the truth.

CLAIRE STOOD AT THE COUNTER in the butler's pantry, arranging the tulips with trembling hands and listening to Devon's purposeful footfalls as he made his way across the foyer and into the dining room. Her stomach roiling, she took a deep breath and desperately tried to decide what she was going to do. Throw herself into his arms and tearfully apologize for being a virgin? Stamp her foot and demand that he choose between her and Darice Lytton? Dissolve into tears and beg him for an annulment—an escape—by sundown? Pretend that she didn't see or hear him? That she wasn't a mass of tangled feelings and jangled nerves?

He came to a sudden stop just inside the little room, and her gaze leapt to meet his. So much for pretending that she wasn't aware of his presence.

"What did she tell you?" he asked, his chest rising and falling, shadows of worry dulling the normal brilliance of his eyes. No sooner had the words left his mouth than he grimaced, threw his hands up in the air, and exclaimed, "Oh hell, you don't have to answer. I know what she said."

Claire stared at him in amazement, her nerves settling with the realization that he was genuinely concerned about how she felt. He was, in fact, just as worried, uncertain, and frightened as she was. A warmth gently, serenely bloomed in the center of her chest. "You don't owe me an explanation, Devon."

"Yes, I do," he countered, stepping closer. "She's come into your home and hurt your feelings." He gently placed his hands on her shoulders and looked deeply into her upturned eyes. "I didn't tell you about her because, for one thing, it was an extremely brief affair. For another, it was purely physical. And thirdly, because it was over well before I met you."

The earnestness of his assurance touched a chord deep inside her and drew her hands to his waist. "You aren't hoping to marry her?" she asked softly, already knowing the answer.

"God, no."

Her pulse skittered wildly. "Does she know how you feel?"

"I was honest to the point of being brutal. Several times. Yes, she knows."

The impulse was strong and she made no effort to

resist it. Stretching up on her toes, she pressed a kiss to his cheek with a murmured "Thank you, Devon."

Never had such a simple expression of gratitude so arrowed into his heart. Words failed him; all he could do was smile down at her and hope she knew how much he appreciated all the goodness that she'd brought to his world. The smile she gave back to him was understanding, but tinged with sadness.

"What is it, Claire?" he asked, tracing the soft curve of her cheek with the back of his hand. "What's troubling you?"

"I feel sorry for Darice in a way. How embarrassed she must be to have made such a strident claim to your affections, only to have—"

"No pity for Darice," he interrupted gently, pressing his fingertips to her lips. "Not only would it be wasted on her, but she'd shred you to ribbons for your efforts at compassion. Stay away from her, please. Plead a headache or exhaustion or something of the like so you can take your midday meal in your room. I'll handle her."

She drew her face back from his touch just enough to quietly say, "I'm not going to hide from her, Devon. I promise that I won't do anything that might create a scene."

"It's not that at all," he protested, placing his hand back on her shoulder. "I don't want your feelings hurt."

A slim brow arched upward as mischief sparkled in her eyes. "You don't think that I can hold my own against her, do you?"

"I know Darice," he explained, admiring her spirit but wanting to protect her at the same time. "You're a much nicer person than she is, Claire. No, you can't hope to match her. And you wouldn't want to."

She considered him, her brows knitted and her lips pursed.

"Claire?" he said warily.

The corners of her mouth edged upward and the impish light in her eyes brightened. His heartbeat accelerated and she rewarded him by deliberately sliding her hands down his hips and then back to slowly caress his backside. He stopped breathing, stopped caring about anything beyond her touch, beyond the wild hope of being seduced.

As though in answer to his unspoken plea, she rose up onto her toes and feathered a kiss across his lips. His eyes drifted closed and she gifted him with another kiss, this one achingly sweeter, deliciously longer than the first.

He gathered her against him, reveling in the feel of her body pressed to his own, wanting more of her, wanting whatever she was willing to give him. His limbs weakened by burgeoning hunger, he twined his fingers in the golden strands of her hair, gently inviting her to possess him more deeply still, silently begging her to feed the desire she'd stirred to life.

She obliged, catching his lower lip between her own, holding it gently captive as she leisurely, boldly stroked it with the tip of her tongue. An exquisite jolt of pleasure shot through him, shattering his reserve. Timeless, primal instincts swept into the void, demanding that he ease her down and lose himself in loving her. God, he'd never wanted anything so desperately in all his life. Right here. Right now. Forever.

"Claire," he gasped between greedy gulps of air as he drew away. "What are you thinking, sweetheart?" he asked, gazing down at her, his senses reeling, his head light. "What do you want?"

"I..." she began, her voice quavering as she released her hold and let her arms fall to her sides. She paused, searching his face and trying to steady her breathing before saying softly, "I don't want to match her, Devon. I want to go her one better."

One? Sweet Jesus, she'd just easily managed a half

dozen. And then his heart cringed as the whole of her admission sank into his brain. "You're jealous?" he asked, incredulous. "Of Darice?"

She looked away, but not before he saw tears shimmering in her eyes. Tenderly taking her chin in hand, he brought her gaze back to meet his own. "You don't have any reason to be," he assured her with a smile. "Is that what just happened—between us—all about? Jealousy?"

"No," she answered on a ragged breath, mustering a tremulous smile for him. "It was in the beginning, but I forgot about it somewhere along the way."

God, she was so beautiful, so honest. And he wanted so badly for her to want him just for himself. "Do you remember when you forgot to be jealous?"

"When I moved my hands and your eyes got big. You stopped breathing and I stopped thinking."

Relief and hope washed over him in an exhilarating, intoxicating wave. Laughing, he pulled her to him, hugging her close and rubbing his cheek into the golden warmth of her hair. She wrapped her arms around his waist and burrowed her face into the linen of his shirt, making him feel oddly, wonderfully complete. And to think he owed this moment and all the possibilities within it to George Seaton-Smythe's nefarious little heart.

"Darice isn't the only woman in my past, you know," he offered casually, grinning.

She eased back in his embrace to look up at him, her brow arched daintily, her smile easy and accepting. "I assumed as much. You're a handsome man. You can even be charming when you put your mind to it."

"If I was willing to make a rough count," he offered, "would you be willing to do them all one better?"

She laughed outright and he watched her, thinking that there had to be a way he could overcome her objections to colonial rebellion, a way of making her forget her home in England. And while she'd never said a word on the subject, he knew that she opposed the institution of slavery. He could see it in her eyes when she looked at Ephram and Hannah. So many obstacles to surmount, to move past . . . How to go about it? He could—

A strangled sound came from behind him, interrupting his thoughts. He frowned, recognizing the voice and resenting the intrusion. Claire sobered and looked up at him, her lower lip caught between her teeth and a shadow of guilt shading her eyes. He winked in reassurance, tightened his embrace, and without giving the woman behind him so much as a glance, tautly asked, "Is there something you need in here, Aunt Elsbeth?"

A low hissing sound was the only response. Claire winced and, with an apologetic smile, leaned around him. He felt her start, felt her heart jump and begin to race. Drawing her back in front of him, shielding her with his body, he looked over his shoulder. And found Darice standing there, her eyes blazing and her hands fisted at her sides.

"Forgive me," he said wryly. "You and Aunt Elsbeth sound remarkably alike when in the throes of pique. Is there something *you* need in here, Darice?"

She glared at him and, through clenched, bared teeth, managed to say, "The Lee brothers have returned from their tour of your fields." Before he could respond, she turned and stomped off.

Devon shrugged and brought his attention back to Claire. "I'd much rather stay here with you than go entertain the Lees."

"But the requirements of hospitality being what they are, you must go anyway," she answered, bringing her arms from around him to place the palms of her hands against his chest. "And I have duties of my own to perform."

Cautiously, he asked, "Perhaps later we could find some time to be alone again?"

She nodded nervously and eased from his embrace.

"If you'd take this to the library with you when you go," she said, taking the vase of flowers from the counter and handing it to him, "I'd be most appreciative."

He considered the bouquet, his lips pursed as he tried to recall the last time anyone had thought to bring the beauty of flowers into Rosewind. "As am I, Claire," he said, his voice uncomfortably tight. With a brief bow, he turned and walked away before he could make an utter and complete fool of himself.

Claire watched him go, her hands pressed hard against her fluttering stomach and knowing that in surrendering to temptation, she'd committed herself to exploring a very dangerous path. And—God help her—the thought of venturing along it thrilled her every bit as much as it frightened her.

IT WAS, WITHOUT DOUBT, the most strained dining affair Claire had ever endured. Wyndom had hobbled in, his limp more pronounced than the day he'd arrived home and the swelling of his face reduced enough that his perpetual scowling was quite evident. He sat at the table between Elsbeth and Darice, each of whom not only shared his unhappy expression but also seemed inclined to wallow in the pool of his glowering silence.

Henrietta and the Lee brothers—bless them—resolutely tried to keep the conversation lively. It centered around trivial matters, mostly upcoming social events planned for the convening of the House of Burgesses. Having nothing to contribute to the discourse, Claire listened attentively, nodding and offering the most general observations and comments when called upon to do so.

And Devon... As Mother Rivard waxed poetic over the ballroom of the Governor's Mansion, Claire slid another quick glance in Devon's direction, finding him as he'd been throughout the course of the meal—casually leaning back in his chair, a secretive smile playing at the corners of his mouth as he watched her. His smile broadened as her gaze skimmed over it, and she looked away, her heart racing.

"And who," Francis Lightfoot asked, "will be squiring you to the Governor's Ball, Lady Lytton?"

"Having so recently returned from Philadelphia," she answered with amazing breeziness, "I have no idea who among the bachelors remains eligible. Devon's courtship and marriage may not be the only one to have happened so hastily."

Francis cocked a brow, but it was Mother Rivard who sailed into the awkward silence. "Wyndom would be honored to escort you, wouldn't you, Wyndom, dear?"

"I'd love to," he replied, his tone and frown belying the assertion. "As long as Darice doesn't mind a cripple hobbling alongside her. My knee is not mending well."

"Perhaps Lady Claire can make a compress that would help," his mother suggested, casting Claire a meaningful look. "Something that might take the swelling down. It would be a shame to attend the ball and not be able to dance. Don't you agree, Lady Claire?"

"Absolutely," she replied politely. "And I'll see to a compress immediately after luncheon. I'm sure what I need can be found in the storehouse. It won't take long at all."

Wyndom perked up a bit at the promise. With something resembling a genuine smile, he grasped his cane and leveraged himself upright. He addressed everyone at the table saying, "If you all would please excuse me, I'll start for my room now so that I have a reasonable chance of being there by the time Lady Claire is ready to work a miracle."

Amidst the murmurs of acceptance and encouragement, he ungracefully edged out from between the chairs and haltingly made his way toward the door.

Everyone fell silent, watching his slow progress. Claire was about to excuse herself to see to the making of the compress when Richard Henry turned to her and inquired as to which medicinal herbs she intended to use. Unable to politely escape, she resigned herself to answering and finishing out the meal with the others.

CLAIRE MAINTAINED a sedate pace as she moved down the pathway toward the storehouse, resisting the urge to gather up her skirts and run. She could feel Darice's gaze burning a hole in her back. Take a walk in the gardens with the woman? Not for all the tea in Boston Harbor. If Mother Rivard hadn't already provided her with an excuse to beg out of the ladies' excursion, she'd have conjured one up on her own.

The door creaked open on stiff hinges, allowing a shaft of bright afternoon light into the dark room. Claire slipped the iron dog into place with her foot, propping open the door so that she had the light necessary to find what she needed. She knew from previous searches that the shelf secured against the farthest wall held the crated bags of dried fruits and vegetables the kitchen garden had produced in years past. The tall shelf that stood as an island in the center of the storeroom's floor was the one packed full of the crocks containing the dried herbs and flowers used for both cooking and medicine.

Claire moved directly to it, scanning the brown paper labels neatly twine-tied around the various containers, searching for marigold, marjoram, thyme, lavender, and parsley. When she had found all of the dried plants, she retrieved an earthenware mixing bowl from the long, freestanding workbench behind her and set about creating the combination she wanted. "Equal parts marjoram, thyme, and parsley," she said quietly to herself, placing a handful of each into the bowl. "Two of lavender—one to reduce the swelling, one just because it smells so good." She smiled and removed the cork from the last of the crocks, adding, "And three of marigold, Mother's instant cure for whatever ails you."

Shifting the dried bits of plants through her fingers, she thoroughly mixed them together, breathing in the sweet fragrance. "Water or apple cider vinegar?" she asked herself aloud, dusting her hands clean over the bowl. Water wouldn't compromise the blend of scents, but neither would it contribute anything to the healing process. Vinegar, on the other hand, was a mild anti-inflammatory in its own right. And what would Wyndom care about scent anyway? All he wanted was to be able to walk without excruciating pain. Vinegar would certainly accomplish that goal much more quickly than water would.

"Vinegar, then," she decided, turning away from the table.

She started at the clank of pottery, the creak of protesting wood, and looked up just as the whole of the world toppled over and came crashing down.

CHAPTER NINETEEN

*G*IVEN LADY LYTTON'S general demeanor at the table," Francis Lightfoot mused, pouring a round of after-dinner brandies, "might I reasonably infer that she's a bit put out with you for having married someone else?"

"Ever the keen observer, Francis," his brother quipped as he settled into a chair beside the library hearth.

Unfazed, the younger Lee handed Devon a snifter and went on with a grin, "You're lucky to have escaped with your life. She's killed three husbands, you know."

"Figuratively speaking, of course," Richard Henry quickly added.

Devon narrowed his eyes and studied the dark spirits in his glass, remembering.

Francis snorted, but it was his brother who actually commented, "You don't honestly suspect foul play, do you, Devon?"

Suspecting murder and proving it were two very different things. And a careful search of Lytton Hall had turned up nothing that could even be considered circumstantial evidence. Devon shrugged and took a sip of his drink before replying, "All I know for sure is that Robert Lytton was barely a score of years older than I and every bit as healthy when he dropped dead last year."

"He might have had a bad heart," Francis suggested. "As I recall, his father died young."

"His father was thrown by a horse and trampled to death," Devon retorted. "According to my mother, his grandfather lived to be well over seventy."

"Lady Lytton has quite the reputation. It could well be that he was simply ridden to death."

"Francis!" his brother censured. "Lurid insinuation is for the pages of *Fanny Hill*. The Widow Lytton is a proper lady."

No, Devon silently corrected. Darice wasn't proper and she wasn't a lady. She just dressed better and had loftier airs than most whores. And while her reputation was indeed the stuff of legends, it was also false and wholly dependent on her lovers being gentleman enough not to share the details of their experiences.

"You don't believe that's possible?" Francis pressed, leaning close. "The bad heart? I heard he died in her bed."

"I didn't say a word," Devon replied. He took another sip of his brandy, trying to banish the memory of Robert Lytton's blue-tinged face, the memory of how the hair on the back of his neck had prickled at the sight of the man lying stiff and cold among the lace-edged pillows of Darice's bed.

"My keen observational skills," Francis said quietly, leaning closer still, "are telling me that there's a story to be told here."

"If you suspect foul play," his brother added, "you have a legal and ethical obligation to speak up, Devon. An inquest can be convened to make a formal inquiry."

An inquest that would require him to publicly admit to having bedded the Widow Lytton in order to conduct his own investigation into Robert's death. He'd come up empty-handed and a group of his peers wasn't likely to do any better. No, hell would have to freeze before he made his suspicions and actions public knowledge. It was bad enough that his friends and family knew what he'd done. Even if they weren't privy to his true motivations. No one—friends, family, and the public alike—would believe them, and in the end he'd look the fool for trying to put a noble light on having bedded the damn woman. Humiliating himself wasn't likely to bring Darice to justice and it sure as hell wasn't going to bring Robert Lytton back from the dead.

Devon polished off the last of his brandy and set the snifter aside. "I don't see any real cause for calling an inquest," he began, choosing his words carefully. "I think—"

The rest of what he'd been about to say died on the tip of his tongue as Mary Margaret Malone staggered into the doorway, gasping for air and clutching the jamb for dear life.

"Meg!" he cried, instantly starting for her, her panic already his own. "What happened?"

"In the storehouse," she rasped. "Lady Claire—"

His heart shot into his throat and he didn't wait to hear any more.

As HANNAH'S FRANTIC efforts succeeded in creating an opening in the debris, Claire summoned a reassuring smile.

"Are you sure you're not injured?" Hannah asked, peering at her face and moving aside yet another handful of shattered pottery.

Claire spat out a bit of what tasted like oregano before carefully turning her head to look up at the underside of the workbench and answering, "I got most of myself under the table. It's just my legs that are sticking out, I think. They don't hurt, but I can't move them for all the weight on my skirts. I can move my arms, but I'm afraid I'll cut myself if I do."

"No, child. Just lie there quietly and let me clear it away."

"Claire!"

Devon. Bless him. He was as terrified as she'd been when the shelf first toppled over.

"I'm all right," she called out as Hannah disappeared from sight. In the next instant, Devon was there, reaching through the opening to cup her cheek in the warmth of his hand. She turned her head, placing a quick kiss in the calloused palm. "Really, Devon," she assured him as she snuggled her cheek back into the comfort of his touch. "I just can't get myself out."

"Don't even try to," he crisply commanded, drawing back. "We'll have you free in just a moment."

Claire winced as she saw him kick aside not only bits of broken pottery but some of the pots that had somehow survived the fall. Her heart sank. All the crocks. All the herbs. Years of labor, lost.

"On three, Richard Henry. One . . . two . . . three!"

There was a sudden groaning of wood, the crash of still more crockery. Bits of dried plants swirled through the air and drifted down around her. Claire held her breath, wondering how many pots there were left to fall. She turned her head to look back over her shoulder and saw Devon's booted, muscled legs amidst the debris. As she watched, he reached down, grabbed a crock in each hand, and flung them away.

"Devon," she protested over their shattering, "please don't do any more damage than has already been done. There's no great hurry. I'm all right."

"By the grace of God, it would appear," she heard Francis Lightfoot say in the vicinity of her head. "How on earth did you bring that shelf down on yourself, Lady Claire?"

"I didn't," she countered, shifting about to see him widening the opening Hannah had made. Over the continued noise of pottery breaking all around her, she said, "At least not by doing anything that I'm aware of. I was working at the table and had turned around to go get vinegar when it simply tilted over and came down."

"Thank goodness the table is a sturdy one," Richard Henry observed from somewhere—judging by the sound—near Devon. "Any less stout and it might not have sheltered you."

"If she'd been any less quick in diving for cover," Devon growled, "the sturdiness of the table wouldn't have mattered."

She'd be dead, Claire silently finished for him. Her stomach twisted and went leaden as a cold certainty swept through her. Telling herself that the danger was past, that she'd survived, didn't ease her trembling in the least. Neither did berating herself for cowardice. Her poise deserted her and she pushed herself up, suddenly desperate to escape the confines of her makeshift shelter.

She'd barely begun to struggle when Devon scooped her up from the debris and cradled her in his arms. She clung to the solid, certain strength of him, burrowing her face into the warm white linen of his shirt and the hard muscled planes beneath. He held her tightly to him and, in the haven of his embrace, the grip of fear began to relax.

"Hang on," he said softly as he turned and kicked his way through the wreckage.

The movement brought her awareness back to the larger reality. They were outside the storehouse before she could make the words in her head tumble off her tongue. "Devon, this isn't necessary," she protested.

"I'm a bit battered and bruised, but I'm perfectly able to stand on my own two feet."

He paused, but instead of setting her down, he shifted his hold so that she rested even closer to his chest. She looked up to see his jaw tighten, a storm gathering in his eyes. Her heart began to race again and she tightened her arms around his neck.

"Meg, will you see to cleaning up?"

"Aye, sir. An' not to worry, Lady Claire, I'll be salvagin' everythin' that I can."

"The compress mixture," Claire whispered, remembering and trying to turn so that she could see past Devon's shoulder into the rubble of the storehouse. "Is it still there?"

Devon stared down at the bundle in his arms, incredulous. She'd damn near been killed and she was worried about the compress she'd been making for Wyndom? "Hannah," he said simply, pulling Claire close again and starting for the house.

"I'll see to it, Lady Claire," the woman called after them. "And that it gets to Mr. Wyndom."

"There," he said gruffly as he carried Claire up the back steps. "It's been taken care of. You needn't give it another thought."

"Devon," she said softly as they emerged from the dining room and entered the foyer. "I'm embarrassed enough at having to be hauled out of the rubble. But to be carried away like a child . . . Please put me down."

"No." He wasn't sure when he'd be able to let go of her. As long as he was holding her, he could feel her heart beating, feel the warmth of her life pressed against him. It was all he'd wanted, all he'd hoped for in those first seconds after reaching the storehouse. Knowing that she was pinned, imagining the shredded flesh and mangled, crushed bones . . . He hugged her as he started up the stairs, feeling again the relief that had washed over him as he'd cleared the last of the debris away and she'd moved her legs. And as it had in the immediate aftermath, rage came again on the heels of gratitude and renewed his strength.

"Why are you angry?" she asked quietly as he carried her down the hall.

"Because at the moment, I could kill," he answered honestly.

"Who do you want to kill? Me?"

He stopped in his tracks and gazed down into wary, troubled eyes. "God, no. Never."

She smiled and relaxed against him. "Then who?"

"Darice comes to mind," he admitted, resuming his course.

"You're not making any sense at all."

He opened the door to her room with one hand and, using his foot to kick it closed behind them, carried her to the bed while explaining, "That shelf weighs a good twenty-five stone, Claire. There are only two ways it could have come over. The first is if someone were to climb up on the shelves to reach for something and his or her weight pulled it over."

"I wasn't climbing on them. I was simply standing there."

"You don't weigh enough to offset the balance, anyway," he declared, settling her into the center of the feather bed. Bracing himself with a hand on either side of her hips, he met her gaze squarely and said quietly, "Which leaves the second alternative as the only reasonable explanation. Someone pushed it over on you."

She considered him briefly and then slowly shook her head. "I was standing in the light of the doorway the entire time I was in there, Devon. No one came in."

"Then someone was in there, waiting for you to arrive," he said. "Waiting for the chance to kill you."

"As much as I dislike Darice, I wish I could say that it was her. But it wasn't, Devon. She and your mother and Elsbeth were walking along the flower beds as I went out. I left them at the back door."

"Wyndom."

She shook her head again and gently brushed a lock of hair off his forehead. "He went to his room while we were all still at the table. And as injured as he is, he doesn't have the strength it would have taken to push over the shelves. Neither does he have the speed and agility it would have required to have escaped the storehouse and be out of sight in the time it took for Meg and Hannah to hear the crash and get there from the kitchen."

God help him, his mind was wandering. He wanted so badly to lean just a little bit forward, to kiss her and gently ease her back into the feathery softness of the bed. "Richard Henry and Francis Lightfoot were with me in the library," he said tightly, pushing himself upright and taking a step back from the edge of temptation.

"We seem to be at a loss for a culprit," she announced, laughing softly.

He took another step back. "Hannah, Meg, and Ephram have yet to be accounted for."

"You can't be serious. Hannah and Meg? They're the only friends I have in this world. Besides, they were together in the kitchen. And Ephram? Why would Ephram want to do me any harm, Devon?"

"He wouldn't." The fear that had gripped him when Meg had rushed into the library tightened around his heart again. Fear of something nameless, faceless, unknown. "But someone had to have pushed that shelf over on you. It didn't just topple all by itself."

She shrugged. "I shifted a good many things around in searching for what I needed for the compress. It could be that I inadvertently upset the balance so that it tipped over on its own."

"You're stretching plausibility."

"And you're not?" she asked, exasperated. "Who, aside from my uncle, would want me dead? And I will remind you that George Seaton-Smythe is in England, no doubt frantically meeting with his barristers."

An entirely new and far more frightening realm of possibilities opened up before his mind's eye. "We don't know that as a certainty."

"So you think there's a possibility that Uncle George is skulking about in the woods of Rosewind, watching me, awaiting an opportunity to do me in?" She didn't give him a chance to answer. "George Seaton-Smythe's only familiarity with woods of any sort comes from having passed through one or two while riding to the hounds. He has neither the ability nor the inclination to play at being a poacher, Devon. Either here or in England."

"He could have hired someone to do the deed for him," Devon suggested, his mind racing. "He does know where you are, Claire."

"True," she admitted. "But that possibility is based on the assumption of several others. The first of which is that he would have had to arrange to have me killed at the same time that he was dispatching me to be your wife. Which presumes that he was aware of the court's investigation of him and that I would be summoned to testify against him.

"I doubt very much that the King's officers politely announced their intentions in advance so that he could set about plotting the demise of witnesses. Then, of course, we have to ask why he would bother to marry me off to you, Devon, when his larger intent is to have me killed. It's a most unnecessary scheme."

"Not if he wanted to be able to tell his hireling precisely where to find you."

She rolled her eyes and began scooting toward the edge of the mattress. The hems of her skirts hiked up as she moved, and despite her one-handed effort to keep them down, Devon was afforded a delightful display of long, shapely legs. If this was God's idea of helping him resist temptation, God was a sadist, pure and simple.

"Would it make you feel better if I agreed with you, Devon?"

Hell, he couldn't remember what they were disagreeing about. And if he had to stand there and watch her fumble with her skirts for one more second, he was going to forget a lot more than that. Devon stepped forward, offering her his hands and saying, "You'll remain here, in this room, with the door bolted, until Darice leaves the house. Is that clear?"

She stood in front of him, the bed brushing against the backs of her legs, her hands gently enveloped in his and wishing he would lean down and kiss her until they tumbled mindlessly onto the bed. That he'd stay with her until Darice left. But it was a fool's hope, a wanton's desire, and so she drew her hands from his and stepped away, blithely saying, "My gown's shredded and I don't have another that's been altered to fit me. It will take me a good hour to make myself presentable."

He seemed to find it hard to swallow and his voice was tight when he replied, "Perfect. You're safe here."

"Someone could put a ladder up against the side of the house, crawl through the window, and attack me," she teased. His gaze instantly went to the window and in the next heartbeat he was moving toward it with long, purposeful strides. "Oh, Devon, really. I was being facetious."

"And I'm being cautious," he shot back, checking the lock. "Humor me."

"Thank you for being concerned."

He slowly turned from the window, his gaze going to the door before it came back to her. Squaring his shoulders and taking a deep breath, he finally said, "I need to go. The Lees are undoubtedly waiting for a report on your condition. It'd be unkind to make them worry unduly."

He obviously didn't want to go, and it lightened her heart. She nodded in understanding and acceptance. "I'll be down as soon as I can."

"I'll check the window locks in my room before I go downstairs. Are you sure you're all right?"

"Yes, Devon. I'm fine."

He hesitated for a moment and then, with a crisp nod, moved to the door connecting their rooms. She watched it close behind him, wondering what would have happened if the Lees hadn't been there. Would he have stayed with her? If he had, would she have thrown caution to the wind and tried to seduce him?

Probably.

Claire sighed and sank down on the edge of the bed, her legs suddenly too weak to hold her. Why did being anywhere near Devon scatter her thinking? What had happened to her sense of purpose, to the dreams that had always sustained her? Casting them aside for an impoverished, slave-owning man willing to commit high treason was beyond irrational. And yet when she was with Devon, when he touched her, reason ceased to exist. Why?

A soft rapping on her door pulled her from her musings. She stared at it, remembering that Devon had wanted her to bolt it and that she hadn't. The knock came again, this time a bit more insistent than before.

"Lady Claire? It's Wyndom."

Claire pushed herself off the bed and crossed to the door, feeling guilty for having been so absorbed in her own worries that she'd forgotten all about Wyndom's. She opened the door to find him leaning heavily on his cane and offering her a heart-wrenchingly painful smile.

"I hope I haven't disturbed you," he said before she could apologize for her selfishness.

"Not at all. Hasn't Hannah brought you the compress yet?"

"Yes, a few minutes ago. And she told me about the

accident in the storeroom. She wanted to apply the compress for me, but I insisted on coming down to your room first, to tell you how terrible I feel that you were endangered while doing a kindness for me."

"There's no need for you to feel anything of the sort, Wyndom," she assured him, her guilt deepening another degree. "Accidents happen. Now please go back to your room, elevate your leg, and put the compress on your knee. I'll bring you a tray this evening so that you don't have to struggle down the stairs. Pushing yourself will only slow the healing process."

He didn't make the slightest effort to move. "You're a very kind woman, Lady Claire. It's been for the benefit of all of us that Devon was forced to marry you."

It was a backhanded compliment if she'd ever heard one. And it was somehow so very Wyndom. And endearing. "Thank you."

"You will be careful around Darice, won't you? She's not the sort of woman who loses gracefully. Especially when it's something she wants so badly and has worked so hard to get. She set her cap for Devon a long time ago. The only reason she married Robert Lytton was to be within casual visiting distance of Rosewind."

"I'll be careful," she promised absently, feeling a deeper sense of pity for the late Robert Lytton than any fear of Darice. "Now, please, Wyndom, go back to your room and put the compress on your knee. If you'd like help with it, I'd be happy to oblige."

"It's most kind of you to offer, but I can manage on my own," he replied, turning away from the door. He winced and sucked a breath through his teeth. Claire cringed in sympathy and he gave her a strained smile, adding, "I'm much too young to be so affected by damp and chill, you know."

Damp and chill? Her brows knitted in consternation, Claire focused her awareness on the air around her and discovered that Wyndom was absolutely right. It was damp and considerably cooler than she recalled it being when she'd crossed the yard to the storehouse. "I'm sure that Meg and Ephram are lighting the downstairs fires already," she said. "I'm equally sure that one of them will be up straightaway to see to the one in your room."

"You're a rare gem, Lady Claire."

Claire softly closed the door and then leaned her forehead against the cool wood. The weather had changed and she hadn't noticed. As the mistress of Rosewind, it was her responsibility to see that the fires were being lit, that the food being prepared for tonight was appropriate for the weather. And she hadn't done any of it because she'd been oblivious to what was happening in the world around her. Dear Lord. If that didn't say something about the depth of her preoccupation with Devon, nothing did. A rare gem, indeed. Her brain was filled with common rocks.

CLAIRE GLANCED out the window to make sure Darice's carriage hadn't returned, and then checked her reflection in the cheval mirror one last time. Deciding that the hastily modified gown was good enough for the time being, she dashed out of her room, resolving yet again to keep her mind steadfastly focused on her duties. She'd barely reached the foyer when the Lee brothers and Devon emerged from the library, hats in hand.

"Ah, Lady Claire," Francis called to her. "We were hoping to see you before we left for home."

"You're leaving Rosewind?" she asked, glancing out the front windows to make sure that she hadn't lost track of the time of day as she had the weather. "But it's so late. Why don't you wait until morning?"

"A storm front is coming in from the northeast,"

Richard Henry said. "We've been watching the line build since before noon."

"Even more reason to stay," she countered. "If you leave now, you'll be drenched to the skin before you're more than a league from the house. And given how chilly it's become, you're likely to catch your deaths of cold."

Devon slipped past the brothers, saying as he came toward her, "This is a slow-moving storm, Claire. It'll be hours before it gets here." Stopping in front of her, he smiled and presented his arm, adding, "And since Richard Henry and Francis Lightfoot will be riding away from it, they can easily beat it home."

She hesitated to take his arm just long enough to remind herself of her determination to keep her wits about her. Just long enough for Devon to cock a brow in silent question and trigger a delightful flutter in the center of her chest.

"Weather this time of year tends to move in and settle, Lady Claire," Francis explained as his brother led the way to the front door. "If we don't leave now, it could well be a week before we have another opportunity to travel. And we've imposed on your gracious hospitality for long enough already."

"You haven't been an imposition at all," she protested as Devon escorted her out of the house in the Lees' wake. "We've thoroughly enjoyed your company."

Richard Henry paused on the front steps to give her a perfunctory bow and what was undoubtedly a traditional rejoinder for the circumstance. "As we have very much enjoyed our time at Rosewind."

"Ah, here comes Ephram," Francis announced as the man came around the side of the house, leading the Lees' horses. "His sense of timing is positively uncanny, isn't it?"

In response, Richard Henry turned to Devon and said, "When you told us two years ago that we were needlessly dependent on slave labor, I honestly thought you'd taken leave of your senses. But having seen for myself the health of your fields and the smooth functioning of your household...all achieved and maintained with only the most minimal labor...If you choose to reintroduce your bill this session of the House, I'd be willing to consider it."

"As would I," seconded Francis as he charged down the steps to take the reins from Ephram.

Devon extended his hand to Richard Henry, saying as the other man grasped it, "Thank you. With your support, it might actually pass this time."

Two years ago? Was this the law Hannah had mentioned? Claire wondered, watching the Lees swing up to their saddles.

Francis called out, "We hope to see you in Williamsburg in two weeks, Lady Claire. Do remember to bring your dancing shoes."

"I will," she promised, waving and knowing that she didn't own any. "It's been a pleasure to have you as our guests, gentlemen. You're always welcome at Rosewind. Godspeed and travel safely."

Richard Henry touched his hand to the brim of his hat and his heels to the horse's flanks. Francis, with one more jaunty wave, took off after his brother.

They were almost to the end of the drive when Devon quietly said, "I thought they'd never leave."

"Devon!" she laughingly chided.

"Well, it's true. I have work to do and instead I've been playing host."

The Lees reached the end of the drive, reined in their mounts, and turned back to wave one more time. While waving in return, Claire observed, "But the time appears to have been well spent. The Lees are willing to vote in favor of your proposed law. Which, apparently, they couldn't bring themselves to do two years ago."

"No one could. You would have thought I was asking them all to slit their own throats."

As the brothers galloped from sight, she looked up at the man who was her husband and decided that there was no time like the present. "What did you ask of them?"

He sighed and, staring off into the distance, answered flatly, "That they change the law to allow a slave owner to free his slaves if he so desires. That they legalize manumission."

"Do you mean to tell me that you couldn't give Hannah and Ephram their freedom even if you wanted to?" she asked, astounded. "That there are laws that say what you can and can't do with your own property? And that you've made these laws yourselves?"

He turned his head to meet her gaze and with a rueful smile replied, "Yes. Yes. And, amazingly, yes."

"My God, Devon. It simply boggles the mind."

He looked back out over the front lawn of Rosewind and his smile faded. "Human bondage is an indefensible practice, Claire. Economically, socially, and philosophically indefensible. If we can't bring ourselves to end it, it will someday be the ruin of us all."

She had misjudged him terribly. "I had no idea you felt that way. I thought you'd reduced the number of slaves you owned simply because you needed the money."

"If money had been my chief motivation," he replied, the rueful smile returning, "I could've made a lot more of it than I did. I sold my people mostly to yeoman farmers out in the Piedmont. They have a better chance of living like free men and women there. Society itself isn't as law-bound on the frontier." With a heavy sigh he shrugged and added, "It was the best I could do."

And he considered the effort a very personal and painful failure. "Sometimes our best is all we can do," she said softly, touching his cheek, wishing with all her heart that she had the power to make the world as right as he wanted it to be.

Devon covered her hand with his own and closed his eyes, reveling in the strength she so lovingly poured into him. With her standing beside him, no pain would ever be too deep to bear, no shame so damning that it had to be borne in silence. "I can't tell you how many nights I've lain awake, staring up at the ceiling and wondering how I'm going to face God and explain just why it was that I owned my half brother." He opened his eyes to gaze down at her. "That would be Ephram, in case you haven't already surmised the truth."

"I have," she replied softly. "And I think God will know what's in your heart, Devon. He knows what efforts you've made to change the situation."

She obviously believed the Maker was a far more attentive and kinder deity than he did. "What's the saying? The road to hell is paved with good intentions?"

"I don't think it applies in this situation," she replied, smiling. "Besides, the Lee brothers are willing to help you make a difference. You'll succeed this time, Devon. And if there's anything I can do, you need only ask."

"You've already done it." He brought her hand from his cheek and pressed a kiss to her fingertips. "You've proven to Richard Henry and Francis Lightfoot that a home can be run without an army of slaves."

Her smile broadened and she made no attempt to pull her hand from his possession. "It's not the men you need to convince of that particular possibility. It's their wives."

"And I have every confidence in your ability to sway them as well. I'll make the case in the House of Burgesses, and you can make it over tea in the meeting room at the Raleigh Tavern. Fair enough?"

"Fair enough, Devon. I'll do my best." She blinked and a pensive shadow tinged the edges of her smile. "I suppose I'll have to do some needlepointing in the course of my mission, won't I?"

He remembered that first day, the carriage ride from Williamsburg and how vehemently she'd declared her loathing of traditional feminine pursuits. "More than likely," he admitted, grinning.

"Only for you, Devon," she whispered, her eyes sparkling. "I wouldn't willingly needlepoint for any other man on earth."

Just how special was he? Devon wondered, his heartbeat suddenly hammering in his ears. "Does it help to know that I'm most appreciative?" he asked, slowly slipping his arm around her waist and drawing her closer.

"Yes, it does."

He brought her fingertips to his lips again, watching her as he feathered another kiss across them. Her breath caught and she leaned into him, her lips parting and her free hand coming to rest lightly over his pounding heart. *Make love to me, Claire.*

Abruptly, she turned her head and frowned. Her shoulders sagging, she asked, "Is that Edmund Cantrell coming up the drive?"

He choked back a snarl of frustration and glared out at the drive, only then hearing the thunder of hooves. "Yes, dammit." Good God Almighty. Had someone put up a sign somewhere inviting the entire world to encamp at Rosewind?

She stepped out of his arms, saying, "I'll leave you to the welcoming while I go tell Hannah and Meg that we're not yet done dispensing hospitality. Do you think he'll be staying the night?"

"More than likely," he answered morosely.

She softly said, "I'm sorry," and then stepped into the house. He watched her go, his chest aching with a strange kind of want, his throat scratchy and tight. And beneath the physical sensations, buried deep, was a sense that some great, glorious treasure was lying just beyond his grasp. That anything and everything a man could ever desire would be his if he only had the wisdom to put a name to the prize and the courage to step forward and take it.

CHAPTER TWENTY

*R*AIN POUNDED against the windows. In the near distance, lightning flashed and thunder rumbled in reply. Claire settled back into her chair, her wineglass in hand, thinking that it really had been a lovely meal. Hannah and Meg had outdone themselves and the food had been divine. Elsbeth and Mother Rivard had pleaded aching joints just after the storm had set in and, like Wyndom, had taken their evening repast in the privacy and comfort of their rooms.

It was something, Claire had decided during the soup course, that she was going to encourage them to do more often. It had been rather nice not to have Elsbeth monopolizing conversations and slinging barbs. And while Mother Rivard was a dear, it had been a relief to pass a meal without having to shepherd her illusions and sensibilities.

Claire's gaze traveled to their guest, who was, at the moment and to Devon's apparent amusement, attempting to bounce a shilling off the tabletop and into his empty wineglass. It was hard to believe this Edmund Cantrell was the same man who so somberly occupied a law office in Williamsburg. For as long as she lived, she'd never forget looking up from her soup to find him grinning at her, his spoon magically dangling from the end of his nose.

The shilling missed the glass and skipped across the white linen toward Devon. Snatching it up before Edmund could, he declared it his turn to try. Edmund produced another shilling from his pocket and was about to make it a true competition when the door to the butler's pantry swung open. He dropped the coin on the table in the same instant that he came to his feet.

Hiding her grin around the rim of her wineglass, Claire waited for the next act of the delightful performance. Act one had begun the instant Meg had brought in the soup. As she'd begun to serve, Edmund had not so subtly kicked Devon in the shin to initiate an introduction. Meg had been surprised, but handled the decidedly unconventional moment with aplomb.

Act two had commenced with the removal of the soup bowls and the serving of the salad. In the course of it, Edmund had established that they were both unattached and currently uninvolved. Meg had blushed, dismissed his obvious interest with a roll of her eyes, and then stolen glances at him when she thought he wasn't looking. He'd caught her every time, and when she finally escaped, her face had been positively flushed.

Act three had been during the removal of the salad plates and the serving of the main course. Edmund had simply grinned and watched her work. Meg had tried— and failed miserably—to ignore him.

Act four . . . dessert. Edmund had lyrically told Meg that any woman who could make such delicious lemon pie deserved the key to his heart. Which he was gladly willing to surrender on the spot. Meg had paused at the door, said she could appreciate such devotion, and promised to introduce him to Hannah.

And now Meg was back and for the last time. If Edmund didn't want the evening to be a waste of persistent flirtation, then he was going to have to take decisive action within the next minute or two. Only dessert plates, silverware, and two empty wineglasses needed to be cleared away. It wouldn't take long for Meg to have it all gathered up and be gone.

Claire glanced at Devon, who was sitting with his elbows propped on the table, watching the scene with evident interest. His gaze slid to hers and he gave her one of his heart-tripping smiles.

"Allow me to assist you in taking these things out, Mistress Malone."

Claire tore her attention away from Devon to find Edmund holding Meg's serving tray. Meg stood on the other side of it, trying to take it away from him. " 'Tisn't necessary, Mr. Cantrell," she protested. "An' 'tisn't appropriate, either. A guest doesn't carry his own dishes to the kitchen."

He grinned and tugged on the tray. "I'm not a guest. I'm one of the family. And if you think I prefer the after-dinner company of Devon over that of a beautiful Irish lass, then we really ought to take this chance for you to get to know me better."

Devon laughed. "Let him help, Meg. But keep that cleaver handy."

"I'll not be a needin' any cleaver, Mr. Devon," the Irishwoman shot back, releasing her claim to the tray. "I'll have a righteous Hannah right by me side. He'll not get away with anythin' untoward."

Edmund, all innocence, freed a hand to press it over his heart. "Untoward? Me? I assure you, Mistress Malone, that my intentions are purely honorable."

"Oh, an' 'tis the first time I've ever heard those

words," Meg scoffed, pushing open the pantry door. He stepped past her with the laden tray and she followed, adding, "Mind the silverware doesn't slip off the plates there, Mr. Cantrell. I don't want to spend hours muckin' about in the mud a lookin' for a fork that's been allowed to go missin' 'cause ye was all moony-eyed."

The door swung closed behind them and then there was only the sound of the wind, the rain, and the rumble of nearing thunder. Claire sipped her wine, feeling Devon's gaze touching her and delighting in the caress.

"We seem to have found ourselves alone," he said quietly, his voice warm velvet, his quirked smile still in place. He rose from his chair and came toward her, adding, "What would you like to do with our evening, Madame Rivard?"

See where a kiss might take us. Reason instantly reminded her that it would take them into a permanent union that would cost her everything. Her heart promised that love would make not only their bodies one, but their minds as well. If she had the courage to take a leap of faith. "Perhaps you could read me some of Mr. Shakespeare's sonnets."

"Perhaps not," he instantly countered, his eyes bright and his smile widening as he held out his hand. "Think of something else."

Make love. She put her hand in his. Her heart—and reason—went with it.

Drawing her to her feet, he whispered, "Something a bit decadent. Maybe even a little wicked."

All night long.

"I'm thinking," she hedged, shocked at the unerring direction of her thoughts. The devilish light that suddenly ignited in his eyes emboldened her enough to confess, "Most unseemly thoughts."

With his free hand, he reached into his coat pocket and produced the coin he'd taken from Edmund. "A shilling if you'll share them with me."

"Oh, they're worth far more than that, sir."

"I might be willing to pay a sovereign," he countered, a delightfully wolfish edge in his smile. "If you'd be willing to give me a small sample to assure me that the coin's worth finding."

Would you give me your heart? Your love? "It's not your money I need, Devon."

He laughed softly. "That's good. Because I don't have any." He blindly tossed Edmund's coin on the table, then slipped his arms around her waist and drew her to him. "I do, however," he murmured, "seem to have recently acquired a great deal of hope."

"About what?" she asked, slipping her hands up and over his shoulders to brazenly undo the bow at his nape. He said nothing, and in his dazzled, breathless silence, she became braver still. Letting the ribbon fall, she threaded her fingers through the silken warmth of his dark hair. "Hope about what, Devon?" she asked again.

"Life," he whispered, gazing down at her, his eyes dark pools of wonder and appreciation. "Claire, I want to—"

They both started at the crash and turned as one toward the sound. Rosewind's front door stood wide open, with wind and leaves and rain and a sodden Darice Lytton blowing in through it.

"Goddamnit!"

Yes, Claire thought. Devon had summed up her own feelings perfectly. She'd never in all her life so resented an intrusion.

"You can't turn me away!" Darice wailed from the threshold, water dripping from all over her and pooling around her feet. "You just can't. The roof of Lytton Hall is leaking like a sieve. There's water everywhere. Everywhere! All my beautiful things are being ruined. I couldn't bear to watch."

Devon quietly growled, "Well, God forbid that she

stay there and put some effort into saving what she could."

"It's too late for her to go back tonight," Claire observed just as privately. "We'll just have to be gracious about it."

Devon swore again, but she ignored him and glided forward with a feigned smile and reassuring words. "I'm so sorry for your loss, Lady Lytton. Of course you're welcome to spend the night here. And in the morning we'll all go over to Lytton Hall and see what we can do to salvage your possessions. I'm sure that, in the light of a new day, things won't seem nearly as disastrous as they do this evening."

"I'm soaked to the skin," she declared, smoothing her bodice down. It had been tight when dry, and was now clinging to her more-than-ample breasts.

Devon, apparently rooted to the dining room floor, indulged in another round of muttered curses. Claire took a candle lamp from a foyer table and moved toward the stairs, saying, "Then let's be about getting you settled into a guest room so that you can change into something dry. I'm sure that we can find you some—"

"Devon," Darice interrupted her to purr, "do be a dear and send your man out to help mine with my baggage. I'll need the blue leather trunk brought up straightaway."

The woman had taken the time to pack her clothes before fleeing her flooding home? Claire stopped on the stairs and looked over her shoulder, incredulous. She was even more stunned to find Darice standing in the doorway with her skirt hiked up to a scandalous degree and wringing the water out of it. Devon, his chin lowered and his hands fisted at his sides, was striding toward the woman. Claire was about to call out, to beg him not to harm her, when he altered his course just enough to avoid running her down as he stormed out of the house. Darice looked after him, a satisfied smile touching the corners of her mouth.

Claire tamped down her anger as best she could. "This way, Lady Darice," she said curtly. She gestured to the top of the stairs, and Darice found the good grace to accede to what was an obvious command.

As Darice followed her, Claire silently chastised herself for rudeness and then made a deliberate, valiant effort to be a bit more cordial. "I hope you don't mind if we lodge you in the room adjoining Mr. Cantrell's. The Lee brothers left just hours ago, and we haven't had time to prepare those chambers for another guest."

"As long as there's a sturdy bolt on the connecting door."

Darice thought Edmund would sneak in and try to seduce her? "I don't think you need be concerned," she replied, unable to keep her amusement suppressed. "Mr. Cantrell seems to be developing an interest in Meg. I rather suspect he'll spend most of the night in the kitchen paying court to her."

"A solicitor courting an indentured servant?" Darice sneered. "A common kitchen maid?"

Hospitality, Claire reminded herself. *Cordial hospitality.* "I don't think the notion of social class means all that much to Mr. Cantrell. He strikes me as a most open-minded man."

"Any man who can court money and chooses not to is a fool."

"Some people simply don't value wealth as much as others do," Claire pointed out, knowing even as she did that the observation was falling on closed ears.

"Well, Devon certainly isn't one of them," Darice asserted, laughing. "Money matters more to Devon than anything else on earth."

No, it didn't, but Darice's ignorance was to her advantage. Stopping, Claire opened the door of the guest room, then turned and handed Darice the candle lamp while saying, "I hope you find the accommodations satisfactory. I'm sure your baggage will be up shortly. Good night, Darice."

"I want some hot tea brought up as soon as possible," Darice announced, making not the slightest effort to move out of Claire's path or into the room. "And some scones. With clotted cream and strawberry jam. I was too distraught to even think of eating before I left Lytton Hall."

You weren't too distraught; you were too busy packing to move into Rosewind. Go to hell, Darice. And take your scones, clotted cream, and strawberry jam with you. Claire stepped around the woman and walked away replying tightly, "I'll see what can be done." *Your Majesty.*

She met Ephram and the blue trunk on their way up the stairs, noting that his clothing was as dry as the proverbial bone. "He's going to kill her," he muttered as she stomped past.

"Good. I'll help him," she shot back, continuing on her way, seething. There was a huge stack of sopping, dripping trunks in the center of the foyer floor, and while Devon was nowhere to be seen, she could hear him swearing above the roar of the wind and rain. She looked out into the darkness, seeing only the slashing of rain and the driver struggling to free the poor, soaked horses from their harnesses.

She went on, knowing there was nothing she could do at the moment to assist Devon in dragging things in. And Lord knew she wouldn't be able to calm him, either. Her own anger was burning just as brightly. Together, they would gleefully murder the Widow Lytton.

The rain was cold and heavy and wind driven. And she was not only drenched but swearing aloud by the time she dragged her sodden, muddy skirts through the ˙tchen door.

Hannah, Meg, and Edmund were leisurely seated in front of the cooking hearth, teacups in hand. All three turned at her entrance, their mouths agape. Edmund recovered first, gaining his feet and saying, "My God. You're steaming. Literally steaming."

"Darice Lytton is back," Claire announced, advancing on the central worktable and the tea service sitting on it. "The roof of Lytton Hall is leaking and it's just too dreadfully wet for Her Highness to stay there tonight. She wants hot tea and scones with clotted cream and strawberry jam brought up to her immediately."

"Scones?" Meg repeated, almost choking. "She wants us to be makin' her scones this time o' the night?"

"What the Princess wants," Claire snapped, slapping a basket of leftover dinner biscuits onto the tray, "and what the Princess is going to get are two very different things. She'll be happy to get tepid tea and cold biscuits, or she can haul herself and her baggage right back to Lytton Hall."

"The Princess isn't here for tea and scones," Edmund calmly announced, setting his teacup on the table. "She's here for Devon. Where is he?"

Claire, accepting a clean but utilitarian cup and saucer from Hannah, replied, "At the moment, he's hauling Her Majesty's considerable wardrobe in out of the rain. And he's none too happy about it, I might add."

Edmund crossed to the door and picked up an oilskin tarp. As Claire headed toward him with the tray, he looked past her and smiled. "The needs of friendship require me to leave you for a bit, my dearest Meg. But keep a light on for me. I'll be back as soon as I have Devon tucked into the solitary safety of his room."

With Edmund at her side and holding the tarp over their heads, Claire stepped back out into the night and the storm. There was no shouting over the wind, and so she waited until they'd entered the butler's panty and closed the door to say, "Devon doesn't need a keeper."

Tossing the tarp aside, Edmund rushed ahead to push open the dining room door. "Agreed. He needs someone to guard his flank. Darice Lytton could have taught the Trojans a thing or two about surprise attacks."

She managed a smile, the first since the woman had burst into the house and shattered the magic moment with Devon. In the foyer they found a mountain of luggage surrounded by a pond of water. Ephram and another dark-skinned man were using sheets and brooms in what appeared to be a largely futile attempt to keep the pond from growing into a lake.

"Ephram," Edmund began, "do you happen to know where—"

"In the library, sir," the other replied without looking up from his task. "And I warn you . . . he's in a bear of a mood."

"Understandably," Edmund conceded, squaring his shoulders as he considered the hall leading to the master's lair.

"I'll deliver the tea," Claire promised, "change into dry clothes, and then relieve you of your protective duties so that you can get back to your dearest Meg."

"You don't really mind, do you? She has the most beautiful smile and a delightful sense of humor."

"I don't mind at all, Edmund," she assured him as she moved resolutely to the stairs. "Actually, you look quite fetching together. And you two have definitely been the high point of our evening."

"That's not saying much, you know."

Yes, she did know. Holding her waterlogged skirts above her ankles while carrying the tray up the stairs sorely taxed what little good humor Edmund had provided. It was fairly well gone by the time she reached Darice's door. She knocked and waited for what seemed an eternity before hearing Darice call out permission to enter. The woman sat on the edge of the bed, dressed in a diaphanous gown and brushing her waist-long hair.

"Tea as per your request, Lady Darice," Claire announced, setting the tray on the small table just inside the door. "And some biscuits."

"I detest biscuits. They're dry and tasteless. I want scones."

Claire paused, her hand on the doorknob. "As my mother frequently reminded me, beggars can't be choosers. Perhaps breakfast will be more to your liking. It will be served at seven. In the dining room. We hope to see you there. Until then, Lady Darice, pleasant dreams."

Darice was sputtering in wordless outrage when Claire stepped out and closed the door. Grinning, she moved down the hall, determined to be rid of the cold, heavy, wet dress as soon as she could. And since there wasn't another gown altered and ready to be worn, there was no choice except to put on her breeches and linen shirt. She was going to be comfortable when she went down to the library and sent Edmund back to the kitchen. And if anyone cared how she looked or what conventions she defied, she didn't care. It had been a very long, very trying day; she deserved a bit of ease and a little tolerance of eccentricity.

The fire had been lit in her room hours ago, and in her absence it had burned to pulsing embers. In the dim light she quickly added several small pieces of wood and then set about the interminable process of peeling off her dress and petticoats. Gathering up the sodden mass of fabric, she carried it all to the armoire, pulled open the door, and unceremoniously dumped it into the wicker hamper.

With a smile of anticipation, she bent down and pulled open the lower drawer. Her fingertips had barely touched the soft doeskin of her breeches when the impact came, tearing a startled cry from her throat and sending her tumbling headfirst into the armoire. Her head struck the back wall of the oaken cabinet hard enough to momentarily daze her, and in those seconds where up seemed down and in seemed out, a pair of hands grasped her about the ankles and spun her around. She landed, breathless and dazed anew. And then there was nothing but darkness and the solid, resonating click of a latch. Blindly, she scrambled to her knees and frantically slid her hands over the wooden walls of the cabinet that had become her prison. She found the door panels easily enough, but no amount of searching or praying revealed an interior latch.

Suddenly, anger replaced the desperation that had driven her to that point. Holding her breath, she pressed her ear to the wood and strained to hear something of the world beyond the confines of her cold, dark cell. Who was out there? Who thought this vicious prank was amusing?

She heard no voice, no footsteps. Only several dull thumping sounds and then, a half dozen heartbeats later, the heavy clang of metal falling against metal. In the silence that followed, Claire knitted her brows, knowing the sounds as familiar but unable put an object or an action to them.

And then she caught a tiny whiff of smoke and she knew.

Pounding on the doors with both fists, Claire screamed for Devon with all her might, all her hope.

CHAPTER TWENTY-ONE

*D*EVON TOOK A HUGE sip of his brandy, slammed the glass back down on the tabletop, then, leaning down to pry off his waterlogged boot, resumed his long rant right where he'd left off. "Enough damn clothes to get her to England and back four times. Jesus. My mother and Aunt Elsbeth don't travel with that goddamn much baggage. Combined. I swear she brought every stitch she owns."

The boot finally came free and he flung it toward the fireplace and the mate that had preceded it. Steam was rising from the other one already. As well as from his jacket that he'd dropped over the woodpile.

" 'Do be a dear,' " he mimicked, yanking his shirttail from his waistband, " 'and send your man out to help mine with my baggage.' " He paused for another drink and glared at Edmund. "As though I could ask Ephram to wade out into the storm and wrestle her damn trunks while I stood inside all nice and dry and watched him."

"You only think you're mad," Edmund said,

swirling his brandy around in the snifter. "You should have seen your wife, Devon. I wouldn't be at all surprised if ol' Darice doesn't end up wearing a teapot for a hat."

Devon sank down onto the chair, his knees suddenly too weak to hold him upright. "What happened?"

"Darice wanted a pot of tea, scones, clotted cream, and strawberry jam. Claire came into the kitchen like a Fury, slamming things about and calling Darice Princess and Her Majesty and threatening to send her packing right back to Lytton Hall." He polished off his drink, sighed, and smiled. "And in case you're wondering, Darice got what was left of a pot of tea Hannah had made for the three of us and the biscuits we didn't eat at dinner. Another brandy?"

"Not quite yet. Help yourself." He picked up his snifter with a smile, pleased by Claire's fiery spirit.

"What are you going to do about Darice?"

"I honestly don't know," Devon admitted, his smile fading. "I suppose I'm going to have to think of something beyond hoping the ground opens up and swallows her. I wish to hell I knew why she was so damn persistent in pursuing me. I'm hardly the prize catch of Virginia."

"She's a loyalist to the marrow. Maybe she's hoping to spy for King and country someday."

Claire was a loyalist. No, that wasn't quite right. Nor was it fair. Claire wasn't a blind follower, waving the Union Jack and singing "God Save the King" just because she'd been born English and it was expected of her. Her objections to colonial rebellion were soundly philosophical. And humanitarian. He understood why she felt the way she did, why she couldn't stand at his side and proclaim the fight worth the price of limbs and lives. She'd endured in a very personal, very daily way the consequences of man's willingness to take up arms.

She'd seen her father's mangled body, and compensating for it had set the course of her life, had made her who she was. And what she was—strong, resilient, daring, and confident. She was a fighter. A survivor.

If only they had more time. Six months to a year was all it would take for Claire to realize that her spirit was more colonial than English, that there were principles more precious than peace. The colonies needed women like her. He needed her. Not to run Rosewind. Hell, Rosewind could burn to the ground and he wouldn't really care all that much. It wasn't the house that mattered, it was the life within it. And Claire was the very heart of it. If she left, Rosewind would go back to being a cold, lifeless, cheerless asylum for the inept. And he'd go back to dreading every sunrise and hoping for a noble excuse to die.

But how to get her to see that this was where she belonged? How was he going to get her to choose to come back to Rosewind once she'd fulfilled her obligations to the court? There wasn't a damn thing he could offer her in the way of traditional inducements. No woman in her right mind would choose impending poverty, insane in-laws, and looming revolution over the serenity and stability of life in an English country cottage. And she wouldn't be alone in that little haven for long, either. Some pasty-faced vicar or schoolmaster would swoon at her feet and Claire—sweet, loving person that she was—would pick them up, dust them off, and then marry them out of pity and compassion.

And eventually she'd be free to marry someone else because there wasn't a damn thing he could do to keep her married to him. Annulment, hell. If Darice Lytton hadn't come barging through the damn door, an annulment would have been an impossibility an hour ago. Darice had only delayed the inevitable, though, and he knew it. As soon as he could get rid of Edmund, he was going to find Claire, start the seduction all over again, and shoot anyone who so much as thought about interrupting it.

Just why she was willing to be his lover was beyond him; it didn't make any sort of rational sense. But she clearly was and he didn't have the ability to resist temptation for the both of them. Not that he'd tried all that hard, he had to admit. He'd wanted her from the beginning.

The only explanation for her willingness to surrender had to be in her having realized that an annulment wasn't her only way out, that she could return to England and petition the Crown for a divorce. If rebellion came, it would be granted on the grounds that he was guilty of high treason. And if she didn't want to wait that long, she could rightly claim that she'd been forced into the union by her uncle. In either case, she could indulge her carnal curiosity and the Crown would free her to walk away. The life would go out of Rosewind. And some pale, simpering English fop would make his way to her door and collapse.

Unless . . . Devon scowled into his brandy, disgusted that the thought had even occurred to him. No, he'd be inordinately careful. More careful than he'd ever been in his life. He wouldn't have Claire coming back to Rosewind because she felt obligated to. And he wouldn't have a child growing up on the other side of the Atlantic without a father. There were far too many Rivard bastards in the world already. His father and brother had seen to that.

"Devon, darling."

He looked up, his blood chilling even before he could bring Darice into clear focus. It turned to ice when he did. She stood in the doorway, an all but transparent dressing gown cinched loosely at the waist and her dark hair spilling in waves over her shoulders.

"No," he said sharply, knowing exactly why she was there. "The answer is *no*."

She slinked toward him, purring, "But you haven't even heard my offer yet."

"I don't want to hear it," he declared, coming to his feet. "Go back to—"

"Then you leave me no choice but to show you."

"I'm not interested in what—"

The wrapper came open at a mere touch and instantly fell to the floor at her feet. He was already scrambling back, barking, "Jesus Christ, Darice! Put your clothes on!" when she held out her arms to better display the wares she was selling.

"Personally," Edmund drawled, "I'd prefer that you didn't."

God, he'd forgotten Edmund was there. Devon sagged with relief even as Darice gasped and snatched up her dressing gown. Clutching it in front of her, she stamped her bare foot and squealed, "You should have made your presence known, sir."

Edmund grinned from ear to ear. "I've been standing right here all along. Not that it's been that long, mind you. All of four, five seconds at the most. The last two of which I've been struck absolutely speechless." He turned to Devon and lifted his glass in salute. "I'm really most impressed, Devon. I had no idea that a woman could get naked so quickly. And you didn't have to do anything except protest."

Darice stamped her foot again and commanded, "Leave us, you odious man."

"And miss an opportunity to learn from a master?" Edmund countered, laughing as he picked up a decanter. "Wild horses couldn't drag me away. I'll be so quiet, you won't even know I'm here. Ready for that next brandy yet, Devon?"

Devon held out his glass for filling while meeting

Darice's gaze squarely. "What little there ever was between us is done, Darice. We've been done for months. Accept it and stop embarrassing both of us."

"There you go. All full up," Edmund announced blithely as he moved away. "I'll be over here if you need more."

Darice stepped closer and lowered her voice to a conspiratorial whisper. "Don't be a fool, Devon. I have so much to offer you. Money, land, slaves. Everything you could possibly want."

"I don't want your money." He pointedly looked her up and down before cocking a brow and adding, "Or anything else you're offering. How many times do I have to say it?"

Snarling wordlessly through her clenched teeth, she fumbled with her wrapper. It wasn't until she found the sleeves and was ramming her arms into them that she also found her voice. "You were forced to marry Claire because you couldn't afford to pay Wyndom's debt. You don't owe her fidelity, Devon. And you certainly don't owe her a real marriage. You don't love her and you don't want her for anything more than one quick tumble. Admit it."

Devon threw the full contents of his snifter down his throat. It seared all the way, taking his breath and filling him with a fire that momentarily burned brighter and hotter than his anger. When the sharpest edge faded, he was marginally in control of his impulses.

"What's between Claire and me is our business, not yours," he declared. "I won't discuss it with you. Not now. Not ever."

"I'm not the least bit interested in talking, Devon," Darice pronounced just before she wheeled around and marched away, her shoulders squared and her nose held high.

If he'd had his head on straight, he'd have ordered her out of the house right that instant. But the idea of going after her to issue the command now...No, it would be far more masterful to issue it in the clear, cool light of morning.

"Well," Edmund said quietly, dryly, "that was certainly an interesting exchange."

"I need to find Claire," he replied, ramming his fingers through his still-damp hair. "She shouldn't be left alone. I don't trust Darice."

"Claire got drenched going out to the kitchen. She's probably still in her room, changing into dry clothes. And speaking of the kitchen...I promised a certain lilting lass that I'd be back. I also promised a wet and indignant English girl that I'd deliver you into her protection before I did." Edmund stepped to the door and indicated the hall leading to the foyer and the stairs. "So if you'd be so kind as to stomp this way..."

Devon brushed his shoulder as he stormed past him, saying, "I can make it to the top of the stairs and down the hall without an escort."

"I am a man of my word," his friend countered as he fell in behind. "And Darice could be lurking in the shadows, waiting to leap out and press her soft, nubile form against the sculpted planes of your—"

"Oh, shut up."

Edmund's laughter was a balm, no doubt helped by the sudden impact of the brandy he'd all but inhaled. Halfway up the stairs, the tightness in his chest began to ease enough that he could fully exhale. Opening his fists, he flexed his hands, forcing the blood to flow back into his fingers.

At the top of the stairs, he slowed and then stopped, grabbing Edmund by the arm and staying him as he tried to figure out what it was that prickled the hair on the back of his neck. It had been there and then it was gone. He listened for a sound, taking slow, deep breaths so he could hear better. He'd almost given up when he tasted the acrid pall.

"Do you smell smoke?" he asked, his heart hammering as he quickly looked along both wings for the smallest signs of fire. He saw nothing. Not even the usual faint light that spilled out from under the doors this time of night.

"God, yes, now that you mention it, I do."

Hadn't Edmund said that Claire was changing her clothes? Would she do that in the dark? Fighting back a rising tide of apprehension, he strode down the corridor that housed himself, Claire, and Wyndom, saying, "You check the rooms on the left side and I'll get those on the right."

He went straight to Claire's bedroom door, vaguely aware of the low rumble of Edmund's voice behind him. "Claire!" he called, knocking hard enough to rattle the frame. There was no answer and he grasped the knob, turned it, and pushed. The door didn't move and dreadful certainty rammed his heart into his throat.

He raced for his own door, throwing it wide and dashing to the door that connected his room to Claire's. The bolt had been thrown and a strip of something lumpy and white had been stuffed into the crack along the lower edge. He kicked the latter aside as he fumbled to push the lock open, his hands shaking and his breathing ragged with burgeoning panic.

The door gave way only a bit, and a dense cloud of bitter smoke rolled over him. He put his shoulder and all of his might into the door, shoving his way into the blackened, roiling room. He froze, holding his arm over his nose and mouth, desperately trying to see, desperately straining to hear anything above the popping and crackling of the fire in the hearth.

"Claire!"

The sound came from his left, small and distant and weak. "Claire!" he called again, moving in the direction of the noise. He heard it more clearly the second time, and hope surged through his veins. Scrambling to the armoire, he kicked aside a wicker basket and yanked open the door. A cry of relief strangled in his throat as Claire, naked and gasping weakly, fell out into his arms. His eyes tearing, his throat tight and raw, he cradled her close and blindly raced for the patch of thinner smoke that marked the entrance to his room and the relatively cleaner air beyond it.

"I'll get the damper and the windows!" he heard Edmund call from somewhere in the blackness.

He didn't care what anyone got, what anyone did. He had Claire and she was alive and that was all that mattered. For now, he amended, carrying her to the window and carefully setting her on her feet. She clung to him weakly, her cheeks stained with smoke and tears, her breathing shallow.

"Devon," she whispered brokenly, sagging into him, a fresh wave of tears washing over her cheeks.

"I'm here. I won't let you go," he promised, holding her steady and close in the circle of one arm as he quickly undid the lock and flung the window open.

"Breathe," he gently commanded, guiding her, holding her, so that they both leaned over the sill and out into the clean, cool air of the night. The rain poured down and the wind whipped her hair, and her tortured gasping turned to silent sobs that wracked her body and battered his heart.

"Deep, deep breaths, sweetheart," he instructed soothingly, trying to hold her hair out of her face. "I know it hurts, but you have to clear your lungs."

Behind him he heard the connecting door slam shut, and with a start he realized both that Edmund was there and that Claire was still as naked as he'd found her. "I'm going to leave you for just a second," he said, pressing a quick kiss to her temple before pushing himself from her side.

Through the haze, he could see that Edmund was diligently shoving the cloth back along the bottom of the door. As Devon tore the coverlet off his bed and wrapped it around Claire's lower half in a single smooth motion, his friend quietly observed, "There's a petticoat just like this one stuffed along the lower inside edge of her door. I left it in place to contain the smoke. Which is dissipating rather quickly now that the damper and the windows are open."

"Thank you."

Edmund said something else, but Devon was already leaning out the window again, gathering Claire back into his arms. She was drenched and shivering, whether from the cold or from the aftereffects of fear, he couldn't tell. He smoothed the wet hair off her forehead and tucked her head under his chin. She snuggled into him and he closed his eyes, thankful for the gift of her survival.

The next window over slid open and Edmund leaned out. "The smoke's almost gone in here. How is she?"

Devon eased back and she smiled up at him. Was there a more dauntless woman on earth? he wondered as he asked, "Better?"

"Yes, much." Her voice quavered, but it was infinitely, blessedly stronger than before. She arched a brow and her voice was stronger still when she added, "All things considered, of course. May I come inside now? I'm beginning to prune."

He planted a quick kiss in the center of her forehead and then loosened his hold on her, saying, "I'll go first so I can manage the coverlet for you. We don't want to offend Edmund's tender sensibilities."

She started and tried to look back over her shoulder. "Oh, God. Did he see—"

"No," Devon quickly assured her, not knowing whether it was true, but certain that it was what she needed and wanted to hear. "The smoke was too thick. And I covered you while he was busy securing the door."

She visibly relaxed and he smiled, drawing the coverlet up around her as she moved back from the sill. How interesting that she didn't seem concerned about *him* having seen her unclothed. And how badly he wanted to throw away the coverlet, wrap her in his arms, and warm her with passion. Reluctantly, mindful of Edmund's presence, he bundled her to her chin, offering a silent promise to kiss her senseless the minute they were alone.

Claire looked up at him, her heart achingly full, her soul begging to be enveloped again in the comfort and strength of his embrace. She wanted to be rid of the coverlet, to twine her arms around his neck and press her body against the warmth of his. She wanted him to kiss her, to touch her and love her until all the horrible memories were gone forever. *Go away, Edmund,* she silently, desperately pleaded. *Please go away.*

As though he'd heard her mention his name, the solicitor quietly asked, "Are you sure you're all right, Claire?"

She nodded and held her breath, waiting and hoping he'd say something about returning to Meg and then excuse himself.

"Good," Devon declared, his jaw slowly turning to granite. "Now, tell me what happened."

No. This wasn't what she wanted. The magic was already slipping away; she could feel it ebbing with every frantic beat of her heart. She closed her eyes, willing the enchantment back and Devon's arms around her.

"Claire." He gently took her chin in hand and tilted her face up. "Open your eyes and tell me what happened."

It was too late to hope; she could hear the distance in his voice, the resolve. She obeyed, her heart heavy. "I was getting my breeches from the drawer when someone came up behind me, pushed me inside the armoire, and closed the door. I heard thumping in the room and then a hard bang, but it wasn't until I began to smell the smoke that I realized that they'd fed the fire and closed the damper. There wasn't anything I could do except beat on the door and scream and hope someone would hear me."

Someone tried to kill me. The words were unspoken but there nonetheless, reverberating softly, clearly audible above the sounds of wind and rain.

His eyes went cold. And as she had known he would, he turned and left her to stand alone. "Stay with her, Edmund," he snapped as he strode out of the room. "Don't let her out of your sight."

She stared into the darkness of the hall, numbly fighting back tears.

Edmund was suddenly at her side, his arm around her shoulders and a measure of quiet urgency in his voice as he said, "Do tell me that you're capable of stumbling along in his wake. Please. If we don't go after him, there won't be anyone to keep him from killing her."

She nodded, realization slowly plowing through the tumult of her emotions. Darice. Devon was on his way to Darice's room. "Go," she instructed, already working to ease the restrictions of the coverlet. "I'll be there as soon as I can move."

He was gone as the sound of splintering wood echoed down the hall. With trembling hands and pounding heart, Claire hastily fashioned a makeshift toga and, at Darice's high-pitched scream, hiked its skirt above her ankles and scrambled out the door.

Wyndom was ahead of her, making his torturously slow way down the center of the hall. She didn't slacken her pace, didn't ask for him to move out of her way. There wasn't time. She could hear Edmund and Devon bellowing. And then the chaos deepened with Elsbeth and Mother Rivard bolting from their rooms, their cries of alarm punctuating Darice's hysterical screams.

Turning sideways, Claire tried to shoot through the narrow space between Wyndom and the wall. He moved toward her in the last second, and despite her yelp of warning and effort to twist out of his way, their shoulders connected. With a cry of pain, he went reeling back.

"Apologies," she shouted, continuing her course, watching Devon's mother and her sister rush into Darice's room as the screaming and bellowing abruptly ceased.

Her lungs and throat burning, her sides aching, Claire reached the shattered doorway and clung to what was left of the jamb as she desperately surveyed the dark shadows of the room. Devon was against the far wall, pinned there by Edmund's shoulder and the full weight of his body and determination. Darice sat in a heap on the floor, sobbing, her hands wrapped loosely around her neck as Elsbeth sat down beside her and gathered her into her arms.

Claire slumped with relief, grateful that Edmund had been there and able to avert disaster. She glanced down the hall to check on Wyndom's condition and found him hobbling along. She recalled how he'd been moving before they'd collided and decided that he was none the worse for the unfortunate encounter. The compress didn't seem to have done any good for him, though; if anything, his limp was more pronounced tonight than it had been this morning.

"I hate you," Darice sobbed. "I hate you all."

Devon, his blood still boiling and his heart trying to hammer itself out of his chest, attempted to push Edmund's weight away.

"You stay right there," Edmund growled, "and hope to hell she doesn't bring charges for battery."

"It's all right, baby," Elsbeth crooned, gently rocking her back and forth. "Hush. Mama's here and she won't let him hurt you."

"Mama?" Devon repeated softly, what little air Edmund had left in him catching high in his throat. Mama? Darice was Aunt Elsbeth's daughter? No. It couldn't be. But...looking at them in that light, he could see a faint resemblance. It wasn't entirely unbelievable. Darice his cousin?

His mother gasped and pressed her hands over her stomach. "Oh, Elsbeth. Oh dear. You never told me..."

"Of course I didn't, you stupid twit," Elsbeth snapped, her eyes obsidian coals. "You were his wife."

Realization struck like a lightning bolt, branching, searing each facet of Devon's world. His stomach clenched and then heaved upward as every ounce of his strength poured out the soles of his feet. "Jesus," he moaned, feeling himself sliding down the wall and unable to care. He'd lain with his half sister, his cousin. "Oh, sweet Jesus."

As though through a fog, he heard Darice screech, saw her slap Elsbeth hard across the face. "Damn your running mouth! This wasn't over! We could have yet had it all the easy way."

And then Edmund was talking, the rumble of his voice passing through his arm and into the center of Devon's chest. "In the name of basic human decency, Darice, you and your mother will be allowed to spend the rest of the night here. But at dawn you will both vacate the premises, never to return. If necessary, I'll file a petition asking that the court bar you from contact of any sort with any member of the Rivard family. Have I made the terms clear?"

"Rosewind belongs to me!" Darice screamed, climbing to her feet and fisting her hands at her sides. Elsbeth huddled on the floor, weeping softly into her hands. "It's more my birthright than it is Devon's and Wyndom's! I'm the firstborn! I'll sue for it if I have to!"

Edmund let go of him and whirled away. Devon caught himself on the edge of the dresser, willing his legs to hold him upright, praying to awaken from this hideous nightmare.

"So you can try to get what you couldn't by the unholiest of schemes?" Edmund raged in Darice's upturned, defiant face. "Go ahead, Darice. Take it to court. I dare you to!"

So all the world could know the blackness of his crime. Darice would do it just for that end. Sickened and reeling, Devon stumbled toward the door, wanting only to escape, now and forever. Better a bullet in his brain than to face the shame and humiliation she'd bring down on him, on Rosewind.

Claire...She stood in the doorway, her eyes huge and searching as she watched him come toward her. What she had to think of him. She knew; he'd told her himself. The best and brightest thing that had ever happened to him, to Rosewind, was lost forever, snuffed out in a single instant of confession and realization.

"Devon," she began, stepping back into the hall and into his path.

Unable to meet her gaze, unwilling to see the loathing in her eyes, he roughly pushed past her and resolutely made his way down the darkened hall toward his room.

CHAPTER TWENTY-TWO

*T*HERE WAS MUCH to be done, and while his strides were long and purposeful, his mind flitted from one task to the other without logic. Zeke needed to be charged with getting the rest of the crops planted. Ephram. He had to do something about Ephram. And Hannah. And rewrite certain provisions of his will. Rosewind couldn't go to Wyndom by default. Claire. He'd leave it to Claire. She'd take care of it. It would be safe in her hands.

He stopped just inside his room as yet another realization hit him. It would be a cruelty to give Claire the responsibility for his mother, brother, and Rosewind. The stain of public scandal would be dark and forever attached to this place, to his name. Why would she want to live the rest of her life with the shame? No, now more than ever, she needed to make her future in England. Better that Rosewind be lost than that Claire be forced to bear the burden of it.

"Devon?"

He started. He needed to talk to her, to be sure she understood all that was going to happen in the days ahead and why the course was unavoidable. But not now. Now he didn't have the strength or the courage to make the words come out right. Without looking back at her, his heart racing and his throat tightening, he stepped further into his room, saying tersely, "Leave me alone."

"No." So soft, so gentle. "I won't."

He wanted to turn on her, to rail and snarl and frighten her away. And he couldn't. It took every measure of his will to stand where he was and keep the tears in his throat from crawling any higher. He was so tired. Closing his eyes, he tried to summon the strength to keep going for just a few moments more.

The touch of her hand against his cheek was startling in its warmth, its tenderness. "Don't touch me, Claire," he commanded, leaning away. "I won't foul—"

She grabbed his shirtfront, twisting the linen tight in her fists and robbing him of words and the ability to do more than stare down at her. With stunning strength, she pulled him toward her. "I don't believe them," she declared, her voice resonating with conviction, her eyes bright with certainty. "The word of two vipers means nothing, Devon. They have to prove it."

She hadn't known his father, didn't understand that it was not only possible, but very likely. "And if they can?" he asked, bracing himself for the telltale flicker of hesitation, the instinctive flinch of disgust.

"It doesn't matter," she answered instantly, her voice still strong and even. Holding him fast with one hand, with the other she gently cupped his cheek again. "You didn't know. If there is a sin, it's hers, Devon. Hers and Elsbeth's."

He hadn't known. He honestly hadn't. The slightest suspicion had never even crossed his mind.

"Claire, how can you bear to touch me?" he asked,

gently extracting his shirt from her grasp. "How can you possibly want me?"

"I simply do," she answered, her arms falling to her sides. "Can't wanting you be enough, Devon?"

If only it were as simple as wanting. And taking. But it wasn't this time; not with this woman. She met his gaze unflinchingly, her eyes filled not with the fires of mindless passion but with the softness of love, of wanting to heal his heart and soul. No other woman had ever looked at him that way. No other woman had ever wanted to give herself to him for the sake of the giving. And he'd never needed to be loved as much as he did in that moment.

He could take; he knew how. It was all he'd ever done, all he'd ever had to do. The women in his past had been conquests. Gaining their surrender had been a matter of deliberate calculation and timing, of subtly negotiating terms that allowed them both to walk away pretending it had never happened. No ties. No bonds.

But with Claire... There was no game to play, no surrender to cajole or manipulate. There was nothing to take. For the first time in his life he had only to accept the gift of another's heart. And he didn't know how to do it.

"Devon?"

His knees weak, he leaned down to feather a kiss across her lips, then drew back to take the hem of his shirt in his hands and peel it over his head. Dropping it blindly to the floor, he reached for her hand and placed it in the center of his chest, holding it over his overbrimming heart. Wonder filled her eyes as her gaze dropped to their hands.

"Feel that?" he asked. Her nod was almost imperceptible. "Do you know why it's beating so hard, so fast?" Her lips formed a "No" but she made no sound. "Because I'm scared."

"Of what?" she whispered, looking up at him.

"I want your first time to be perfect," he confessed. "And I know it can't be. There'll be pain and there's nothing I can do to spare you. I'll be the cause of it."

"Then make it quick, one moment that can be lost in a thousand moments of pleasure. I want to make you happy, Devon. I've never wanted anything more in my life."

His heart swelled, pressing the air from his lungs. He wasn't alone in this moment. She stood with him, willing to risk everything for the chance of giving from the heart. And asking only that he take the same risk for her.

He reached out and lifted the end of the coverlet draped over her shoulder, drawing it back and letting it fall from his hand. The whole of it unwound and slipped away from her, pooling at her feet and baring her to his gaze. She didn't flinch, didn't blush, but stood silently before him, her hand still pressed to his heart and smiling so softly, so invitingly.

Where his eyes went, his hands followed. The curve of her cheek, her shoulders, her breasts. He cupped her in his hands and watched the dark crests harden and peak. Lifting his gaze to her face, he traced the pads of his thumbs over the tips and watched her lips soften and part, watched her eyes darken with yearning.

He brushed her once more and she moaned softly and arched into the caress. Achingly hard, he released his claim to her breasts to undo the buttons at his hips, his breath catching as she drew the fabric aside.

He lowered his head to reverently kiss her as he discarded his breeches. She touched her tongue to his and he was undone. There was nothing beyond her and that moment; no past, no future. Only the sweet taste of her lips, the heady promise of losing himself in her. Pledge and consequence were cindered and swirled away as need became hunger, reverence abandon.

He wrapped her in his arms, kissing her deeply, and

drawing her against the length of his body. She melded into him, her breasts an exquisite heat branding his chest, her hands slipping back to grasp his hips and bring them hard against her own. He ravaged her mouth, his tongue probing, twining with hers. She arched into him, moaning, settling her hips closer. His arms went around her and he cupped her backside as he caught her lower lip between his teeth and slowly shifted his hips against hers, pressing and stroking in a dance as old as time.

Flawlessly catching the rhythm, she moved with him, faster and harder, her breathing ragged and tiny, whispered pleas brushing over his lips. And he obeyed. Lifting her from her feet, he turned and laid her on the edge of the bed. Quickly, regretting the necessity, he got a lambskin sheath from the nightstand drawer and protected them both. Returning to her, he kissed her and settled himself between her parted legs. Shuddering at the warmth and tightness of her closing around him, he pressed into her as slowly as he could, trying to give her time to adjust to the fullness of his possession, savoring the perfect friction as she shifted to accommodate him.

"Oh God, Devon," she moaned, arching up to invite him deeper. "It doesn't hurt at all."

But he knew that it would. He drew back a bit and then gently pressed forward again, being mindful of going no farther than he already had. With each stroke she arched another degree higher, fisted the sheets just a little bit tighter. He shivered once with the strain of holding back and then surrendered, letting her draw him deep and against her maidenhead. She gasped at the contact and that was all the time he gave her. Clenching his teeth, he pulled her hips hard against his and thrust past the barrier, filling her completely and making her his.

She cried out, instinctively trying to pull away from him. He held her gently but firmly in place, going still inside her. Only when she stopped struggling did he release his hold. Slowly leaning forward, he put his hands on either side of her head, then eased down to kiss the tears from her cheeks and whisper, "It's done, sweetheart. The pain will fade in just a minute or two. And it will never hurt like that again."

She took a shuddering breath and bravely tried to smile for him. "I won't move until you want me to," he promised, searching her eyes. "You tell me when the pain is gone."

She nodded and touched the tip of her tongue to her lower lip. He lowered his head and kissed her lightly. His reward was a contented sigh as her arms twined around his neck.

Claire clung to him, her desires stirred and fueled by the tender hunger of his kisses. She groaned in protest as he drew his lips from hers, sighed as he pressed a trail of kisses down her throat and lower, to her breasts. He suckled a peak, gently at first and then harder, sending waves of pleasure washing over her to steal her breath and ignite her blood.

Her senses consumed by a need to touch him, to lose herself in him, she arched up in instinctive plea. The sensation was sudden and exquisitely intense, arcing from her womb to her breasts and then deep into her soul. She gasped in wonder and deliberately arched again, driven by a wholly new kind of hunger.

"Oh, yes, sweetheart."

She opened her eyes to find Devon smiling down at her, his eyes bright and his breathing every bit as shallow and uneven as her own.

"Do it again."

Her heart thundering, she obliged. Slowly she arched up, reveling in the sweet heat, feeling it swell when Devon deliberately drove down to meet it. And then there was only the ghost of it, and Devon pulled back, smiling, whispering, "Again."

He matched her, met her, and the heat was heavier and brighter, the swell larger and more compelling. It faded again, but not as quickly; the promise of it was still there when she arched again. And again Devon matched and met her, his smile ebbing away as he held himself deep within her, as his eyes widened and the swell of sensation rose higher still.

There was more, she could feel it building, beckoning, just beyond her reach. "Devon," she cried, grasping his shoulders, desperately straining up. He answered with his body, knowing what she wanted, giving her what she needed. The swells came one right after the other, ever closer, sweeping through her, each more engulfing than the one before, each propelling her higher, closer. And then they came a hundredfold, one on top of the other, all at once, shuddering through her, consuming her in a blinding burst of completion.

Her fulfillment caught him and held him deep, pulling him over the crest and into his own long, explosive culmination. Gasping and spent, he lowered himself, covering Claire with his body and wrapping her in his arms. Pressing a kiss to her forehead, he rolled onto his side with her, holding her close and wanting to never let her go. Her head pillowed in his arm, she snuggled against him and laid her hand on his hip.

He was in heaven, blissfully satisfied and complete. God, that every day of the rest of his life could be so gratifying. Claire stirred, rubbing her cheek against his chest, and he kissed the top of her head.

"Are you all right?" she asked softly.

It took every ounce of his remaining energy to smile. "Am I all right? Sweetheart, only you would think to ask that." He sighed and kissed her again. "Yes, I'm all right. And you? Did I abuse you?"

"Hardly," she answered with a quiet chuckle. Then she slowly drew back so that she could meet this gaze. "But you did frighten me, Devon. The look in your eyes when you left Darice's room...I was afraid you'd harm yourself."

It seemed so long ago. A memory borrowed from the lifetime of another man. "I think the thought crossed my mind."

"Has it gone now?"

"Is that why you sacrificed yourself?" he asked, the mere possibility tearing at his heart. "To distract me?"

"I don't think that anything so enjoyable can be considered a sacrifice," she replied, her sigh utterly satisfied. "And when it comes to being distracted...I've never met anyone else who can make me so completely forget the reasons I begin a course."

"Then it's a miracle that anything gets done around here at all," he observed. She settled back against him, wriggling to press as much of herself along him as she could. "Are you cold?"

It took effort to focus her attention on anything beyond the contentment. It was still raining outside and the wind was still blowing. And yes, her feet were chilled. "A little."

He hugged her tight and then slipped away from her, saying. "Wait right here while I close the windows and add a log to the fire."

Forced out of her stupor, she sat up, starting at the protest of muscles she hadn't known she possessed.

"Not that closing windows and stoking the fire are going to help matters all that much," Devon went on cheerfully as he moved around the room and she gingerly slipped off the bed to retrieve the coverlet. "This is the draftiest damn house I've ever been in. Someday I'm going to tear out every window in it and replace them with some that actually keep out the wind and dirt."

"I don't think it's all that bad," she countered, putting the coverlet back on the bed and then sliding beneath it. "It's certainly not the draftiest house I've ever been in."

"But it could be so much better than it is."

He teetered on bankruptcy and was thinking about the day when he could make Rosewind the house of his expectations and dreams. He'd do it. There wasn't a doubt in her mind. Devon was a very determined man. And a delight for the eyes, too. She smiled, watching his shoulder muscles bunch and flex as he closed the last window, thrilling to the sight of his thighs and buttocks as he crossed to the hearth, bent down, and added a good-sized piece of wood to the dwindling fire. He was the most magnificent creature she'd ever seen. Sleek and rippled, powerful. And he was hers. Her husband, her lover. And to think how much she'd resented being forced to marry him, how badly she'd once wanted to escape.

He slipped back into bed and drew her into his arms, asking, "What do you know about cattle?"

She had no idea where the question had come from or where it was going. Laughing, she answered, "You keep an eye on their hooves when you're milking them."

"I meant about managing a herd. I've been thinking that I need to get some cattle. Food crops are a good start in broadening the base of Rosewind's production, but it still seems like a matter of having all my eggs in one basket."

She'd never seen this side of him—the lighthearted dreamer. And she loved him all the more for his being able to do it. "You should probably get some more chickens, too."

"You're right. How about a couple more pigs while we're diversifying?"

"And what are you going to feed all these animals, Noah?"

"I need to set aside some land for forage crops, don't I?"

"And build sheds and pens for your menagerie as well," she pointed out. "You can't properly care for an animal if it's allowed to run willy-nilly through the woods and fields. British farmers consider that American practice to be an appalling thing, you know."

He chuckled dryly. "Not to mention that they have a tendency to wander off and never return. The very last thing I ever said to my father was that instead of buying another cow, he ought to just tie the money to the tail of a kite and let it go into the wind."

"Did he buy the cow anyway?"

"I have no idea," he replied with another chuckle. "He went to James City on the pretext of doing so." He paused and when he spoke again his voice was somber. "His heart gave out while administering to the needs of his mistress, and rather than risk the embarrassment of being found in her bed, he stumbled out of her house to drop dead on a main street. Absolutely stark naked. Given the general nature of public comment when I went to retrieve him...Well, I wasn't inclined to tarry long enough to make any inquiries about a cow."

"Oh, Devon. How awful. I hope your mother never heard the story."

"I certainly didn't tell her. But funerals being the kind of affairs they are, I'm sure she heard the whispers. I suspect that she wasn't all that shocked by the circumstances of his passing. The mistress that killed him wasn't the first one he'd ever had. He spent his entire life pursuing women and illusions of grandeur. Mother's spent hers cultivating blindness to an art."

"So I've noticed," Claire admitted sadly. "I suppose, though, that it was the only way she knew how to cope with the heartache of his betrayals."

Devon drew back and gently tilted her face up. "I promise you that there will never be a mistress. Only you, Claire."

"You're planning to keep me?"

For as long as I can. But now wasn't the time to talk of war and the hard decisions it would require. He wanted to live in hope until he didn't have any other choice. "I do believe we've burnt the annulment bridge."

Her eyes sparkled. "Could we burn it again? Just to be sure?"

Laughing, happier than he had ever been in his life, Devon rolled onto his back, drawing her with him and settling her across his hips.

THE WORLD WAS STILL BLACK, still wet, when Claire rolled over in her sleep and reached out for him. Her eyes came instantly open and he stepped back to the bed. "I didn't mean to wake you," he whispered, leaning over to kiss her. "Go back to sleep."

"Where are you going?" she asked groggily. "It's still dark."

"Darice and Elsbeth are leaving at dawn and I'll be damned if anything delays their departure. I'm off to put baggage into the carriage while her driver tries to put her horses back into their traces."

She thought about it a minute, daintily stifled a yawn with the back of her hand, and then asked, "When you're done, you'll come back to bed?"

"Will you still be in it?"

"Yes."

"Then I won't waste any time," he promised, kissing her again and then stepping away. "Sleep while you can."

She smiled and her eyes drifted closed. Grinning, Devon slipped silently out of the room and made his way down the hall, listening to the sounds of the house coming awake. He could hear Wyndom moving behind his closed door, could hear the sounds of hasty packing from the end of the hall where Elsbeth and Darice were. And from the floor below there drifted up the delicious scent of food along with the unmistakable sounds of

Edmund Cantrell's cursing and trunks being dragged across the foyer floor.

Making his way down the stairs to join his friend at the task of hauling Darice Lytton's baggage back out into the rain, Devon silently resolved to do no more than load the carriage. With the vehicle having been left out all night, getting the horses hitched back into the drenched harnesses was going to be miserable, time-consuming work.

Devon smiled. A choice between wresting horses and fighting wet leather or climbing into bed and making love with Claire wasn't a choice at all.

Chapter Twenty-three

*T*HE RATTLING OF CHINA called her from sleep. Claire smiled, stretched languidly, and slowly opened her eyes. And immediately wished she hadn't.

"I was on my way downstairs and saw that a breakfast had been left outside your door," Mother Rivard announced breezily, carrying the laden tray to the table in front of the far window. "It wouldn't do to let it get cold. Not when someone was thoughtful enough to go to the effort of preparing it and bringing it up. Probably that Mary Margaret woman trying to atone for her early days of ineptitude."

"Good morning, Mother Rivard," Claire offered, trying to get herself upright, covered, and reasonably composed. Somehow knowing that she had every right to be in Devon's bed didn't make being found there by his mother any less uncomfortable.

"I'm not disturbing your sleep, am I?"

"No," she lied, summoning good manners. "I've

been fairly well awake since Devon went downstairs to get Darice's carriage ready."

"Tea?"

It was something to do with her hands besides pleating the bedcovers. "Yes. Thank you."

"I'm glad to find you in Devon's bed this morning. Given the set of your chin when you left Darice's room last night, I thought there might be a reasonable chance of finding you here. I hope that he had the good sense to fully share it with you."

Heat suffusing her cheeks, Claire managed a strained smile while her mind stumbled about in search of words. Never in her wildest dreams had she ever considered the likelihood of having this kind of conversation with anyone.

"Wonderful," Mother Rivard declared, beaming as she handed her the teacup and turned back to the tray. "Then we can forget all the nonsense of an annulment. It would have been so unpleasant. Not to mention embarrassing. Both of you would have borne considerable social stains for having failed to make a go of it. Toast?"

"I'm never hungry first thing in the morning," Claire said, watching her heap strawberry jam onto a thick slice of well-buttered bread. "But please feel free to have some if you'd like."

"I do believe I will," she said, adding yet more jam. "I always wake up famished. I swear, if for some reason I couldn't get out of my room, I'd eat my pillow."

Claire smiled, lifted her cup from the saucer, and then set it back down as Devon strode through the door, drenched to the skin, but his smile broad and his eyes bright. At the sight of his mother, he stopped in his tracks and grinned.

"Ah, good morning, Devon," Henrietta said, turning to him and holding out the toast she'd prepared. "Are you hungry?"

"Morning, Mother," he replied, shaking his head and moving to his armoire. "Darice and Aunt Elsbeth are downstairs in the foyer, and as soon as the driver's finished getting the horses into harness, they'll be gone. If you want to go say your farewells, now's probably the time to do it."

Mother Rivard stared down at the toast for a long moment, then looked up and put a pleasant smile on her face. "I think I'd prefer to avoid seeing either of them. Under the circumstances, it would be exceptionally awkward, don't you think?"

"I'm sorry, Mother," Devon said softly, turning to face her, a clean, dry shirt in each hand. "If I'd had even the slightest inkling, I would have done everything I could to have spared you."

"You've always been very good about trying to shield me, Devon. Such a sweet gesture on your part." She shrugged and her smile turned bittersweet. "And, for the most part, ineffective."

Claire watched the emotions play over his features: first surprise, then sadness and then the shock of realization. He cleared his throat and swallowed hard before he asked, "You knew about Elsbeth and Darice?"

"That Darice was her daughter and one of your father's bastards?" Henrietta asked. "For heavens sakes, Devon. Elsbeth had more lovers than your father did. Darice could be the child of any one of at *least* a hundred men. If, for one moment, I had thought that Darice was your half-sister, I would have said something to you the very first time you glared in the direction of Lytton Hall. But I did know that Elsbeth had been one of your father's lovers. It's almost impossible to meet any woman who wasn't."

The latter assertion he knew to be true; he'd have to accept his mother's word on the former. The tightness that had coiled in the pit of his stomach began to ease, and he crossed to the bed, handing Claire one of the shirts so that she could cover herself. Appreciation shimmered in her eyes and warmed his heart. He watched her set her tea on the bedside table. God, she was beautiful. The pale light of dawn bathing her bare shoulders, the inviting swells of her breasts...He considered the shirt as she pulled it on, wondering how long it would take him to get rid of it once they were alone.

His mother's hard sigh pulled his attention back to her. She was staring down at the toast in her hand again, and when she finally spoke, her voice came as though from a great distance. "You've asked me many a time why I've tolerated Elsbeth's abrasive manner. She hated your father for throwing her away like he did all the others, Devon. And she was my voice. She would say the things that I lacked the courage to say for myself. Having her under this roof and sharing our table made your father acutely uncomfortable, and it pleased me that he could be made to pay some small price for his actions. I never let on that I knew of their past relationship, of course. It was my private vengeance and made all the sweeter for it being a secret."

God, he'd never even considered the possibilities. His mind clicked back through time, counting the years. Fifteen. Elsbeth had lived with them for the last fifteen years. Two since his father had died, thirteen before that. To have been so completely blind for so long... What else had he missed seeing? What else didn't he understand? "But she stayed even after Father died. Why?"

She looked up at him with a patient smile. "I'd used her for years, Devon. Was I supposed to toss her out simply because I no longer had a practical need for her? That wouldn't have been very nice of me. Actually, it would have been very much in the vein of your father's treatment of her. And I'm a better person than your father was."

His heart said that it was a difference of small degrees, and ached with the loss of what tiny illusions had always comforted him. "Why didn't you ever stand up to him on your own?"

"I truly didn't care that he slept with other women," she replied with a dismissive shrug. "It was a relief to be spared having to render the service myself. But the public whispering behind my back...The only thing about my life that I didn't like was the embarrassment I suffered because of his lack of discretion. Everyone knew what he was doing, with whom, when, and where. But, as you've no doubt noticed, I'm a shallow woman, Devon. I wasn't willing to risk all my pretty things in a protest over his infidelities. So I endured."

She smiled tightly and absently took a bite of the toast. With a grimace, she chewed, swallowed, then said, "With Elsbeth's unwitting but enthusiastic help, of course." Wrinkling her nose, she cleared her throat and set the toast back onto the breakfast tray, saying, "Lady Claire, when you see Mary Margaret, please tell her that the jam has gone sour. I'd be horrified if it were to be served to a guest."

Jam. The expectations of hospitality. The thin facade of civility that hid all the tangled, dark realities of life at Rosewind, that made honest exchanges an aberration and trusting relationships an impossibility. Devon closed his eyes as anger warred with compassion, as he told himself that his mother had lived too long with the facade to abandon it at his command, that putting the torch to Rosewind today wouldn't undo all of its yesterdays.

"I heard voices. Are we having a family meeting?"

Wyndom. Devon stifled a groan and opened his eyes. His brother stood in the doorway, his arm in the sling and his weight leaning heavily on the cane. When he buttoned his frock coat, he'd be suitably attired for sharing breakfast with the likes of the Royal Governor.

"We have good news, Wyndom," his mother said. "There won't be an annulment. Devon and—"

Devon whirled about. His mother stood as still and stiff as a statue, her eyes rolled back into their sockets, her lips blue.

"Mother!"

Claire watched in horror as the woman toppled into Devon's arms. Flinging the covers aside, she scrambled over the bed toward them, hearing Wyndom call her name above the pounding of her heart. She glanced in his direction and froze, her heart seizing with fearful realization as she stared down the muzzle of a flintlock pistol.

She blinked hard. Wyndom's arm was out of the sling. The cane lay on the floor at his feet. Her gaze snapped up to meet his, searching his eyes in the desperate hope that she was wrong.

"You were supposed to eat the toast and jam," he said calmly. "The rat poison was for you. Not Mother."

No. No, she wasn't hearing this. This wasn't happening. Frantic, she looked to Devon for reassurance and found him kneeling on the floor, holding his mother's contorted form tight in his arms, looking down at her, his face twisted with sadness, disbelief, and rage.

"Oh God, Wyndom," Claire groaned. "Why?"

He shrugged and sighed. "Your uncle wants you dead so that you can't testify against him. I happened to have been in the position of owing either another large sum of money or a very big favor to your uncle. His men in James City were very blunt about it all, and when it came down to it, the only choice I had was between your life and mine. I chose mine, of course."

She stared at him, stunned by the dispassion in his voice. The muzzle of the pistol remained level and pointed at her heart, his hand as steady as his manner. Claire anxiously looked over at Devon, at Henrietta, not knowing what to do for herself or anyone else, not knowing how to make the nightmare end.

And, as though Henrietta Rivard had heard her plea, the woman stiffened, made another deep gurgling sound, and then slowly went limp and silent. Claire choked back a sob and met Devon's gaze. Cold, hard, unflinching. A silent promise of deliverance and ruthless retribution. Her heart skittered, but she knew there wasn't any other course. Forcing herself to swallow, she lifted her chin, just as silently promising Devon whatever he needed of her.

He reverently laid his mother's body on the floor and deliberately gained his feet as Wyndom blithely went on, "It was a well-considered plan, you know. Put into motion some months ago. Devon was forced to marry you so that it'd be easier for me to eliminate you. I must admit to being pleased to see him so neatly boxed against his will. And then, when I threw the brandy on your flaming skirts . . ."

Wyndom glanced briefly over at his brother and smiled. "Devon acted the gallant knight, you were the appreciative maiden, and I saw the possibility for a little retribution of my own. I figured that if I bided my time, I stood a fairly good chance of watching my dear brother weep genuine tears over your grave and then die quickly thereafter of heartbreak.

"Unfortunately," he added with a little shake of his head, "the gentlemen in James City couldn't appreciate my own goals in the matter needing to be done and insisted that I come back and get on with it in earnest. I didn't have any choice but to comply with their wishes."

"Yes, you did," Devon said quietly, flexing his hands at his sides. "You could have told me. I would have protected you."

"In your infinitely condescending way," Wyndom countered, the heat of anger suddenly flooding his voice. "I hate you, you know. The always perfect Devon."

He paused, visibly struggling to control his breathing, to steady his suddenly trembling hand. After a moment he smiled and went on, "It occurred to me—after I'd pushed the storeroom shelves over on Claire—that I was being a bit too narrow in my thinking and passing up a wonderful opportunity to . . . well, to use the old expression . . . to kill two birds with one stone. It's a considerable understatement to say that I was terribly distressed last night to discover that neither of you had succumbed to the smoke."

With his free hand, he motioned toward the breakfast tray. "Hence this morning's impromptu attempt with the poisoned toast and jam."

"Which," Devon drawled, "you managed with your typical degree of competence."

"See?" Wyndom snarled. "That's what I'm talking about. Always condescending, always critical."

"That's because you're always an idiot," Devon replied, unruffled. "Right now, you're standing there with a pistol in your hand, no doubt feeling smug and superior. You have two of us to kill, Wyndom, and one shot. Which of us will you choose?"

Wyndom frowned and Devon smiled in grim satisfaction. Before his brother could gather his scattered wits, he said, "Let me tell you what's going to happen, Wyndom. There are two loaded pistols in the top drawer of my bureau. If you shoot me, Claire's going to open it up, take one out, and shoot you dead before you can blink or run. If you're stupid enough to decide to shoot her, know that I'm going to choke the life out of you with my bare hands. Very slowly."

He saw Claire's gaze dart to the drawer and then to Wyndom. He inched forward, forcing Wyndom's attention back to him.

"Well, given the options," his brother said with a quick sigh, "I can clearly see that my best chance lies in killing you." The muzzle moved quickly and chaos erupted. A scream, a flash, a cloud of smoke, and then there was nothing beyond a searing, thundering impact ripping through his shoulder and knocking him off his feet.

"Devon!"

Claire was beside him and he vaguely heard his shirt being ripped open. There was nothing vague about the pain it caused, though. It took everything he had to catch his breath, to clear the red haze from his vision and lift his head.

"He was gone before you hit the floor," she said, pushing him back down before he could see for himself. "Let me look at your shoulder."

If she touched him, he'd scream. Or pass out. Neither of which he had the time for. "It's just a flesh wound. I'll live," he assured her, rolling over, willing himself onto his knees. "The bastard never could shoot worth a damn," he added through gritted teeth, painfully gaining his feet.

The world spun around him but he plowed through it anyway, doggedly heading for the bureau and his pistols. He almost lost his balance pulling open the drawer, but he pitched himself forward, driving his hand into the space and wrapping it around the familiar, smooth wooden butt of the weapon.

"Devon, no," she said softly from beside him as she slipped her hand around his. "You can't. He's your brother. Let others do what has to be done now."

No, justice was his responsibility and his alone. But he didn't have the strength to explain it to her. Not now. If he paused for so much as a single second, he'd never move again. "Stay with Mother," he said tersely, drawing his hand from her grasp and stepping past her.

Claire turned to go after him, watching him bleed and knowing that he wasn't strong enough to deal with Wyndom's madness. And then Edmund suddenly filled the doorway.

"Oh, Jesus," the lawyer whispered, his eyes widening as he took in Devon's bloody shirt. His gaze swept on, touching Claire briefly, his relief at seeing her whole and sound existing only until he saw the still, silent body of Mother Rivard on the bedroom floor. His knees buckled. "Sweet Almighty Jesus."

"Sir! No! Don't!"

A stranger's voice, startled and fearful. She and Edmund turned at once in the direction from which it had come, but it was Devon who took the first steps toward the window that overlooked the front drive, Devon who reached the window first.

And it was Devon who bellowed in warning as Wyndom stood in the carriage box and viciously slapped a set of reins against the horses' backs, Devon who fumbled to raise the window as the horses bolted from their unfastened traces.

The horror unfolded with a slowness that pressed each detail forever into Claire's memory. The lead reins being pulled from Wyndom's hands, his moment of relief. Another set of reins popping tight, the terror on his face as he pitched backward and his feet were yanked from under him. The stiffness of his body as he was jerked out and down from the box, the hard snap of his neck against the edge. Darice's and Elsbeth's piercing screams. The horses running furiously on, terrified of the broken, lifeless burden they dragged in their wake, heedless of her ragged pleas for them to stop.

Devon gingerly laid the pistol down on the tray, his heart aching and heavy, his body and mind past exhaustion, past endurance. "Edmund," he said softly.

"I'll see to it," his friend answered, gently squeezing his good shoulder before slipping out of the room.

He turned to Claire and saw the unspoken words shimmering in her eyes. "It's not your fault, sweetheart," he said, feeling his strength ebbing away, his knees weakening. "Don't blame yourself for any of this."

"But—"

"Hold me, Claire," he begged, reaching for her. "Please."

Her arms came around him, and knowing he was safe in her care, he let the darkness steal over him and take away his pain.

FROM THEIR VANTAGE POINT on the rise, the breadth of the devastation was easy to see. Devon glanced to his left, first at Edmund and then past him to Ephram, noting that both were scowling as they surveyed the labyrinth of small streams cutting deep courses across the newly planted fields.

A man couldn't ask for better friends, he thought, shifting his attention back to the wreckage of his hopes. Rain pouring down, their horses mired in mud up to their hocks, and not a word of complaint out of either one of them. Just stoic silence. The third day of stoic silence, in fact. And constant, hovering companionship. The kindness, concern, and unspoken fears were beginning to wear on him.

"Amazing what damage four straight days of rain can do, isn't it?" he ventured.

Ephram grimaced, but Edmund found the wherewithal to quietly ask, "Can you replant?"

"Some of it," Devon answered, relieved to be talking about something other than death and funerals. "I've got a few sacks of seed left. The problem isn't so much seed as it is timing, though. God only knows when it'll stop raining. Then the ground has to dry enough so that we can get back in there and work it without sinking up to our knees. And reseeding so late in the growing season will put me more at the mercy of the weather than usual. Replanting will be a complete waste of effort if the summer's dry or winter comes early."

"At least you're not growing tobacco," Edmund offered with a sigh and a shake of his head. "Think of how much those poor bastards have lost the last few days and how long it'll take them to recoup. Years."

Devon nodded slowly, his mind tracking along the course of consequence. "Rosewind won't be the only estate facing bankruptcy. And if there's anything positive in that reality, it's that she'll be one of the last carcasses the creditors come to pick. I've got more time to find a solution than others do."

"Have any ideas as to what you're going to do?" Edmund asked.

With a rueful smile, Devon admitted, "Not a one that doesn't involve spending money I don't have."

"I have a bit of savings set aside," his friend offered. "It's certainly not much, but if you need it, it's yours."

He'd expected the offer to come, and readily replied, "Thank you. But if Rosewind can't stand on her own, then she deserves to fall. I'll figure something out. I always have."

But he'd never been this deep in the hole. In the past, he'd counted on his fellow Virginians to have the money necessary to buy the things he was forced to sell in order to pay his bills. And they had. They'd bought his slaves, his tobacco production equipment, and some long-stored household goods he'd had discreetly auctioned to pay the taxes. But with their own fields awash and their own pockets cleaned out, he couldn't count on them to bail him out this time. He was on his own and the odds of success weren't good. The only thing to be done was to salvage what he could and whom he could.

"Ephram?"

"Yes?"

"Claire sails for Boston next week," he said, his gaze fixed on the ruined fields below. "I want you and your mother to go with her."

"I beg your pardon?"

"I'll admit to not following that one, either,"

Edmund chimed in. "I know you can't go, since the House of Burgesses will be in session and you're required to be there. And I can see why you'd want someone to go with her. A woman shouldn't travel alone. But why Ephram and Hannah? Why not me?"

"Because you're not a slave."

"And what difference does that make?"

"None in Boston. But all the world in London." He leaned forward to look around Edmund and meet his half brother's gaze. "Ephram, if I can't make a miracle for Rosewind, she goes on the auction block for debts and taxes. You know that just as well as I do. And you also know that you're listed on the asset ledger. Would you rather be sold off on the block or live as a free man in England?"

"I'd rather stay and count on you to gain passage of your manumission law."

"Not a wise gamble, Ephram," he answered, looking away. "Time and circumstances are against it. The House agenda is going to be filled with matters relating to the support of Boston and the preservation of our liberties. A manumission bill isn't likely to be considered this session. And, barring a divine intervention of Red Sea proportions, Rosewind will be on the block before the next one. I appreciate your confidence in me, but it's groundless. You and Hannah need to go to England."

"Might I point out that you don't own my mother anymore?" Ephram asked quietly. "That she's not yours to send anywhere for any reason."

Devon smiled. "Slaves run away all the time."

Edmund cleared his throat. "And it's a crime to aid and abet them in doing so."

Sliding a glance over at his friend, Devon grinned. "Are you planning to testify against me?"

"God, Devon."

"I'm a desperate man," he quipped. "We're known to take desperate actions."

The wariness that had clouded their gazes for the last three days was instantly back. Weary of the fear that had hung silently between them, he forced himself to laugh and chide, "There's no need for the two of you to look so damn grim. I'm not about to put a pistol to my head just yet. I have a few things left to do." He cocked a brow and more somberly added, "One of which is to bury Mother and Wyndom. We should probably be heading back to the house."

He wheeled his horse and set off down the trail through the woods, hearing the others fall in behind him, not having to see their faces to know the expressions they wore. That was the worst of it—people trying so hard to mourn as they thought he was mourning. Everyone except Claire. She didn't hover over him like the others did, didn't creep around the house as though she was afraid to remind him that others went on with living. Life had taught her about death and how to move on, how to get through the dark days. She attended to the somber tasks she needed to and then looked past them to deliberately see the simple joys of today, the promise of better tomorrows.

"I haven't asked you today, Dev . . . How's the shoulder feeling?"

"Better than yesterday," Devon answered truthfully.

"The rain's not bothering it?"

"No. But I'm sure the weather's a concern for other people. Any bets on whether Reverend McDowell makes it out for the service?"

"The creeks are running high and fast," Ephram pointed out. "They'll be almost impossible to cross."

"Hell," Edmund groused, "the land's running high and fast. It's just going to be us at the service. Us, a hundred pairs of funeral gloves, and a mountain of food."

And no river of tears, Devon silently added. No one would cry for the two lives ended. Elsbeth hadn't shed a single tear. Neither had Darice. Both had looked past

Wyndom's broken body and ordered the horses put back in the traces. The death of family hadn't mattered to them at all.

That was the sadness that haunted him: knowing that his mother and brother had lived their years without truly touching the lives of others, that their passing created no holes in the world of those left behind. Even if the sun had been shining, a hundred pairs of funeral gloves would have been at least ninety pairs too many.

CHAPTER TWENTY-FOUR

*T*HE SUN WAS ACTUALLY SHINING. For the second straight day. Not that it made any difference to how she felt. Devon had made arrangements for her to sail out in three days. And she didn't want to go. Something deep inside her said that leaving was dangerous, that if she turned her back and walked away, she'd never see Devon again. It was a fear she carried alone, not wanting to add her fears to the burdens Devon already bore. His grief and regrets ran deep and silent, hidden beneath his more open concerns for his fields and Rosewind's future.

Claire looked around the second-story meeting room at the Raleigh Tavern, resenting that she was ensconced among the dozen or so well-dressed women with handiwork projects. She'd been formally introduced to everyone, but her thinking had already been scrambled by that point and none of the names she remembered went with the faces. Each was the wife of a burgess, but which wife went with which burgess was well beyond her.

"Well," Gray Mitten Knitter was saying, "a day of fasting and prayer seems like such a small thing to do for those poor people. Surely we Virginians can do more than that. Our going hungry doesn't feed the children of Boston."

"And the only prayer I seem to be able to muster," said Coat-of-Arms Needlepoint, "is that of asking God to please smite the King and his advisors with the jawbone of an ass."

"Which would be the jawbone of Governor Dunmore."

Claire squinted to better see across the room. Ah, Cross-Stitch Sampler.

Cabbage Rose Needlepoint added, "John tells me that today they'll discuss supplying Boston overland and sending out a call for the other colonies to do likewise."

"My Robert stands prepared to run the British blockade if necessary," said Shirt Woman. "His brothers, William and Henry, are of the same resolve. Henry left for James City last night with the intent of seeing additional cannons mounted on the decks of our merchantmen."

"It would be pointless to run the blockade with an empty vessel," Gray Mitten Knitter interjected, putting her work in her lap and looking around the room. "Ladies, we must see that necessary supplies are gathered. Men, being the creatures they are, will see to the amassing of gunpowder and weapons and never once think beyond that. It's up to us to attend to the daily, practical needs of Boston."

"Food is the most important," noted the very rotund Pomander Maker. "If each of us was to contribute a barrel of flour and five hams from our smokehouses—"

"And medicines," interrupted Tatter. "We mustn't forget that. If the blockade continues through the winter, they'll have need of remedies for common ailments."

Gray Mitten Knitter nodded. "And shoes and gloves and cloth. We all have leather sitting in our warehouses that we can contribute, bolts of fabric in our sewing cottages. I, for one, am willing to do without a new dress so that someone in Boston can be warm this winter."

There was a chorus of agreement, which Claire absently joined. She had gloves to contribute. Already made. Ninety-three pairs to be exact. Mourning gloves she and Hannah and Meg had spent three days making for those who would attend the funerals. And no one had, outside the family.

Oh, everyone had been quick to offer their condolences to Devon when they'd arrived in Williamsburg yesterday for the opening session of the House of Burgesses. And just as quick to offer an explanation for why they hadn't been able to attend the funeral for "dear Henrietta" and "poor Wyndom." Devon had politely accepted all the stories and then made up one of his own. Wyndom had had a pistol in the waistband of his trousers, and when he'd been dragged from the carriage box, it had fallen out, hit the ground, and discharged, and the lead ball had struck and passed through Devon's shoulder. His mother, on seeing one son's neck broken and the other shot, had clasped her heart and fallen dead. And everyone had not only accepted it but had spent the first half of the day trading the lie back and forth.

The true cause of her troubled spirit, Claire admitted to herself as she glanced around at the assembled wives, was that she didn't want to be in Williamsburg or around other people. She wanted to be at Rosewind, locked with Devon in the conservatory she'd converted into their bedchamber the day of that horrible morning.

She wanted to hold him and heal his battered heart, to care for his torn shoulder. In time, with love, the light would come back into his eyes.

But time was something she didn't have. Three days. And Devon's sense of duty had called him to Williamsburg and required what little time they had to be sacrificed for the betterment of Virginia. Claire frowned down at the needlework in her lap. Her father would have understood perfectly, she realized. They were very much alike, her late father and her husband. Quiet, intelligent, and wholly committed to honor, duty, and principle.

"What is it, Anna?"

The tone of the question abruptly pulled Claire from her musing. She watched as the others tossed down their work and moved toward the window overlooking the Duke of Gloucester street.

"Our men are coming from the capitol. En masse," someone—presumably Lookout Anna—announced.

Claire frowned, remembering that Devon had told her that the House had a full agenda for the morning session. If they were out within an hour of convening... Her stomach leaden and her heart in her throat, Claire quickly put her needlepoint tulip in her carrying bag and was already heading toward the stairs leading down to the main room when one of the other ladies observed, "They look angry. Something awful must have happened."

DEVON FILED INTO THE TAVERN with his fellow burgesses, searching the chattering crowd of women for Claire. She was off to the right of the stairs, pale and silent and wide-eyed. His heart twisted at the sight of her distress, knowing that this moment was just the beginning of her heartache. And his. He had to be strong for her, resolute for them both. He threaded his way through the group of angry men, wincing when his shoulder connected with another's. He'd worked his way halfway to her when Mrs. Randolph, standing on the third step up, called above the noise, "Peyton, an explanation please."

The room fell silent as their president turned to his wife, bowed slightly, and answered, "Governor Dunmore has formally dissolved the Virginia Assembly."

The women gasped and Mrs. Randolph asked for all of them, "Why?"

"He apparently considers the House of Burgesses' resolution calling for a day of fasting and praying on behalf of Boston to be seditious."

The room erupted with outrage.

"Seditious!"

"To pray and fast?"

Devon never took his eyes off Claire. She worked her way through the crowd to his side, coming into the circle of his arms just as an indignant and defiant female voice demanded, "And if we were to send them a ham or a pair of shoes, would we be guilty of high treason and hanged for it?"

Out of the corner of his eye he saw someone step up onto a chair. "I have ten hams for Boston! Who is willing to hang with me?"

He recognized the voice, felt Claire start. Amid the chorus of offers, Devon leaned down and whispered in her ear, "That's Patrick Henry. If we run out of cannonballs, he'll volunteer and manage to incite a riot before we can get him tamped down the barrel. Cooler heads will prevail, sweetheart."

"Gentlemen! Ladies! Please!" It took a moment, but the room stilled and quieted. When it had, Peyton Randolph went on. "By a show of hands, gentlemen members . . . all those in favor of convening the Virginia Assembly extralegally, please signify."

The price they would pay would be dear. Devon

lifted his right hand and saw that every man in the room had solemnly done the same. The die had now been cast.

"All those opposed?"

The raised hands came down. Not a single one went up.

"I can see," Peyton went on, scanning the crowd, "that while we have the quorum necessary for the vote to stand, we're lacking a member or two from our numbers. So that the business of the colony of Virginia can be conducted in a rightful manner, this body will recess until nine o'clock tomorrow morning. Mr. Richard Henry Lee will see that the missing members are notified and present at this place and at that time for the conduct of legislative business. Come prepared to work without rest, gentlemen. For the present, we stand adjourned."

As his fellow burgesses found their wives and began to go, Devon gave Claire a quick hug and then stepped from her side and into the path of Peyton Randolph. "Mr. Randolph, a moment of your time please."

"Rivard," Randolph said, nodding slowly, "I have a special task in mind for you. I'd be most appreciative if you'd work on a committee with Mr. Jefferson for the purpose of drafting a document detailing for the world our present grievances with Parliament. Along with that, I'd like for the committee to prepare a list of possible actions we may reasonably take in response to both our own crisis and that facing the citizens of Boston. I'll open tomorrow's session by formally proposing the formation of the committee and the nature of its task. Are you agreeable to serving?"

"I am. With one request." Randolph cocked a brow in silent question, and Devon took the first deliberate step. "My wife has been summoned to Philadelphia and then on to England as a witness in a legal matter. I'd thought to see her aboard a ship bound that way in three days' time. But given today's events and the potential consequences on my time, I think it best if she departs as soon as possible. With your permission, I'll be absent from tomorrow's morning session so that I can see her safely departed from the James City docks."

Behind him, he heard Claire stifle a cry. Taking a deep breath, he endured the pang that shot through his heart.

"It's a thoroughly reasonable request, Rivard. And a wise, thoughtful decision on your part. We have much to discuss and decide in the coming days, and better you be gone from our ranks at the first of it than in the more critical days that will follow."

"My thinking exactly, sir."

Peyton Randolph nodded and then, to Devon's dismay, turned to Claire. Offering her a bow, the president of the House of Burgesses said, "My sincerest apologies, Madam Rivard, for the disruption of your travel plans. And my deepest appreciation for your willingness to understand and accommodate the needs of Virginia and the American colonies. I wish you a safe and speedy journey to England and back."

Claire's chin came up a tiny notch and she found a gracious smile. "Thank you, Mr. Randolph."

Feeling her strain, Devon stepped to her side and slipped his arm around her waist. "Should there be anything requiring my immediate attention, sir, I'll be on the road to James City today. Several of my servants will be en route there from Rosewind in the early hours of the morning if you need to send a message through them."

"Safe travels to you as well, Mr. Rivard. I'll see you tomorrow afternoon." With another quick bow, Randolph left them.

She looked up at him and took a breath.

"Not here and not now, sweetheart," he gently admonished, drawing her toward the door. "I need to find Edmund and get our bags into the carriage. When we're on the road, we can talk."

He saw anger spark in her eyes. For a second he regretted his high-handed approach and then just as quickly changed his mind. Anger would serve them both better in the short term. They'd have eternity for the tears.

Ever so predictably, Edmund stood with Zeke and the carriage. "I heard," he said as Devon and Claire drew near.

Devon shot him a warning look and handed Claire into the carriage. "I'll be gone only a few minutes. You stay right here," he commanded, closing the door before she could object. But not before she shot him a look that promised that he wasn't going to come back to kisses and contented sighs.

"Zeke, please stay with the carriage and Lady Claire. If she tries to run off, tackle her," he instructed as he motioned for Edmund to come away from the carriage. When they were out of earshot, he took a steadying breath and met his friend's gaze squarely. "I need you to do a couple things for me. First, I need the petition that I asked you to draw up for Claire. Is it ready?"

Edmund hesitated before saying quietly, "I wrote it that morning. It's in my desk drawer." He paused, then shook his head and drew himself up to his full height. "But that was before, Devon. When you and Claire were still strangers. Circumstances between you have changed since then."

"Yes," Devon admitted, resenting the challenge, "and they changed again this morning. I need the petition."

"You can't do this, Devon. It's wrong."

Anger surged through him, borne on a soul-deep wave of certainty and sorrow. He looked away, not wanting to wound their friendship. "A week ago I buried my mother and my brother," he said when he had his emotions reasonably under control again. "I can't bear the thought of having to bury Claire, too. I'd sooner die than face that."

He turned to meet the other's gaze and softly confessed, "Edmund, I love her. I love her with all my heart. If she's in England, she's safe. I'd rather live without her, knowing she's alive and well, than keep her with me and put her life at risk."

"It's her choice to make."

"No, it's mine," he snapped, squaring his shoulders and dredging up another measure of resolve. "And as hard as it is, I've made it. Go get the petition and take it out to Ephram. Tell him to pack his things and be at the James City docks tomorrow morning at dawn."

"Devon, please don't do this. You're not thinking clearly."

"I'll be back tomorrow afternoon. We can argue about it then." He didn't give Edmund a chance to say anything else. Turning on his heel, he walked away, heading for the King's Arms to see to the retrieval of his and Claire's meager baggage.

Claire stared at the far wall of the coach and blinked back furious tears. She didn't want to be on the road. Not to James City. She wanted to go to Rosewind, with Devon. She wanted to hide in their room and let the world go crazy without them. To hell with her uncle and the courts of England. To hell with the House of Burgesses, Governor Dunmore, and Peyton Randolph. To hell with the King and all his addlepated advisors.

And to hell with Devon, too! With his damn determination to hide his grief so stoically. With his oh-so-noble sense of duty and responsibility. And especially with his imperial decrees! *You stay right here.* The hell she would. If he wanted to go to James City, then he could go without her. He couldn't drag her there by brute force. And if he wanted to try, then he'd have to find and catch her first. And damned if Zeke was going to stand in her way.

Cautiously, she lifted the curtain to see just where Zeke had taken up his watch and the best way to get past him. She found him easily enough; he was standing with Devon some fifteen feet away. Swearing under her breath, she watched Zeke nod, take their bags from Devon, and head toward the rear of the carriage. Devon didn't follow. He stood there, his sadness so profound, so visible on his face that her anger instantly dissolved into heartache.

As he gathered himself and heaved a sigh, she did the same, letting the curtain fall back and settling into the seat. It would take them hours to get to James City, and she'd use them as best she could. And maybe, just maybe, by the time they reached their destination she'd have convinced him to change it. If she couldn't... Claire blinked back tears and lifted her chin. She loved him too much to make his pain any deeper than it already was.

He climbed into the coach with a smile that didn't soften the hard lines of his jaw or brighten his eyes. As he sat opposite her, the carriage began to roll forward. "All right, Claire," he said with a resigned sigh. "I'll entertain your protests now."

"Well, to begin with," she replied, hoping that he couldn't hear the desperate pounding of her heart, "I doubt very much that General Gates will be inclined to come looking for me if I don't arrive on his doorstep when I'm supposed to. And surely my testimony isn't the only evidence they have against my uncle. Their case won't crumble for the lack of it. In short, I don't have to go."

His answer came instantly, no less firm for the gentleness of his voice. "The rule of law is all that separates civilization from anarchy, sweetheart. We don't have the luxury of picking and choosing when we'll honor our laws and fulfill our duty. You've been summoned to testify. It's your duty as a citizen to obey that summons, to provide what the government needs to right a wrong. You know that. And you know that you have to go."

"Would it insult you terribly if I asked you to come with me?"

"No, it wouldn't insult me at all," he replied, the tiniest flicker of a real smile lifting the corners of his mouth. "I'd give anything to be able to go with you. But I can't. Just as you have your duty, I have mine. And I can't step away from it any more than you can yours. Not now. Especially not now."

"The work on the committee Mr. Randolph is going to form."

Devon considered her, trying to gauge how much she was ready to hear, how best to soften her illusions and hopes so that she wasn't shattered when he reached the point of having to destroy them.

"It's much larger than that, sweetheart," he began, leaning forward to take her hands in his. "When Governor Dunmore dissolved the assembly, he changed the course of our lives. All our lives. We don't have to like it. No one cares that we had our own dreams and plans for the years ahead. It's done and can't be undone."

He looked down at their hands. "I recall that a very wise woman once gave me a credo that suits the situation perfectly. Circumstances frequently require adaptation."

"The woman clearly lacked good sense."

He heard regret in her voice. But also an acceptance that their world had indeed been altered and that they had to accept it. And it was all the further he was willing to push her for now. What time they had left was too precious to spend it in tears or flinging angry, useless words at each other.

"I don't know about good sense," he began, his heart filling with a bittersweet ache as he grazed her knuckles with the pads of his thumbs. "On the day I met her, she was running about town masquerading as a boy. She did a very fine job of it, too. I was the only one who knew."

"She sounds like an absolute hoyden."

"Oh, most definitely," he agreed, still studying their hands, committing the sight to his memory. "Opinionated, too. And demanding. I couldn't believe that I was being forced to marry her. It turns out that she's the best thing that's ever happened to me." He looked up to meet Claire's gaze. "I love her."

"And I love you, Devon."

He didn't need to hear the words; he could see them in her eyes. Her beautiful deep-blue eyes. No other woman on earth would ever look at him like that, no other woman would ever love him as deeply, completely, and without condition as his beautiful, brave Claire. The enormity of what lay ahead squeezed around his heart.

"Come here," he whispered, drawing her into his arms, determined to gather as much as he could of her into his soul before he had to let her go.

CHAPTER TWENTY-FIVE

*C*LAIRE WALKED ALONG THE DOCK, her every breath shuddering in and out of her lungs, her knees threatening to give out on her at any moment. They hadn't slept but in fits and starts the night before, and her limbs felt as though they'd been weighted with stones. But her emotions... They were painfully alert; so sensitive, so tightly coiled that she felt as if she might explode at any moment. But she couldn't allow it. Just couldn't. Devon was teetering on his own brink; she could feel it in his touch. It passed through his palm and into the small of her back as he guided her through the predawn crowd.

Ahead, amidst the bobbing sea of bodies, she saw familiar faces. Edmund and Meg. And to their right, Hannah. Hot tears welled in Claire's eyes and sent her running for the haven of the old woman's arms.

"Hannah," she sobbed into her shoulder. "Help me. Please help me."

"You have to be strong, Lady Claire," Hannah said in her ear, patting her back. "His whole world is tumbling down around him, and he can't find his way in it and yours, too."

"But I can help him," Claire protested, pulling back to look Hannah in the eyes. "I have the strength. Help me make him see that."

Brushing away the tears with gentle fingertips, Hannah shook her head. "Child, as long as you're standing beside him, he won't let himself crumble. And he's got to do that. He needs to grieve for everyone and everything he's lost before he can begin to heal. If you love him, then you'll give him the solitude he needs, the time he needs. He can't be half of a marriage until he's a man whole unto himself. And you can't do that for him. No one can."

"I'm afraid for him, Hannah."

"We'll watch him. Mr. Cantrell, Meg, and me. You can trust us."

Swallowing back another wave of tears, Claire choked out, "But you're not going to be at Rosewind to watch over him. You're going back to Mrs. Vobe's."

"No, she isn't," Meg corrected, gently laying her hand on Claire's shoulder. "When she stamped down her foot an' refused to go with ye an' Ephram to England, Edmund stamped his own feet at Mrs. Vobe's an' bought her. An' where Edmund goes, she goes. An' he's takin' up residence at Rosewind with us."

Stunned, she looked between the two women. "Ephram's sailing with me?"

Meg nodded. "Ye didn't think Mr. Devon was 'bout to let ye go off alone, did ye? Ye've been so wrapped up in a worryin' about him the last week or so that ye've missed a wee bit of what else has been goin' on."

"One of them apparently being that you've moved to a first-name acquaintance with my husband's attorney."

Meg blushed and managed to control her smile enough to say, "Aye, that I have."

"I wish you every happiness in the world, Meg."

"An' I the same for you, Lady Claire. Don't you worry about Mr. Devon. Hannah's tellin' ye the truth. We'll watch him an' make sure he comes out of this all right."

She felt better, somehow reassured that life would indeed go on and everything would turn out well in the end. Buoyed, she nodded and found a smile for her friend. "You won't get married until I get back, will you? I promise I'll return as soon as I can."

"No, child," Hannah said quietly, touching her cheek. "I know you mean well, but coming back before his heart is mended enough to hold you will only tear him apart again. When he's ready, he'll reach out for you. Until then, you have to be strong. It's the only thing you can do for him."

Claire bowed her head as another wave of tears swelled her throat.

"What your own heart and mind tell you is right doesn't matter, child," Hannah went on sternly. "Not today. Tell him what he wants to hear. Agree to do what he asks of you. Give him the peace of mind he needs for now. In the days to come, things will change and the promises you make today can be set aside. But you both have to survive today to get there. Do you understand what I'm telling you?"

She did. "It hurts so badly, Hannah."

"I know. But you pull up that chin of yours and be brave for our Devon. You keep your eyes firmly fixed on tomorrow. It'll be a better one. And remember that the good Lord doesn't give us any burdens that He knows we can't bear."

Ephram stepped to his mother's side and slipped his arm around her shoulders, saying, "They're calling for passengers to board, Lady Claire. Our bags are stowed. So whenever you're ready . . ."

Her voice quavered when she said, "Thank you,

Ephram," but she squared her shoulders, hugged Hannah and Meg, and then turned away from them.

Devon stood waiting for her, his eyes dark and unreadable. Determined to be brave as Hannah had instructed, she stepped forward and slipped her arms around his waist. As always, his arms came around her shoulders to draw her close. Laying her cheek against his chest, she closed her eyes and listened to the beat of his heart. "I'll come back just a soon as the court frees me to leave," she offered, hoping he'd prove Hannah wrong.

"No, Claire."

She drew back to look at him, and the hardness of his jaw frightened her. "But I'm your wife. My place is here."

He shook his head, his lips a thin line of resolution.

"Devon..."

He sighed and stepped back to stand with his hands on her shoulders. "Claire, sweetheart, listen to me and hear what I'm saying. And know that I'd give my life not to have to say these things to you."

Her heart skittered and she tried to back away. He held her fast and coolly said, "In the next day or so, the Virginia Assembly will send a communication to every other colony, calling for them to meet—probably in Philadelphia at the end of the summer. They'll come and we will, by necessity, consider armed rebellion as a course of action. Whether we make one last effort at peaceful settlement of our differences with England remains to be seen. But I know in my heart that even if we do, it'll fail, Claire. War is coming. It's inevitable."

Oh, God. She knew what he was going to say, what decisions he'd made.

"It's my duty to stand for right, Claire, to lead however I can in the struggle, and I won't shirk it. All that I have will be forfeited when that day comes. Rosewind will be gone, either seized by the Crown or razed by its soldiers." He smiled weakly and his laugh was dry and hard. "Frankly, that doesn't matter to me in the least. The damn thing's an unprofitable, drafty beast, and I'd welcome the chance to build another house and do it right."

"I'd like to help you do that," she offered, grasping at hope.

"I know you would," he said sadly, brushing the back of his hand over her cheek. "But the plain truth is that it's not likely to happen, sweetheart. Great Britain is the mightiest, wealthiest nation in the world."

He motioned with his chin toward the ship and the people streaming up its gangplank. "Look around you. Look at the people standing with us here. Just ordinary people. This is our army, Claire. These merchantmen tied along the dock are our navy. That's all we have to throw against the greatest power on earth. You know as well as I do what chances we have for success."

"Then why make the fight, Devon?"

"Because the choice is between living as voiceless slaves or dying as free men. We choose the latter. And yes, I remember your objection. How can I say that when we hold others in chains? We're not perfect, Claire, and we know it. But we also know what perfection is, and we're determined to someday achieve it. It'll take time and a thousand small steps along the road of reason and compromise. But the first step has to be securing the right to make those decisions for ourselves. Richard Henry is absolutely correct. We cannot give to others what we don't ourselves possess."

He was right; what she hadn't once believed of him, of his fellows, she now did. "Then let—"

He put his fingertips over her lips and shook his head. Only when she'd sighed in resignation did he take them away. Reaching into his coat, he extracted a folded piece of parchment and handed it to her, explaining, "I asked Edmund to draft a petition for you to present to the court when you get there. It asks the court to grant you title to Crossbridge Manor in recompense for your service to England. I think they're likely to do so. Ephram will stay with you until you're safely settled there."

She stared up at him, the paper clutched numbly in her hand. Crossbridge. He wanted her to go to Crossbridge. So he'd know where she was. So he'd know where to send the letter to call her home. Relief flooded over her. It wasn't forever. She could endure.

"Will you, in turn, see that Ephram strikes out on his own as a free man?"

"Of course."

"And I'll ask you to do something for me when you reach England."

"Anything."

"I want you to petition the Crown for a divorce."

The words struck like a physical blow, shattering her hope. "No. I will *not* do that," she declared, stepping back.

His fingers tightened on her shoulders, holding her firmly in front of him. "Yes, you will. I'm going to commit treason, Claire. Knowingly and willfully. If you remain my wife, you're subject to the same punishments that'll be brought down on me. Crossbridge Manor will be seized and you'll be thrown into prison. There will be no one to come to your rescue, no one to petition the Crown for leniency and mercy. You'll die there." His eyes darkening and his breathing ragged, he gave her a tiny shake, demanding, "Do you hear me?"

"I hear you," she answered, her eyes filling with tears. "But you can't make me do that, Devon. You can't make me abandon you."

He closed his eyes and pulled her hard into his arms, holding her tight for a long moment before he exhaled a shuddering breath and said quietly, "If you truly love me, you'll remove yourself from harm's way so that I'm not constantly worried about you. Please, Claire. Ask for a divorce, either on the grounds that you were forced into the union against your will or that I'm a rebel leader. They'll grant it for either cause and you'll be safe."

"Why should I be safe when you're not?" she demanded.

He set her from him tenderly, taking her face in his hands and tilting her head up until she met his gaze. "You were thrown into my life, my circumstances, against your will. This isn't your fight, Claire. And you shouldn't have to suffer the consequences of it because of a twist of fate. You have nothing to gain in standing with me except certain poverty and likely widowhood. I love you too much to want that for you. Please give my soul some peace. Promise me that you'll stay in England, that you'll petition for the divorce, and make a happy life for yourself."

Her heart was tearing. She couldn't breathe and didn't want to. "But I—"

"Promise me," he whispered raggedly. "Give me that as the last of the gifts of your heart."

"I love you, Devon."

The boatswain's final call rang out over the dock, chilling her blood and draining the strength from her body. As though from a great distance she heard Ephram say, "Sir, there's no more time."

The longing and heartache in Devon's eyes was an echo of that resounding through her soul as he bent down and kissed her. She clung to him, desperately willing him to relent.

"Sir." Ephram's voice was anxious. "They're getting ready to haul up the gangplank."

God, if she could hold him just a few seconds longer. It would be too late. Her body trembling, she gathered his lapels into her fists. And then his lips were gone and he was pulling away from her grasp.

"Take care of her," he said, his voice rough as he thrust her, stumbling, into Ephram's hands.

Through the blur of her tears she saw him turn and walk away. "No, Devon," she whispered as Ephram pulled her toward the boat. "No. Please." He didn't pause, didn't look back, and what was left of her heart shattered into a thousand jagged pieces as Ephram picked her up and carried her over the plank.

"BACK TO WILLIAMSBURG, ZEKE," Devon barked, ripping open the door of the carriage and vaulting in. "I have work to do."

"Yes, sir."

He slammed the door closed behind himself, stumbling onto the seat, blinded by scalding tears. And as the carriage started forward, he sagged into the corner and surrendered to the wracking sobs of a grief deeper and more abiding than any he'd ever known.

CHAPTER TWENTY-SIX

CLAIRE TWEAKED THE POSITION of a salad fork and then stepped back to survey the table. Her mother's best china glowed in the late morning light streaming in through the windows. The silver that had been blackened from years of disuse now gleamed. The linens, so long packed away, were white again and crisply pressed. The food—an assortment of cold meats and cheeses, breads, puddings, and salads of which Hannah would be proud—was prepared and carefully covered with damp towels to keep it fresh. Claire smiled ruefully and turned away.

As she stood in the doorway of the dining room, her gaze passed slowly over the main room of Crossbridge, touching the familiar objects of her childhood. The settle, the hearth, the wheeled chair. Her father's pipe. Her mother's prized crystal vase. The small, gilt-framed drawing a traveling artist had done of her brothers the year before they'd died. They were such small things, their value in shillings and pounds nothing when compared to the beautiful and costly furnishings of Rosewind.

Tears welled in her eyes and she quickly brushed them away, sternly reminding herself that it wouldn't do to have Reverend Graves and his wife arrive for luncheon to find their hostess crying. Squaring her shoulders, she took her shawl from the peg beside the front door and marched outside, resolving to use what time she had to get on with her too-long-delayed survey of Crossbridge's gardens.

She walked along the front of the house, her mind wandering not among the plantings but along the paths of memory. The Reverend Reginald Graves had been older than the hills since she could remember. He'd outlived two wives. His third, Cornelia, a timid, quiet, altogether invisible woman, was only a handful of years older than she was. Reverend Graves spoke for Cornelia whenever he wasn't too busy speaking for God. And if Reverend Graves wasn't free to offer Cornelia's opinion, then Cornelia didn't have one.

Claire sighed. What had she been thinking to invite them to luncheon? Why hadn't she simply responded to their request to call by saying that Crossbridge wasn't yet ready to receive visitors? Because, she answered herself, that wouldn't have been the truth. Crossbridge was ready. For the last three weeks she'd spent her every waking moment trying to make it all that she remembered it once being. It had never looked better. And never had it felt so empty, so lifeless.

No, the truth was that *she* wasn't ready to receive visitors, wasn't ready to pretend that her life was serene and that she was happy. She'd invited the Graveses to dine in the hope that having to fulfill social obligations would engage not only her mind but her heart. It had been so long since she'd felt anything except a kind of numbness. In the beginning it had been a blessing, wrapping first her voyage and then her appearance before the grand jury in a soft, gentle fog.

It had dissipated a bit when she'd been handed the title to Crossbridge; she'd actually had the wherewithal to stammer some genuine words of gratitude. It had cleared a little more when she'd walked back in through the door and realized that she'd achieved all that she'd so long hoped for. But no matter how hard she worked, no matter how hard she tried to smile and dream, her heart remained distant and shrouded. Out of reach and numb. Fearfully numb.

And so, in a moment of weakness and desperation, she'd invited Reverend Graves and his mute-as-a-post wife to luncheon. God. Better numb than bored mindless. Or having to hear of God's lowly opinion of mankind in general and of womankind in particular. If he mentioned that damn apple...A tiny smile tickled the corners of her mouth as she imagined leaping across the dining room table to choke the good and very righteous Reverend Reginald Graves. Perhaps it wasn't such a bad idea to have invited him to dine after all. There were some in the community who would be forever grateful if she put an end to their weekly dose of misery.

A gust of cool, damp wind whipped around the corner of the house and Claire pulled the shawl closer about her shoulders, breathing deeply the scent of turning leaves. Were they changing colors in Virginia, too? In her mind's eye she saw the drive of Rosewind canopied in gold and rust, the warm brick of the house glowing in the morning light, the smoke curling up from the chimneys. And Devon riding toward her, coming in from the fields, his shirtsleeves rolled up, his jacket draped over the pommel. She watched him draw near, the beat of her heart matching the rolling cadence of hooves...

"Good day to you, madam!"

Shoving her thoughts aside, Claire turned to the couple coming up the front walk and forced herself to smile. Reverend Graves hadn't aged a day since she'd last seen him. Cornelia, as always, floated along on his arm looking both dazed and a trifle apprehensive. Claire looked past them for a second to see whether the carriage was the same one as always and if the ancient horse was still alive. They were. Four, almost five years gone since her father's death, and nothing had changed. It was a comforting realization, and holding it close, she moved forward to meet her guests.

"Please forgive my inattention," Claire began, extending her hand. "Plans for putting Crossbridge Manor back to rights have a tendency to make me oblivious to anything else. Welcome. It's lovely to see you again after all these years."

"We had hoped to see you in church this past Sunday," Reverend Graves said, the censure in his voice belying his smile as he wrapped her hand in a nest of wrinkled, bony flesh.

Claire resisted the urge to pull away from his grasp. With a shrug, she gave him the simple truth. "Coming home has brought back memories. Unfortunately, not all of them have been good ones. The last time I was in Good Shepherd Church was for my father's funeral. I'm afraid that I haven't had the strength necessary to face that particular memory yet. I'm sure I will in time."

His hands tightened around hers. "The sooner you face the demons of the past, the better. The less power they have over you. When I look out from the pulpit next Sunday, I will expect to see you sitting in your family's pew."

Deep inside her, something sparked. It was a startling sensation, quick and unexpected, but delightful in its warmth and vibrancy. Extracting her hand from his grasp, she gestured toward the door, saying politely,

"Won't you and Cornelia come inside? Our meal is prepared and waiting."

As she expected, the minister cocked a bushy gray brow at her small rebellion. The spark inside her brightened, and reveling in it, she turned and started up the steps of Crossbridge, not caring whether they followed or not.

They did, though, stopping just inside the door. Reverend Graves glanced about the interior. "Have you given your servant a holiday?" he asked, stepping behind Cornelia and divesting her of her shawl.

"Ephram isn't my servant," Claire explained, tossing her own shawl over the back of a chair. "He was my husband's business manager and accompanied me on my journey back to England. He saw me safely settled here and then returned to London. He's accepted employment with a bookkeeping firm there."

"Your husband didn't accompany you himself?"

She heard the condemnation in his voice, and the spark flickered into a flame. "Circumstances made that impossible," she supplied tightly, unwilling to dignify his presumption with a detailed explanation, unwilling to share her life with Devon with anyone outside it. "Won't you come to the table?" Again she turned and led the way. Only this time her earlier ambivalence was gone; she hoped that the minister and his wife would decide not to follow.

"Your own circumstances have been quite extraordinary," said a soft, tremulous voice from behind her. "I've been following the tales avidly."

Claire stopped in her tracks. Good God, Cornelia Graves had not only spoken, but actually uttered two complete sentences. Hoping to encourage the unusual show of bravery, Claire turned and asked with a smile, "What tales have you heard, Cornelia?"

Cornelia blanched beneath her husband's withering

look and dropped her gaze to the floor. Claire clenched her teeth as Reverend Graves replied, "Women have always been weak to temptation. Satan offers many apples. Of which gossip is only one."

That damned apple. And always the weakness of women. Poor Cornelia. To be interested in something beyond the narrow world of Crossbridge and rebuked for it . . . It wasn't fair and it wasn't right. And she wasn't going to let it pass unchallenged. "Tell me something, Reverend. Is it considered a sin to speak the truth?"

"Of course not," Graves replied, seating his wife at the table. "God demands that we speak the truth in all things."

"Good." Lifting the covers from the food, she said brightly, "Cornelia, let me tell you the truth of what's happened to me in the last few months. It has indeed been extraordinary. As I'm sure you've heard, my uncle has long been engaged in cheating the Crown and made me a party to his crimes. When the King's ministers discovered his perfidy, they moved to bring an indictment against him and sought my testimony to that end."

The woman glanced up for only a scant second, but it was long enough for Claire to see the silent plea for her to continue. Claire smiled, seated herself, ignored the reverend's scowl, and obliged. "I imagine that it's at this point that the story's become a bit blurred for everyone. I doubt that it's been exaggerated, though. It would be extremely difficult to make the tale any more harrowing or horrific than it was. You see, my uncle, in trying to prevent my giving testimony and evidence against him, contracted to have me murdered in a place and under circumstances that would cast suspicion in a direction far removed from himself."

Claire paused, considering the road she'd traveled and realizing that she'd never before attempted to put into words those days, those events and how deeply they'd affected her. In that place deep within her where the flame flickered, the warmth of it intensified and began to gently thrum.

"To that end," she continued, both strengthened and unsettled by the sensation, "my uncle forced me into a marriage with a stranger, an American farmer, a decent, caring, intelligent man who didn't hold my uncle's scheming against me. A man whose brother was assigned the gruesome task of disposing of me. His brother and my uncle failed only because of the brave actions and hard choices my husband was willing to make in order to protect me. He paid a high price for his devotion to me. A devotion he had no reason to offer and every reason to withhold. I owe him my life many times over."

Bits and pieces of memories flitted through her mind, blessedly fractured. Darice. Elsbeth. Wyndom. Meg and Hannah and Edmund. Mother Rivard. And Devon. The sadness in his eyes as he'd stood on the dock at James City, the hardness of his jaw as he'd told her farewell. The longing and tenderness in his final kiss.

And suddenly the numbness surrounding her heart shattered, and the soul-deep ache of that moment came flooding back over her. She closed her eyes, welcoming it as proof that she could still feel, struggling to bear with dignity the overwhelming sense of loss that came in its wake. Unwilling to lose her composure and embarrass the reverend and his wife, Claire seized a deep breath, willed a smile onto her face and dispassionate words from her tongue.

"I didn't want to leave him, but he insisted that I respect the rule of law and fulfill my duty to the court. And so I left the colonies and returned to England to render my testimony before the grand jury. I understand that the indictment has already been handed down and that my uncle has been arrested. I'll be required to testify against him in the trial, of course. The Crown has given me two weeks to return to London."

"Will your husband be joining you there?" Cornelia asked softly, seemingly oblivious to her own husband's disapproving frown.

God, how deeply she wanted to see Devon, to be in his arms again. How deeply it hurt to know that it wasn't at all likely to happen. "I rather doubt it," she forced herself to say around the thickening in her throat. "He has great responsibilities to attend to in the colonies."

"Will you be returning to him after the trial? Or will you be coming home to Crossbridge?"

"Home," Claire admitted sadly, "seems to be something I've lately found difficult to identify. I find myself torn between two shores."

"It would appear that you escaped that wretched American shore just in time," Graves intoned. "God obviously had a hand in bringing you back to England. In time and with guidance, you will undoubtedly come to appreciate His infinite wisdom."

Claire stared at him blankly. "Wretched? I don't think of America in that manner at all."

"Then you haven't heard about recent developments in the American colonies."

Her heart lurched upward. "Apparently not," she heard herself say over the rapid clicking of her thoughts. Devon had said that they were on the brink of war, that Virginia would send out a call for all the colonies to send delegations to a meeting at the end of summer.

"Let us bless this food and thank the good Lord for your timely rescue."

She nodded absently, and while the reverend and his wife bowed their heads, she gazed at the leaves outside. It was the beginning of October now, and if they'd met when Devon had said they would ... Time enough to declare war, time enough for word of it to have reached London. The drone of the minister's voice ended, and she offered up a quiet "Amen" for it.

Picking up the platter of meats and cheeses, Claire held it out for Graves and, with a wholly feigned nonchalance, said, "You were about to tell me what's happened in the colonies."

"I was in London just five days ago for a meeting of church elders," he said while helping himself to generous portions, "and I had occasion to read for myself the reports in the London papers. The American colonists have fallen into the depths of utter stupidity. The consequence of which will be the full wrath and power of His Majesty's Royal Army and Navy being brought down upon them."

Her heart tripped even as she told herself that she wouldn't panic, wouldn't assume the worst. As she presented the platter to Cornelia, she pressed for more information. "Might I ask you to be a bit more specific as to what they've done that's so appalling?"

"They have met in an illegal assembly and authored some bit of rubbish they call the Declaration and Resolutions of the Continental Congress. In this document, they whine and carry on concerning legitimate acts of Parliament and declare themselves above the law and absolved of obedience."

Claire expelled the breath she'd been holding. Not a declaration of war. Light-headed with relief, she blindly filled her own plate and then, with a trembling hand, reached for her glass of white wine. She should have known they wouldn't have acted so rashly. Devon was resolved to fight a war if he had no other choice, but he didn't *want* war.

"And then," Graves went on as she sipped, "in a pathetically empty gesture of defiance, they vow to cease all trade with us until our blessed King George grovels for their forgiveness."

Empty gesture? Devon never made empty gestures. He never made a threat, either; he made promises that he always saw through to the bitter end. Claire smiled.

Except for the matter of her breeches and boots. That contest he'd conceded. But her wearing breeches and boots was a world apart from the conflict arising between the colonies and England. On those issues, Devon would never yield.

Reverend Graves snorted and snatched up the crystal jar of ground mustard. All but flinging a spoonful of the stuff onto his plate, he added, "They won't last through the winter without the materials we supply them. They cannot survive without the might of Britain to defend and support them. And—should they go so far as to commit actual treason and take up arms—they certainly won't be able to stand against the mightiest military power in the history of the world."

Claire thought of the stores at Rosewind, of the women at the Raleigh Tavern and all that they'd been so instantly willing to send for the support of Boston.

"I respectfully beg to differ with you, sir," she said quietly, studying the pale color of her wine. "Unless the Crown has wanted the coins out of their pockets, the colonies have been largely ignored. Because of that neglect, they've learned to make their own way and to take care of themselves. Their lives are entirely sustainable without England's assistance. And while it remains to be seen whether they can emerge victorious in any military contest with Great Britain, I can assure you that if they choose to take up arms, they'll fight until the last man falls."

"Then they're pitiful fools."

With a sigh, she shook her head and said, "Forgive my bluntness, Reverend, but you know nothing of the American colonists. I've been there. I've lived among them. I can assure you that, by and large, they're a thoughtful, well-educated, and very deliberate people."

"Any man, any people," he shot back, "who oppose the rule of law and the authority of our King and

Parliament are fools. And not just fools, Madam Rivard, but also an ungrateful scourge that must be eradicated from our kingdom lest it infect and rot from within the tradition and tenets of common law."

Anger surged through her. "And for what should they be grateful?" she demanded. "That they're being taxed into poverty and ruin? That they've been denied the most fundamental right of Englishmen, the right to representation in Parliament and a voice in the formulation of the laws that govern them? That their freedoms are being stripped from them?"

Graves sardonically observed, "It would seem that there is something in colonial air which is contagious."

"Perhaps there is," she admitted, ignoring Cornelia's frightened look. "I can't help but admire them for being an incredibly resilient, independent people, sir. They've carved their existence out of the land by their own efforts and freely, gladly contributed the fruits of their labors to England's glory and power. They've asked only to live in peace, to enjoy the bounty they've worked so hard to attain, and to have their considerable contributions to the empire respected and rewarded by representation in Parliament. They've given much and asked for very little in return.

"The same can't be said for the King and his advisors. They give little and demand everything the colonists have won for themselves. And not for need, either, Reverend. But simply because the Crown believes it has the right to take what it pleases from whom it pleases when it pleases to spend as it pleases."

Graves glowered at her and, beside him, Cornelia cowered and shrunk into herself. "And it will please the Crown to no end when—at the sight of our power bearing down upon them—the seditious vermin turn tail and run."

"They're not going to run. I know my husband and

his fellows. If the King and his advisors refuse to address the concerns expressed in their most recent declaration, then the Americans will pronounce themselves a free nation. They have nothing to lose in fighting for their principles."

"Principles mean nothing when cities are smoldering rubble and people are starving."

"Understand this, Reverend. The Americans are a very different breed of people. They consider it a sacred duty to serve Right and the principles of freedom. The English talk of liberty and the rights of free men. The Americans live it. Freedom is more precious to them than peace, more precious than life itself. If England doesn't now understand that about her American colonists, they'll soon teach her."

Through gritted teeth, he retorted, "And we will teach them humility."

She tried to picture Devon on bended knee, his head bowed. "Never, sir," she replied with a short laugh. "They know what they've accomplished and against what odds. Great achievement doesn't lead to humility."

"Then they will leave us no choice but to destroy them."

Destroy Devon? Destroy Rosewind? Not as long as there was breath in her body. Claire met the reverend's gaze for a long moment before she replied solemnly, "Should England have the sorry misjudgment to make war on her own people, it won't be the first grave hardship visited upon the Americans. One of the most fascinating and wonderful things about them is their ability to see the opportunity that lies on the other side of a great misfortune. You can tear down their cities, burn their farms and plantations to the ground, and they will turn to their fellows and happily say, 'Now we can build something else, something even better than before.' They're an utterly undauntable people. They believe in themselves and in their ability to forge a tomorrow of their dreams. Try as England might, she will *never* destroy that."

"God is always on England's side."

"God, Reverend, is always on the side of right. And in the treatment of the Americans, England is not right. She's absolutely, blindly, stupidly wrong. And I, for one, will not stand by and permit the Americans to be wronged. To do so would be unconscionable."

"If I might offer you a word of advice, Madam Rivard?" Graves said, abruptly rising from his chair. He didn't wait for her assent, but took a cringing Cornelia by the elbow and all but hauled her to her feet while saying, "You would be wise to keep your rabid colonial sympathies to yourself. In the coming days, they will not be at all popular among your fellow citizens."

"Thank you. I'll bear that in mind," she replied, rising to follow them into the main room. She opened the door and held it for them, waiting until they were down the steps and moving along the walk before she called out, "Oh, and Reverend?" He turned back, his eyes blazing. She smiled. "I won't be in church on Sunday."

She didn't wait to see them the rest of the way down the walk and into their carriage. Wrapped in an abiding sense of satisfaction, she stepped back and smartly closed the door. "No one tells me where to be and when," she declared, striding into the dining room to snatch up plates of half-eaten food. "No one tells me what to think and what I can say. I've earned the right to make those decisions for myself. It might well be that nothing around here has changed in almost five years, but I certainly have and—"

Claire slowed and then stopped, stunned by the quiet potency of realization. She *had* changed. She wasn't the same Claire Curran who had grown up in this house. Crossbridge was beautiful and held precious memories, but it was the home of someone else, someone who didn't exist anymore. That's why all the weeks of housekeeping and homemaking hadn't given her the sense of peace and happiness she'd hoped to find. And, oddly enough, the fact that she'd tried made her angry. Truly angry.

CHAPTER TWENTY-SEVEN

$\mathcal{D}$EVON STOOD AT THE WINDOW and looked out into the night. From the second floor, he could see only so far, but it was far enough to know that London was a sprawling giant and the largest city he would see in his life. It only slumbered through the night, never really sleeping. On the streets below, lamplit carriages rolled by, and people, bundled against the damp chill, made their way along the walks. By light of day the city bustled, its streets and walks clogged to the point of near impassability. It was an interesting place, full of sights and sounds and smells. He could see how some would be drawn to it, wanting to immerse themselves in the hectic pace of the life it offered. He couldn't, though.

He'd been here for a week, moving through and around the city and yet constantly finding himself gazing off to the west and north, in the direction the maps said Herefordshire lay. Roughly two hundred miles if the maps were accurate. Five days of hard riding. Maybe four if the roads were as good as people said they were. Not that he had any reason to travel them. He'd just been making conversation.

"Well, here's an interesting bit of news," Edmund called out from his seat beside the hearth. He folded his newspaper and angled it into the firelight. "Lady Darice Lytton, late of the British American colony of Virginia, has been arrested and charged with the murder of one Sir William Grayson, Earl of Something-shire, Lord of Something-wick, and a distant cousin of the King. According to Grayson's closest relatives—presumably *not* the King—Grayson and ol' Darice were having an affair and had differing views on the appropriate way to end it."

Devon smiled wryly, thinking that Darice had apparently won the contest. "Does it say how she killed him?" he asked, looking over his shoulder.

Edmund read a bit, then pursed his lips and cast a quick glance in his direction. Devon recognized the hesitancy and had seen it often enough in the last few months to know the cause. Everyone at Rosewind had developed the habit of censoring their conversation. And no one mentioned Claire at all. They were very, very careful about that.

"Given the look on your face," he said, turning to look out the window again, "I'd guess it was by poison. Am I right?"

"You'd think that people could be just a bit more creative with mayhem," Edmund observed. "Just a little more original. Do you think they'd be interested in knowing your suspicions about how Robert Lytton died?"

Devon shrugged. "I don't know. And I don't know if it'd make any difference in the end. They can only hang her once. Does it say where they're holding her?"

"Newgate Prison."

Devon nodded. There were some aspects of the British legal and penal system of which he didn't approve, but their willingness to toss Darice into the pits of hell was something he couldn't help but appreciate. He'd thought she'd been the one trying to kill Claire, but it was the only sin of which she was innocent. All things considered, Newgate was where Darice belonged. "Does it say anything about dear Aunt Elsbeth?"

Edmund rustled through his paper, supplying, "Nothing beyond the fact that she's apparently living in Charleston these days." There was a long pause and then Edmund mused aloud, "Wouldn't it be ironic if we ended up in chains beside Darice?"

Devon snorted and, watching a carriage roll past, replied, "I'm just a businessman here to discuss the ramifications of war with my British counterparts. You're my legal advisor. Unless we rob or murder one of them, we're not going to land in Newgate." *And once we rebel, they won't bother with hauling us across to prison. They'll just hang us from the nearest tree.*

"It's gratifying to know that your counterparts are hearing what we're saying," Edmund observed, frustration creeping into his voice. "And that they can see the consequences just as clearly as we can. But I doubt that the King and his ministers will be any more willing to hear their own merchants' protests than they've been willing to hear ours. We've wasted the trip, the whole effort, you know. All of us."

"We've tried to make peace, Edmund. From every direction possible. Our conscience is clear. When we take up arms, they won't be able to say that we didn't tell them that we would and why. They won't be able to say that we didn't give them a chance to choose another way."

There was a quiet knock at the door, and Edmund

threw his paper aside, saying, "Maybe that's the King," and heading off to see.

Or maybe Claire, Devon thought before he could censor hope. He scowled out at the darkness, reminding himself that she didn't know he was in England and didn't know to come looking for him. Of course, it was best if she didn't, and he should damn well stop scanning the faces in crowds, looking for her.

"Ephram! Damn, it's good to see you! Come in, come in. How are you?"

His heart suddenly racing, Devon turned away from the window to see Edmund furiously pumping Ephram's hand and dragging the man across the threshold.

"Just fine, sir," Ephram was saying. "And you?"

"Well, I'm here with Devon," he replied, freeing his hand to gesture in his direction. "Need I say more?"

Ephram's gaze met his and Devon advanced, smiling, his hand out. "Freedom seems to agree with you. You look good, Ephram."

"I wish I could honestly say the same thing about you, sir. You look . . . tired."

No, he looked beaten and he knew it. Shaking his half brother's hand and clapping him on the shoulder, he changed the subject. "It's Devon, not 'sir.' Not anymore. It never felt right, anyway."

"How's my mother?"

"Fine," Devon replied, stepping away. "As strong and opinionated as ever. She sent along some things for you on the chance that we'd be able to find each other. Let me get the package for you."

He was moving to his trunk in the corner when Edmund asked, "How's Claire? Did the Crown grant her petition for Crossbridge?"

Devon's step faltered and his heart lurched, but he quickly resumed his track, determined that no one know how deep the pain still went.

"Yes, sir, they did," Ephram answered as Devon snagged the string-wrapped bundle. "It's a very nice house by British standards, and I saw her settled in before I came back to London."

Edmund was nodding and looking acutely regretful that he had brought up the subject of Claire. Devon felt sorry for him. Asking about her was a natural thing to do, since Ephram had been the last of them to see her. Handing the bundle to his half brother, Devon asked as casually as he could, "Is she happy?"

"No."

A flat statement of certain fact. Having a knife thrust into his heart would have hurt far less. Devon dredged up a smile and admitted what truth he could. "That's not what I wanted to hear."

"I know," Ephram countered with a dismissive shrug. "But I'm a free man now and I don't have to worry about what you want to hear and what you don't."

He knew what was coming; he could feel it in the air. "Have you ever worried about my opinion?" he asked, forcing a chuckle and moving back to the window.

"Not really." There was a momentary pause, followed by a deep breath. Devon braced himself to endure the criticism from without and the heartache from within, and then Ephram began, "I came here this evening because I have to say what I think about all this. Lady Claire has been at Crossbridge spending every minute of her days and most of her nights putting things back to the way she remembers them. But her heart's not in it. The light in her eyes went out the minute you walked away from her on the James City dock."

Oh, God. He didn't have to sleep to have that moment torment his mind. The nightmare was with him constantly, ever twisting his heart. Time hadn't blurred the image or dulled the pain one little bit. "And you think I ought to go to Crossbridge, get her, and take her home with me," he said, moving to the inevitable conclusion in the desperate hope of getting the conversation done before he had to actually fight back the tears.

"She's not at Crossbridge at the moment. She's been summoned back to London for the trial that begins in two days. She arrived yesterday evening."

His heart jolted and the blood shot through his veins. Claire was in London?

"How do you know that?" he heard Edmund ask.

"She came by my office to say hello this afternoon when she finished her meetings with the barristers."

"Did you tell her Devon was here?"

His heart twisted with fear even as his breath caught hard on a wild, foolish hope.

"There was no need to," Ephram answered. "She's read the newspapers. She knows you're both here and why."

His heart was going to explode. Just after his knees gave out.

"Did she say anything about trying to find him?" Edmund went on.

"Why would she need or want to?" Devon asked, desperately gazing out the window and trying to sound as though he were unaffected by the conversation. "We're no longer bound to each other."

Ephram cleared his throat. "Which brings me to the other reason I've come to see you this evening. You need to know that Lady Claire hasn't petitioned for a divorce and has absolutely no intention of doing so."

Pain fled in the face of shock and concern. Devon stepped away from the window, abandoning the pretense of nonchalance. "She promised me that she would."

"No, she didn't," he countered. "I was standing right there and she didn't promise you anything of the sort."

Edmund nodded in silent, irritating agreement.

Surprise and concern gave way to anger. "Didn't you arrange for a solicitor to take care of it as I asked you to?"

"No." Ephram reached into his coat pocket and produced the paper-wrapped bundle of bills he'd been given on the dock in James City. "She was adamant about the matter and I have to admire and respect her decision. Here's your money," he said, tossing it down on a nearby tabletop. "Handing it to a solicitor would be the same as stuffing it down a rat hole. I know that you have better uses for it than that."

Devon stared at the bundle, his teeth clenched, his heartbeat thundering. "She's got to divorce me."

"You know," Ephram drawled, "even when we were boys, the only way to do things was your way. Most of the time your course is the right one for all the right reasons, so people go along with you. But you're not always right, Devon. Sometimes your way isn't the only way. This is one of those times."

"Good God," he railed. "This is a matter of common sense and good judgment. If she doesn't divorce me, they'll toss her into Newgate just for being the wife of a rebel. Claire is the most intelligent woman I've ever met. Why the hell is she being so stupidly stubborn?"

"That's a very good question," his half brother calmly conceded. "But why are you asking me? Why aren't you asking Lady Claire?"

Because he wasn't strong enough to go anywhere near her. Because he loved her so much and missed her so badly that he'd sell his soul and all thirteen colonies to have her back again. And in succumbing to selfishness, he'd be condemning her to an existence even more hellish than that inside Newgate Prison.

"He does have a point, Dev," Edmund said.

He looked back and forth between them, seeing the expectancy in their eyes. With a snarl, he stamped to the hat rack and snatched his tricorn from the peg.

"Are you going to go find her?" Edmund asked hopefully.

"No," he snapped, yanking open the door. "I'm going to the nearest pub and I'm going to drink myself into a goddamn stupor."

"We'll go with you," Edmund announced, following after him. "That way, when you finally come to your senses, you'll have someone who can at least carry you to her doorstep and beg for forgiveness."

"There's nothing to be forgiven for," Devon retorted. But even as he said it he knew it for the lie it was and that it was going to take an ocean of ale to drown his regrets.

CLAIRE PACED THE PARLOR of her rented room, from time to time glancing over at the untouched meal sitting on the table. She really should eat; she'd probably feel ever so much better, more capable if she did. But, as usual, the very suggestion made her already knotted stomach clench that much tighter. She stopped in front of the fireplace and stared into the flames, trying to calm her nerves.

It was really very simple, she told herself. All she had to do was put on her cloak and bonnet and gloves, open the door, and tell the court-appointed guard that she wanted to make a social call. He'd blink over the lateness of the hour, but he wouldn't say anything as he fell in beside her and made sure that she got to the Cavalier Inn without incident. Once she was safely there, though . . .

Claire swallowed and glanced at the crates and trunks stacked in the corner. She hadn't once dithered or questioned her decision while she'd packed her belongings and prepared to come to London. Her way had been clear, her goal well defined and certain in her mind. But now that she stood on the precipice of actually taking action, she was all but paralyzed by unexpected fear.

"And it's just plain silly," she declared, squaring her shoulders and turning away from the warmth of the fire. "What's the worst that could happen?" she asked as she marched toward the coat tree beside the door.

Her step faltered in the center of the room. Devon could say that in her absence he'd discovered that he didn't love her; that he'd found another woman and given her his heart. Tears welled in her eyes and she blinked them back, assuring herself that not only was it the worst that could happen but it was also the remotest of possibilities. No, it was far more likely that Devon—her handsome, noble, self-sacrificing, stubborn husband—would have spent the last four and a half months carving his own decision in stone and would refuse to hear a word she said.

Perhaps wisdom lay in being patient a while longer, in trusting Ephram to effectively speak on her behalf. Or maybe Devon would come to his senses on his own and come to find her.

"And maybe someday pigs will fly," she muttered. Shaking her head, she resumed her course to the coat tree. She was just lifting her cloak from the peg when she heard the low rumble of voices in the hall outside. She paused, listening, but was unable to make out any words, to identify the sounds as belonging to anyone in particular. Holding her breath, Claire glanced at the clock on the mantel. Half past ten. Ephram had said he would see Devon in the early evening. Perhaps...

A knock at the door sent her hopes flaring and her

heart into her throat. "Bless you, Ephram," she happily whispered, putting the cloak back and then throwing open the door.

Her heart seized and her blood turned to ice.

"Good evening, dear niece. May I come in?"

Chapter Twenty-eight

GEORGE SEATON-SMYTHE didn't wait for Claire's assent. He advanced, leaving her with no choice but to hastily step back in order to stay out of his reach. She felt her heart thundering frantically in her chest, but the chaotic chatter of her thoughts was all she could hear. He'd changed so much in the months since she'd last seen him. He was dressed as magnificently as always, but he was heavier, his face ruddier, and his arms and legs seemingly even thicker and shorter than before. The greatest change, however, was in his eyes. The blue was brighter, almost transparent. And through them she saw the wild flickering of desperation and madness. Her blood chilled another painful degree.

"What are you doing here, Uncle George?" she heard herself ask.

"A rather naive question, don't you think?" he replied, pausing to push the door closed behind him.

The cold click of the key in the lock sent her thoughts racing. Where was the guard? Her uncle alone couldn't have overpowered the younger, stronger man. Dear God, what was she going to do? She couldn't run past him. By the time she got the door unlocked and open he'd be upon her. And even if by some miracle she made it into the hall, it was a certainty that she'd be dashing into the arms of her uncle's henchmen.

Scream? The inn was old and the walls were thick. No one would hear her. And even if they did, by the time they got past the men in the hall, any rescuer would be too late to help her. She needed to slow matters down. She had to have time to think, to find herself a weapon.

It took all the control she had to force herself to inch her way toward the hearth while calmly observing, "I was told that you were under house arrest."

"I am," he answered with a smile broad enough to pull tight the wide, ugly scar across his forehead. "But it's a large house with many doors, and the guards at those doors are only men. One or two of them were happy to look the other way for a price. And do stay away from the hearth, Claire. I well recall the last time we had this dance."

As did she. And he appeared to be no better armed this time than he had been the last. "You should know that Devon—my husband—is on his way here," she bluffed, hoping her wishing him there would bring him. "You won't get away with harming me."

"Harm?" he snorted, advancing. "Dear niece, I intend to kill you. And since your colonial bumpkin is not presently battering down the door, I'll have sufficient time to do it."

Kill her how? she wondered. With his bare hands? Or did he have a pistol or a knife under his frock coat? A knife... "Killing me isn't going to result in the charges against you being dismissed," she reminded him, very slowly, very nonchalantly backing toward the table and her untouched meal. "I'm not the only one the Crown has called to testify against you."

"Betrayal is utterly unforgivable," he declared, his watery blue gaze never leaving hers as he reached into his pocket and took another step closer.

She watched him take the end of a red silk scarf in each of his hands. So it was to be strangulation. Which would require him to be very close. Claire inched toward the table, mentally picturing the various items on it. The china was heavy. The teapot had a handle that would make it easy to swing. And there was the very stout but serviceable knife placed to the right side of the plate. Bless British beef for being as tough as it was.

"No one sells me for thirty coins and lives to enjoy them," her uncle said, popping the fabric taut. He smiled at the sound and repeated the gesture while adding, "One of the advantages of having great wealth is that it will buy you justice in any form you so desire. I can assure you that you'll not be the only witness found dead by morrow's light, dear niece."

"There are scores of us. You can't possibly kill us all in a single night," she pointed out, knowing even as she did that no logic would penetrate the madness that enveloped his mind.

"Yes, that indeed would be impossible. So I decided that I'd hire the other work done and personally see to dispensing justice for only the most personal of all the betrayals. That would be you, Claire."

"I'm honored," she said dryly as her backside connected with the edge of the table.

"As well you should be," her uncle replied, popping the scarf again and advancing another step. "I've already put a considerable amount of time and money into ridding myself of you. If only that idiot in Virginia had been even fairly competent."

"Wyndom?" she asked, watching her uncle, trying to keep his attention on conversation so that it didn't wander toward a consideration of what might lie behind her and within her reach.

Slowly closing the distance between them, he shrugged. "I don't recall his name. I don't bother with such unnecessary details. I made inquiries of my people in James City, and they found a situation that perfectly fit my objectives. Had the fellow done as he was supposed to, you wouldn't have been available to answer the Crown's summons."

Claire forced herself to swallow and remain where she was, to wait for him to come close enough. "If I might ask . . . why did you blackmail Devon into marrying me? Why not Wyndom?"

"My people felt that the younger Rivard—the one who ever so fortunately owed me very large sums of money—was of such weak character that he would confess everything if he was suspected of being involved in his wife's sudden demise."

He stopped, the lower edges of his frock coat brushing against the fullness of her skirt. "The elder brother," he went on, "knowing nothing of the larger plan, wouldn't be able to do so under the same circumstances. His only purpose was to insulate me from suspicion."

"You won't have anyone to insulate you from tonight's crimes," Claire said breathlessly, leaning back slightly as though she were trying to get away from him. Slipping her hands behind herself, she made a pretense of trying to use the table to keep herself from toppling over. "The Crown will know who is behind my death and the deaths of all the others. You can't get away with this."

"True, but I can get away from England," he admitted as he flipped the center of the silk scarf over her head. The cool fabric slid over her bare nape as he added, "Once we're done with our business here, I'm boarding a ship bound for Algeria. English justice doesn't reach to the north of Africa."

He'd crossed the ends and was drawing the silk tight when her fingers closed around the handle of the teapot.

"I don't need any keepers," Devon groused as he neared the top of the stairs. "And I damn sure don't need an audience."

"We promise," Edmund retorted dryly from behind him, "to leave as soon as she lets you in."

"Trusting you, of course," Ephram chimed in, "to do the right thing in our absence."

"Of course," Devon agreed tightly. He had every intention of doing the right thing, of saying what needed to be said. The four and a half months without Claire had been the most miserable of his life, but they hadn't altered his decision any more than had the pint of ale and sometimes slightly less than friendly persuasion. Not that Ephram's and Edmund's words had made any difference. He'd known when he'd left his rooms that he was going to end up here, that he didn't have any choice.

Claire was safe in England. He was more convinced of it now than he'd been the morning Governor Dunmore had suspended the House of Burgesses. War was coming. It was inevitable and Claire needed to be well out of harm's way. And for her own safety, she had to stay in England and she damn well had to divorce him. One way or the other, he was going to convince her of those certainties before the night was over.

He vaulted up the last of the steps, reaching the second floor and turning to start down the lamplit corridor on his right. Ahead of him, midway down the hall, a well-dressed man lay in a crumpled heap on the floor. Another man—stocky and thick-browed—lounged against the door frame beside him, apparently unconcerned for his companion's welfare.

Devon froze, instantly wary, his gaze quickly sweeping the hall beyond. Just the one man. Scruffy coat, poorly mended stockings, battered short boots. A man who didn't belong in this place. A lazy glance up, then a start. The man straightened quickly, stepping into the hall as though to block it and then casting a nervous glance back to the door.

"I don't like this," Edmund said softly from behind Devon's right shoulder.

"By the numbers," Ephram said just as quietly from his left, "that door would be Lady Claire's."

Certainty and horrifying possibility instantly melded in Devon's mind. Claire was in London to testify against her uncle. The uncle who had once tried to kill her to keep her from doing so. If he were to make another attempt before it was too late ... The man on the floor was likely the court-appointed guard, and the man who looked like a hired thug ...

Devon moved instinctively, his only thought of getting to Claire before it was too late. The stranger stood his ground, but only until Devon's fist connected with the center of his face. He was still falling when Devon whirled toward the door, grabbed the knob, turned it, and threw his shoulder into the solid wood panel. The mechanism squeaked and the timber groaned, but didn't grant him entrance.

He could hear Ephram's and Edmund's voices, but their words were only a low rumble lost in the rushing of his frantic heartbeat. Stepping back from the door, he focused his attention on a point just to the left of the handle. And then he kicked it with every ounce of strength and determination in his body.

It splintered into long, jagged pieces and sagged away from the frame as the world stood still. Claire was in the center of the room, staring down at her blood-covered hands. Her gown was soaked with it. So much blood. Too much to long survive its loss. Dear God, he was too late.

She looked up then, her gaze slowly meeting his. Recognition flickered and in its wake silent tears spilled over her lashes. He wished the distance between them gone and it was. Her hands were in his and he was desperately looking for the wound, demanding, "Where are you hurt, Claire? Tell me where!"

"I'm all right," she said weakly, her voice quavering. "It's *his* blood."

His? Devon started, realizing that once he'd seen her, he hadn't given any thought to her assailant. He quickly looked over his shoulder and sagged in relief to see Edmund standing between them and the figure lying stone still in a widening pool of blood.

"My uncle," she said quietly as Devon turned back to her. "He was trying to kill me." What was left of her composure crumbled. Tremors wracked her body and a sob caught deep in her throat as a fresh flood of tears poured over her cheeks. In the face of her need, all of his resolve and good intentions were undone.

"Edmund," he began, sweeping her up into his arms and carrying her toward the bedroom.

"Ephram's gone for the constables," his friend replied crisply. "It's too late to send for a doctor. Just see to Claire and I'll manage in here."

Claire sighed and let her eyes drift closed, too exhausted to think, too weak to move on her own. Devon was there and the horrible nightmare had come to an end. It was all that mattered now. She would be all right. Her world would be mended and made whole. Devon had come for her. He loved her. She could feel it wrapping around her and radiating through her. She was in his arms and he'd never again let her go.

"I want to go home, Devon," she whispered into the curve of his neck.

"And you will, sweetheart," he promised, gently placing her in the center of the bed. "You will."

He drew back and she tried to protest his leaving, but couldn't make the words come off her tongue. Her limbs were leaden and her eyes wouldn't open.

"Sleep now and we'll talk later," he said softly as he pressed a kiss to her lips. "I'll be here when you wake."

He would be. She knew it to the center of her soul. And as long as they were together, she'd have the strength and courage to face whatever happened next. The worst was over. She'd endured and survived. She was going home. With Devon. To Rosewind.

CLAIRE AWAKENED with a start, not knowing for a moment where she was. The first light of a new day trickled through the small parting between the curtain panels, and she sat up in bed and stared at it, waiting for a sense of place to come to her. The cold draft on her shoulders slowly brought her awareness back to herself. She wasn't wearing a nightrail. She wasn't wearing anything at all. Even odder, she didn't remember retiring last night. It was very strange indeed. She looked back to the window and studied the fabric of the curtains.

London? Yes, she—

The floodgates of memory opened and deluged her. Her uncle. The scarf. The teapot and his rage. The sickening feel and sound of the knife as he threw himself on her, on it. And the blood. Oh, God, the blood. Everywhere. The heat and smell of it. The look on his face as he'd staggered back, his hands red and fumbling at the hilt.

Devon had been there. Her handsome husband, striding through the splintered door, taking her into his arms. After that . . .

Her heart pounding, Claire looked around the room, hoping to find him there and choking back a cry of disappointment when she didn't. No, she couldn't have dreamed him, she assured herself as she flung back the covers. Her feet hit the cold floor and she stopped, her mind racing.

Her gown had been drenched with blood; that she

remembered. She looked at her hands. Clean. Devon had to have undressed and bathed her. Who else would have? She didn't remember doing it for herself, didn't remember anything after he'd wrapped her in his arms except for a sense of finally being safe.

She glanced around the room, but saw no sign of the dress anywhere. In fact, everything she'd been wearing last night was gone without a trace. No stockings, no stays, no shift, no petticoats. Had Devon taken it all away? Was he still here? Had he come to his senses? Had he come to take her home?

A snippet of memory, foggy and dim, came to her. Her own voice saying she wanted to go home. Devon promising her that she'd get there.

Claire started toward the parlor door, her heart filled with hope and excitement. She stopped halfway across the room and frowned. Her uncle was dead at her hand. There was a very good chance that London constables might be waiting with Devon. The first question they'd think to ask her would be whether she made a habit of bursting into rooms naked.

Smiling, she dashed to the armoire and took out the easiest clothing she could pull on.

DEVON LOOKED AWAY from the window to find her standing in the doorway of the bedchamber, silently studying him, her hair tumbling wildly over her shoulders, the swells of her breasts draped in the linen of her shirt, the length of her legs and the curve of her hips encased in the doeskin of her breeches. And to think that at one time he'd been appalled by her boy's clothing.

He filled his senses with her even as his brain reminded him yet again that he couldn't have her and that the price he paid for coming here was his heart breaking all over again. But it was one he was willing to pay for the chance to look into those beautiful eyes again, to try one more time to protect her the only way he knew how.

God, that he could do that just by holding her in his arms. If only he could wrap her in his love and know that it would be enough to keep her safe. And if wishes were horses . . . He looked away from her, not wanting her to see his regrets and misery, not knowing what to say or how to begin.

Claire watched the sadness settle over his features, and the hope that filled her withered away. He wasn't here to tell her that he'd made a mistake, to ask her to come back to Rosewind with him. She stood frozen, desperately wanting to run to him and throw herself into his arms. And just as badly wanting to find something heavy and throw it at him. Unable to decide which she wanted to do more, she remained where she was, swallowing down her heartache.

After a long moment, he gestured to the main door and said, "As you can see, they've replaced it already. And put the place back to rights." The silence stretched taut between them, and he stepped away from the window, asking, "Are you all right, Claire?"

She nodded, touched the tip of her tongue to her lower lip, and then asked, "Where are the constables?"

"They've been here and gone," he answered, hooking his thumbs over the waistband of his breeches. "Your uncle's hireling told them everything they either needed or wanted to hear. Edmund went with them to do the necessary paperwork. Ephram went along to show him a bit of London when they were done. Edmund asked me to tell you that the court will send you something official tomorrow—" He glanced toward the window and smiled weakly. "Make that today—that releases you from any obligation to remain in London on its behalf."

"So I'll be free to return to Crossbridge," she ventured, needing to know what he was thinking and desperately hoping to hear him protest.

"Yes."

No single word had ever hurt as deeply. Pride was all that kept her from running away. "Why are you here, Devon?"

He looked out the window as he replied, "Edmund and I were sent to talk with British businessmen in London to see if we could get them to make the King and Parliament exercise good judgment."

"Yes, I know. I've read the newspapers. I imagine that they'll make an appeal," she said, exasperated, knowing an evasion when she heard one. "It's in their best interests to keep relations between England and her colonies peaceful. I don't expect it will do any good, though. Why did you come to my room last night?"

Squaring his shoulders, he finally met her gaze again. His jaw the same hard granite it had been the morning she'd last seen him, he answered, "Ephram came by the inn yesterday evening. He told me that you don't intend to petition for a divorce."

Ah, there it was. The divorce. He'd come to see finished what he'd begun on the James City dock. She'd made it easy on him that day; she'd been too hurt and afraid and confused to put up a real fight. He wasn't going to walk away unscathed this time. She hadn't been angry that morning. She was now. "I think Ephram has done quite well for himself as a freedman. Don't you?"

Her eyes had turned the color of steel. Despite the hair prickling on the back of his neck, Devon doggedly held to his course and answered, "He looks good. I forgot to ask about his job. Why won't you do the sensible thing?"

"Meg and Hannah?" she asked breezily. "How are they? Has Edmund asked Meg to marry him yet?"

"They're fine," he supplied, struggling to contain a

burning mixture of hunger and anger as he watched her amble toward the hearth. "And yes. The wedding's to be this spring. Now answer my question. Why won't you petition for a divorce?"

"I'd offer you a cup of tea," she said, not bothering to look at him as she warmed her hands before the fire. "But I broke the pot over my uncle's head. Not that it'd be at all palatable at this point even if I hadn't. I could order some sent up if you'd like."

Claire started as a settee pillow sailed past her, hitting the mantel in front of her as from behind her he bellowed, "Dammit, Claire! Talk to me!"

She whirled around, furious. "Why should I talk?" she demanded, marching to stand toe to toe with him. Tilting her head up to meet a gaze every bit as angry as her own, she charged on, not caring what damage she did with her words. There wasn't any damage that hadn't already been done.

"You don't talk, Devon. And you don't listen, either," she accused. "You issue decrees and everyone is expected to obey. You decide what's important and what isn't, and what anyone else thinks or feels doesn't matter. Almost five months ago we stood on the dock at James City and you made one of your kingly pronouncements. I was to go to England, petition for a divorce, and be happy. What I wanted didn't matter. King Devon decreed and I was to see his wisdom and obey."

She paused to seize a breath, and then, jabbing a finger into the center of his chest, she declared, "Well, I'm not going to obey and there's not a damn thing you can do about it." She turned around and marched off to the bedchamber, saying, "If you want tea, send for it yourself!"

Devon watched her storm away, stunned, his heart racing. Sweet Jesus Christ. He'd had no idea that she saw his decisions as being presumptive and heartless.

He'd thought he'd made his motives so clear that day. She had to understand; he couldn't bear her resentment.

He stopped just inside the bedchamber door. "Claire, all I've done..." His throat swelled and he swallowed hard to clear it, to say, "All I want is for you to be safe."

Her back to him, she quietly asked, "What does being safe matter when you're so miserably unhappy that you'd rather be dead?"

It didn't. Living wasn't worth the bother if there wasn't even the hope of happiness in it. He'd known that before she'd come into his life, and he'd learned the lesson again the day he'd sent her away. But not once since then had he ever stopped to consider that her pain might be as deep as his own, her heartbreak as raw, her life just as forever empty. He'd been so damn wrapped up in his own misery that he hadn't thought about hers. He was a selfish ass. Guilty of every callous, pompous crime of which she'd accused him.

"What would make you happy?" he asked, willing to do or say anything, grant any request she made of him.

"So that you can decree it for me?" she asked.

He deserved that slap. And he'd invite and endure a thousand more of them if that's what it took to get her to talk to him, to tell him what was in her heart. "When was the last time you were happy, Claire?"

"When you took me in your arms last night and carried me in here," she answered, her voice quavering with tears, "and I thought that you'd come to take me home."

Relief flooded over him. There was road to go yet, but they were at last on the same one. Devon stepped forward, gently placing his hands on her shoulders. "I've been such a damn fool," he confessed.

Turning under his hands, she looked up at him defiantly, tears rolling down over her cheeks. "Yes, you have. And I've been a fool to let you get away with it for as long as I have."

No, she'd been a saint to endure the consequences of his stupidity. Cradling her face in his hands, he gently brushed her tears away with the pads of his thumbs. "Can you ever forgive me for what I've done to us? For the heartache I've caused?"

The defiance left her eyes and the hope that came into them filled his heart. "Do you still love me?" she whispered.

He answered her with a kiss, tender with apology, fierce with a hunger too long denied. With a moan, she melted into him, her arms twining around his neck, her love and forgiveness healing his heart and soul.

ROUSED FROM SATED BLISS, Claire smiled as Devon gently shifted beside her on the bed, swore softly, found and then tossed a boot aside. Gathering her back into his arms, he held her close and whispered, "I love you, Claire. I will to my dying day."

"And I, you," she replied, placing her hand over his heart.

Covering her hand with his own, he sighed contentedly. "I feel it's only fair to remind you that I have absolutely nothing to offer you except hope, my love, impending bankruptcy, and the real possibility of committing treason. If you want to rethink your commitment to a life with me, I'll understand."

She shook her head in the tender confines of his embrace. "Hope and love are all that matters, Devon. I don't need anything more than that to be happy."

"If you're sure..." He hesitated and then asked, "Will you come home with me, Madam Rivard?"

They were the dearest words she'd ever heard. She smiled and snuggled closer to him, listening to, feeling, the steady, strong beat of his heart and discovering a fundamental truth. "Home isn't bricks and boards and glass, Devon. It's wherever you are."

"It's good that you look at it that way, sweetheart," he said, pressing a kiss into her hair. "Because odds are that you'll be living with me in a military campaign tent before the next year is out. War is coming."

His greatest hope, his greatest fear. Propping herself on her elbow, Claire looked down at his handsome, beard-shadowed face. "And I'll stand with you on the day that war arrives. What you need me to do in the defense of freedom, I will. Where you go, Devon, I will go with you. No matter what happens, I will never again leave your side."

She was the most magnificent light that had ever come into his life, and he would spend the rest of it making sure that she never once regretted loving him. "Always together, Claire," he promised softly. "From this day forward. Come what may."

ABOUT THE AUTHOR

Leslie LaFoy grew up loving to read and living to write. A former high-school history teacher and department chair, she made the difficult decision to leave academia in 1996 to follow her dream of writing full-time. When not made utterly oblivious to the real world by her current work in progress, she dabbles at being a domestic goddess, and gives a fairly credible performance as a Hockey Mom. A fourth generation Kansan, she happily lives on ten windswept acres of native prairie with her husband and son and assorted animals.

You can find Leslie on the web at:
http://www.authorsmansion.com/lafoy.html

Experience the enchanting wit of *New York Times* bestseller

Betina Krahn

"Krahn has a delightful, smart touch." —*Publishers Weekly*

THE PERFECT MISTRESS
___56523-0 $6.99/$9.99 Canada

THE LAST BACHELOR
___56522-2 $5.99/$7.50 Canada

THE UNLIKELY ANGEL
___56524-9 $5.99/$7.99 Canada

THE MERMAID
___57617-8 $5.99/$7.99 Canada

THE SOFT TOUCH
___57618-6 $6.50/$8.99 Canada

SWEET TALKING MAN
___57619-4 $6.50/$9.99 Canada

THE HUSBAND TEST
___58386-7 $6.50/$9.99 Canada